UP SHE RISES

UP SHE RISES

David Garnett

ST. MARTIN'S PRESS
NEW YORK

TO
THE MEMORY OF
MY MOTHER
CONSTANCE
TRANSLATOR OF RUSSIAN

AUTHOR'S NOTE

THE heroine of this book is my mother's paternal grandmother, my great-grandmother, and the events of her and her husband's lives are recorded here with considerable accuracy. But this is a novel – not a family history.

In the preface to my book *Pocahontas*, a historical novel written forty-four years ago, I wrote:

'Such a reconstruction is inevitably a work of fiction; for what, after all, are men's names and what are their deeds when weighed in the scale against their emotions?'

I have here changed many of the surnames lest I should give offence to some distant cousin, but I have kept the given names of the characters. I have helped myself to a song from George Borrow's *Romano Lavo-Lil*, where the interested reader will find a translation.

I owe an immense debt of gratitude to my cousin, Jane Gregory, who has traced Peter's naval and subsequent career with pertinacity and skill and I have benefited greatly by her advice and interest. I owe much help also to my son Richard, and I thank them both.

David Garnett

29 February 1976   Le Verger de Charry, Montcuq, France

CHAPTER ONE

THE SEA was always there, cutting off half the land and often angry, seeming spiteful that it could not wash away all Scotland. And in winter it needed courage in the young girl, Clementina, to stand on the shore and watch the grey waves explode in white towers of spray over the belt of rocks that held them back on that part of the coast. Often, after the roller broke, the wind swept the spray in, and the watcher's face was stung hurtfully and her clothes drenched. She would watch a leaden bar in the sea define itself into a wave, then grow to being a breaker that burst in towers of spray upon the rocks and rush between them down the channel, a pathway of boiling milk. Then, as the sea withdrew, the channel was left a dull blue, with a network of white bands of foam, like the brindled skin of a sea-serpent, all to be obliterated a moment later by another roller exploding on the rocks and come roaring down. And so without end. She learned early that the sea was the lifelong enemy.

The coast there ran straight for many miles. The shore was a high bank of sand, tumbled loose and slippery, held together by grassroots on the land side, on the other steeply concave with a wide stretch of firm wet sand, reaching almost to the belt of rocks, exposed at low tide, but with only a black point or two showing after it had come in.

Along the shore objects were visible for a long way, and from East Haven, where she stood, it was possible to know what the men at West Haven were doing. She could watch them, two miles away, come out, gather in a knot, then separate come together again, to run Master Lamond's boat down to the shore. A rock stopped her from seeing them launch her into the water, but a few minutes later she was clear of the rocks and she could see the red patched sails fluttering for a moment before they drew, and the boat move off, under a new impetus for a day's fishing. Master Lamond's boat might stay out all night and then come back loaded to the gunwale with herring. There was no boat then like Master Lamond's *Eliza* at East Haven.

At each of the Havens there were perhaps eight or ten boats in regular use, which meant a community of forty to fifty fishermen who were not crofters but lived from harvests of the sea. There was no safe anchorage at either Haven : the boats had to be drawn up on shore. Men scarcely venture to use the two Havens today. Each is just wide enough for skilled men to take an open boat through the channel of rocks out to sea, and until the mid-nineteenth century no decked or half-decked boats were used for fishing.

At the end of the eighteenth century, when this history opens, the boats used were shallow skiffs, sometimes with one mast and a square sail. They were about twenty or twenty-five feet long, not more than six foot in beam, and drew under two foot of water. The stem was straight and the stern raked steeply. They were manned by a crew of five, four men at the oars and a steersman, who was skipper. Master Lamond had built the first of the new type to be used at West Haven : the North Isle vole. It was the same length as the Fair Isle skiff, but it was almost twice as full in the beam, with nearly twice the draught, and it had two masts fitted with lugsails and a jib. It had the same straight stem and raking stern and like its predecessor was clinker built of Scottish oak and larch. It carried the same number of men.

The fishing was seasonal and the girl watching knew that the boat was setting out line-fishing for haddock. Each of the men had a line fifty fathoms in length, with a hundred snoods or droppers, each with a baited hook, one every yard along its length. At East Haven and West Haven too, in spring and summer, the chief fishing was for lobsters which were caught in wickerwork pots. It was the safest fishing, for the rows of pots were sunk just outside the belt of rocks, and no boat was far from land in case a sudden squall blew up.

And the lobsters fetched good prices. Their claws were tied and they were packed in hampers full of seaweed, and, if a passing vessel responded to a signal and shortened sail, a skiff would dash out with the men rowing like fury, and the hampers or boxes would be handed over the side and carried off to distant markets: Edinburgh or even London. And very often the skiff would pull round to the seaward side of the ship, so that what was going on could not be seen from the shore. Then you might guess that it was a two-way trade. Selling lobsters was a good cover for smuggling.

The girl who watched the launching of the boat knew all these things: how the snoods were fastened, how the hook was tied on and how each was baited with a mussel and how the long line was coiled up in the boat so that it could be fed into the sea without a single snood tangling with another.

She was not a fisherman's daughter: her father was a crofter who had never been out in a boat; for the crofters and fisher-folk kept apart. But her father was a great friend of an older man: old Peter Lamond, who had settled there many years before, soon after the Forty-five, and whose only son was the Master Lamond who had built the first North Isle vole at West Haven.

Everyone in East Haven, West Haven and Panbride knew part of that story; no one but Old Peter and Master Lamond knew it all. Perhaps the girl's grandfather, James Carey, had known bits of it that were now forgotten. What was undeniable was that Old Man Lamond had settled about two hundred yards east of East Haven, between the seashore and David Carey's cow pasture, thirty or forty years before. He had built himself a bothy and had married a woman who had died soon after giving him a son. And that son Patrick had walked out of his father's cottage when he was a lad of sixteen, had gone to Edinburgh and had come back twelve years later, married, to settle at West Haven. He had fished and he had prospered and had built the first of the North Isle voles. She was more seaworthy than the Fair Isle skiff, much faster under canvas, and could venture further afield after the herring.

His wife, Elizabeth, had given him two sons. He had not been out to sea for eight years, but had given his time to salting, curing and marketing the catches of fish landed at the Havens. He was a silent, quiet, bald-headed man, ruled by his wife. She had first changed his name from Patrick, which she disliked, to Peter. Then she had turned him from a fisherman, first into a boat-builder and then into a fish-curer and fish-factor, for he handled the catches made in other boats than his own. Thanks to his steady reliable character, Master Lamond was a respected man. He ranked after the Minister and had been called in to arbitrate in disputes as far away as Arbroath and Dundee.

Perhaps to keep him further away from the sea, Elizabeth had made him buy a house with a big garden next to the manse in the little town of Panbride, after which Marr, the skipper of the *Eliza*, moved into the slate-roofed cottage near the beach where they had lived after their marriage.

In all the years since Master Lamond had brought his wife home from Edinburgh, he had never been the two miles up the beach to see his father, and in all that time Old Lamond had not spoken to his son except in the kirkyard on a Sunday. The Old Man would bow to his daughter-in-law, but he had never talked with her, entered her house, or sat down with her to a meal.

But there had never been a quarrel, or even a harsh word spoken between them. That was strange, for the old man had a fiery temper and his reputation in East Haven was that of a bad neighbour.

No one in Panbride had any blame for Master Lamond's un-filial behaviour. The Old Man was known to have had gypsy women living in the bothy after his wife's death, he reeked of whisky and his uncombed beard sparkled when a ray of sunlight caught the scales of herring lodged among the bristles. That the sister of a Professor in Edinburgh, who visited on equal terms at the manse, should bow to her husband's father as they passed each other in the kirkyard was graciousness enough to show the reprobate.

But though Elizabeth had had her own way with her husband and had raised him from a poor fisherman to a respected house-holder, with a garden full of flowers as well as its kailyard, she had trouble with her sons. There was no keeping them away from the sea, the rockpools at low tide, fishing off the rocks, crabbing and prawning. They even learned to swim. Elizabeth did what she could, but in this instance her husband did not support her. Master Lamond had a sense of justice. If the boys did their schoolwork and satisfied the dominie, they had a right to freedom at other times, and perhaps he was not sorry to see them living, in those hours, the life he had been born to, but had abandoned for one of buying and selling the work done by other men.

At first their mother had been more successful in keeping the boys away from their grandfather – from the old man of the sea – than from the sea itself. But that was because seeing him meant trudging along the beach two miles there and two back, from West Haven, and then another mile to their home in Panbride. Also Old Lamond did not welcome the company of small children. One day, however, when Peter was fourteen and Robert twelve, the two made an expedition to East Haven. It was hot. The tide was out and on their arrival they paddled about among the rock pools and splashed into the deeper channels between them. Suddenly Robert gave a piercing scream. Peter got hold of him and pulled him out, but his brother went on screaming. He was in agony. Peter carried him back, slipping and staggering from rock to rock until at last he was on the firm wet sand directly below his grandfather's bothy. He had fallen twice, and his own knee and elbow were bleeding. But he was unaware of that, for to his horror Robert had fainted. He laid him on the sand thinking that he was dead, then gave a shout for help. It was the late afternoon. Clementina was milking, with her head pressed hard into the flank of the little blue-black Angus cow, when she heard a distant cry. She knew it was very wrong to leave a cow before you had her stripped. But it had sounded like 'Help!' She ran out of the byre, then across the cow pasture, through a gap in the hedge by Old Lamond's bothy. From the top of the bank she beheld a sight which she never forgot: young Peter Lamond with his brother lying dead at his feet. She would have flung herself down the bank, if Old Lamond had not done so first. She saw then that Robert was not drowned, for his hair and shirt were not wet.

Old Lamond reached the boys; he picked Robert up, slung him over his shoulder and started back up the bank. Clementina stepped back from the path and stood watching. First came the old man, puffing under his burden, then Peter with his black curls and sunburned shoulders. She could have touched him as he went past. When they had gone into the bothy, she went back to the byre. No one had noticed her absence and she finished stripping Arabella. All that evening she was desperate to find out what had happened to the boy : there was no way, unless she was sent on a message to the bothy. She dared not tell what she had seen. Her father might have struck her for leaving the milking. As it was, noticing her restlessness, he exclaimed : 'What's got into the girl?' And her Auntie growled : 'Sit quiet or I lose count.' David Carey and his aunt were playing cribbage.

It was a long while before Clementina fell asleep.

Next morning Old Lamond was on the doorstep before Clementina had swallowed a mouthful of porridge and he was calling to her father : 'David, I want a pony and that girl of yours to lead it to take my young grandson home. He ought not to put a foot to the ground yet awhile.'

So she was to see the grand Lamond house in Panbride. She might see Peter again, perhaps even talk to him. She did not think to run and change her frock until it was too late and she was leading the pony. She had no shoes, but the lack of shoes did not trouble her. None of the girls she knew wore shoes in summer. She herself went barefoot all the year round, unless she could borrow an old pair of her Auntie's boots when there was snow on the ground. Soon Robert was sitting sideways on the pony, telling of his experiences.

'Was that your Auntie who came last night when I was greeting with the pain? She put a plaster of seaweeds on my foot and the pain went after she had talked very strangely. My Grandpa called her Mother Carey and said she was a wise woman who called cousins with the Devil, but that I was not to breathe a word about her.'

'Did he now? That was bonny of him!' Clementina would have said more but Robert was too full of the marvels he had seen to wait.

'Grandpapa has two guns : a fowling piece over the chimney and an army musket hidden away in the tall clock. And he has a Highland dirk and a case of pistols. But he keeps them hidden too, and he made me promise not to tell my mamma, or anyone, what I had seen.'

Clementina looked at the little boy scornfully.

'So, after promising, you are blabbing about it already? I see that you aren't to be trusted.'

Robert looked surprised and his mouth puckered.

'Grandpapa didn't say it was a secret from you.'

'You don't know what is secret and what isn't. If you don't want to make trouble, you must learn to hold your jaw.'

Clementina led the pony in silence for some minutes.

Then Robert asked timidly : 'Why don't I see you in the Sunday school?'

'I have to work for my father.'

'What work do you do?'

'I milk the cows, feed the calves, muck out the byre and the stable in winter, feed the pigs and watch that the stock don't break through the hedge into your Grandpa's garden.'

'It sounds like you did all the work.'

'I do my full share.'

'What does your papa do?'

'David is a fine man. But he likes going to markets and sing-songs with the gypsies. He is free-handed.'

Clementina would have liked to have boasted about her father, to have implied that it was better to be a full man with whom women went willingly, pleased and silent, a man who after taking the whisky, would leap up, catch hold of a girl and dance until he tripped and fell. She would have liked to boast, but with the Lamonds it would not do. The full man, her father, had only a few shillings at most times. Quiet Master Lamond had half-a-dozen men working for him, his fishing boats and his curing sheds. And his sons were decent and wore boots and went to the school from which she had been taken before she could read, though she knew the alphabet and had learned to write her long name, though why it started with a C instead of a K, she did not know. A trap perhaps.

Robert soon recovered his spirits and Clementina and he were firm friends by the time they reached the Lamond house which stood back in its garden with flowers in the beds in front.

Clementina was scared as Master Lamond came out of the door and hurried up, followed by Peter.

His father lifted Robert off the pony.

'How's your foot, Robbie? If the pain has gone, it will soon be well. Come in, my girl: I'm glad to see you. Peter, take the pony round to the stable.'

Carrying Robert in his arms, he led the way through the front door and down a passage to the big kitchen where he laid his son on an oak settle.

Clementina followed. She marvelled at a tall clock with a brass face above the polished wood case and at an engraving of Robert Bruce sitting in a dungeon contemplating a spider. Then she was in a big room with a coal fire burning and a large table covered with a white linen tablecloth and fine polished wooden chairs round it, with bowls set out for porridge.

'Your mother has just stepped round to the manse with a basket of the first broad beans for Mrs Henderland,' Master Lamond was telling Robert.

'She had ordered the pony to be put into the trap and was all for fetching you back at once, directly Peter had told us about your treading on the stingray. But I stood out against her. I knew you needed rest until the pain was over and there was less risk of the poison spreading; it was better for you to spend the night in the bothy. Did your Grandpapa look after you well?'

'Yes, Papa, indeed he did.' With Clementina's rebuke in his mind he would not enlarge on the wonders he had seen.

Then Peter was back in the room, and Master Lamond had them all sitting round the table while he ladled out thick porridge and told them to fill their cups with fresh milk in which to dip their spoonfuls and to pass each other the salt. And Clementina was awed because the spoons were silver spoons and the salt cellar was silver also.

'And how many cows has your father got in milk now?' Master Lamond asked.

'Only the three,' replied Clementina.

'There was never such cream as from the Careys' cows. I loved going round to your farm when I was a boy. David and I were a pair of rascals. Many a bird's-nest we robbed together.

And then the crabbing and the shrimping....'

Soon he had set Clementina at her ease. She liked Master Lamond fine and kept eyeing Peter on the other side of the table. What blue eyes he had behind the black lashes and what a noble forehead with the black curls clustering round it, and that fine nose with a high bridge and his firm mouth, sitting there, so proud and silent and never a look for her. How unlike his small, bald-headed father, so kind and hospitable. Peter would be a full man like her own Papa.

There was a sound of a door opening and shutting and there was Mistress Lamond back from her neighbourly visit to the manse.

Clementina rose in her seat and dropped her a curtsey.

'This is Clemmie, David Carey's daughter who brought Robert back on her pony this morning,' said Master Lamond.

His wife barely noticed the girl but turned to Robert. After she had assured herself that the pain had gone, though the foot was still very swollen, she said to him: 'I was afraid that you would think that we had forgotten you when I did not come at once to fetch you home. But I insisted, and I feel sure that I was right, that it was wiser to leave you undisturbed to rest the foot, even though it meant leaving you in that filthy hovel with that old man. You must have had a horrible time. Forgive me and you may be sure that now I have got you back I shan't let you run such a risk again.'

Clementina was watching Peter and saw his expression change. A smile of contempt greeted his mother's first words. And indeed they contradicted what Master Lamond had said earlier. But her last words were greeted by a look not merely of contempt, but of dislike or disgust.

Soon they had finished breakfast. Oatcake and marmalade had followed the porridge, and then Mistress Lamond turned to Clementina with a gracious air, as though she had observed her presence at the table for the first time.

'You will be going as a fisher-lassie soon, I suppose.'

It was rare for the daughters of the crofters to go with the fishergirls, or for their sons to turn fishermen. But Mistress Lamond, a lady from Edinburgh, might well not know it.

17

'Aye, Mistress Lamond, I might think about it. And your lads will soon be going as fishermen, no doubt,' replied Clementina, anxious to be civil.

But Mistress Lamond laughed scornfully.

'You've made a big mistake there, though I don't suppose you meant to be insolent. Peter is entered for the University in Edinburgh and will be leaving us next term,' said the lady of the house, but with such anger that a long silence fell round the table. Then Clementina rose and said to Master Lamond, 'Thank you, sir, for your kindness and the parritches.'

Mistress Lamond rose also and was saying:

'I would like to give you something for bringing Robert back. I have an old pair of shoes which might do for you.' She got up and went out of the room.

'Go and fetch Clementina's pony from the stable, Peter,' said Master Lamond. Then his wife was back with a pair of old black leather shoes, worn down on the inner sides of the heels, in her hands. 'Here you are, my girl,' she said, handing them to Clementina. Then: 'Robert, you won't be seeing her again, so thank her nicely for bringing you home on her pony.'

'I do thank you, and I thank you for all that you said,' Robert spoke in a low voice. Clementina held the shoes which had been thrust into her hand. She curtseyed to Mistress Lamond and went out quickly into the yard where Peter was holding the pony.

'Hold these, Peter,' she said, giving him the shoes. Then she gripped the pony's mane, put her other hand on his back and swung herself up. And at once she stuck her heels in his flanks and started to ride off.

Peter ran after her with the shoes in his hands and caught up with her in the lane outside the gate. 'You've forgotten these.'

Clementina reined up the pony and looked at him.

'Do you really think that I want a pair of your mother's cast-offs?' she asked the handsome boy standing with the shoes in his hands looking at her and very much aware of her bare leg with her frock riding half-way up the thigh. She always rode her pony astride. She waited for the answer to her question. But Peter gazed speechless, seeing her strong nose between red cheeks, her wide mouth open, showing even white teeth, blue eyes, dark curls clustering, the high breasts and then the white thigh, naked. He looked at her breathless as though he were seeing her for the first time. Clementina was laughing at him, knowing the turmoil that he was in.

'Surely you know that I don't want gifts of that sort,' she said gently.

'What shall I do with them?' he asked in tones of distress.

'Throw them in the ditch!' She rode off laughing. Peter looked so pitiful and ashamed.

He did not follow her advice, and a week later he was suddenly confronting her at the gap in the pasture with a parcel under his arm.

'My mother meant to be kind. It did not occur to her that she would offend you,' he said.

Clementina stared astonished. The shoes again!

'So I have had them heeled and brought them to you. Please accept them.'

She shook her head.

'No! It is very kind of you, Peter. But when I want shoes I shall choose my own.'

Peter was getting angry. 'You do not show much humility. My mother's intention was to help, and to show gratitude, not to insult you. I only brought them and had them repaired because I am grateful and want to help.'

Clementina made him a little mocking curtsey. 'Thank your mother and thank you, Master Peter, for your charitable interest in a poor barefoot girl. And, by the way, does your mother know that you had them heeled?'

Peter's face turned red. They looked at each other silently. At last Clementina said reflectively: 'Your mother is quite right. Shoes *are* important. You judge people by their shoes: if they wear thick boots or shoes with silver buckles.' She looked down at her feet and wriggled her toes. 'But there's only one judgement to be made about bare feet.' She laughed, but Peter's face remained stern. Laughter suited Clementina, her cheeks grew redder, her eyes sparkled, her white teeth flashed. She was laughing at him, and she would not take the shoes he had paid for having heeled.

'You had better please your mother and keep away from barefoot girls!' she said softly so he could only just hear.

'I am very sorry for the misunderstanding,' he said stiffly. Then he gave a slight bow and walked away carrying his parcel.

When he had gone fifty yards Clementina shook her fist at his back and then turned to wipe away a tear – not a tear of laughter, but of rage.

Lying on the grass on the top of the bank, Clementina could see Peter Lamond start off from West Haven along the beach towards her. He was down below the high tide mark, so he could walk on the firm wet sand and he was carrying something that looked like a stick in one hand.

'Anyway it's not those shoes,' she thought and laughed. At intervals she turned her head and looked back at the pasture to make sure that the cows and young stots were grazing peacefully. There were two big gaps in the hedge that her father never found the time to mend. So Clementina had to be always on the watch when the cattle were in that field.

Peter came steadily along the beach. He passed the boats drawn up opposite the entrance to East Haven and then, when he was almost below her, he climbed up the bank. He was so close that in another twenty yards he would reach her. He must be coming to see her, but he gave no greeting and she did not move. Then, when he was only fifteen yards away, he stopped short and turned his back. He unrolled the two little sticks he was carrying: they had white flags on the ends, and he began going into curious attitudes, holding the flags at arm's length. Clementina could not imagine what he was doing. After a while he stopped and she saw a small figure outlined against the sky at West Haven had begun to make similar movements. They were signalling to each other. But how did they signal? she wondered.

While she was still watching, there was a footstep near her and Old Lamond subsided into the grass by her side. Peter had begun again. Three-quarters of an hour later he rolled up his little flags and walked off, then ran down the bank on to the damp sand, and so back to West Haven.

He had not given his grandfather or Clementina a look or a word, though he must have known that they were lying in the grass just behind him.

'Well, we can't read the telegraph, can we, lassie?' asked Old Lamond. Then as she made no reply, he went on: 'Have you forgot your alphabet?'

Clementina turned away her head, ashamed. Then her mood changed, and she said defiantly: 'I know my letters. I can write my name. But I cannot read. And there aren't any books I can learn from.'

Old Lamond looked at her with a curious expression, amused but with a queer friendliness. 'Well, I'll lend you my Bible. I can't read those new signals myself, so I can't help there.'

Clementina felt the tall grasses tickling her cheek, felt the sun warming it, saw the white clouds stuck in the blue sky, heard the low hiss of the breaking waves of the incoming tide, and all the time she was thinking of Peter suddenly turning himself into a living signpost – what wouldn't he think of next? And there was the white-faced stot coming to the gap. She had to spring up, break the spell and drive him back.

Next day the boys were at it again. It was not enough to just watch, so Clementina went back to the croft and fetched her old school slate and slate pencil, and, as Robert stayed for a moment in the same position, she was able to note down the angles at which he held his arms. She guessed that they represented the letters of words that he was spelling out. Thus:

Also that he waved the flag across between the words to show where one ended and the next began.

That night Clementina lay awake and decided she would change her life. She would teach herself to read; she would learn the code of the telegraph; she would make young Peter Lamond respect her.

She would make her Auntie, who was bone lazy, do part of the milking; she would force her father to mend the gaps in the fence – or else – or else – I'll go off with the gippos— The idea of going off with Pyramus Lee and his wife made her laugh when she thought of how Mistress Lamond would take the news. 'If I did that she would have no fears of her sons seeing me again.'

Next morning she found her mother's old Prayer Book, which luckily opened at the Lord's Prayer which she knew by heart.

She stared at the words and soon identified them and read them easily :

GIVE US THIS DAY OUR DAILY BREAD

It was easy. And once she had the idea, she found that she could read, though some words were puzzles and words of three syllables or more were too difficult. She took the Prayer Book with her when she went to guard the gaps in the cow pasture. It was blowing a gale. The north wind carried handfuls of sand along the bank so that she moved further inland where the hedge gave shelter. There was nothing moving at West Haven : in such weather a boat could not put out to sea, or if at sea, could not make a landing. If the sea rose, any boat caught out would run down and take shelter in the Firth of Tay.

Peter and Robert did not come down to the beach that day, but on the morrow they were back, and for the week after kept up signalling to each other. She went on noting the angles down. Perhaps one day she would learn the code and would be able to break up Robert's messages into words and read them. Peter's she did not attempt to note because she was sitting in the grass behind him and to be sure of the angles she had, at that time, to be facing the signaller.

One day Peter was not visible, but intent on Robert, she did not notice. She was taking down one angle after another, when Robert stopped, and there was Peter, almost looking over her shoulder. Clementina snatched away the slate for which he had held out his hand.

'So you have been reading our messages ! Let me see.'

'No, not reading them. Just taking them down.'

'You can't read the telegraph?'

'No. But I can guess it is something you are spelling out in letters. I'll find out one day,' she added defiantly.

'It's just wonderful! Please let me see your slate. I did not know that you could even read or write.'

'Well, I know the alphabet, and I have taught myself to read the Lord's Prayer.' Clementina blushed and reluctantly gave up the slate covered with angles. Peter scanned it.

'Yes, it is all one message, so that I can read it. You have got it all down. There are only two letters wrong.' He gave her back the slate.

'You aren't angry, are you, Peter? I didn't mean to be spying on you. But I wanted to teach myself. I was taken away from school before I could read. But I haven't forgotten the alphabet. And I can read the short words in the Prayer Book. I've taught myself that.'

'You are a bonny lassie with the best head on your shoulders of any in Angus,' said Peter gallantly. Though she was older than he was, he felt as though he would like to take her for a pupil and teach her. Clementina had blushed scarlet at his praise. Then he stopped and turned.

'It's good-bye for now. I'm being sent to Edinburgh tomorrow.'

CHAPTER TWO

DAVID CAREY'S croft consisted of a farmhouse, byres, shippons, sties and hay-barns with a hundred acres of rough grazing and ten acres of sandy ploughland which needed all the dung and kelp he could put on it if it were to raise a decent crop of oats, barley or turnips. If he had farmed his croft well and worked hard, David could have lived comfortably. But instead of a herd of milch-cows, or a flock of sheep, instead of a harvest of oats, or a field of turnips to keep his cows in milk during the winter, or for the lambing ewes, he harboured a score of gypsy ponies, whose owners paid him in flashing smiles and promises only to be broken.

David Carey was a tall man. His hair, once black, was now a mass of grey curls. He shaved the red bristles of his beard on Sunday mornings. He had a light in his blue-grey eyes, and when he spoke solemnly, Clementina knew that he was out to tease.

His household consisted of his Aunt, called 'Mother Carey' whose powers as a witch, able to raise storms and sell fair winds, were articles of faith to the older generation of Scottish seamen on the East Coast. Then there was his only legitimate child – Clementina – whose mother had died in bringing her into the world – in spite of, or because of, Mother Carey's ministrations.

David had not married again – though he had had a series of gypsy mistresses, who never lasted long, as they quarrelled with Mother Carey and were afraid of her putting a spell on them.

Four or five times a year the croft was invaded by Romanies; sometimes as many as twenty men with their women and brats innumerable would drive up with vans and covered carts, with mares and foals running free, and lurchers on rope leads trotting between the back wheels of the carts. They would set up their tents in the horse meadow and light fires.

Then David would kill a pig or a sheep and they would feast and drink, and the younger women would sing and dance, lit up by the flames of a big bonfire.

When the 'travellers' came nothing was the same. David went out to meet them laughing, all smiles for a crowd of men and women who found no welcome elsewhere. David himself was a Highlander with no Roman blood, but he treated them as though they were his clansmen, and for the couple of weeks that they stayed they could help themselves to hay and straw, their ponies could graze on his land, and on winter evenings the older men and women would crowd into his big kitchen and smoke and drink and listen to some long tale, which provoked nods and quiet comments but seldom laughter. And then a space would be cleared and they would start dancing again.

The Romanies were the earliest of Clementina's memories: she was sitting in the grass covered in daisies, so that it must have been early summer – and then, through the open gate came a rush of ponies – a white one leading, a piebald next and then, cantering up close to her, a sorrel which stopped short, snorted and stared at her and then turned away to graze, flickering its tail.

On the edge of the great horse-field where the gypsies ranged their vans and covered carts and where they put up a little street of tents, stood a row of beeches, among them a gigantic pollarded one, hollow, but with a crown from which sprang four great boles, each as large as a forest tree.

While the gypsies were there, the children were Clementina's playmates, and soon she had a bosom companion all to herself. Sarah was the daughter of Pyramus Lee, the leader of the gypsies, though not the oldest amongst them, for the 'kingship' went by birth.

Sarah was small, nutbrown, her skin the colour of a ripe hazelnut, her hair brown too and not black, like many of the women. Her little face had high cheekbones and a triangular chin below lips as red as rose-hips, and her eyes sparkled with intelligence. Like all little girls they played 'houses'. When Sarah was mistress their house was a covered cart, and in it they set out their plates made of oyster shells, the knives of razor shells, the cups of limpets, and so on.

But when it was Clementina's turn the house was in the hollow beech which she called 'Carey's Castle', with their treasures set out on an old keg as a table, with two stones on which they crouched with their backs against the wooden wall of the hollow beech. There was a top storey to Carey's Castle also, for they could lie stretched out, as on a sofa, between the great boles which sprang from the edges of the crown of the tree. In all their games they spoke Romany, and as their intimacy was renewed on every visit, by the time Clementina was eight she could speak the language as well as any of the gypsy children.

It was when Clementina was about ten years old that she overheard a conversation that puzzled her, but which she thought about and never forgot. It was market day at Arbroath and most of the gypsies had gone there, Sarah among them. Clementina, however, climbed up on to the crown of Carey's Castle and lay there idly gazing at the patterns of the beech leaves high above her. Then she heard two women talking directly below her. They were Sarah's mother Jessica and an older woman always known as 'Martha Polecat', perhaps because she was not as clean in her habits as most of the gypsy women and smelled strongly, or maybe because of her disposition.

The Polecat was saying: 'You let Sarah run about too much with that Gorgio lassie.'

'There's no harm in Clementina, or in their friendship,' replied Jessica.

'Great harm may come of it.'

'David and my Pyramus are like brothers. Why shouldn't their daughters grow up like sisters?'

'It is not David I am speaking of,' said the Polecat. 'It's his Auntie, Mother Carey. She's a witch and an evil one.'

'Clementina is a sweet child. She knows nothing of her Auntie's doings.'

'That sweet child is only living now because her Auntie means to make her a witch and as evil as she is herself.'

26

Jessica began to say something but the Polecat went on in a hoarse whisper that Clementina could just hear.

'We all know that Mother Carey gave David's wife ergot at her confinement, so that poor woman bled to death. And we may be sure that if the child had been a boy, Mother Carey would have strangled it. She saved the baby because she was a girl, and when the time comes she will hand her over to the Devil to make a witch of her. And you don't want Sarah growing up bedfellows with a young witch.'

'No, I would not. But that is looking years ahead.'

'Not more than four or five.'

'Anything may happen before then. But I'll talk to Pyramus about it.'

The two women moved away. At first Clementina felt nothing but anger that anyone should interfere in her friendship. But she did not tell Sarah for fear that the thought of her wicked Auntie should come between them. Curiously enough she never doubted that what Martha Polecat had said about her Auntie bringing about her mother's death was true. It was only later on that the conversation came back as a warning to herself – a warning that her Auntie would hand her over to the Devil to make a witch of her.

The life in the gypsy encampment was not always idyllic. One scene Clementina never forgot. It was summer, a year or two after she had overheard Martha Polecat's words. She was sitting up with Sarah watching two of the young women dancing in the light of a great bonfire, with the starry sky above, but no moon. Suddenly the dance stopped; the dancers ran aside and where they had been dancing, two men were standing exchanging angry words.

'Pig!' 'Ponce!' 'Informer!' Then they were dancing round each other with knives in their hands. But before either had struck, David Carey, a dozen years older than either gypsy, had rushed in. He felled one man with a blow from the whisky bottle he held in his right hand, and then stepping up close to the other man, knocked him insensible with a left hook to the chin. The affray only lasted a few seconds after his intervention.

Pyramus Lee the gypsy 'king' had run up to help from the far

27

side of the field. He pulled up short, then opened his arms, threw them round David and kissed him.

'Oh, my brother. You are still the man you were, ten years ago! You remember ...'

'I remember that day, Pyramus. But no more about it, before that young fellow there.'

Pyramus went and picked up the knife lying beside the man whom Carey had knocked out. Then he went up to the man whose temples were bathed in blood and wrenched the knife out of his hand.

Later the girls came back and began dancing again while the man with the bloody head had it tied up in rags, and sat and glowered at David Carey. Suddenly her father turned on Clementina and ordered her off to bed and soon afterwards all was quiet in the encampment. But before it was dawn the man with the bloody head had driven off with his old mother and his two children in a covered cart and his wife carrying her basket trudging along behind.

When the gypsies were gone the croft was quiet and in summer the house most often empty; Mother Carey would go off on some secret journey and was away for a month or more. Although the house had few rooms, it was large – of one storey with an attic reached by a ladder above the living-room. It was built partly of brick, partly of clay and wattle, roughly plastered inside and roofed with thatch, plaited and sewn down against the wind. Over all, tarred fishnets had been spread and pegged down as an extra precaution, for if, during a winter gale, the wind loosened a corner of thatch and gained entry, it was likely that the whole roof would go, leaving naked rafters. So David's roof was well-protected against such a disaster. The walls were whitewashed. There were only two little windows with glass in them, but there were two others, permanently closed, with oiled sailcloth which let in light if the protecting outer shutters were thrown open.

On each side of the big open fireplace were two shut beds with elegant frames and clean curtains. Curiously enough they were seldom occupied: David slept in the little room at the west end

28

of the house in which his father had died, and Mother Carey had her own crib in a little alcove which was scarcely a room. Clementina had recently partitioned the attic and established herself in the smaller half for the sake of privacy. The drawback was that it was dark and that she had to maintain a constant warfare against spiders.

Downstairs the big living-room was sparsely furnished with well-made ash and elm chairs standing round a fine oak table. A handsome dresser stood against one wall and opposite the Spanish tallboy, both of which had come out of Lord Lovat's castle. David Carey's mother had brought them and some silver and china long since lost, stolen or smashed. It was owing to his Fraser blood that David regarded himself not as a dissolute Lowland crofter, but as a 'shentleman' and he was recognised as such by Old Lamond whose own claims could not be pressed or openly discussed.

The fisherfolk at both Havens called such pretensions just plain daft. In spite of his gentility, the cockerel stalked through the open door and his hens flew up on to the table if Clementina or her Auntie were out of the room before it was cleared. But it was not the way in which he lived that was thought daft: it was the notion that lairds and gentry were a class above. That was as nonsensical as the French saying that all men were equal. Everyone knew that the man who stood to his oar when the boat was half swamped was a better man than the Joe who threw up with fear. And everyone knew that some men were born leaders and you would follow such a skipper through any weather. And there were men like Andy Gatt whom you could trust to follow but hadn't the head to lead or give an order. No, men were not equal, and the lairds and the gentry bred as many cowards as their clansmen. But among the fisherfolk there was no room for any such. There were the quick men and the slow ones, but there was no man in the Havens you could not trust to stand to his oar in a gale. The boys who were no good went inland. Master Lamond had been as good as any – better than most: it was his wife who had ruined him. And David Carey was all right on land, though he had never been tested in a full

29

gale in an open boat. But a lot of the gentry's heads might fall and not be missed.

Clementina's plans for a new life of study and self-improvement were not easy. Any spare moment she might have was needed for sweeping out the rooms, washing and mending clothes. Her Auntie resisted attempts to make her work, and Clementina was wise enough not to speak of her plan to educate herself. But in this she found unexpected help. Though Peter had been sent to Edinburgh, Robert had remained at school in Panbride. His mother had given him a pony, hoping that a love of riding would help to keep him from the sea. Peter had told him about the Carey girl copying down their messages, though she could not read them, and they had laughed over it. Then, after Peter had gone, it occurred to Robert that if he were to teach the girl the code, he could get her to go on practising it with him in Peter's absence.

So one Saturday afternoon when there was no school, he rode over and found Clementina sitting by the gap in the cow pasture, puzzling out some of the long words in the Bible. So many of them turned out to be names and she could not always be sure if they were people or places, or things that she had never heard of. Were the Urim and Thummim people? Or what?

She looked up at the sound of hoofs and Robert slid off his pony. He was carrying the sticks with the little white flags on them.

'Peter told me that you had been watching our signalling. I wondered whether, if I taught you the code, you would care to practise with me now that Peter is away?'

Clementina agreed and was thrilled when he told her that the telegraph was a new invention made by the French, but now used by the British Admiralty, with huge flags on masts put up on the tops of hills to send orders instantly from London to Portsmouth. Of course it could only be used on clear days. Peter had been told about it and given the code by his mathematics master.

But Robert soon discovered that the big girl, who was two years older than Peter, could only read long words with difficulty – and then that she only knew the figures but not the multiplication tables, or long division, and had never even heard of fractions. When he told her to add up three-quarters and two-thirds, she understood well enough what he meant, but said that the only way was to measure three-quarters of a pound and two-thirds of a pound of flour and then weigh it. But when he explained that three-quarters was the same thing as nine-twelfths, and two-thirds the same as eight-twelfths, her eyes sparkled and she said:

'Then the answer is seventeen-twelfths, or one and five-twelfths exactly.' And she added: 'Thank you so much for showing me. I shan't forget that.'

Robert loved having a pupil and one who immediately grasped his explanations and very seldom forgot anything that he taught her. Simple mathematics and the first two books of Euclid were delights which she raced through.

Robert gained as much from these lessons as Clementina. For there is no way of learning and of really understanding a subject better than teaching it. As a result he soon found himself top of his class and making rapid progress at school.

He gave Clementina lessons twice a week in term time. On Saturday and Sunday afternoons nobody was sufficiently interested to become aware of them except Old Lamond. Once when there was a sudden unexpected burst of hail, he came out and said: 'Come on in. I shan't listen. I learned my tables sixty years ago and haven't bothered with them since.' Then as they looked questioningly at each other he said: 'And I'll give each of you a stuffed plum sent from France.'

But when the school holidays came, Elizabeth began to inquire into Robert's absences from home, and when Peter came back, it became obvious that the two boys were constantly going off together to East Haven. Fortunately Mistress Lamond did not suspect that it was the Carey girl who was the attraction, she put it down to the old scoundrel, her father-in-law, and asked her husband to forbid his sons to go and see their grandfather. But Master Lamond shilly-shallied and while not actually refusing to speak to the boys, said that he must find a suitable opportunity.

Peter was much impressed by Robert's pedagogy and still more impressed when he questioned Clementina. She knew her tables, could deal with vulgar fractions and extract a square root. Her logical mind had enjoyed and remembered the proofs of many of Euclid's propositions. Her weakest point was spelling, and there were a great many words of which she did not know the meaning, as she had never heard them used and read no books.

It was this that led to her first quarrel with Peter.

'Why doesn't your mother call your father by his substantive?' she asked him one day.

'By what?'

'My Dad says your father's substantive is Patrick.'

Robert began laughing, but Peter asked: 'Do you mean his name?'

'You told me substantive meant a noun and a noun was the name of a thing. So what's wrong?'

Both boys roared with laughter. Clementina turned scarlet. The boys were telling her things that weren't true so as to make game of her. She ran off. She would have no more to do with them. The gypsies would not treat her so.

When a gypsy covered cart or van went through a village, the women would go from door to door with their baskets in which shoelaces and buttons were sometimes lifted aside to reveal a piece of real lace smuggled in from France or the Low Countries. If the girl who opened the door was young and pretty a bottle of scent might be opened for her to sniff, or with whining caressing voice, the offer was to read the lines on her palm. Besides the gypsies there were tramps – often crazy Highland pipers – and pedlars of various descriptions. Most of them made their rounds – reappearing twice in a year at most.

Rather more frequent was a pedlar for whom Clementina had felt a peculiar horror ever since she could remember. He was a hunchback with a sallow dirty skin; his skull was nearly bald, but with a few locks of greasy black hair dividing it, to make up for which thick tufts of black hair sprouted from his nostrils and his ears.

But his eyes were what Clementina most dreaded: they were brown but curiously flat with never a gleam or sparkle of life in them: they might have been the eyes of a cuttlefish. But by

32

contrast this hunchback pedlar carried a box wrapped in black tarpaulin, and when it was uncovered, he drew out tray after tray of rings and earrings and brooches set with sparkling diamonds or paste, or green glass emeralds and blood red rubies, and there were trays of beads, jet and turquoise and amber, and it was an agony of childhood to long to look and touch them and yet to keep as far away from the pedlar as possible.

Those flat, dead expressionless eyes knew just what she was feeling. Of that fact she was certain.

David could not endure the sight of the hunchback pedlar who came to the croft to see his Auntie and usually timed his visits when he was sure David would be absent. But one day just when the pedlar had parted from her – she never bought his beads but they had long whispered conversations – just as he was hobbling out of the yard, David came clattering up on his grey mare with a young fellow he met on the road and who came from the forest land beyond Friockheim. They had been drinking together, and the stranger had agreed to buy three stots which he would fatten up for beef. David was more than half-drunk. He could always keep his seat on a horse but he staggered around after he had dismounted. Then he noticed the pedlar and gave a defiant cat-call.

'Look at that filthy hunchback fellow. You would never guess that he has had more bonnie lasses – and gude wives also – than any man in Angus. If he ever comes to your farm with his box of sparklers, you set the dog on him.'

The stranger chuckled.

'Women have odd likings, I know. But I don't believe that for a tale,' he said.

David spat earnestly and said : 'It's God's truth. He is the Black Doctor – the witches' Devil and every young witch is his whore when he cares to have her. On the Sabbath he has the whole coven – one after the other – and when he can't do it himself any more, he uses a stone prick.'

The strange young farmer laughed loud at this and asked : 'How should you come to know all this?'

'Have you never heard of Mother Carey? She is my Auntie and

33

I got it out of her when she was drunk. She is inside there, if you want to see her.'

At the name of Mother Carey the stranger's expression had changed. He was shaking with fear and anxious to get away quickly. Five minutes later he had paid for the stots and was driving them before him along the road, but he was still scared. The stots looked like being a good bargain, but he would have no more dealings with David Carey and never go near that croft at East Haven again.

The most constant of David Carey's mistresses was Agnes, a tall handsome Highland woman, past her first youth. When she came to the croft David would be sure to have no other woman around. Agnes would stay for a month and then suddenly be away for three or four, and even though they might have parted angrily – with David glad to see the back of her – they always fell into each other's arms when she returned and for a few days life seemed richer and more delightful for everyone.

Agnes always made a great pet of Clementina, treated her as a favourite daughter, shared secrets with her, and at sixteen Clementina would have sacrificed her life for Agnes and believed that she was the greatest of her friends.

It was midsummer eve: Clementina had done a hard day's work in the hayfield and went to her bed before it was quite dark. But before she was asleep, Agnes had come and, squatting down, laid her head beside Clementina's on the pillow.

'I had to come and say good night, my sweet. You are so innocent and so good. You will love me always, won't you? Even though something changes you?'

Clementina was sleepy, but she wondered what Agnes meant. Very soon the older woman had stroked her hair, kissed her, sighed and disappeared. Clementina would have dropped off to sleep then, if her great friend Thomas, the cat, had not leapt on to her bed and begun digging his claws into the quilt and then nudging her with his muzzle under her chin. Clementina put him off her bed on to the floor. Thomas ran to the door and mewed. It was shut. Well, Thomas wanted to go out. Clementina climbed out of bed, walked to the door and opened it. The cat did not go out, but stood on the threshold, turning his head up to look at her and mewing. She pushed him out with her foot over the doorstep into the moonlight, but he turned his head to look at her and mewed his invitation once again. She could see that he wanted her to follow him, so she stepped outside, closing the door very gently behind her, and Thomas ran ahead, his tail erect, and every few yards turned his head to see that she was following. So they proceeded until, before they reached the edge of the hollow by the standing stone, Thomas hesitated. Clementina could hear voices. The cat lay flat on his belly and crawled forward as though stalking a mouse. The girl went down on hands and knees, imitating him.

When she peered over the rim of the hollow she saw Old Mother Carey and five women, unknown to her, sitting in a circle.

It seemed that one of them was deaf, for she cupped her hand to her ear and her neighbour shouted into it what the others had been saying. Thanks to this, Clementina heard it all.

'She is a powerful strong lassie,' Mother Carey was saying. 'You'll have to hold her down and give our Master help. He could not manage her by himself. There will be a lot of fight in her.'

'Maybe it would be better to wait another year,' said another woman.

'No, I think unless he gets Clemmie now, he might miss her altogether. She is so taken up with book-learning,' said Mother Carey.

'He'll be here in an hour, and some of the younger girls will come to watch the sport.'

'And to get their share after Master has finished with the lassie,' said the harsh voice of an old crone who had not spoken till then.

'You'll keep her for three or four days after she has been given the draught, Christina, you have a good padlock, for she will be bound to try and get away when she comes to,' said Mother Carey.

Clementina had heard enough. She backed away from the hollow on all fours. Then she rose and ran, in her nightgown, to the bothy. She rapped on the door and pushed it open and in the darkness heard Old Lamond sit up in bed and ask:

'What is it, lassie?' For Clementina was outlined in the moonlight.

'Gi'e me a gun to shoot the de'il,' she cried.

Old Lamond laughed, and climbed out of his bed. He was stark naked, but Clementina's words had sobered him.

'What's your quarrel with him? Tell me about it,' he commanded.

'Mother Carey and some grey sisters are sitting round the standing stone, waiting for that filthy pedlar fellow to come, and they mean to hold me down while he makes me into a witch. I'll kill the fellow rather than let him touch me.' There was a hysterical note in the girl's voice.

'So it has come to that, has it? You did well to come to me. I'll gi'e you a pocket pistol if you promise not to shoot him above the knee. We don't want a dead devil on your father's croft. It would spell trouble. And in case you miss him I'll give you a dirk and you can hit him in the face with it.'

Clementina looked up at the old man as he came into the streak of moonlight. He was still, at seventy-two, a splendidly built man, with magnificent shoulders and chest and a hollow belly. He had long hair and a short beard, but there was little hair on his body. He went to his grandfather clock, bent down and drew out a case of pocket pistols.

'I'll load this one with a light charge of bird-shot, so it won't smash his bones. Get yourself a jacket or a shawl to hide it when he comes for you and don't shoot until you are out in the open. You don't want blood in the croft.'

Clementina took the pistol and the skene-dhu silently and looked into the old man's eyes. It was only then that she realised that he was stark naked, like a god of the old days.

'Have no fear, lassie. It will be better for you to dispose of him yourself than to take shelter behind me. But I'll listen for the shot, and I'll be there if things go amiss.'

Clementina stole back to the croft. She was surprised to see that Thomas was still with her. His eyes shone in the moonlight. He did not mew or try to lead her but walked sedately by her

36

side. She put on an old jacket before she lay down in her bed, putting the pistol in one pocket and the skene-dhu in the other. Then she lay still. There was a sound, then her Auntie's voice:

'Clemmie, Clemmie. Come and help me. I've fallen and twisted my ankle.' Clementina went out.

'All right, Auntie. I know what you want with me tonight. I've been waiting and am ready.'

'Clever girl!' Mother Carey rose without help from the grass plot. 'Come with me and give me your arm.'

But Clementina kept out of her grasp. In the hollow there were ten women with the dark hunched figure of the pedlar in the middle of them. Without waiting, Clementina went straight up to him, took the cocked pistol out of her pocket, pressed the muzzle on to his knee and pulled the trigger. The Devil gave a scream that almost drowned the report of the pistol and fell on to the ground, and Clementina turned and ran for the croft, almost knocking down Old Lamond who was in waiting with a drawn claymore in his hand. He had had time to scramble into his breeches and shirt.

'I heard him screech. Where did you plug him?'

'In the knee.' The old man had taken the pistol and would have taken the knife. But Clementina clung to the latter.

'Keep the skene-dhu if it makes you feel safer. But you are in no danger now. And I shall talk to David in the morning.'

Clementina did not sleep that night and rose early. When she had finished milking she went into the croft and there was Agnes, who on seeing her, gave a cry of astonishment spreading out her arms. It was clear that she had not expected to see her. It was some minutes before Clementina realised that Agnes had known, the night before, that she was to be carried off and raped by the pedlar. She had come to her bedside to stroke her hair, to kiss her, to hope that Clementina would always love her – but not to give the warning that one could rely on from any true friend. She had known and had not told her. That was unforgivable.

Clementina said nothing but went to her father's room. Old Lamond was already there, and David was red in the face. The two men looked at the girl silently. Then Clementina said: 'Agnes came and kissed me when I was in bed last night; she knew that I was going to be taken but she did not tell me. I have finished with her.'

She turned and went out into the open air where she could breathe, and as she stood looking at the sea, Old Lamond came up.

'David has sent that old Highland trout packing. And Mother Carey will have to find another corner. David won't have her back in the croft again.' They walked in silence, and then the old man asked: 'But if Agnes did not tell you, and you knew nothing when you went to bed, what made you guess?'

'It was Thomas.' And Clementina described how the cat had come to her bed and made her follow him.

'Aye. I never believed much in witchcraft. But that is proof that there is something in it, after all. I'll give Thomas a bit of fish when he next comes round to the bothy.' As they parted he said: 'You are a fine lass to have shot the Devil. But I fear that Mother Carey will have her revenge.'

But the months went by. Rumours came that the pedlar had died of gangrene. But Mother Carey gave no sign of life.

It was the summer of 1801. Clementina was twenty-one. The first herring had just come south from Shetland. The Napoleonic wars were in full swing, but some of the inhabitants of East Haven, in particular Old Lamond and David Carey, were less elated by the British command of the sea than worried by the fact that the war had enormously increased the hazards of smuggling, which ranked not only as defrauding the revenue, but also as trading with the enemy. Moreover the excisemen were sometimes able to call on reinforcements from the navy.

This did not worry Clementina, who was in a mood to enjoy herself when the gypsies drove up.

There were bundles of contraband waiting for them to carry inland, and David and Pyramus were soon busy carrying out parcels and apportioning them among the men whose carts were least likely to be stopped and searched. While the older women cut up the pig that David had slaughtered for them, and made roasts and stews with mushrooms cooked over juniper faggots, the younger women put on their finery.

Later two of the men helped roll out a barrel of home-brewed ale flavoured with heather, while David himself carried out bottles of whisky. The men talked and drank in a group until the women called them that food was ready. Then they separated and all began eating in little groups as each family's meal was ready, though the sun had not set. Then when it disappeared over the hills inland the moon rose, seeming very large and blood-red.

All seemed to be gay and good tempered: then suddenly came Clementina's first quarrel with Sarah, who was with her boy Jonathan, a gentle fellow who would have been handsome except that he had lost an eye as a small boy.

Sarah came up smiling and said: 'Tonight you and I will dance together for everyone to see.'

Clementina shook her head. 'No, I won't dance.'

Sarah stamped her foot and said: 'You are as beautiful as any girl here and you can dance as well as I can. So, no nonsense!' And catching Clementina by the wrists she tried to drag her forward.

'No, I will not dance. You cannot force me to do what I do not wish to do. Stop, you are hurting me with your nails.'

'Don't force her against her will,' said Jonathan.

'So you are siding with the silly girl.'

Clementina tried to explain. 'I would love to dance, but Peter would not like my dancing in front of everyone.'

'So it is that stuck-up Peter! Peter this and Peter that! Peter decides what dress you wear and whether you wear shoes! And I am sure he has never given one thought to you and will come back married to an Edinburgh lady like his hen-pecked father.'

'You are not kind, Sarah.'

'I am trying to open your eyes. Supposing your Peter was caught passing bad money and was put in the tolbooth – you would wait ten years for him, I suppose?'

Clementina was crying but she bowed her head and said defiantly through her tears: 'Yes, I would wait ten years for him.'

'Oh, no, you wouldn't. You're too careful a girl.'

'I am careful where I love,' sobbed Clementina.

39

'I spit on your carefulness.' And Sarah did actually spit on to the ground.

Clementina turned away and walked out of the horse-field and watched none of the dancing. She climbed up the ladder to her attic, but she could not sleep. Doubts about her own sense in being in love with a man who had forgotten she existed, and resentment at the way Sarah had treated her, kept her tossing and turning and every little while thinking of some caustic remark which would have made Sarah ashamed. Perhaps at last she did sleep a little, for it was daylight; she got up restlessly. She put on the clothes she had thrown off, climbed down the ladder and went out.

The sun was already high, but not a figure stirred in the gypsy encampment after the night's debauch. The air was warm and the wind gentle. She walked away from the sleeping gypsies, through the cow pasture to the seashore. There were pale lilac milkmaids or cuckoo-flowers growing in the grass. They were one of her favourite flowers, though they wilted quickly, and Clementina stopped to pick herself a bunch. It was almost low tide, and the retreating sea made little deprecatory sounds of breaking wavelets and sucking withdrawal over the sand.

Clementina looked up towards East Haven and saw to her astonishment three white boats loaded with naval sailors, and she noticed Old Lamond's skiff being rowed behind them by a sailor. They were pulling down the channel, and further off she saw a party of men riding down the beach from West Haven.

Clementina turned and ran. She did not attempt to find her father, who might be snoring anywhere with his fancy woman in his arms, but ran straight to the tent where Pyramus and Jessica were asleep. She broke into the tent still holding the cuckoo-flowers in her hand.

'The excisemen and three boatloads of sailors pulling in to East Haven,' she cried.

Pyramus scrambled past her on to his feet and in two minutes the camp was alive: ponies being caught and harnessed, half-dressed men scrambling into their jackets. As each cart was ready it was driven off – keeping away from the road but through the field gate and then from field to field – some along the cattle drift to Arbroath, others turning aside to spread out over a wide area of country. The last but one of the carts loaded with contraband was well away when a band of sailors came running across the horse-field headed by a warrant officer with a bare cutlass in his hand.

'Halt, or I fire,' he shouted as Pyramus and Jessica with Sarah aboard – the last to leave – disappeared through the field gate, nearly knocking down a sailor who had run to it.

The man waved his cutlass ineffectually, and Pyramus slashed him with his whip.

And then – without warning – seeming to have sprung from nowhere, David Carey was standing in the gateway with a musket in his hands.

'I'll shoot the first man who tries to get past me,' he shouted. Everything was confusion: gypsy women screaming, children running for the ditches. Some revenue officers on horseback who had come along the beach rode up to David and shouted at him. Minutes went by. Suddenly a sailor who had climbed through a gap in the hedge stole up behind David and knocked him down with a blow from a bludgeon. His musket was seized; later he was pulled to his feet and handcuffed. But even to the last his body barred the gateway and had to be dragged aside before the pursuit began. It was hopeless. David was the only important prisoner, but two young gypsy boys were press-ganged for the navy. No contraband was found in the croft.

Old Lamond was the other prisoner. He had had his breakfast of oatcake, a bit of Dunlop cheese and a dram of whisky, then he hauled his skiff down the shore and pulled round the rocks to his row of lobster pots. He had taken a fine lobster, had picked him out and tied his claws and was baiting the pot again when he heard oars and before he could get rid of the pot and start rowing for the shore, a boatload of navy men came straight on him. He was ordered out of his skiff and told that it would be the worse for him if he resisted. A sailor jumped into his skiff, nearly swamping it, and pulled it along behind. Two other boats had come up by then.

'You'll never get into East Haven with a boat of this draught at low tide,' he said to the midshipman commanding.

'What do you mean?' asked the young man, though his meaning was clear enough.

'She draws too much water and the tide is going out; you'll be stranded.'

It was not true, but it was possible, and his warning made the naval coxswains hesitate, and a sailor was stationed in front to test the depth of water with an oar. Just then Clementina put her head over the bank, but not being opposite the East Haven entrance, she was not noticed.

Old Lamond was questioned and gave truthful answers.

'You are one of the men we want. We are to search your place.'

'Have you a warrant?' the Old Man asked.

'We are working for the excisemen. You can ask their officer about warrants.'

'Does David Carey live in the croft behind you?' was the next question.

'Cairns? No Cairnses around here.'

'Not Cairns. Carey.'

'No fisherman of that name at East Haven.' The boats grounded. Old Lamond had his wrists tied behind him with yarn and was held by the boats. After the scuffle with Carey was over, he was taken to his bothy, which was searched.

Three bundles of silk, lace and silver were found. Then the Brown Bess in the tall clock and the dirk.

'How do you come by these arms? You know they are illegal?'

'I fought under His Royal Highness the Duke of Cumberland at Culloden Moor, and the Duke was glad enough that I had them then,' answered Old Lamond.

'Can you prove it?'

'Ask the minister at Inverness where I was living at that time. (One lie will do as well as another, and it is so long since that these young men have never heard of Culloden Moor, or of the Prince either),' Old Lamond growled to himself.

He and David Carey were taken to Dundee to await trial. By midday old Mother Carey was back in the croft, rubbing her hands together and cackling unintelligibly. It was she, Clementina felt instinctively, who had betrayed David to the excisemen and who had revenged herself by so doing. And with Mother Carey there, she was not safe, though she did not give much thought to that. For her father whom she loved was likely to be hanged for armed resistance to the officers of the Crown. The least that might be hoped for was that he should be transported for the rest of his natural life to Botany Bay, or Tasmania.

Peter got back from Edinburgh that afternoon to hear the news of his grandfather's and David Carey's arrest and of the escape of the gypsies from the revenue officers. Without waiting to change out of his town clothes, he went to the paddock, caught Robert's pony, saddled her and rode off to East Haven. Clementina was not in the croft, or in the farmbuildings, so he hurried down to Old Lamond's bothy. The sun, near setting, sent a shaft of light through the door, blinding Clementina who was sitting facing him with a strange look on her face. She grabbed at a dirk lying on the table beside her, then sprang up saying: 'Oh, it's you, Peter,' and shaken with sobs, ran forward and threw her arms round him. Then looking him in the eyes, with the tears streaming from hers, she exclaimed: 'Oh, what shall I do? They will hang them both. And I can do nothing.' He pressed her to his chest and then kissed her and she lifted her head and kissed him, and for Peter the salt taste of her tears was something that he never forgot.

When he released her she looked at him and swallowed her sobbing to say: 'How grand you are, Peter, in those yellow breeches and with buckles on your shoes.'

He explained that he got home and heard the news less than an hour ago.

'Oh, darling Peter, how good of you to come.' She gulped at a glass of whisky and poured him a generous tumbler full of the neat spirit. He drank it off, still holding her with his other hand. The whisky ran like fire in him. He had seldom tasted it, having a father who never drank it in the home and himself disliking, from childhood, the sight of drunk men and the smell on the breath and the rowdiness of fishermen that followed drink. But this fire was wonderful and Clementina was looking into his eyes. He poured himself another glass. Soon afterwards

Clementina had shut the outside door and they were lying in each other's arms upon Old Lamond's bed, in the dark.

Clementina opened her bodice and he kissed her breasts. She sighed and allowed him to lay her body bare. He gulped more whisky and suddenly tore open the flap of his yellow breeches. Clementina let him pull off her linen drawers and helped the stiff hot rod of flesh to find the way. Then she could not repress a cry of pain, a moan, then lay passive and slowly, slowly every movement that he made built up into a mountain, and she cried out in ecstasy and her convulsive movements frightened Peter and she had to try and reassure him, but without success. It was cold, she got under the quilts and he lay for a little while beside her and she fell asleep, not hearing him stumble to the door and go.

She slept late and was dismayed when she found that Peter had gone. But it was wonderful. It was happiness. He would come again. Meanwhile the cows would have to be milked. She washed her face and seeing her thighs were streaked with blood did some more washing before she set her clothes to rights and went to the cowshed. She had just finished milking when she heard a pony trap being driven into the yard and went to see who it was.

There was a smart couple in a neat dogcart: a young woman in a fashionable hat beside a young man in a tall white beaver. It was Sarah with her one-eyed boy, Jonathan. Sarah leaped down and the two girls embraced. 'I've come to fetch you. Put any belongings you may need together quickly. You'll be better off and safer on the roads with us than living under the same roof as Mother Carey.'

'Come in, Sarah. Come in, Jonathan. You'll have a bite of oatcake and some tea, unless Jonathan prefers a dram of whisky.'

'No thank you, darling. And I would not touch any tea where your Auntie could have got at the canister.' Sarah was urgent to be off, as there would be search parties of excisemen on all the roads within a few hours and their disguises might be penetrated. There was no safety until they were well away into the Highlands, or over the Border into England.

Clementina explained that much as she loved Sarah and the

44

Romanies, she would not go with them.

'It's that same Peter. Be damned to his good looks,' exclaimed Sarah.

'Yes it is. He has come back from Edinburgh – and I've not heard of his bringing a wife with him,' Clementina added slyly.

'Well, Jonathan, I must not risk your neck any longer,' exclaimed Sarah. 'But if you ever change your mind and want to live with us, you may find some of our people if you cross into England. Jonathan has a friend near Bellingham who makes the real soft pipes worth all the Highland pipes of the boasted MacCrimmons. He's a shepherd called Armstrong. Don't forget.' The two girls kissed. Sarah jumped up into the dogcart and they whirled away. Clementina was going to make herself some tea. Then she remembered Sarah's words and drank a pint of new milk, still warm, instead.

There were things to do in the croft house which in her despair Clementina had neglected the previous day, and when they were done she went to the bothy and gave that a good turn-out. So it was past midday when she walked down the beach to West Haven. She walked happily, singing and feeling sure that she would soon see Peter, and, when they met, they would look into each other's eyes exchanging their secret. But at West Haven there were only Willie Windram and the two Hossacks standing together.

Willie beckoned to her. 'There is some more bad news, lassie. We reckoned on having young Peter in our boat since Angus has broken his thumb joint. But the devil must have got into the silly fool! He ran off this morning after telling his Dad that he was shipping himself before the mast in some merchant vessel, going overseas.'

Clementina stood stunned, white as a sheet, and only came to herself when she heard Willie say : 'If it's your doing, lassie, you have done everyone a wrong – not barring your own self, for you will never find a finer Joe than young Peter.'

'Shut your trap, Willie. Canna you see the poor lass is dazed with sorrow and her father taken only yesterday,' said Duncan Hossack in a kind voice. Then he went on : 'And since you are here, Clementina, I may as well tell you what my brother and I have been asking ourselves. Could young Peter have been doing any risky work to oblige his grandad – so that he would be safer away until the trial is over? If so, he has been uncommonly clever, and no one has ever had a suspicion.'

Clementina burst into tears and could not answer, but she shook her head and turned back towards East Haven. Later on she reflected that the Hossack rumour might be just as well: it would help keep her secret which would only come out if Peter had got her with child. But she could not understand why he should have gone. With any other man or boy, the explanation would have been obvious. They would have run away so as not to have to marry her. But that could not hold for Peter. He was a man of honour. And even if he were not, there was no one now to make him marry her, since her father was to be hanged. Besides which, he must surely know that she would not demand it if he were unwilling? She would accept his love in any form. Thinking of her father suddenly brought Clementina to a sense of reality. What was she going to do with herself?

It was madness now to go back to the croft, or the bothy. She must get someone to milk the cows. Her Auntie might be up to any of the Devil's tricks. She turned round and walked past the three men who were still in debate and went on to the curing sheds where she found Elspeth Marr, who had been her great friend before she was taken away from school and with whom she had kept up a warm friendship ever since.

Elspeth and a dozen other women were washing down the long tables after the day's work of gutting herrings. Clementina beckoned to her and when she came out, asked if she could come to work as one of the fisher-lassies.

'We work in threes, and Grace and I would be glad to have you with us. Mistress Wilson is a loud mouth and grabs the biggest fish. Where will you lodge? Not back in your father's croft?'

'I have come to you to get away from it and from my Auntie.'

'Well, Grace and I sleep in my uncle's attic. You are welcome to come and bed down with us. There will be room in the bed. Grace has a boy and she lets him come up sometimes if Uncle and Auntie are away. But he's a nicely behaved lad and Grace takes care that I don't get any of him, though I would not mind.'

46

So it was settled. That night Clementina slept in the same bed as Grace and Elspeth, and next morning waited to see the foreman of the sheds, who said that she could start work as soon as she had found someone to milk the cows and feed the stock on the croft.

It was almost midday before she got back to East Haven. The farm had been stripped as though by witchcraft. All the livestock was gone – all the poultry, even the two cats. Ploughs and harrows, farm implements, the hay waggon, the scythes and pitchforks, harness and ropes – all were gone. Only an old stone grass roller had proved too heavy to be flown away with. Inside the house there was not a stick of furniture, not a chair or a table, not a sheet nor a counterpane, not a saucepan or a broom. Mother Carey, if it were she, had done her work well.

But it seemed unlikely that it was her – for Clementina's clothes and her few possessions had been left untouched.

A week later the farm was occupied by bailiffs sent to seize all David Carey's goods and chattels on behalf of his creditors, by order of the court. They found nothing.

The contents of the bothy had not been touched. But then Old Lamond did not owe anyone a penny.

As a fisher-lassie Clementina earned the same wages as Elspeth and Grace, and the three girls shared in everything – except the boy Alan, if Grace brought him up to the attic. They worked so hard that they scarcely had time to break off and eat a bannock, or swallow a glass of beer or buttermilk, once a boatload of herring had come in. But they were happy together and were always laughing when they were not so tired that they could do no more at the end of the day but wash off the herring blood and try to comb the witches' stirrups out of their hair before they climbed into bed and fell asleep.

Clementina had learned her job quickly, and she had been in the curing sheds for three months. It had seemed a lifetime and the herring season was nearly over, for the boats were now fishing all the way down the Northumberland coast and into Yorkshire, when one day, just after the trough had been filled with the shining silver fish with their bloodshot eyes, she became aware that Elspeth had stopped work and was looking at her.

47

Then she felt that someone was standing behind her. She dropped the herring, but still holding the knife, turned to see who it might be.

It was young Peter Lamond, dressed like a fisherman but in new clothes: coarse blue breeches with the thick stockings pulled up and gartered above the knees, and wearing slippers like all the men when not in their seaboots. Clementina took in all that before she dared look up into his face. She began to tremble. He was not wearing a bonnet over his curly locks of black hair – for he was holding it in his hand. She looked at last into his dark blue eyes and saw that they were troubled and that he was frowning.

'Why are you working here, Clementina?' he asked in a voice so soft and gentle that she was astonished.

'I'm working while we still have the herring,' was all that she could think of to say.

'I did not expect you to become a fisher-lassie.'

'Why are you dressed like a fisherman? I heard you had run off to be a sailor.'

'So I did. Because I did one wrong, I did wrong again. The ship I was on was wrecked in Norway but we were fortunate and no one was drowned. I have come to beg forgiveness.'

'I thought you had come to pity me, because my father is waiting to be hanged. I can do nothing for him, and he can do nothing for me,' she burst out.

'If you deserve pity, so do I. My grandfather is in the Tolbooth and on trial with him. But your conscience is clear, and mine is not.' Peter spoke with dignity, and Clementina recovered herself and waited silently.

'I thought you would be working on a croft. It was Willie who told me where to find you.' Again he was speaking with a strange gentleness.

Clementina laughed. She had been on the point of tears a moment before.

'So I might. But on what croft? Not my father's. My Auntie has flown away with every stick on the farm or in the house; she would have flown away with me too if I had stayed a day longer after David was taken....'

48

'Yes, I heard that.'

'She would have dated me with the Devil too. But there'll be another to take his place. Except that he was murdered, I'm told. I would rather be a fisher-lassie, like my good friends here.'

'You might have found something better ...' Peter began.

'What's it to do with you, Master Peter, where I work?' she asked angrily, for his words reflected on the two girls beside her. She had turned her back on the troughs of fish and was facing him, and the two girls working beside her had stopped work and had turned towards him to listen.

Peter turned rather red in the face, but behaved as though neither girl were there.

'I have a great respect and a great liking for you, Clementina,' he said, speaking in the same gentle voice. The remark astonished her, but if he could ignore the existence of her companions, she could not.

'Does that give you the right to ask me about what I choose to do?' she asked, half hoping that he would answer: 'Yes, it does.'

'Not any right. But you might forgive an interest.'

There was a silence. Then for the first time Peter looked at each of the listening girls beside them and gave to each a slight inclination of the head; it was less than a bow, but it was an acknowledgement of their presence. Then he asked with quiet dignity: 'May I meet and talk with you on Sunday after kirk, Miss Carey?'

Clementina flashed him a warm smile. 'Indeed you may.'

He was gone.

CHAPTER THREE

DISASTERS had fallen thickly upon the head of Mistress Lamond. She had married a poor man and had raised him up in the world. Poverty she could have borne. If Master Lamond's boats had been wrecked or his curing sheds swept by fire, if ruin had come, she could still have held her head high. But disgrace she could not endure, and it was disgrace that had come upon her. With her father-in-law in prison, how could she escape the pity of kindly folk and the contempt of those who had previously looked at her with envy in their hearts?

The trial was not yet – but it was clear that since goods had been found in his possession he would be condemned. He might be hanged, and Mistress Lamond would have wasted no pity on him if he had gone to the scaffold. There was a chance, however, that as he had made no resistance he might only be transported to Botany Bay. It was the best that could be hoped for, since after a few years it would be forgotten.

After all, the grandfathers of many men highly respected today had committed treason. Lord Lovat had even had his head cut off, and no one thought the worse of the family. But, of course, they were great folks.

But the disgrace that Master Lamond's father had brought upon her was the least of Elizabeth's troubles. Her son Peter, about whom they had received most encouraging reports from Edinburgh, had taken no advantage of his opportunities, but had run away to sea, been wrecked, and on his return had declared that he was going to be a fisherman. It was madness and perhaps a madness that was in the blood. For his father, who, as she knew only too well, could be crazily obstinate, had backed the boy up and had promised him, later on, the command of his new boat *Patience* which had been building for more than a year and was just finished.

Storm succeeded storm in the Lamond house. Elizabeth raged,

and her husband said little in reply, but he refused to give way.

But when he said: 'Peter is old enough to choose for himself, and he might have chosen a lot worse. I indeed would rather live the life of a fisherman than that of an apothecary,' it was too much.

Mistress Lamond's brother was the famous professor of surgery and was known all over the civilised world; her husband's reference was insolent.

'You may not be in the Tolbooth yourself, thanks to me, but you come from a family of criminals. Whatever lies he may tell, your father is a Jacobite at heart, and he has lived by lying and smuggling – which is no better than thieving – ever since he escaped from Culloden. And now the criminal taint is coming out in my son.'

'You have said enough for today. You had better retire, Madam,' said her husband in the quiet voice that made her despair.

To her son Peter she repeated her description of the Lamonds as a family descended from criminals – a clan of miscreants no better than the MacGregors – who had been driven out by the great Duke of Argyll. And only her influence had saved his father from continuing in the family tradition. But for her, he would be in the Tolbooth along with his father now.

But her son interrupted the flow of words.

'I respect my father. You must say no more if you wish me to continue to respect my mother.' And with that he walked out of the room.

For the first time in her life Mistress Lamond broke into a flood of hysterical weeping. They could hear her all over the house and even in the garden. What did it matter now that all Panbride should know of her disgrace? How could she face Mrs Henderland in the kirk? She who had been so proud and her equal must show herself as a broken and defeated woman!

And with that prospect in mind she decided to go and stay in Edinburgh with her brother until her husband returned to a sense of their position in the world and of what was fit and proper.

Master Lamond raised no objection to her plan when it was

put before him, and next morning, sitting stern and upright, she was driven to where the stage coach took on passengers for Dundee where she would take the coach for Edinburgh. She hoped to find Robert there, but his school had broken up, and he might have left his uncle's roof. Robert was her last hope! But nonsense! Her husband was a careful man, and he must surely come to his senses before long.

On the day of her departure Robert returned home. He must have passed her coach on the road. Next morning, when they were alone together, Peter asked his father if he thought that his grandfather would be hanged or if he would be transported, and whether something ought not to be done to help in his defence. Master Lamond eyed his son without enthusiasm, but showed no hostility at the question.

'You know as well as I do, Peter, that there is smuggling all along the east coast of Scotland. I have no great moral objection to it. But when I was a boy I decided that I should be better off if I had no hand in it. And that is why I walked out and went to Edinburgh, and you can see that, by worldly standards, I was right.'

There was a silence, Peter waiting for his question to be answered. Then his father went on:

'I am a good deal surprised that the excisemen should have found contraband goods in the bothy. My father was, and is, a very careful man. A musket and a dirk – that is all sentimental nonsense, and the judge will see it like that. Your grandfather fought for the Prince at Culloden when he was a lad of your age. He has never acknowledged the Hanoverians in his heart – and he makes that a sort of excuse for defrauding their revenue. But it is not like him to have been taken with the goods on him. As to helping him, there is not much I would care to do, or that needs doing. He won't be short of guineas to fee an advocate.'

Robert had come into the room unperceived by his father or his brother. Peter said: 'I can see it would be difficult for you to do anything, because there have been no goings and comings between you, but perhaps I ...'

'Well, when I brought your mother here I made her a promise that I have greatly regretted. But that's the way it is.'

52

Robert's young voice interrupted them with the words: 'That promise does not hold for me. I went to see Grandpapa in the Tolbooth before I came home.'

'You did, Robbie?' His father was astounded.

'They kept me waiting for a very long while, and I began to be afraid that he would not want to see me. But he was pleased. He was very pleased. He held me in his arms. I had taken him some oatcake and a black bun, but he sent me out to buy him a clean shirt, which was what he wanted most.'

'You did very well, Robbie,' said his father. Suddenly he looked up. 'Well, the men are waiting for you, Peter. There is work to be done. The shoal of herring won't wait.'

In the absence of Mistress Lamond, Peter's meeting with Clementina after kirk caused very little sensation among the Panbride congregation. Peter went up to her as they came out of the porch and led her up to his father, who was standing among the gravestones talking to Duncan Hossack and Willie Windram who had taken shares in the new boat *Patience* and would be members of the crew.

'Well, Clementina, you have grown into a bonnie lass – and so now you've thrown in your lot with us fishermen.'

Willie Windram was clearly amused at Master Lamond calling himself a fisherman, since he had not been to sea for ten years.

'Well, Master Lamond, Miss Clemmie is not the only one. Here's Peter come back to join us and a bonnier pair you never saw. Don't spend too long over the courting, Peter.'

'That's enough from you, Willie,' said Clementina. 'I don't care for that sort of joking while my father is waiting to be hanged.'

Willie Windram mumbled something and Peter and she turned away and walked side by side up the hill to the great beech-wood.

'You are angry, my dear,' said Peter.

'Not angry, but a fellow like that ought to know better.'

'If I could do anything for David. . . .' Peter began but Clementina looked at him in sudden fury. 'It's just words, all words. . . .' Peter then told her of Robert's visit to the Tolbooth, and of Old Lamond's pleasure at seeing him, and of his sending him out to buy him a clean shirt.

Clementina's whole mood changed, and she laughed with delight.

'I love your Robbie. He has the warmest heart of all of ye.'

'Indeed he has,' Peter agreed enthusiastically. 'I was talking to my father about getting some help at the trial for my Grandpapa, and as you say it was just words, all words. And then Robbie burst in having done the thing I was only talking about. He is worth ten of me!'

Clementina laughed aloud. 'Don't think too badly of yourself, Peter. I dare say you have your points if one only had time enough to find them out.'

Peter took hold of her arm almost roughly, and turned her about to face him.

'You can have all the time you like.' She saw that there were tears in his eyes.

'It sounds as though you were proposing a very long engagement.' She was laughing.

'Only until I can earn good wages. My father has promised me that I shall skipper *Patience* when the crew trust my seamanship.'

He took her in his arms and kissed her, but she pushed herself free and, laughing, repeated the name *'Patience! Patience.* Your boat is well named. How many years will it be before four men are fools enough to trust their lives to you?'

Then as her teasing had made his face a picture of misery and doubt, she threw her arms round his neck and kissed him again and again. They held hands after that and walked a few yards in silence. She was the first to speak.

'You have made me happy. And I thought I should never be happy again. And what right have I to be happy with my father ...'

'I'll go and see him and try and get his blessing,' Peter interrupted.

'Would you do that?' Clementina was astonished.

'I'll put a hare or a salmon in the boat next Friday. Then Duncan Hossack will never go out to sea that day.'

'He would be a rash man who did,' said Clementina seriously.

'Do you believe all these superstitions?' asked Peter, laughing.

'But it's known, isn't it? If you meet a dog, or the minister, or there is a salmon or a rabbit in the boat, you may as well not go out. There'll be no fish.'

'That is all nonsense. Like buying a good wind from Mother Carey.'

'You don't believe that either?' she asked, awed.

'Of course not. It's against the laws of nature. Think. Try and think and you'll see what nonsense all these superstitions are.' Clementina was silent. Peter must be right, but how could she discard all her beliefs at a word from him?

Meanwhile *Patience* was to be launched, and this was an occasion in which ceremony and superstition played their part. The open North Isles vole boat was twenty-five feet in length overall. She was dragged and pushed out of the builders' yard on rollers. Then she was run down to the beach at ebb tide. Master Lamond was cheerfully supervising all the operation. At the actual launching, he broke a bottle of whisky over her stern and Willie Windram recited:

> 'Frae rocks and sands
> An' barren lands
> An' ill men's hands
> Keep's free,
> Weel oot, weel in
> Wi' a gude shot.'

At the last line the crew of five men rushed her into the sea and leapt in. Duncan Hossack was at the tiller, and the four men at the oars were his son Donald, Peter Lamond, Willie Windram and Andy Gatt. The crew had not yet chosen their skipper, and Duncan's position at the tiller was only temporary. After rowing *Patience* down the entrance of the channel they rowed her back and ran her up above the high-tide mark. The masts had yet to be fitted.

David Carey was looking very glum when Peter went to see him. And when Peter told him that he and Clementina wanted to be married as soon as he was made skipper of the new boat *Patience*, he looked glummer still.

'You see that I am in no position to do what I would like for my daughter. You are a good lad, but she is lowering herself by marrying a fisherman. And why have you chosen to be one? You could have got away from all that. Were there no opportunities for something better in Edinburgh?'

'It's my choice. I like the sea.'

'You have chosen badly, and I would not give my consent to the marriage if it were not that your grandfather is a gentleman of good blood and was a close friend of my father's and has been like a father to me ever since James Carey died. The Lamonds are not fisher stock. They are gentlemen like the Frasers.'

'Thank you for the good opinion of my family,' said Peter.

David Carey dismissed the subject of his daughter and revealed what was on his mind.

'I shall be convicted. There's no doubt of that. And it will be a public hanging, and for that, my boy, I must have blue velvet breeches, a white ruffled shirt, white stockings and silver buckles on my shoes. And where am I to get them? Every penny I have in the world has been taken from me by my rascally creditors. If I am to be hanged, I must be decent or I could not bear it. And I would not be found wanting. . . .'

'Before the trial I promise that I'll send you a tailor to take your measurements, a shoemaker and a shirtmaker. You have my promise,' said Peter.

'You are a good lad, though I am sorry you are to be a fisherman. And thanks for the snuff. As to Clementina, she has a mind of her own. But if she is satisfied with a fisherman, there is no help for it. You have my blessing, though none of the Careys or the Frasers have married fisherfolk before.'

Much to his surprise Peter was chosen skipper by the four older men who manned *Patience*. He had studied navigation at Edinburgh and knew more than they, and they chose rightly. But it was nevertheless an extraordinary choice because Duncan Hossack, his son Donald, Willie Windram and the huge Andy Gatt who was a mandrake man – that is he mixed the powdered and roasted root of white bryony in his food – he believed that it kept away rheumatic pains – were all men ten to fifteen years older than Peter and yet were ready to accept his authority. It was not because he was Master Lamond's son – though that helped a little. It was because they felt safe in Peter's hands.

Directly Peter was chosen skipper, he asked Clementina to marry him at once.

'The trial is coming on in a month's time, and it may last a month or two. It would not look well for us to be married while it was going on,' he argued.

'Nor directly it is over when we shall both be in mourning,' said Clementina.

Peter muttered something about funeral bakemeats.

'What are you saying, Peter?'

'Words from a play I saw while I was in Edinburgh. One day I'll read it to you.'

But married, they must have a roof over their heads, and Peter went off to see his grandfather in the Tolbooth.

He came to the point at once: he had been chosen skipper of *Patience*, he was marrying Clementina just as soon as they could find somewhere to live in. 'So I have come to ask you if I may have the bothy.'

'No, Peter. You cannot. I shall be back there directly this trial is over.'

'I am glad you are so confident.'

'I am certain to be acquitted. If I knew that I was going to be hanged, as you seem to think, then you would be welcome to it for your honeymoon.'

'No, Grandpapa. There can be no question of hanging. But I think that transportation is almost a certainty.'

'You are wrong on both points. There are many who would like to see me taking the jump. If they could convict, they would hang. There would be no mercy. But they will be disappointed.'

'Well, I do pray that you are right. And please forgive my asking,' said Peter.

'There's nothing to forgive. Clementina has a warm heart and I have loved the girl since she was a baby. To tell the truth she deserves better than you.'

'You are right there,' said Peter.

'Well, before you go, I will say that there is an old shippon on my land. The roof is still sound. You could build on to it as you need. I'll give Clementina the shippon as a wedding present.'

'That is very generous. Thank you. Clementina and I will go and look at it tomorrow.'

'Is she still working as a fisher-lassie gutting your father's herrings?'

'No. I have made her stop that now she is marrying me.'

'And the Hossacks and that poor creature Willie Windram and that fellow Gatt have chosen you as skipper?'

'They have shown that trust in me, Grandpapa.'

'Well, I expect they are as good judges as any in East or West Haven.' The old man nodded in dismissal.

When Peter returned from his visit, Clementina was shocked by his having asked his grandfather point-blank for the bothy.

'You showed him that you believed that he was going to be hanged or transported.'

'It seems reasonable to think the latter. But he is perfectly certain that he will be acquitted. He said that he would be back in the bothy directly the trial was over.'

'If he is so certain, I am sure that he is right. But how generous to give me the shippon although you went begging, presuming his death.'

Peter did not try to justify himself and they went off to look at the shippon at once.

It had been used for sheep for half a century. It was small, built of stone, with a roof of thatch. A big fireplace almost filled one wall, with a brick oven on one side of the hearth. There were two windows, but they had not been glazed because of the tax. Peter measured them. He would get putty and glass from Dundee and glaze them at once. When the inches of filth on the floor had been shovelled and scraped out, it was revealed as made of black polished flagstones split from the great belt of rock that encircled the land. Clementina scraped down the walls and scrubbed the floor, while Peter oiled the hinges and put a lock on the door, though he would have to chisel a piece out of the doorpost

58

later to take the ward. The room was big enough for two people to live comfortably, but furniture would be needed: a bed, a table, chairs.

Peter had to go out with *Patience* next day, but Robert arranged to meet Clementina at the shippon and to help her.

He got there first and came running and in great excitement.

'You must shut your eyes and let me lead you.'

'How did it happen?' exclaimed Clementina when she opened her eyes. There on the floor which she had scrubbed so carefully the day before, stood a table and beside it chairs. Both table and chairs were familiar enough; they had been in the croft and had only been spirited away in time to avoid their being seized by the bailiffs. Now they had magically reappeared. And in the alcove on the far side of the hearth was the larger of the two shut beds. There were pots and pans, knives, forks and spoons, cups and saucers, plates and a breadboard, all familiar to her since childhood.

'How did it happen? Who was the good angel?' Robert was agog.

'I shall not inquire too closely. But it seems that Peter and I will have good neighbours,' said Clementina.

The two of them worked away, lit a fire, and next morning when they came it was scarcely a surprise to find the fire made up and blazing and that curtains had been hung beside the windows and linen and quilts spread upon the bed.

The day fixed for the wedding arrived. They had decided not to be married in the kirk at Panbride, but in a chapel at Carnoustie. Peter's mother was still in Edinburgh, and Master Lamond did not wish to attend in her absence without her knowledge, which he would have been bound to do if the wedding had taken place in the kirk within a stone's throw of his garden. Grace and Elspeth came as bridesmaids. And then, just as the wedding party were setting off, there was a clattering of hoofs and Clementina saw with dread a red-faced, red-haired fellow ride up on a tall rangy animal. He dismounted and announced in a loud but husky voice, 'I'm Fraser. Jamie Fraser, come to give the bride away *in loco parentis* as I was taught at school.' Then, pouncing on Clementina, he gave her a kiss reeking of whisky.

'Oh, my bonnie, bonnie lassie. The spit of your loved mother, a Lindsay. I was her first Joe and am a cousin of your father's, no less.' And Fraser planted another kiss on the bride's lips.

He had planned, it seemed, to take a leading part in the ceremony and insisted on making an incoherent speech in which he claimed that Clementina being half a Lindsay on her mother's side and a quarter Fraser on her father's, was the social equal of any lassie in the land.

'Peter, my boy, I've been on a stud farm all of my life and I know what I'm talking about. You are a very lucky fellow to have such fine breeding stock to your bed.'

After the simple ceremony was over, Jamie Fraser brought out a bottle and declared he would pledge them all in the best malt whisky. Then, catching sight of Elspeth who was giggling, he descended upon her and after a noisy kiss, began whispering in her ear. 'Help!' cried Elspeth. But Mr Fraser had attached himself, and a dirty hand began to fondle her breast. She resisted, and he began to twist her right arm, which brought him a resounding box on the ear from her left hand.

'I'll whip some sense into the bitch, by God I will.' And he might have attempted the feat if Willie Windram and Donald Hossack had not taken him by the elbows and run him into the little vestry where bride and bridegroom had just signed their names, and there they locked him in.

The intrusion of Clementina's uncle was soon forgotten, and at a party given by Skipper Marr, master of the *Eliza*, and his wife, they sat down to a spread of oysters, crab and lobsters, haggis and kale, plum bun, bannocks and seedcake, washed down with a flowing bowl of home-brewed ale and ending with a dish of flummery, that is cream, whipped up with heather honey and malt whisky. Jigs, reels and fishermen's hornpipes followed, but after an hour or two, the married pair stole away unperceived.

They were flushed from the dancing and the unaccustomed rich food and stood for a little while on the high bank above the shore looking at the waves. They paused when they reached Peter's boat *Patience*.

'Fine built. Scottish oak and larch,' said Peter, stroking the gunwale. Then sensing something in the girl beside him, he said : 'My mother's actions are unforgivable. But bear no ill-will against my father. He knows his duty is to live with her when she returns, and if he had come to our wedding, as he would have liked to do, he would never have had another hour's peace. It will be hard enough for Robert to put up with her, as he will have to do for a few more years. But of course he is her ewe-lamb, and if he becomes in time a surgeon, it will make up for my relapse.' Then they walked together back the two miles to East Haven.

In the shippon the fire was still glowing. Peter blew up the embers and put on more logs. They looked at each other. Peter locked the door. It was almost dark except when a flame shot up throwing shadows. Soon they were in the narrow bed together. The flames flickered, throwing shadowy patterns on the ceiling.

The courthouse was cold and draughty, and the Clerk of the Court blew his nose between every sentence that he spoke, and the Judge looked as though he were carved from granite. Old Lamond's case came first. He had made a few concessions to the importance of the occasion. He had been shaved, head, chin-beard and all, and was wearing a small neat old-fashioned wig with side rolls and a queue tied with a black silk ribbon. But his clothes were those of every day : dark blue woollen breeches with thick stockings gartered above the knee, and over his knitted woollen jerseys the leather sword-proof coat that he had worn on Culloden Moor. He was obviously in excellent spirits with a mocking smile on his tight lips as he bowed to the Judge and a lively eye that took in everyone in the Court. He looked round from the dock and blew a kiss to Clementina after he had been sworn.

'Not guilty, my lord.'

The prosecution called evidence as to the finding of three bundles of contraband, of their examination, and with a list of their contents read out:

61

'Item: twenty-six silver spoons, not hall-marked in Great Britain or Ireland.

'Item: a pearl and ruby necklace set in gold, apparently of Italian workmanship.

'Item: one ivory fan and one of black lace and jet beads. . . .'

So the lists went on.

The defence was a surprise.

Monsieur Antoine Laval was called and sworn in. He was a tall spare man with a little straw-coloured wig, and a long pale face on which was a permanently supercilious expression.

'Monsieur Laval, are you the valet of the Marquis of Lautréamont?' asked Old Lamond's advocate.

'*Oui* – yes.'

'Have you seen any of the articles in these bundles before?'

'Yes, sir. They belong to my master the Marquis.'

'Is the Marquis within the realm?' asked the Judge.

The question had to be repeated as Monsieur Laval had not understood it.

'Is the Marquis in Scotland?'

'Yes, my lord. 'E would have gone to the guillotine if 'e 'ad rested in France.'

'And you swear that these articles are his property?'

Monsieur Laval swore it.

Old Lamond was called and swore that he had received the bundles from a Breton fishing-boat and that he was waiting to restore them to their owner. The Judge raised his hand.

'I rule that on the evidence just given the articles seized are not contraband, for although smuggled out of France they are not merchandise, but the private property of a French nobleman in exile.'

The prosecutor intervened: 'I submit, my lord, that there is a strong presumption that the accused, though in this case smuggling private property, is a professional smuggler and should be convicted accordingly.'

'I am not trying the accused on your presumptions, Mr Gavin, but on the facts. Any other charges against the accused?' asked the Judge.

The musket and the Highland dirk were produced.

Old Lamond acknowledged that he had owned them for very many years. The jury found him not guilty of having contraband in his possession and that the case in regard to the musket and dirk was not proven. Old Lamond was discharged. A new jury was sworn, and David Carey took Old Lamond's place in the dock.

He was a very fine gentleman indeed, with his white ruffled shirt, his blue velvet breeches, white stockings and silver buckled shoes. Since no contraband had been seized at the croft, the case against him was of possessing an illegal firearm, to wit a musket, and of taking up arms against the officers of the Crown. The prosecution demanded the death penalty.

The advocate for the defence asked:

'You are a famous horseman, Master Carey?'

'I am a horseman, and I own, or owned, a stud of horses.'

'Do you own the musket?'

'Yes, sir.'

'Why?'

'If a horse of mine breaks a leg or for some reason has to be destroyed, I shoot it. I think the pole-axe is cruel, and I would hate to use it.'

'Do you admit that while holding the musket you defied the excise officers to go past you?'

'Yes, sir, I do.'

'What explanation can you give of such conduct?'

'I was suddenly woken from a deep sleep, still more than half drunk. I looked out and saw women and children flying in all directions. The musket stood by my bed. I seized it and ran out and challenged the intruders.'

'Your defence is then that you were drunk?' asked the Judge.

'I was startled out of a deep sleep after I had been drinking deeply.'

The jury were in retirement for an hour. Then the foreman appeared and said: 'One of the jurors will not agree to have the accused hanged. But he will agree to bring him in guilty if he is only to be transported.'

'That is not possible. The jury must bring him in guilty, not guilty or the case not proven. The Judge pronounces the sentence if he is guilty.' There were long consultations. Then rather than discharge the jury, empanel a new one and start the trial anew, the prosecutor said: 'In view of the fact that the musket was not discharged and was indeed unloaded, we are ready to withdraw the capital charge and ask for a sentence of transportation for life.'

'You would have saved the Court a great deal of time if you had said so earlier, Mr Gavin,' said the Judge. His last words were: 'I hereby sentence you, David Carey, to transportation to His Majesty's dominions beyond the seas for the remainder of your natural life.'

CHAPTER FOUR

MISTRESS LAMOND was a broken woman. She had confided her troubles to her brother, who listened carefully, questioned her with sympathy and gave his opinion after pushing his spectacles up to the top of his forehead and then shutting his eyes.

'There is no blinking the fact, Elizabeth,' he began, and paused for so long that his sister looked at him to see whether he were in fact blinking – but no – the eyes were tightly shut.

'There is no blinking the fact that your duty is with your husband, and that as you have made your bed, so you must lie on it.'

'But ...' began Elizabeth.

'Listen to me, my dear sister. You have done well by your husband and he has done well by himself. Now that his father has been acquitted, no one can hold up a finger. All is as before.'

'Everyone knows that he has been the head of the smuggling gang at East Haven....'

'You say that everyone knows it, but the Judge was quite right to dismiss Master Gavin's presumptions. And now that David Carey is to be transported and the gypsies cleared out, there will be little smuggling at East Haven for some time to come.'

'It is not the smuggling I care about. It is my son Peter!' And Mistress Lamond sobbed aloud.

'Peter is a fine young man but headstrong, and he has apparently made a bad choice in the matter of a wife and in that of a profession.'

'I shall never speak to that girl,' declared Elizabeth.

'I trust that you will think better of that. But you have two sons and you must place your hopes in Robert. He spoke of wishing to become a surgeon. I will do all I can to help him in his studies. As for Peter, he may be taken into, and greatly extend, his father's business. I have always felt that Patrick....'

'Peter,' interrupted his sister. 'You know that I cannot bear the name of Patrick....'

'I remember. Well, I have always thought that your husband erred on the careful side. He has done well with the fish curing, but he would have done far more if he had agreed to introduce the new chemical method of curing that I suggested and the yellow dye for haddock would help the fish to sell better. Perhaps Peter may be less rooted in old ways than his father.'

The professor opened his eyes, and pulled his spectacles down on to his nose. Then he picked up a little book.

'I was looking up the coaches. There is one coach which only waits half an hour in Dundee before going on to Montrose. It will take you to the staging point at Muirdrum, not three miles from Panbride, where Patrick will meet you. I wrote to him directly after his father's acquittal.'

Mistress Lamond was being dismissed from her brother's house. The shock was so great that when he again called her husband by the name of Patrick, she had not the heart to correct him. Next morning she took her place in the coach for Montrose.

There was little chance of Clementina accidentally meeting with Mistress Lamond for several reasons. That lady seldom went to West, and never to East, Haven, and *Patience* was berthed at East Haven where all the members of her crew had their homes. Since their marriage Peter and Clementina seldom went to Panbride, having exchanged attendance at the Panbride church for the Carnoustie chapel.

Peter rarely saw his father either, and the link between the grand house next to the manse and the humble shippon was Robert. He indeed spent most of his time helping Clementina to whitewash the outside walls, to dig a patch for kale and turnips and to plant a herb garden with roots of parsley, mint, sage and scallions filched from his mother's garden in Panbride.

Then he would run over to the bothy on some errand : perhaps to return an iron girdle for baking oatcake in the ashes which Grandpapa had lent until Peter bought one of their own.

The shoals of herring had swum out of northerly waters

and the West and East Haven boats did not attempt to follow them beyond the Yorkshire coast but went back to line fishing for cod and haddock.

Old Lamond had caught cold in prison and after his return to the bothy stayed indoors coughing and wheezing. He could look after himself with a little help from Clementina, who brought him a quart of milk and sometimes a pat of butter and a batch of oatcake. He trusted to warmth and whisky to put him to rights, but he could not row out in his skiff to look at his lobster-pots. So, one Sunday when Peter was not fishing, he and Robert, taking Clementina with them, ran their grandfather's skiff down to the shore and set out to collect the catch and bait his pots again. The wind was fresh, and the sea a bit choppy.

'I'll take the oars; you steer, you know the channel better,' said Robert.

Soon after they reached the row of pots Robert was in difficulties: he had to keep the skiff head to wind, and stop her from being blown sideways, while Clementina pulled in a cork marker with a boathook and then hauled up the pot below. She then had to open the pot and shake out the crabs and lobsters into the big bucket they had brought. Some pots were full up with the catch, and she had to use tongs to pull the lobsters out. Then she baited the pot, fastened it up and threw it overboard. She got three pots emptied. Then at one moment she was pulling a big black lobster out with the tongs and in the next there was a crash. A wave had tipped the skiff just as Robert was putting all his strength into pulling his left-hand oar; the blade had lifted above the surface and Robert had fallen backwards, hitting his head against a thwart.

Peter leapt forward from the stern, but he was too late. The skiff, sideways to the wind, was drifting very fast on to the belt of rock only a few yards away. The oar with which Robert had 'caught a crab' had floated out of the rowlock and was a yard away. Robert struggled up, lost his balance, and the skiff tipped and began to fill with water as Peter fended her off the rocks with the remaining oar. Suddenly he dropped it, pulled his knife out of its sheath and sticking it through Clementina's waist belt ripped off her skirt. 'We shall have to swim for it,' he was saying.

The point of the knife had made a scratch from the small of her back to her buttock. Next moment they were in the water. The sun was almost blinding, the waves sparkled blue and green and broke in foam on the black slimy rock beside them, the seaweed floated up green, brilliant.

Clementina felt no fear: it was all too sudden and too brilliant.

'Catch hold of this and don't struggle,' Peter ordered, pushing an oar towards her. 'And don't swallow more water than you can help.' As a child she had learned to swim a few yards, and now she obeyed Peter. She held on to the oar and Peter pushed it and her along. Her skirt and petticoat had slid off, but her cotton drawers clung round her knees. At last she got one leg free and the garment clung to her other ankle.

Neither Robert nor Peter had been wearing seaboots, and Peter succeeded in getting out of his thick jacket and was making every effort. But, though he said nothing, Clementina knew that they were making little progress. Both wind and tide were against them as Peter struggled to get away from the belt of rocks. They had to keep clear until they could round the rocks guarding the entrance to East Haven. For every yard Peter gained, the tide would roll the oar and them back a couple of feet. Clementina began kicking and that, little as it was, turned the scale. They drew past the guard rocks, and then the wind and tide were with them and they were swept down the channel. Still clinging to the oar and kicking gently, they were able to get their breath and recover. Then in shallow water they used the oar as a punt pole to push themselves forward and stop the undertow carrying them back. At last they crawled ashore. They lay exhausted, side by side, their hearts thumping, and fighting for breath and at moments, as the sun warmed them, sinking almost into unconsciousness.

It seemed to her absurd that all this should have happened when the sun was so warm and everything so brilliant; even the wind was warm, though it was blowing harder.

Peter staggered to his feet and pulled Clementina up beside him. She was naked from the waist down except for a bit of linen still clinging to one foot. They looked down the narrow channel with the waves dancing and breaking in patches of foam over the rocks. There was no sign of Robert.

'I'll muster a crew and we'll take *Patience* out to search.' Then, staggering with difficulty up the bank, Peter went off to collect men to man *Patience*.

Clementina pulled the remaining rag of her linen drawers off her ankle and tried to run to the shippon. But she was surprised that she could only walk. A boy playing tip-cat looked up and watched the half-naked woman pass. He was puzzled. In the shippon she tore off her wet blouse and jersey, dressed herself fast and ran – she could run now – back to *Patience*, carrying with her a pair of breeches and stockings, a smock, a blanket and a bottle of whisky.

Peter had raised a scratch crew: the Hossacks, Willie Windram's nephew Colin Swankie, and old Job Soutar, who could still pull an oar in an emergency. Peter pulled off his wet clothes, put on the dry ones and took a swig out of the bottle while the crew pushed *Patience* down and launched her in the channel. Peter climbed on board, and they pushed off.

Clementina stood on the shore among a little crowd which had gathered. *Patience* shot down the channel, breasting the bigger waves that came at high tide. Once clear of the rocks, she turned and disappeared. A long wait followed. Clementina felt, for the first time, the pain of the scratch made by the point of Peter's knife stinging with the salt of the sea water. It stung and it ached, and she hoped it was not bleeding into the clean drawers she had pulled on. Children who had come out began larking about and were sternly reproved by their elders. At last, when the sun had already begun to cast shadows of the rocks on to the sea and the beach itself was in deep shadow, she could see *Patience* slowly draw out past the rocks to the mouth of the channel. She was towing something: the overturned skiff, or what was left of it. And then when she was nearing the shore she could see the blanket, covering something stretched out in the prow of the boat. She ran down as the boat touched and then was run up on to the sand. The blanket was lifted, and there was Robert's body. He had a bad wound in the temple. The blood had washed away and only marked the edges of the

69

wound. He must have been stunned by being thrown on the rocks, before he drowned.

The body was lifted out, carried up the bank, covered with the blanket and deposited in the dray that was used to carry a catch of fish to the curing sheds. Peter sent off Colin Swankie to run to Panbride to break the news to his parents and to tell them that Robert's body was on its way. Peter himself rode in the dray, stern, silent, frozen. Clementina went to the bothy to break the news to Old Lamond.

While she had been clinging to the oar and kicking to help Peter, she had felt gay without a particle of fear. She had in fact enjoyed the danger, and the near proximity of death had been a stimulant. Then, while she was watching, a revulsion had set in, and when Robert's body, still dripping with sea water, was carried up and she had seen his bloodless face and the long deep cleft in his temple, she would have liked to have killed herself. Nothing could alter what had happened. She felt torn in pieces, and if it had not been for the knowledge that she must help Peter, she would have run back into the sea and drowned herself. When she went into the bothy she stood wringing her hands and it was some moments before she could tell the story of the disaster through her gulping sobs.

It was midnight before she heard a step, and Peter entered the shippon.

'Thank God you are back!' And she held out her arms.

But he brushed her aside. 'I broke God's command by going out on a Sunday.' Then, after a silence: 'If I had taken the oars, Robert would be with us. By my thoughtlessness, my wicked thoughtlessness, I have killed my brother. I am Cain, the guilty man. I have killed my brother.'

While waiting for her husband, Clementina had cooked a pot of mutton broth with barley, but Peter would not sit at table or eat. He walked up and down the room erect and silent and his short precise steps were those of an officer on the quarter-deck. Once after glancing at her, she heard him say with terrible bitterness: 'If you had not been there, I could have saved him.' At these cruel words, Clementina burst into tears and buried her face in the pillow of the bed. She could hear him pacing up and down. At last he said, as though speaking to himself: 'That is not fair. He must have been thrown head first on the rock at once, for he could swim as well, or better than I can, but once he had got that wound, nothing I did could have saved him from drowning.'

Clementina stifled her sobs.

'Have a bowl of broth and come to bed.' But Peter refused, and went on pacing. At last, seeing him waver in his walk, she caught him by the arm and pulled him down into a chair and said:

'You are to do what I tell you. If you will not let me help you, I shall run back into the sea and drown myself. I mean that.'

Peter looked at her strangely. That she was suffering and torn with grief had not occurred to him, taken up as he was with his own guilt.

Now he lifted the bowl of barley broth and gulped it down, and then let her lead him to the bed. She took off his boots and unbuckled his belt, and pulled his smock off over his head. He lay there on his back awake for a long while after she had blown out the candles and crept in beside him with her head on his shoulder. Soon afterwards she fell asleep. The sound of his wife's gentle breathing changed the direction of Peter's thoughts from his own guilt to Clementina's innocence and his duty to protect her. Then came a sudden tenderness and love for her as she lay asleep, and mixed with his deep unchangeable love, there was the pity that one feels for a sleeping child. But the belief in his own guilt soon came back and was to stay with him all his life.

All Panbride and most of the inhabitants of East and West Haven came to Robert's funeral. The most notable exception was Old Lamond whose cold had developed into bronchitis. He lay feverish and half stupefied by whisky on his little bed.

The crowd, almost all of them in black, was gathered in the gateway and garden of Master Lamond's house. Every little while a pair of mourners would emerge from the front door, and after proper hesitations another pair would enter to view Robert before the lid of the coffin was screwed down. When they had gazed their fill, and embarrassment had grown as curiosity was

71

satisfied, they would pass on to where Master Lamond was awaiting them.

Ever since Colin Swankie had burst in with the news of his son's death, he had been saying to Elizabeth: 'You must keep up your strength, my dear,' at the same time offering her a bite of solid and a nip of liquid sustenance.

Now the words issued mechanically from his lips, and every brawny fisherman and tub-like fishwife was urged in the same way to take a bite of smoked eel or an oatcake spread with cod's roe and a nip of whisky in the words: 'You must keep up your strength, you know.'

None of those so addressed thought that the words were unsuitable.

When all had looked on Robert for the last time and the last pair had come blinking into the sunlight, the coffin lid was screwed down, and six of the strongest fishermen, chosen as bearers, emerged carrying it.

As they waited for a moment in the garden a procession formed: Master and Mistress Lamond first, the Professor and his wife from Edinburgh, Mrs Henderland and her sister, then the fishing community, headed by Skipper Marr, his wife, Elspeth Marr and her new sweetheart, Donald Hossack, the rest of the crews of the *Eliza* and the *Patience*, the men, women and girls from the curing sheds.

But when the bearers and the first couples had come out into the street, Peter suddenly stepped forward with Clementina, and holding up his hand, took the second place, in front of his uncle and his wife.

He led Clementina to the far side of the grave with his father and mother opposite. It was only after the coffin had been lowered, and the bands of cloth supporting it withdrawn, that Elizabeth lifted her eyes from the grave and saw her son and his wife opposite her. She tottered, and, as Master Lamond took hold of her arm to support her, said aloud:

'Drive them away! They murdered him!'

None of the mourners appeared to have heard these dreadful words, and the possibility of her saying more was ended by the Reverend Mr Henderland plunging into the burial service. After the clods of earth had been thrown into the grave, both Peter and Clementina contributing their mites of clay, and the service was over, they left the churchyard, going outside the village to where they had tethered their pony, harnessed to the light trap. Meanwhile the more privileged walked back to the Lamond house to partake of the funeral tea. Peter and Clementina did not speak until they reached East Haven, when she said:

'I'll just pop in to the bothy and see that Grandpapa is comfortable.'

After Robert's funeral the division in the Lamond family was greater that ever before: there was an open wound and there seemed no possibility of its being healed. Yet this division did not lead at once to a greater intimacy and understanding between Peter and his wife, or to a greater sympathy between grandfather and grandson.

The autumn gales came, and no boat could go to sea. Winter came, the days grew short. Peter put up a new fence to stop the cattle belonging to the new owner of the croft from breaking into Old Lamond's garden and pasture. Clementina prepared the long lines for fishing, fastening a snood and hook every yard of its length: a hundred snoods to the whole line.

Peter became more and more silent; he was obsessed by his own guilt, and on the days when *Patience* could go out, he would come back frozen with the weather: the boat often loaded to the gunwales with cod, hake, ling or haddock. It would be unloaded by the women, the drays full of fish driven off to the curing sheds, and the boat cleaned out. Meanwhile Peter had gone back to the shippon where Clementina was waiting. He would strip off his working clothes, soaked with sea water in spite of his oilskins. He would stand at the table and wash in a bucket of hot water, put on dry clothes and slippers and sit down to his supper, all without a word.

After a week during which Peter scarcely spoke to her, Clementina asked him: 'Do you think that Robert would like to see us living like this?'

Peter was silent, but she could see that he was reflecting. To her surprise he took hold of her by both hands and said: 'I must

73

not compound one crime with another, as I did before.'

'There was no crime. You might have been thrown against the rocks, or I might have been, instead of Robert. It was predestined.' Clementina used a word she had often heard in the minister's mouth.

'It was a punishment for breaking the Sabbath.'

'Why should Robert lose his life so that you should be punished for helping your grandfather?' asked Clementina.

'It may be that I was born predestined to bear the curse of Cain. I feel my guilt. My mother called me a murderer at the grave's side.'

'If you believed all that she does, you would accuse me and put me on trial as a witch. If you are going to side with her....'

She could not finish what she was going to say, but instead of bursting into tears as Peter expected, she mastered her emotion and drawing herself up to her full height, looked her husband in the eyes and said : 'Be honest. Do you, who laugh at the superstitions of the Hossacks, believe that I, your loving wife, am a witch?'

'No. I love and trust you more than anyone in the world.'

'Remember that my great-aunt Mother Carey was a witch and would have liked me to join her coven.' And Clementina laughed.

Peter laughed also, and put his arms round her and kissed her as she said, 'Swear that you have as much faith in me as I have in you.'

'Yes, I swear that. And I promise that I will not add to my guilt by being cruel to you, or by any doubts.'

In the following weeks and months he talked and even laughed with her when she told him of something that had amused her during the day. She loved him passionately, and there was much to love. For he had great courage and perfect command of himself, and, in spite of his natural sternness, he was tender with her and tolerant of the faults of others. Himself he did not spare. He made her practise her reading and was always patient when she made mistakes, so that learning with him was for her a pleasure. He never made her think that he thought her stupid; indeed it was the opposite, for he was full of praise for her quickness and intelligence.

They had been married for only a few months before she became pregnant.

'If it is a boy, we must call him Robert,' she said.

Peter shuddered. 'No, not Robert. There will never be another Robbie. I could not bear always to be hearing that name and using it.'

Clementina only said : 'After all he may be a girl.' But she was convinced that it would be a male child.

Clementina had always been strong, but during her pregnancy she felt even stronger and spent two or three hours every day digging the potato patch and the kailyard. And her gaiety and warmth and desire for love-making helped Peter to throw off his obsession of guilt and his inability to show his love for her. He was happy, and the harmony and comradeship which held together the crew of the *Patience* and the trust and affection which the older men showed him were a source of pride and self-assurance.

When the March winds blew, and sea and rocks were hidden by flurries of snow, and the boats, drawn high up, were protected under their canvas covers, Peter would sit at the table in the shippon, studying his textbooks of mathematics and the tattered volume of Mackenzie's *Maritime Surveying*, from which he learned the uses of the chronometer and the sextant. He also studied a sidereal chart which gave the positions of the stars at all times and in all latitudes. He had actually handled Hadley's sextant at a shop in Edinburgh, but he had not been able to afford to buy such an expensive instrument – which was an unnecessary luxury for the skipper of a fishing boat that seldom went out of sight of land.

Meanwhile Clementina sat knitting the little garments which would keep her baby warm. Sometimes she would put the needles aside and ask Peter to explain what he had been learning about the movement of the earth and the planets. And, just as Robert had learned by teaching her the multiplication table and Euclid, so Peter found that after explaining – let us say – the precession of the equinoxes, to Clementina and seeing that she thoroughly understood the subject, he had fixed it firmly in his

75

own head. She might have only a hazy idea about it in later life, but he had made it clear to himself forever by teaching it.

The baby was to be born at the beginning of May. Peter was away on the *Patience* when Clementina felt the first pains, but Martha Hossack and Clementina's friend Elspeth Marr came in as promised. Martha was an experienced woman, and when the pains came on again and labour started, she encouraged Clementina to hold on to a towel tied at the head of the bedstead and to press down – and by talking sensibly she kept her from feeling frightened. And then, just after the baby – a boy – had been born, Peter was heard at the door, which Elspeth had bolted. She would have denied him entrance, but he pushed her aside and came in to the heated room still wearing his tarpaulin jacket and long seaboots. There was a pool of blood on the bed and a dark red object – a baby streaked with blood and smeared with creamy white bands.

'Shut that door, you dolt,' cried Martha. 'You've a son.'

But Peter had no thoughts for the child. 'Is Clementina...? Is she alive?'

'Yes, Peter,' came a faint answer, and he pushed Martha roughly aside and at the head of the bed saw Clementina with her hair and face and nightgown soaked in sweat, and her lip bleeding where she had bitten it to stop herself from screaming. At the first moment her eyes were wild with pain. But as Peter looked into them they grew gentle.

'Tell Martha to give him here,' she whispered. But the child had to have his mouth and nostrils wiped free from mucus and to be smacked to make him cry and then washed and dried and powdered, before he was put beside her and his nagging whimpers stopped by a swollen nipple pushed into his mouth. Soon he was sucking – but not for long. His father was turned out into the darkness outside, while the bloodstained sheets and the bit of tarpaulin under them, were taken off the bed and bundled into a bucket of cold water and Clementina washed and bandaged tightly and put into a clean nightgown. While all this was going on Peter could hear his son's uncertain little cries, and as he pulled off his seaboots in the darkness, he burst into tears. Then, when all was tidy and the baby's cries had been stilled by being put to the breast, he was allowed in again and his emotions made him behave with anger and not with gratitude to Martha. She had done all that was necessary, and she and Elspeth were putting on their cloaks, ready to go, but he almost pushed them out of the room while they were lighting their lantern.

Only when the door had been shut behind them was he free to kneel by the bed, and to take in the fact that he had a son – a creature with a big back to his head and a tiny wrinkled face and hands with fingers that moved and shut into little fists by themselves – in fact that he was alive and would be a third person, binding them closer than ever to each other, but unaware.

Peter made up a bed for himself in front of the fire, but Clementina called to him: 'You must lie beside me for a little while.' Soon she was asleep and then with infinite care not to wake her, or to disturb his son, Peter crept out of the bed and first putting some more peats on the glowing ashes, lay down. But it was a long while before he fell asleep.

Next morning, after he had made the porridge and each of them had eaten a bowlful and drunk a pint of milk, he went to his boat. They would not be out long that day, and Martha Hossack would be sure to look in during the morning.

Soon after he had gone Clementina heard the trundling of wheels, and there was a tap at the door.

To her astonishment it was Master Lamond, a little flustered and out of breath. He smiled, but avoided catching Clementina's eye, glanced at his grandson and then told her that he had brought her the model of a ship which he had made when he was a boy of sixteen. 'I've taken out the masts and the upper and lower decks, and it will be just the thing to hold an active child to prevent him from crawling about and tumbling into the fire or getting into mischief.' Then Master Lamond went out and came back staggering with the hull of his model ship. It was over two foot wide and five foot long and stood as high as the table. Along the sides were three rows of ports for the guns – for it had been designed as the model of a first-rate man-o'-war.

'Well, good-bye, Clemmie, you are a fine lass, and I hope this will give the lad a taste for the sea early on.'

With these words Master Lamond took himself off, and she heard the pony trap driven away.

When Peter came back he gazed at his father's gift in dismay. It was far too big to be kept in the living-room, and he had already bought a cradle of basketwork. So the hull of the model man-o'-war was dragged out into the shed.

'All the same, it is astonishing that my father should part with that model and take out the decks and the masts and the rigging and the guns. That model was the apple of his eye, and neither Robert nor I was allowed to touch it, or go alone into the little parlour where he kept it on show. It proves he has a great feeling for you and the boy.'

Clementina laughed and then said: 'But it's terrible. Your father gives us the thing he values most in the world, and we want to get rid of it. I shall feel to blame whenever I go into the woodshed.'

The year that followed was a happy one. The summer was warm, and when Peter was not at sea, Clementina and he would take the baby and climb over the rocks to a shallow pool with a white sandy bottom encircled by the smooth black water-worn walls. Clementina would pull off the child's woolly breeches, unpin the napkin before first dandling his legs, and then let him sit down with the water up to his armpits. Little Peter would shout and flail the water with his arms.

'I'll teach him to swim before he can walk,' said his father. 'They can't learn too young, for he'll be tumbling in and out of boats by the time he is three years old.'

He was only a year old when Clementina found that she was pregnant again.

'A good thing to have them close together: they will keep each other company and both be learning the same lessons at the same time,' said his father.

CHAPTER FIVE

REPAIRS to the fishing boats were always done at West Haven, for that was where they had been built. Peter had not been satisfied with the rudder and had beached *Patience* at West Haven for a new one to be fitted. That had been done, and on a sunny morning in March 1805, Clementina walked over with Peter to watch the two boats being launched, leaving the baby asleep in the model ship.

There was a pleasant breeze which would be stronger out at sea than under the land. *Eliza* was the first boat to be run down to the water, and directly she was afloat *Patience* was run down after her. Although, or perhaps because, the breeze was light, Skipper Marr hoisted the sails before *Eliza* was rowed down the channel. They fluttered loose, hiding the faces of the crew at the oars. Peter did not give the order to hoist sail, and *Patience* was rowed down the channel with bare masts. Clementina and Martha Hossack and one or two children watched the departure. *Eliza*'s sails were hauled up tight as she drew level with the rocks. Suddenly there was the sound of a musket shot and as *Patience* cleared the rocks into the open sea, a naval whaler with six men at the oars, shot out and barred the entrance.

Two more shots were fired; the crew of *Patience* were rowing madly; spray dashed up at each stroke. Then she rounded the rocks with the whaler only a cable's length behind. Then they were out of sight.

Clementina ran back up the bank in the hope of seeing over the rocks. But *Patience* was invisible. Whatever was going on was close inshore. But a little way out a naval pinnace was sailing on a course parallel to *Eliza* and obviously trying to head her off. There were two musket shots, but *Eliza* kept on her course, and it looked as though she were slowly drawing away from her pursuer. A puff of smoke from a small cannon was visible in the bows of the pinnace, and Clementina could see the splash where the chain-shot fell wide of *Eliza*. The report came almost at the same moment. Then the pinnace fell in behind, but it was clear that the fishing boat was outsailing her. *Eliza* was one of the fastest boats on the East Coast, and Skipper Marr was a helmsman who could catch every puff of wind. The group watching had grown rapidly until there was a crowd of thirty or forty, and the words 'press gang' were on everyone's lips. But where was *Patience*?

After an hour the pinnace returned, having abandoned the chase. She stood in close to the belt of rocks and anchored. Her masts and rigging were visible, but her hull was concealed by the rocks. Another hour went by: it was long past midday. Then the pinnace weighed anchor, set sail and soon disappeared to the southward. Suddenly the bows of *Patience* poked past the rocks and veered to enter the channel. There were three men at the oars, and Clementina saw that Duncan Hossack was at the tiller. Peter was not on board. From the bank she was high enough up to see that he was not lying in the bottom of the boat. The group on shore ran down to the beach.

Hossack climbed over the side and went up to Clementina.

'Skipper has been pressed,' he said slowly, deliberately.

Clementina waited. She was, without being aware of it, wringing her hands and tearing up a handkerchief she was holding.

'At first they could not decide which one to take. Willie Windram and I were too old to suit them. Donald is left-handed, and that let him out. They nearly fixed on Andy, then the officer said what is true enough: "That big fellow is clumsy. The young dark one is the smarter man and ought to do well." So they settled on Skipper. I said what I could: that he was married with a baby and his wife expecting....' Duncan bowed his head; his face was contorted and he snuffled. 'Believe me, I did what I could to save Peter, but they would not listen....'

Clementina turned away and walked slowly up the bank and then along it to East Haven. She repeated to herself, 'Peter taken,' but she could not understand.

When she got near the shippon she quickened her paces, for little Peter was crying with a puddle of piss in the bilges of his ship. Clementina picked him up and changed his napkin mechanically.

'I'll not let him follow the sea. They can make a scholar of him. And perhaps the next one will be a girl.'

For the first time in her life she felt the morning sickness of pregnancy.

'They have taken Peter,' she repeated and sat motionless. The fire lit in the morning, to heat the porridge, had gone out. She must light it and warm some milk for little Peter, who was weaned. But she did not move and remained sitting with her hands in her lap. Once she had begun wringing them, but becoming aware of her action, she forced herself to stop.

There was a tap on the door, then, before she had moved, it was pushed open and Willie Windram had come into the room.

'Don't fash yourself to move, dearie,' he said. Then, while she sat trying to smile at him, he went down on his knees by the hearth, laid and lit a fire and presently had the kettle boiling. Without asking her a question, he found the teapot and the canister of tea, the sugar and milk and brought her a cup.

'A drop of whisky will help,' he decided, and pulled out a flask from his pocket. He knew that Peter drank but rarely and there might be no whisky in the shippon.

'Thank you, Willie,' she said, and drank down the cup of sweet strong tea laced with whisky.

Little Peter woke up and gave a cry. In the inert state into which she had fallen, Willie's presence had not seemed strange. But little Peter's cry and the drink restored her. She got up out of the chair and said:

'You have been very kind to come, Willie. I shall never forget it. But I shall be all right now.'

'Be damned to kindness,' cried Willie. 'We all loved Peter. I would have given my life for him. Why couldn't they have taken that crazy oaf, Andy Gatt?'

'Thank you, Willie. I promise I shall be all right now.'

'Well, I'll be going the now. But I shall just pop in first thing to see that all's well.'

Next morning she asked herself for the first time what she should

81

do to support herself now Peter was gone. She could not go back to the curing sheds and work as a fisher-lassie. And with the baby coming, she could not take any job for very long. She was still puzzling over her future when Mrs Henderland came to the door.

Clementina stood looking at her visitor; she did not say : 'Shall you come in?' but stood waiting.

'I have brought you a letter from dear Elizabeth. Shall I read it to you?'

'I would prefer to read it myself, Madam,' said Clementina dourly, holding out her hand to take the envelope which Mrs Henderland kept hold of.

'It would be best if I read it to you. Elizabeth said you could not read.'

'I am surely very much obliged to her, but she is mistaken. Give me the letter, Madam.'

'It is a very gracious letter,' said Mrs Henderland.

'How could it be otherwise?' asked Clementina.

Mrs Henderland snorted, handed over the letter and with a curt 'Good day,' departed.

Clementina watched her until she was out of sight, then she broke the seal, a simple E.L. intertwined on black wax, pulled out the letter and with some difficulty deciphered :

My dear Clementina,
    Our hearts are with you in the unexpected event.
    If our recognition of you as our son's wife would help you, my husband suggests that you should pay us a visit which would silence the evil tongues now spreading rumours of my son having deserted you,
                    Yours in sympathy,
                            Elizabeth Lamond

Clementina read and reread the note and pondered long over her reply. At last she wrote :

Madam,
    I have read your letter and understand the spirit in which

it was written. I think it is for my husband to decide about visiting, which he will, when he is free to do so.

Yours faithfully,

Clementina Lamond

Before sealing and sending her reply – she would ask one of Andy Gatt's children to take it – Clementina thought good to consult Old Lamond.

Though grey in the face, he was, he said, 'on the mend' but still staying indoors. There had been a growl when she knocked, but when she went in to the bothy, he stood up, put his arms on her shoulders and kissed her.

She showed him Elizabeth's letter of invitation and her reply.

'The dirty, stinking, crazy bitch! So she is trying to make people believe that Peter got himself press ganged on purpose! Yes, and your reply could not be bettered. It is for Peter to settle with his own mother!'

Clementina told him of her doubts about taking any job until after her baby was born.

'If Patrick has a spark of decency left in him after living with that harridan, he will pay you Peter's wages. And, if not, you can come and earn enough to keep you in victuals working for me. I waste half my time washing clothes and doing housework when I ought to be out crabbing, or working in the garden. And I can keep you in fish,' he laughed.

Then he said something that astonished her, and which she thought much about in the months and years that followed.

'Don't grieve too much about Peter. If he lives, he will be none the worse for seeing the world. And he may do well in the navy.'

So for the following months Clementina went on living in the shippon, spending a couple of hours every day working for Old Lamond.

She washed the floors of the bothy, unwashed for many years; she dusted and tidied the rooms, taking care to put each object she handled back in the place where she had found it. She washed the old man's linen and his long woollen pants. She darned his stockings, though her darning was no neater than his. Then she worked a little in his garden.

The old man grew vegetables from seed given him by French-men. His beans were of a sort never seen in Angus; he grew celery and roots of which no one knew the name, and salads that he ate raw. He would chop up dandelions, fry a rasher of bacon and pour the bacon-fat over the leaves and eat them all together. Yet he had never been in France, or out of Scotland. For her work he rewarded Clementina with sixpence a week and as many fine crabs and lobsters as she could eat, vegetables too. She had her own nanny goat and a few fowls carefully enclosed in a netted yard lest they stray into Old Lamond's garden and start scratching up his plants. One afternoon, on returning to the shippon after working at the bothy, she found a surprise awaiting her. She never bothered to lock her door, and someone had entered during her absence. On the table was a parcel containing a pile of linen and a letter. It was from Master Lamond, and it contained a one-pound note on the Bank of Scotland. She read with some difficulty:

My dear Daughter,

I have brought you the family long-clothes which the new-comer will soon be needing. Peter and Robert wore the lace bonnets as babies. I would have brought them before, but Elizabeth could not remember where she had put them. I am glad to think they will be worn by my grandson or grand-daughter. I have also brought some other linen and a bit of money so that neither you nor the bairns need go short.

With my very best wishes for you during your approaching confinement,

P. Lamond

Clementina laughed when she saw the signature, knowing that Master Lamond would not offend his wife by signing 'Patrick', but was too scrupulous to use the name Peter, which was not his own.

Master Lamond had timed his gifts well, for four days after their arrival, Clementina was taken with pains as she was working with Old Lamond in the garden.

'Get you to bed. I'll let the womenfolk know.'

But there was no hurry, and for an hour after Mollie Soutar, and the midwife, Mistress Jappy, and Martha Hossack, Duncan's wife, had come to the shippon, Clementina sat out in the sunlight gossiping with them. Then, when the pains came on again, they kept her walking up and down before letting her go indoors and putting her to bed.

They had shifted the shut bed out of the alcove so that they could get at both sides of it. They had hung a towel on a cord from a rafter above the head of the bed, so that Clementina could hold on to it during the worst pains. Kettles of water were steaming on the hearth. Labour lasted four hours, and in the intervals between the worst pains, Clementina longed desperately for Peter. If only he had been there, she felt that she could have borne the pain.

She moaned, and once or twice she screamed and bit hard on the linen pad that Mistress Jappy gave her.

The waters broke. Then in the last agony she was a wild creature torn asunder in a trap, and then, when she was almost senseless, she heard Martha Hossack say:

'What a fine baby girl!'

Mollie Soutar sat up for the rest of that night in front of the fire, but Mistress Jappy packed her basket and went away. Martha Hossack had not waited after the birth, but had hurried off to spread the news that Clementina had a daughter this time. She called the child Isabella.

For the first months and during the early winter, she went on working for Old Lamond. But before the spring young Peter was able to climb out of the model ship and it was not safe to leave him alone in the shippon. So she had to take him with her to the bothy. The old man so hated having children around, making a noise and treading on his plants, that there was a quarrel.

'Be damned to you, Clemmie! I won't have your bairn treading down my onion bed,' he exclaimed. 'Take the blasted brat out of here and don't bring him back again.'

'You are an old heathen savage to speak so of your own great-grandson,' replied Clementina, trembling with rage. Then she picked up the little boy and, carrying him in her arms, left the bothy and did not return.

Old Lamond tried to make amends by leaving vegetables and fish on her doorstep, for he went out line fishing when the crabbing season was over. Clementina silently accepted his gifts, but she would not speak to him unless he asked her pardon. That the old man would not do, though the breach between them grieved him. He thought it was for her to ask forgiveness for calling him a heathen savage. He was fifty years older than she, and it was for a woman to show humility and respect. But he loved her and often cursed her proud spirit and loved her all the more.

Lacking his sixpence a week, Clementina turned her hand to baiting the long lines for fishermen whose wives had not the time. For baiting the five hundred hooks on a fishing boat's five long lines with mussels she got twopence, or sixpence if she provided the bait. If Elspeth would let Peter crawl and play with her little daughter, she could sometimes earn fourpence in a day.

Lacking money she went back to the ways of her childhood. She gave up wearing boots except in the depths of winter. She breakfasted on porridge and goat's milk with an egg for Peter and Isabella. But life was easy in the summer. Old Lamond left her gifts of beans or lettuce, and a big cabbage would last her a week. At low tide she sometimes collected bags of mussels from the rocks, and they made a good dish steamed in a little water with parsley and a chopped-up shallot.

But winter would be coming: she needed a store of food for her goat, a pile of potatoes and another of turnips, and some sacks of gleanings, after the barley and the oats were harvested, to give her fowls. Oatmeal and flour she had to buy – then candles, though she made rush lights. The pennies she earned baiting the long lines would only just provide the necessities of life. She could not afford to treat herself to a pot of tea.

She went round the hedges collecting the tufts of wool that had been pulled off the sheep's fleeces on to the brambles, before shearing. When she had a sackful she washed the wool half-a-dozen times, carded it and spun it into worsted thread. From the balls of wool she knitted clothes to keep her children warm.

As a little girl she had learned a lot from the gypsies, and this was now put to good use. She put down snares for hares, and sometimes got one which she would sell if she could find a buyer. If not, it was a fine change from fish. She knew every berry, and collected the field mushrooms and the blewits, and cooked them fresh, or dried a string of them against the winter. She borrowed Duncan Hossack's fowling-piece, and one summer night, up in the beechwood beyond Panbride, she shot a roe deer. She pickled the haunch in brine and hung it up the chimney to smoke as though it were a ham.

She laid in a big pile of logs. Once when she was splitting the big branches of a beech tree that had fallen inside the hedge of the croft, the new owner came up and said : 'Who gave you permission to take that timber?'

Clementina leant on her big axe and laughed at him, before replying : 'My Auntie.'

'Well, you can take what you've cut. But don't let me see you on my land again.'

He could hear her laughing at him as he beat a retreat. When he was gone, Clementina went on sawing and splitting logs and piling them on her wheelbarrow.

There was a wreck, and the ship's spars and timbers were washed into the channel at East Haven. At low tide the women came with ropes and dragged up a supply of firing for the winter. The seasoned wood would burn better, when it had dried out, than newly felled timber.

The winter was bitter cold, the days very short and the nights far too long to spend all their hours in bed. But candles were expensive, and Clementina often sat in front of the fire looking into the embers for long hours with Peter asleep in his cot and Isabella in her rush basket beside her. At such times she would knit. When all her wool was used up, she unravelled a pair of her husband's old long stockings, winding it into balls. Afterwards she would knit the wool up again into stockings for herself. Occasionally she would strain her eyes by the stump of a candle or a rushlight to read the Prayer Book.

In the middle of November, the year that Peter had been pressed, news came at last. Clementina was rolling out oatcake, and could see Peter playing about in the sand outside, when Mollie Soutar and Elspeth came bursting through the open door.

'There has been a great victory. Lord Nelson has lost his life. The French and Spanish fleets have been destroyed. Our fleet will be coming back to Portsmouth to refit.'

Clementina was bewildered. Then she asked: 'How do you know?'

'They got the news at Dundee yesterday. Young Willie MacLennan was there and came back this morning with a news-sheet. It is all written in it.'

'The men are reading it now at my uncle's,' added Elspeth.

Clementina picked up Isabella, took young Peter by the hand and hurried to Skipper Marr's house. Before they reached it Elspeth said: 'I'll look after young Peter. The baby is all that you can manage.'

The room was crowded with men, the air thick with tobacco smoke. They were celebrating, drinking whisky. Many of the men were half drunk, but they made way when Clementina, carrying her baby, and Elspeth with the little boy, came in. She had more concern than any of them: her man might have fallen like Lord Nelson. She went up to where Marr was sitting, wearing spectacles, behind the table where the news-sheet was spread out in front of him. The talk stopped while he said: 'This concerns you, my dearie. If your Peter is alive it is a hundred to one that he will be in Portsmouth in a month's time. The whole of the British fleet is putting in to refit after the biggest sea fight ever, and they are bringing in their prizes too. It will be a slow business from the South of Spain, Cape Trafalgar, across the Bay of Biscay at this season with nearly half the fleet under jury rig.'

'When the fleet comes in, there is a chance that you may get word of Skipper,' said Willie Windram.

'How far is Portsmouth?' asked Clementina.

CHAPTER SIX

'IF PETER is alive, he will write to me,' Clementina was thinking, as she walked away from the room full of excited men drinking and shouting. And immediately she was terrified by her thought. He might not be able to get a letter franked. He might be lying wounded, among dozens of dying men, in an old hulk used as a naval hospital. She felt it was tempting Providence, and making it more unlikely that he would write, if she should believe that he would send her word directly after the fleet got in.

It is weary work waiting for news that may never come.

She had good neighbours, and after Trafalgar they were more aware that she needed help. Very slowly the dark days passed. There was no word through the whole of December. The New Year came, and Donald Hossack, a dark man, was the first to cross her threshold to be offered a piece of black bun she had baked in her brick oven and a dram of whisky from the bottle that Willie Windram had given her at Christmas. There was merrymaking in Elspeth's house, but Clementina was not in the mood for it. It was blowing a full gale, and she was thinking of Peter, if he was alive, out at sea in a crippled ship, under jury rig and leaking like a sieve.

Snow came and covered the land and lay for two months. Clementina was well-found, but the spring was frozen. She broke the ice with the back of her axe, filled her bucket with lumps and set them to melt by the fire indoors. It was after the snowfall that she began snaring hares and trapping birds under a sieve. She plucked their tiny bodies and grilled them in front of the red-hot embers. It was something that she had learned from the Romanies. None of the crofters or fisherfolk would be bothered with such morsels. Peter taught himself to walk: she had to make a firescreen as he always tried to toddle on to the

hearth. He was a dark-haired, blue-eyed child. He was small and
did not look as though he would grow into a big man like his
father. But he was a Lamond through and through, more like the
dutiful Master Lamond than like David Carey, the full man
who could not face being hanged unless he had blue velvet
breeches and silver buckles to his shoes.

It was not till the middle of January that a black-edged copy
of the *Gazette* came with details of Lord Nelson's funeral. She
had gone again to Duncan's to hear parts of it read aloud, and
had scarcely made up the fire in the shippon, when there was a
knock at the door, and there was the guard of the mail-coach
who had come all that way himself, with a letter in his hand. It
read:

Frigate *Naiad*, January 1st 1806
Spithead

My Dearest Wife,

At last there is an opportunity to write and a hope that I
may get news of my loved ones if you are able to reply. Ask my
father, *in my name*, to frank a letter to me. If he, or my
mother, makes difficulties, go to our minister, William Baird.
The Almighty God, whose arm is strength, was pleased to give
us complete victory over the French and Spanish fleets at
Cape Trafalgar. It is to His Mercy alone that I owe my life,
though I was wounded in my right arm, in trying to board *Le
Redoutable* and am only just able to hold a pen. Fortune
has favoured me from the beginning. Owing to my having
been Skipper of *Patience*, I was rated as Able Seaman and
drafted to Lord Nelson's flagship, *Victory*. Now that I have
come out of Hospital, I have been drafted to this frigate.
Owing to my having been on *Victory*, the Captain and Master
have taken notice of me, and if my good fortune continues, I
may rise to being a Petty Officer.

Naiad is one of the eyes of the fleet, and if, as seems probable,
we shall be resuming blockade of the French ports, we are
likely to be employed in carrying messages and attending on
the squadrons blockading Cherbourg and Brest.

Now that we have beat the French, the Admiralty may

reduce the establishment. But that would apply to Capital Ships and not Auxiliaries, so that I have little hope of getting my discharge, particularly as my wounds have healed well.

Captain Dundas has shown his interest, by franking this letter.

Your affectionate husband

Peter Lamond

P.S. Most of the crew have been informed that we are to transfer to the sloop *Weasel*, while *Naiad* refits.

Give young Peter a kiss from me.

This letter put Clementina into a ferment of joy. That night she lay awake longing to see Peter. Somehow she must see him. The only way was for her to go to Portsmouth when his ship was in port. Somehow she would find him. It would not be easy : she had only the few shillings saved and could not book a coach fare, or a carrier. She would have to walk. It would be a few weeks before Isabella was weaned. She could not take the children with her. Perhaps Elspeth, now that she was married to Donald, would mind the children while she was away. It was no good thinking of going while there was snow on the ground, and she saw that she would have to wait until spring. But she would ask Elspeth at once : she would be more likely to agree if she was not to take them for a month or so. Next day she put the question bluntly, first telling her of her determination and then, would she mind the bairns?

'Aye, that I will, dearie.' And Elspeth put her arms round her and tried to persuade her from her purpose. The road was full of dangers, and she was an unprotected woman. The notion seemed to her heroic, and her love for Clementina swelled in her and her eyes grew moist.

'But if any woman can do it, you can.'

Later when Elspeth broke the news to Donald that they would be having little Peter and the baby Isabel staying with them for a month or two when spring came, she said : 'I could not refuse her. She has the heart of a lion, and she loves that silent fellow.'

'What if something befalls her on the road? We cannot keep her children forever.'

'If the worst happens, I shall go to Master Lamond with his grandchildren.'

'Why doesn't Clementina go now and ask him for the coach fare?'

'She would not ask a favour, and they would ask for the bairns. Clementina would rather die a thousand deaths than hand little Peter over to Mistress Lamond.'

'I can understand that. Well, we must do what we can, but it is a wild goose chase she's on. And I am afeared that you will want to keep them if Clemmie doesn't ever come back.'

'I'll tell her then that we'll mind them while she is gone.'

'There must be a term. Say we'll keep them till ...' Donald thought for a little. 'Well, say we'll keep them till the end of July. But not a day later.'

Elspeth laughed. She guessed that when the time came it would be Donald that would be for keeping them, and that it would be she who would be glad to be quit of the children.

Meanwhile there was for Clementina a month or more of waiting during which she had to feed the goat and the fowls, carry in enough turfs or logs to keep alight through the night, wean Isabella, bake oatcake, set the morning's parritches among the ashes before she went to bed, wash Isabella's drawers and pray it would be a fine day for them to dry outside.

Although she determined not to start until spring had come and there was little chance of finding the roads blocked with drifted snow on the hills, Clementina began to make ready for her journey. She would take with her a change of linen, soap, comb and towel, needles and thread, darning wool, scissors and three pairs of thick stockings, for she would wear her winter boots. Then a small tin pan and a flint and steel. All these would go into a satchel, and she would strap her cloak round it.

Before the day came Elspeth sent a message to Grace telling her to put Clementina up for the night at Burntisland, which was on her road. For their old companion in the gutting sheds had thrown over her boy Allan and married a widower who lived down the coast.

And the night before she left Willie Windram came round with two gifts: a fisherman's sheath-knife sharpened to a fine edge and a small bottle of the best malt whisky from Inverness.

The most important of her preparations Clementina left until she was on her way. For if it were refused, she would not turn back. It was to call on the Minister at the chapel at Carnoustie and ask him for a certificate of good character. Since her great-aunt was a known witch and her father a transported criminal, she feared a refusal. But the Minister, William Baird, raised no difficulties. Clementina explained the reason for her projected journey, and he highly approved. Then he led her into his study and taking a sheet of paper wrote for a little, paused and wrote again. At last, when he had finished, he said: 'I trust that this will be sufficient,' and read aloud:

TO THOSE WHOM IT MAY CONCERN

The bearer of this certificate of GOOD CHARACTER, Mistress CLEMENTINA LAMOND, is a respected member of the village of East Haven, County of FORFAR and a regular attendant at Divine Service. Her husband, Master PETER LAMOND, a respectable and God-fearing young man, Skipper of the fishing boat *PATIENCE*, was pressed for the Navy. Mistress Lamond is making the journey to PORTSMOUTH in England in the hope of seeing her husband who fought and was wounded in H.M.S. *VICTORY* at the crowning victory at Trafalgar.

Since her husband was pressed, Mistress Lamond has, to my personal knowledge, led an exemplary life and deserves the assistance of all the constituted AUTHORITIES.

William Baird, Minister of the Presbyterian Chapel at CARNOUSTIE in the county of FORFAR, SCOTLAND.

Mr Baird folded the paper, and saying, 'May you be under God's protection, young woman,' showed her to the door.

He had not said a word about her father: a backslider who consorted with gypsies and loose women, a smuggler who had threatened the revenue officers and been lucky to be transported and not hanged, nor about her great-aunt Mother Carey, nor how she herself had shot the witches' Devil in the knee, of which he died. All that had been passed over. Why?

Then Clementina realised that it was because of the great sea-fight at Trafalgar, and that she was setting out to see her husband, a hero who had fought beside Lord Nelson on the *Victory*.

She left the highway almost at once to follow a track that led across the grassy plain of Barry, where the men of Carnoustie played golf and the fishermen also, when the boats could not go to sea. There was a herd of cattle with a bull among them, but he only stood and looked at Clementina and let her go past. She carried a stick against dogs, but knew that most dogs run when one stoops to pick up a stone. In an hour she was at Monifieth, and another half-hour brought her to Broughty Ferry. The boat was on the other side of the Firth, and she sat waiting on a stone wall and ate some of the bread and cheese that she had brought with her. A woman came out of the ferryman's cottage and looked at her. So she asked her for a cup of water and was given a mug of small beer. When the ferryman's wife asked if she were going far, she laughed and told her story. At last the ferry boat came over. Five men disembarked, and half-a-dozen rams were driven ashore. The ferryman's wife went up to her husband and said something that Clementina could not hear. There was a wait until six other passengers had collected, one of them with a pony which was blindfolded before being dragged and prodded on board. When Clementina held out her fourpenny bit for the passage, the ferryman would not take it.

'The wife tells me your man was pressed. My son was taken three years ago, and we have had no word from him since; if you meet with Tom Liston tell him we are all well and that his sister married Andy Tough last midsummer.'

Two hours had passed since she had reached the ferry, and as they disembarked at Tayport it was getting dark. But she set out on the road to St Andrews all the same, for she had hopes of finding a free lodging there. But it was night when she reached the town, and it took her a while before she found the harbour and the few fishermen's huts beside it – only a row of six or seven where she had expected a whole street.

She knocked at a door where a light showed, and an old man unbarred it and looked at her doubtfully.

'Where does Mistress Logie live?' she asked.

'What Logie is that?'

'The good man's slug-name was White Wine.'

'You should ken that White Wine Logie died two months ago.'

'But is his wife living here?'

'She went back to live with her mother in Cellardyke.'

'I was seeking a night's lodging with her.'

'You'll get no lodging in St Andrews at this time o' night.' Then he paused and asked: 'What sort of woman are you traipsing he roads after nightfall?'

'Have you ever heard of Master Lamond who has the curing heds at West Haven and lives in Panbride?'

'No. I don't mind him.'

'I am married to his son, skipper of the boat *Patience*. He was pressed and I am walking to Portsmouth to find him when the fleet comes in.'

'That for a likely tale! Mistress Spouse,' called the man to someone inside the hut.

An old woman hobbled to the door and peered at Clementina from under the man's shoulder.

'Do you mind a new-made boat called *Patience* that put in here o buy bait?' he asked. 'This traipsing woman says she is the skipper's wife.'

Clementina would have gone away, but she was too tired to move and stood waiting for whatever might come.

A sharp young voice called out: 'Let her in and shut the door. Or else shut her out. Don't stand there gawping. It's freezing cold.'

'Yes, I mind *Patience*. The skipper was a handsome gallant. Come in, dearie. You look tired with walking.'

Clementina entered, and the man shut the door. The hut was a but and a ben', one larger room and one small one, with an earth floor and a hearth with a coal fire. It was very dark, lit only by three rushlights. Sitting by the fire was a young girl whose face was invisible. She greeted Clementina with the words, 'I was just catching hold of the Cockie Coo when you must come in and frighten him away. What made you come here anyway?'

'I hoped for a lodging from Mistress Logie. She's cousin to

Duncan Hossack, who is skipper now my husband has been pressed.'

'Didn't you know St Andrews is no place for fishing? The haddock is all gone, and White Wine Logie only stayed because he owed debts and there was a warrant out for him in Anstruther.'

'Why was his slug-name White Wine?'

'All the Logies have slug-names: there's thirty Logies at Buckhaven and most christened Archie.' The girl paused. 'Not but there's a reason why it was White Wine. He went as a boy from Leith on a brig sailing to France, and he got treated rough, so he ran away when they put in at Bordeaux. After that he stayed in France, fishing the sardines. He came back to Scotland after they chopped off the heads of the French King and Queen. He settled in Cellardyke, but after France nothing was good enough. He would not touch porridge, he drank brandy not whisky, and wanted white wine with every haddock or herring. He would cook himself: no one else could do things right. Every penny he earned went for food and wine: then he ran up debts in Dundee and finally left Angus and came to St Andrews. It was the same thing over again here, and when he died he left debts everywhere.'

Clementina slept before the fire wrapped in her cloak. Next morning the old woman gave her a bowl of heaped-up porridge and a piece of haddock for breakfast, and she set out in the half dark, before the sun had risen, and before Archie Spouse was up, or the girl awake. Clementina walked fast and made steady progress; she was at Largo by ten o'clock and stopped for her dinner at Buckhaven. When she asked at a hut for a drink of water, she was invited in by the woman, an old fish-wife, who gave her a smoked bloater and a plate of shrimps. She ate them quickly, thanked the giver and hurried on, taking the coast road through Dysart to Kirkcaldy and then striking across country to Burntisland where she reckoned to pass the night with Grace.

Clementina had never seen so many boats and curing sheds as at Burntisland. She asked for Jacob Criggie's house, and Grace came to the doorway and stood in it.

'Oh Clemmie,' she cried. 'I got Elspeth's message, and I have been praying you wouldn't come!'

96

Clementina stood bewildered. She was very tired and moved forward to enter, but Grace stood barring the way.

'The good man says that I am not to ask you in.'

Clementina stood dumbly bewildered.

'He says he will have no hand in wrong-doing and that you are doing wrong – that you ought not to expose your good name and Peter's by walking the roads. Will you not be advised by him and turn back? He's a good man, though he is hard on evil-doers. He's very down on the fisher-lassies and the dancing. I am sair madden doon, but I cannot take you in. A wife must do the bidding of her man.'

'Why should he think so badly of me?'

'Because you are David Carey's daughter and grew up with the gypsies on his croft, and David has been transported, and you can talk the gypsies' cant, and Master Criggie is set against all vagrants and breakers of the law.'

'Thank your good man for caring so much about my good name. Tell him that I have a certificate of my respectability from the Minister at Carnoustie.'

Grace sank her voice to a whisper. 'I had a word with my neighbour, Mistress Reekie, three doors down the street. She is a widow and will give you a bed for twopence.'

'Thank you, Grace,' Clementina turned away. While Grace had been talking she had listened patiently, but suddenly anger boiled up. She was exhausted, and she was trembling uncontrollably when she knocked at Mistress Reekie's door. When it was opened she could hardly utter the words: 'Grace said ... she said you would give me a bed for twopence.'

Seeing the figure tired and trembling, Mistress Reekie exclaimed: 'Come in, dearie, come in. Sit down and I'll give you a drop of whisky. You look done in.'

Clementina sat down, and a moment later a mug of hot whisky and water was put before her.

Clementina drank it and it restored her. She stopped trembling and was able to thank her hostess when she said: 'I am glad to have you. You see I'm not such a good Christian that I have to turn a tired woman from my door. Come and sit in front of the

fire and you'll soon be better. My boys will be back soon. I have
got their supper ready.'

Clementina stretched out her legs in front of the fire and fell
asleep.

The door was thrown open and Clementina woke at the sound
of men's voices. Mistress Reekie's two sons were pulling off their
seaboots in the entrance before coming in to the room.

Alastair and Angus Reekie were twins, both big men and
identical, except that Alastair was left-handed and always wore
a blue guernsey, while Angus was right-handed and wore a red
one, to enable their shipmates to distinguish them. They moved
about slowly indoors and sat down with care, and the chairs
creaked under their weight. Their shyness in Clementina's
presence kept them dumb, but their mother made up for it by
never stopping talking. Soon she was saying: 'The navy men
came here and pressed thirty men – but I outwitted them. They
won't take a left-handed man. So when they came to the door,
Angus hid in the ben and Alastair was called out. When they
found he was left-handed they sent him back. As soon as he got
inside he whipped off his guernsey and put on Angus's red one,
and Angus put on the blue one and went out and walked past
them down to his boat. I just had time to put some oil on
Alastair's hair and brush it back when they were at my door
again.

' "You have two sons, old wife."

' "Yes," I said. "Angus, they have come back for you."

'Alastair came forward again; they found out he was left
handed and let him go, for they will not take a left-handed man
if they can pick on a right-handed one. That is how I kept my
two sons.

'Grace tells me that they took your husband off his boat in
spite of his being the skipper – because he was the youngest
and smartest man. Oh that Boney! And now we've lost Lord
Nelson. . . .'

Next morning, as they sat eating, first porridge and then two
buttered kippers, she questioned Clementina, who told her she
was going to try and find her husband, now the Fleet was coming
in.

'What is your next stage?' asked Mistress Reekie.

'I was wondering if I could find a boat that would take me cross.'

'Charlie is going across to Fisherrow to buy bait,' said Angus, his first utterance.

'Go and tell him to wait until Mistress Lamond is ready, Alastair,' said his mother.

Ten minutes later Clementina went down to the shore with Mistress Reekie and her two sons, Angus in his red guernsey insisting on carrying her satchel. Clementina had shyly offered twopence to her hostess who refused it with a laugh.

'You can pay me when you come back. You'll need all your pennies when you get to England. The further south you go, the meaner people are, and the more cold-hearted.'

Clementina got into a little boat with two old men who hoisted sail; the widow and her big sons waved farewell, and they were away. The sea was choppy, and presently it began to blow harder and the rain came in a sheet of grey, making all invisible. Clementina unstrapped her cloak and then saw that her satchel was bursting with gifts of food: boiled eggs, cod's roe, two pairs of smoked haddocks, oatcake, apples and a little flask of what turned out to be a syrup of heather honey and malt whisky. She wrapped herself in her long cloak, but dollops of water came striking her in the face, soaking her hair and running in trickles down her spine. And the little boat slid, lurched, fell sideways, rode up the sides of waves at an angle, when it seemed as though everything in it must tumble out into the abyss below. But still Old Charlie at the tiller held on and did not lower the sail or take a reef in it. Soon Clementina was wet and cold. They drew level with Inchkeith and could see the seas breaking mountains high on the rocks. She felt nausea, everything swam in front of her eyes. She subsided from the thwart into the bottom of the boat, gripped the gunwale and was sick over the side. Gulls following screamed and descended to fight over her vomit. She was sick again. Then she dizzily clung to the gunwale and though she was constantly sitting in a pool of water, had not the strength to hoist herself on to the thwart. The old man Enoch, who had been sitting in the bows, suddenly poked her in the ribs with the neck of a bottle and at his insistence she gulped down a mouthful of raw whisky. Soon she recovered enough to sit on the thwart, bowing her head whenever a lump of sea-water came aboard. She sat rigid for hours, wet through and chilled to the bone. At last, when she had given up hope, the sea moderated the mist cleared and she saw that they were coming into a harbour with a row of fishermen's huts behind the harbour wall, on which stood three Amazons with baskets of bait, waiting for them. They disembarked and as Clementina followed last up the steps, she was greeted with a laugh and heard the question:

'Who is your sweetheart, Charlie?'

Then as she stepped on to the quay came the words: 'A braw lass you've chosen, but she's a bit green the now,' which was followed by: 'She'll never make a good wife for you, Charlie, if she cannot stand up to a bit of breeze.'

Charlie was unable to reply to these jokes, but Enoch broke in with: 'She's a braw lassie: you could not match her with any fisherwife in Fisherrow. She's walking all the way to Portsmouth in England to find her man.'

The three women burst into roars of laughter.

'And how far is Portsmouth?' asked one.

'All of four hundred miles,' said Charlie, finding his voice.

'She must want a Joe pretty bad to go all that a way!' exclaimed the second virago.

'The lassies have always run after the men but I've never heard of one that had to run that far.'

'Are you looking for the sailors with prize money when they come ashore?' the third woman asked Clementina.

'You had better stick to Charlie here: he's a careful lad and would only bother you on Saturday nights when he has taken a wee drop.'

'If you took Enoch too you might get enough to satisfy you. Enoch has a fine yard; ask him to show it.'

'That's right, Mollie. If she married both of them she would have enough.'

Clementina turned a deaf ear to these bawdy remarks, paid Charlie three pence and then walked off with a last:

'Stay here and do Charlie and Enoch's business and let the navy alone. Portsmouth has all the whores that's needed for the Fleet.' She had flushed with indignation at these foul-mouthed fishwives and felt the better for it.

Now she took the road to Melrose. But it was getting late and she was tired and her wet skirt hung heavy. When she got a mile beyond Crichton she struck across a field to a solitary hay-barn with no buildings near it. Fine rain was still falling, and she was wet through. The barn was built of stone and filled up to the eaves with dry bracken, cut for litter. There was some dry wood in a corner, and after clearing a space, Clementina built a fire with bracken below and dry branches above. She struck a spark from her flint and steel and caught it on a piece of tinder, blew it to a flame and soon had a fire blazing. Then she sat down and took off her boots and wet stockings. She drank some whisky, then had a meal of hard-boiled eggs, buttered oat-cake and apples. She would have cooked one of the haddocks, but there was no water. Then, after putting more wood on the fire, she curled up in the bracken and fell asleep.

A wind got up and blew in at the open doorway, scattering sparks and embers. There was a blaze of light, the smell of fire and she jumped up to find one whole side of the stacked bracken was alight. The fire had got too big a hold for her to attempt to put it out. It was reaching out to her, and she had only time to save herself and her few belongings. Already the flame was curling round one of her boots. She threw it out, then its fellow, snatched her stockings from where she had hung them to dry, then her satchel and cloak; saw her knife in the flames and swept it out with her bare foot. Luckily she had put it back in its sheath. She could not save the apples, and the butter had melted. She stood outside the barn and started to pull on a stocking, then had to run further back as a breath of scorching air blew out of the door.

At a safe distance she finished dressing, put her things together and ran to the road. For the first time in her life she felt panic fear. Somehow she must get away from the awful thing she had done. She was responsible – but if she confessed, she would be put in prison, perhaps hanged for arson. There would be no chance of finding Peter. She hurried along the empty road in the darkness. It was still dark when she passed through Tyne-head, and there was not a light in any window, and no dog barked at her. Soon afterwards she took a side road – lest by ill luck she were being pursued. It was not until she had covered another four miles that the sun rose and she felt safe to stop and have a few mouthfuls of food and a drink from a burn that ran over the road. She rested then for a little while and repacked her satchel and began to wonder at herself and her guilt.

Suddenly she remembered what Grace had said to her of her husband's horror of criminals and vagabonds walking the roads. How right the good man was!

'I'm a gypsy walking the roads and would be hanged for arson if the crime were traced to me! That's the truth,' she said aloud, and she wondered if she would ever confess what had happened to Peter, or would she keep it hidden all her life?

'I don't think anyone saw me go to the barn – or come away from it. So why be so frightened?' And she laughed again and thought that there was a good deal of her father in herself.

Soon after she reached the main road from Haddington she came to high ground and took the track to Melrose on the left. She walked steadily, but stopped before she got to Lauder and washed herself and made herself tidy in Leader Water before she went on. That afternoon she walked fast, and it was as though the accident of burning the barn had set her free, and she felt happy and sure of herself.

The weather had cleared, and soon after leaving Melrose on her right she began to look about for somewhere to spend the night. The little hamlets she passed did not look hospitable, and she thought it might be safer to sleep out and not have people talking about a single woman walking the roads in case anyone connected her with the burned barn. So she would push on till she found a good place.

Then a little way ahead a flock of sheep broke out from the moor, and came towards her with a woman on a pony riding after.

'Turn them back, will you? Turn them back!' the woman shouted.

Clementina brandished her stick at the front rank, and the sheep halted and huddled in an uncertain mass. Then the woman rode back on to the moor, and trotted along to a gate behind Clementina, and rode up while two slinky collies hustled the sheep the way that Clementina was going along the road.

'Thank you most kindly. You saved me an hour's work trying to head them back.'

Clementina trudged along beside the rough-coated pony, and felt at ease with the woman.

'Pass up that cloak and satchel. The pony can carry them for you, and you look tired. Are you going far?'

Clementina was cautious about her reply. 'All the way into England to meet my husband.'

She was too tired to talk much as they climbed a hill. And then, directly they had passed the summit, the flock of sheep broke into a gallop, the collies in trying to get by drove them faster, and the shepherd woman gave a shout, dug her heels into the pony and galloped after them. When Clementina had reached the crest of the hill there was nothing in sight but a cloud of dust disappearing round the corner of the road.

Her cloak, her satchel and all her possessions with the little food she had for her supper and her breakfast had vanished.

The sun had set, Clementina was tired and footsore, but her situation was so ridiculous that she stood still in the middle of the road and laughed and laughed, but her laughter only made her feel weaker and more helpless.

'I'll rest awhile,' she said to herself, and went to the side of the road and sat down on the bank under the wall.

She dozed a little, and deciding she was too tired to go further, climbed over the wall to be out of sight, lay down and fell asleep.

It was night when she woke up, and the moon had risen. She was chilled through, hungry and very thirsty. She could not sleep in that state of misery and decided to walk on to warm herself, hoping to find a stream or water of some sort at the bottom of the hill. But she was so weak and cold that she could not keep a straight course but wavered from one side of the road to the other. The moon shone brilliantly, and after she had turned the corner of the road she saw something black in the middle of it. She thought it must be a dog and grasped her stick firmly as she approached, and picked up a stone to throw. But the black lump did not move, and when she was a yard from it she saw that it was her cloak wrapped round her satchel, which the shepherd woman had left where she thought Clementina was bound to find it within a few minutes. Wrapped up in the cloak there was also the head of a cottage loaf, a big lump of cheese and an apple.

Clementina ate the apple first, then had a swallow of whisky, some bread and cheese, and, once more climbing over the wall which ran beside the road on to the moor, wrapped herself in her cloak and fell asleep.

She slept late and woke after the sun had risen. She was stiff, but when she got up and looked at the satchel which she had used as a pillow, she smiled, and then, as the memory of her misery when she thought she had lost it for ever came back, she laughed and a wave of confidence swept over her. She stretched, stood on tiptoe, and spread her arms wide to the sun. The first thing was to find water; and in this country of fells and moorland the search would not be long.

Sure enough a beck ran across the road before she reached the bottom of the hill. She left the road and followed the stream down to where there were trees growing and a pool had formed above a rocky fall. She gathered twigs and branches and soon had a fire and her little tin pot boiling. A haddock had to be cut into pieces to go into the boiling water, and in a minute or two she saw it lift from the bone, and it was done. Nothing was more delicious, and when she had eaten all the fish, she drank the water in which it had been boiled. After that there was the moorland water, ice-cold and sparkling. In the shelter the winter sun warmed her.

The country rose in great hills ahead of her; patches of heather appeared dark among the grey of the bent grass. Grouse rose with a whirr of wings and their call, 'Go back! Go back!' mocked at her.

The road wound between great hills, and she made good progress. That night she stayed in a shepherd's hut, and for the twopence she offered she was given not only a bed, but was invited to share a supper with a mutton cutlet and mashed turnips: a meal better than any she had tasted for months. She changed her linen, the shepherd's wife lent her the washtub, and she washed her soiled clothes and stockings. She was late in starting, so they could dry, and, before she left, the woman, who had been churning the day before, gave her a fine pat of butter.

She did not get far that day and had the luck to see an unfinished cottage standing some way back from the road under a big sycamore. The doorway was barred by a plank, easy to dislodge. Inside, the rooms were finished, except for whitewashing. There were heaps of shavings and bits of wood lying about where a carpenter had been fitting a door to a cupboard. Clementina lit a fire and cooked her second haddock and buttered it. After her supper it was dark and she lay down in front of the fire she had made and fell asleep at once. She woke before dawn and was out on the road long before workmen would be coming to finish putting in the doors and shutters.

It was up and down hill walking over the moors. There were lapwings flying and falling over sideways and crying. She walked far that day, and, after cresting a steep hill, met a gypsy with two ponies and a covered cart coming up the hill. He was a rough-looking fellow with a red handkerchief round his neck, dressed in old corduroy moleskins with an old-fashioned waistcoat that flapped on to his thighs. He could see that she was alone and that there was not a man in sight for a mile. He came up to her, and Clementina saw that there was a heavy cudgel in his hand.

'Give the poor man a piece of silver, or you will have bad luck on the road, lady,' he whined, but there was a menace in the whine.

'Put down that cudgel, or it may do you a mischief. You would not like it if it sprang out of your hand and broke your nose? *Te ratfullo pooro jookel. Maurova toot,*' said Clementina.

The man looked aghast. He still held the cudgel, but he was shaking with fear.

'Did you ever go so far as East Haven in Angus?' Clementina asked, again speaking in Romany.

The man stepped back a pace and stared, and the woman, who

had been dragging at the pony, walked up to them.

'It's you who should be giving me the bit of silver. I'm David Carey's daughter – David Carey who was transported for helping the Roman people. Have you ever heard of Pyramus Lee? His daughter Sarah was like my sister.'

'Give the woman what she asks, Anselm,' said the woman to her husband. 'David Carey was a good friend to all our people.'

Then, as the man hesitated, still staring dumbfounded at Clementina, she whispered a few words of which Clementina only heard '... one like her Auntie.'

The man's expression changed. He was frightened, and putting his fingers into the great pocket of his waistcoat, pulled out a coin. 'Take this, lady, in memory of your father and wish us no harm.'

'Put it on the stone wall and go your way.'

He did as she had said, and when she had taken the coin she said: 'I wish you good fortune in all your dealings. But have you heard of Pyramus, or Sarah and her one-eyed man?'

'They are in England, kind lady. Not far from Kendal or Appleby.'

She walked on down the hill towards Carlisle, and the man and woman stood, giving their ponies a rest and staring after her until she was out of sight. Only then did she permit herself to examine the coin to see if it were a gilt sixpence, or if it had been clipped. But it was a bright new guinea, minted in 1792, with George the Third's head on it. Clementina skipped with pleasure, and then went on laughing to think that her Auntie had helped her to such wealth.

That night she slept between two boulders beside a burn. It came on to rain, and the fire she had lit had been put out when she woke next morning. Although her cloak kept her dry, it became heavy with water. After a miserable breakfast, she walked on in the rain. It came in grey sheets that blotted out the fells and the moors. There was sleet, and it stung the cheeks spitefully, and numbed her hands. It ran down her neck. Slowly it penetrated her clothes which clung sodden and heavy. There was nothing she could do but push on, leaning forward against the gale driving the endless sheets of rain, lowering her head as the sleet stung her cheeks. All the time her skirt grew heavier and clung more stickily to her knees. Her boots filled with water and squelched at every step. When she thought it was midday, she crouched in a hollow with her back to the gale and swallowed some sodden oatcake and some cheese. Then there was nothing for it but to stand up and struggle on.

At last, wet through and exhausted, after she had come to lower ground, she saw a building. It was a pot-house. Three waggons were drawn up in front of it, and when Clementina pushed open the door, she saw that it was full of men, the air thick with tobacco-smoke and heavy with the smell of beer, the floor slippery with spittle. She stepped in. Men turned their heads, and her appearance was greeted with coarse laughter.

'Can't come in here! Men only!' shouted one.

'Don't let her in,' cried another.

'Looks like she was dipped as a witch and couldn't drown,' said a humorist.

'Too wet to burn till she be dried out,' said another, keeping up the joke.

'No help for it, we shall have to hang her since she won't burn. Lend us a rope, Sam.'

'Don't you mind them, Missus. Jack here was a sailor. He likes a mermaid. You'll suit Jack.'

'Give the woman a tot of rum. She'll do when she's warmed up. I'm not particular. Any whore in a storm.'

Clementina kept her eyes on the floor and gently threaded her way to the back of the room, where the landlord was drawing a tankard of beer. Before she reached him, she took a shilling out of her purse and held it between her thumb and forefinger.

'Get out, Missus, I don't serve....'

But without replying, Clementina held up the coin. The man looked at the shilling. He would have liked to have turned her out into the rain – but that would have meant turning out the shilling also.

'A double of rum,' she said quietly. The landlord reached for a bottle and poured out two measures.

Clementina sipped her rum, aware of the hostility of the roomful of men. She felt better when she had finished her glass. 'Dutch courage,' she said to herself. Then she lifted her eyes to the land-lord who was fumbling with her change and asked: 'Can I have some bread and cheese?'

The man did not answer, but opened a side door and shouted: 'Mother.'

An old woman hobbled to the doorway and looked in. Her son jerked his thumb at Clementina and said: 'She's asking for bread and cheese.'

The old woman stared at Clementina, who looked her full in the face and smiled. The old woman beckoned to her, and Clementina went up to her.

'Where you from?'

'I'm walking to meet my husband. He's in England.'

'Don't you know that you're in England now?'

'It's giving me a fine welcome,' said Clementina. The old woman cackled with pleasure. 'Come in here. You look pretty wet. You can dry yourself by the kitchen fire.'

Clementina sat steaming in front of a coal stove and ate a hunk of bread and a slice of better cheese than she had tasted in Scotland.

'Can I spend the night here and get my clothes dry? I can pay.'

'You can lay down on my bed upstairs. The men won't bother you there and there's a bolt on the door. And give me your things to dry. And what is your husband, pray?' she asked with sudden suspicion.

'He was pressed for the navy.'

'And where will you meet him?'

'I'm walking to Portsmouth. The Fleet has put in.'

'You'll need something hot or you'll be getting a chill.'

A bowl of mutton broth was dipped out of an iron pot. When Clementina had drunk it, she went up to the old woman's room, undressed and handed out her wet clothes. Then she bolted the door, lay down and covered herself with two quilts and fell asleep. She was woken up once by someone rattling the door and a man's voice saying, 'Open up.' But she gave no sign of life and soon fell asleep again.

In the morning the rain had stopped, her clothes were dry

and the old woman had washed and ironed her underwear. She was given a good breakfast of ham and eggs and a tankard of ale.

'That will be a shilling.' It was a lot of money, but Clementina paid gladly. There was not a man about the place when she set out for Carlisle.

The road wound through flat country, the hills had been left behind, and by midday she was on the outskirts of the city. Clementina had never been to Dundee or Edinburgh, and Carlisle seemed vast. She looked about her suspiciously, afraid of attracting notice, fearing to take the wrong road when there were so many, yet not daring to ask her way. Nobody looked at her, nobody spoke to her. She went into a Presbyterian chapel; service was over, so she prayed for five minutes and came out. She had not gone far when a brindled greyhound came bounding up to her, as though greeting a long-lost friend. At first Clementina accepted his friendliness and spoke kindly to him and patted his serpent-like head. But after he had followed her down a long street, she turned and shouted firmly : 'Go home! Go home!'

The dog stood looking at her, puzzled, but when she resumed her walk, she found him at her heels. She waved her stick at him, but when she would have struck him, the dog rolled over on his back and she could not bring herself to strike him in that position. Seeing her threatening the dog and arguing with it, two passers-by stopped to watch. Clementina wanted above all things to avoid notice, lest a constable arrest her as a vagrant, so she walked on at once and found the beautiful greyhound once more at her heels.

When they came out of the city, and streets and houses gave place to fields and trees, the dog ran on ahead, turning often to see that she followed.

The road to Penrith ran past an encampment of soldiers. Clementina saw a line of horses, a man in a shirt and striped breeches carrying a bucket, and in the distance a line of tents. She passed a sentry standing with musket and fixed bayonet in front of his box. The sight of soldiers was something new to her, and she stopped to look. She went on, but a man called out and afraid that she was breaking some rule, she stood still. Suddenly two soldiers, who had crept up behind her, ran at her, and before she knew what was happening had seized her by her arms and were dragging her backwards into the camp. She called out for help and twisted her head to appeal to the sentry, but he was grinning.

The breath of one soldier blew in her face with a stink of beer, and she saw his red face was set and excited. She struggled but could do nothing, and then, suddenly, the soldier holding her right arm gave a yell and a curse and let her go. Clementina swung round and struck with extended fingers at the eyes of the man holding her left arm. He also gave a yell and let go. As Clementina took to her heels she saw that the greyhound had come to her rescue, and that the first soldier was hopping on one leg back to the camp. The sentry fired a shot, aimed she supposed at the dog, but missed, and then the animal was beside her as she ran down the road towards the mountains ahead of her. There was no pursuit, and when she felt safe she stopped and threw her arms round the dog's swan neck and kissed him on the muzzle. That night he slept beside her in a hay-barn. She had stopped at Hesket to buy a loaf of bread and two slices of green bacon and two eggs. They had a good supper. Next morning, within ten minutes of setting out, the greyhound had caught her a hare.

Soon after midday she was in Penrith, where she was lucky to see two gypsy women in their gay coloured dresses going from door to door with baskets on their arms, selling clothes-pegs and rush mats. Clementina stopped one of them, and speaking Romany, asked whether Pyramus Lee or his daughter were camped near. The woman gazed at her suspiciously and asked: 'Who are you that you speak Roman?'

'David Carey's daughter. My father and Pyramus....'

The woman nodded and told her that Pyramus and all his family were camped above Appleby – along the hill road to Alston.

So Clementina took the Appleby road and got to the town soon after sunset. Following the woman's directions she turned back left-handed. The road was narrow, but soon she came in sight of several fires burning on a piece of waste land beside it.

She was very tired, and the road ran steeply uphill, so she walked slowly, resting and turning sometimes to look at the new moon that was shining now that the last light had gone. As she drew nearer she could see the shapes of the low gypsy tents behind the fires, and there were hobbled ponies grazing along the verge. The greyhound bounded forward, and suddenly there was a woman's voice calling out: 'Why, it's Jasper! Jasper has found his way to us.'

There was movement of people in the darkness, voices of excited children, dogs barked. A man swore and exclaimed: 'That dog must have come all of forty miles!'

Then, when Clementina approached, the little crowd which had gathered to admire Jasper, turned to stare at her, but when she asked, 'Are Sarah and Jonathan here?' a woman rushed towards her, and she was in Sarah's arms. Her cloak and satchel and the hare were carried for her, and she was led to a further fire. Branches were thrown on the glowing peats, and she was sat down on a pile of coats and harness. Soon a mug of hot whisky and water was put into her hand by Pyramus, and she was assailed with questions. While she sipped it, she told her story and heard the sad news that Jonathan had been killed riding. His horse had fallen at a fence and had rolled on him, crushing his ribs. Also, that Jasper's master Joseph Hearn had been caught passing bad coin and was in Carlisle prison. The greyhound had hung about in Carlisle for nearly a month. He must have recognised Clementina, for he had lived for a whole summer at the croft when he was a puppy. So he had thrown in his lot with her.

Sarah's mother, Jessica, brought out a roast grouse, which Sarah and Clementina ate while they talked, and soon after that they crawled into Sarah's little tent and fell asleep.

CHAPTER SEVEN

WHEN she woke up the whole camp had been stirring for hours, and it was almost deserted. A gypsy encampment sends out foragers during the day like a hive of bees: the women who sell from door to door or tell fortunes, the men who go to bargain over a pony, the poachers who visit the snares they set the night before, the older men who drive round to buy old iron, the knife-grinders who wheel their barrows.

When Clementina had dashed some water on her face and brushed her hair, Sarah gave her breakfast and told her that Pyramus would drive her as far as Orton, and that she would come with him.

As she ate the two fried eggs with a slice of bread fried crisp in bacon fat, Pyramus came along and threw himself on the ground beside her. Soon he was asking her what road she meant to take – a subject on which she needed all the advice that he could give, for he knew the roads of England.

He told her that she would do best to keep clear of the big towns like Birmingham and London and to take the smaller roads whenever she could – the people who live on main roads would never give a tramping woman a night's lodging or a crust of bread. Then she should make for Settle, Keighley, Sheffield, Derby, Oxford, Alton and Petersfield. He warned her not to trust to the gypsies she would meet in the south. They would never have heard of her father and might resent her speaking their language, think she was a spy and rob her. Still more dangerous were deserters from the navy, but she would have the dog Jasper with her. Two or three men walking the roads together were much more like to attack her, rape her and rob her than one man alone – for in company men harden their hearts.

After giving Clementina warnings and advice, Pyramus screwed up his eyes and looked at her quizzically.

'If we ever meet again, you will be a grand lady dressed in silk, carrying a sunshade. If you recognise the old gypsy I wonder if you will stop and say hullo?'

The unclipped skewbald pony was harnessed, Clementina got up and sat beside Pyramus who was smiling, but dark and taciturn, and Sarah climbed into the back of the cart; and while they went down the steep hill into Appleby, the shafts rose and Clementina was afraid the weight would lift the pony off its feet. When they got to the bottom of the hill by the river, Pyramus pulled up to speak to two young men who were riding horses out into the river so that they were out of their depth and swimming, before turning downstream and scrambling out on the shelving beach below.

Pyramus picked up the reins, cracked his whip, and they set off at a sharp trot through the little town. Jasper followed with his nose under the back of the cart. Pyramus saluted some of the people in the street and a shopkeeper standing at his door by lifting his whip and whirling the lash around. The king of the gypsies was a well-known man in Appleby.

At Orton they pulled up and got out. Then Sarah looked at Clementina with a curious expression and said: 'Romanies don't give presents, but I want you to take this. I will ask you to pay me back when we meet again.' She handed her a half pound of tea, a very small teapot, some loaf sugar and a cup. It was an extravagance that Clementina had not allowed herself. For the rest of the journey she could enjoy the refreshing luxury. The two women embraced. 'I shan't forget your face, Pyramus,' said Clementina with a laugh, and set off on the road to Kirkby Lonsdale.

She got there before dark, and after crossing the bridge, turned off on a path which led up the river into Barbondale. Just beyond the Devil's Bridge she found a nook sheltered by willows. There she lit a fire and made herself a cup of Sarah's delicious scented China tea and drank it with a knob of sugar in it, but no milk. While she drank her tea, Jasper went to the river and lapped. Then they shared a meal of the hare he had caught and Jessica had stewed. The sun had set by then. Only the flickering flames lit up the darkness. The moon had not risen. And sitting for a little while beside the fire on a boulder, listening to the river, Clementina felt happy to be alone and undisturbed. She loved and longed for Peter; Sarah was as near a sister as she would ever know. But at that moment she was glad to be alone, and to enjoy perfect peace with no interference from a loved one. If Peter was still alive, she would love him dutifully and be happy to share his life. If he had been killed she would live her gypsy life, bringing up her children. But in her heart she knew that she was sufficient unto herself. For that night at any rate Jasper, curled up and asleep near the fire, was company enough. No one came to disturb them.

In the morning she washed herself in the cold river, made herself another cup of tea, ate a crust and some Wensleydale cheese and set off. She was not afraid.

That day she walked fast and far and slept out by the River Ribble, beyond Settle. She woke up cold to find there was a mist, and it came on to rain. But she pushed on past Skipton and Keighley, and got to Haworth as the rain began in earnest. There she found a cottage where a woman took her in, dried her clothes, gave her a hot meal and bed and breakfast for fivepence. She set off in dry clothes, but the rain came on again, and when she reached Halifax she was wet to the skin. She knocked on the door of one of a row of new houses and was directed to another. There a friendly woman called Mrs Collins listened to her story and took her in, though Jasper had to be tied up in an empty outhouse. Mrs Collins was a laundress and presently said: 'Well, dear, my son is driving to Sheffield the day after tomorrow. If you will help me with the washing and ironing tomorrow, I'll speak to him and he'll take you in to Sheffield the day after.'

As Sheffield was more than two days' walk, Clementina agreed.

Next morning the copper was lit and provided plenty of hot water. Then, in the steaming scullery, Clementina spent all day at the washtub, only breaking off for a wretched meal of beans and a bit of bacon. The rain stopped in the afternoon and sheets and pillow cases, shirts and drawers were hung out on the line to dry.

Next morning she asked Mrs Collins when her son would be starting for Sheffield.

'He's in no hurry. And another basket of washing has just come in from the factory manager's wife. You can wash that while you are waiting.'

Soon afterwards Mrs Collins went out. But Clementina was impatient to get to Sheffield and before long she rolled down her sleeves and inquired from a neighbour where young Mr Collins lived. It was a mile away. Young Collins was at home eating his dinner, and he stared astonished when Clementina pushed her way in and asked: 'When are you starting for Sheffield?'

'What business is it of yours, Missus?'

Clementina explained that she had done a day's work for his mother and been promised a lift to Sheffield.

The young man roared with laughter.

'You can go back to the washtub. I'm not going to Sheffield till next week.'

Clementina went out in a rage. She gathered up her belongings and was leaving the house when Mrs Collins came back.

'You are not leaving now, Scotchwoman. You haven't done the ironing!'

'The Devil take you and all Halifax to hell. I have a mind to smash up all your china,' shouted Clementina. She had wasted a day and a half and worked hard, and she laughed at herself for a fool. That night she got the other side of Huddersfield. She wanted no more charitable washerwomen, so she slept out on the open moor. Next morning, before she was fully awake, Jasper had caught a rabbit and brought it to her. She paunched, skinned and roasted it while it was still warm, and then shared it for breakfast with her dog. After that she walked fast over the moors, trying to make up the time she had wasted at the washtub. But at Deepcar she stopped, for the sole of her left boot was coming off. It was Sunday – and would any cobbler hammer on the sole on the sabbath? She could but try and find such a man. However, as she walked disconsolately along the street, lifting the left foot high so that the flapping sole should not catch, she saw over the door of one of the houses in a row, the words, 'William Sell – Bootmaker.' She tapped gently at the door, lifted the latch and went in. A grey little man with sharp eyes looked up. He was making a cast for a fishing-line out of the long hairs of a horse's tail. Clementina smiled and told him that she was on a long journey and hoped to reach Derby where her father was dying. Then she held up her left boot.

'I know that it is a Sunday, the day of rest, but it would be a Christian act if you would hammer on the sole and enable me to reach Derby before my father dies.'

The sharp eyes looked her up and down, but his words were kinder than his looks.

'Luckily for you, Missus, I'm a freethinker. Take off those boots and I'll see what can be done.'

Clementina was astonished by his words, but she took off her boots and stockings.

'I'm going fishing. I keep the Lord's day in my own fashion.'

Clementina slipped out of the cobbler's shop and as she had to wait an hour, went into the church and remained there in prayer. It was the first time she had met a freethinker. Her father seldom went to a service – and the gypsies only when they were married or baptised. Old Mother Carey worshipped the Devil, but Peter and she were dutiful worshippers on Sunday. But all believed that God was there, watching all their actions and that His Commandments must be obeyed. But this cobbler was ready to ignore them and take the consequences – and he went off fishing on a Sunday. Clementina felt sure that the Lord would pardon a man who was like the Good Samaritan in the parable. But she included him in her prayers.

When, an hour later, she lifted the latch of the cobbler's shop, she was faced by a woman who looked at her bare feet and then slammed the door in her face and shouted: 'Nothing for tramps here.' Clementina beat on the door and shouted: 'I've come for my boots.' But all she heard was the bolt being pushed home.

The cobbler's shop was one of a row of little brick houses, and hearing Clementina hammering at the door, first one neighbour and then another came out to see what was going on.

'You had better go away or we'll call the constable and have you up for making a disturbance on a Sunday,' one of the women warned her.

'I've come for my boots. Mr Sell is mending them and told me that they would be ready by now,' explained Clementina.

'You've never worn boots in your life,' said the woman on the other side.

'I saw Mr Sell go out with his fishing rod,' a little boy who had come up volunteered.

'Well, you will find him by the river,' said the first neighbour. 'It's no good your standing here. Mrs Sell won't let you in.'

Clementina turned to the little boy, and gave him a smile.

'You run to the river and tell Mr Sell that the Scotchwoman has come for her boots, and that his wife won't let her have them. I'll give you an apple if you'll do that for me.'

An hour went by, and Clementina knocked at the neighbour's house and asked to be directed to the river. She had just got out of the street when she saw the cobbler and the boy returning. By this time she was so angry that she did not wait for him, but turned round and preceded him to his shop.

He knocked, and his wife unbolted the door. Clementina pushed past the woman, who would have shut her out again.

'The leather of the uppers is so rotten that it will not hold the stitches,' said the cobbler. 'If you want boots you will have to buy a new pair. Try these and see if they fit.'

'You should have said that before you undertook the job. Now give me my old boots back,' said Clementina.

The cobbler went to his bench and handed them to her. But he had torn off both of the soles, preparatory to resoling them, and had then abandoned the attempt.

Clementina looked at them, and the sight of the uppers without soles or heels was so appalling that she burst out into laughter and then said: 'God damn you to hell!'

The cobbler shook his finger at her.

'You must not take the Lord's name in vain – though I doubt if He is there listening. It's a fact that your boots were not worth the leather and the thread and the brads that I might have put in were I not an honest man. They would have pulled out after a mile. You are disappointed, but if you have far to go, you had better buy a new pair. I'll sell them to you cheap.'

'You'll do nothing of the sort,' exclaimed his wife. 'Not

while I am standing by. Turn the tramp woman out and throw her rotten boots after her.'

Perhaps if she had not spoken, Clementina, in the mixture of rage with the cobbler and amused contempt with herself for being made a fool of twice by the Yorkshire people, would have flung out of the little shop. But at the words, 'turn her out', she looked at the angry wife of the cobbler, laughed and said: 'I will put a curse on you so that you have warts all over your nose.'

Then she sat down on the only chair, pulled on her stockings and tried on the boot the cobbler handed her. He was chuckling, and his wife had left the shop.

The first pair of boots was too loose, the second pair impossibly tight, but the third pair, though tight, were comfortable once she was in them.

Clementina's cursing his wife had delighted the cobbler.

'She believes in all that nonsense: witchcraft and good luck and bad luck. You have settled her, and for the next month she will be feeling her nose for the warts. You can have that pair for one shilling and ninepence. And I should have charged you ninepence for the soling and heeling if it had been possible to do.'

Clementina finished lacing up the boots and paid for them, but before she left the shop the cobbler put his arms round her and kissed her on the cheek, saying: 'Your husband is a lucky fellow. You are a fine lass. But why did you tell that lie about your father dying at Derby? Tell the truth if you can't lie better than that.'

It was the best part of another day wasted, but she pushed on after the sun had set until she could see the lights of Sheffield. Then she left the road and walked down to the river. In the dark it was difficult to find sticks for a fire, and she had to content herself with twigs sufficient to boil up her little pot and make a cup of tea, but not enough to warm her through the night. She was depressed, and for some reason Jasper shared her feelings. She lay down close to the river, and Jasper, shivering, lay close to her in a close circle of nose to tail.

That night she could not sleep.

'What am I doing here?' she asked herself. 'Even if I get to Portsmouth in time, I shall never find Peter. It will be a miracle if we meet among the thousands of sailors in the Fleet. I shall have spent every penny, and how can I ever get myself back to East Haven?'

The ground struck up cold, and her limbs grew numb. A wet mist rose over the little river. She grew so cold that she sat up and with shaking fingers pulled out the little flask of whisky and honey syrup that Mistress Reekie had given her at Burntisland. She swallowed a big mouthful, then a second and then a third. Then she pulled on her new boots, which she had taken off to rest her feet while sleeping, laced them up, put her things together, and with Jasper following reluctantly, climbed back on to the road. She walked through Sheffield just as dawn broke. The streets were full of men and boys and half-grown girls hurrying to work at the steelworks, the forges and the grinding-shops. None of them gave her a second glance.

She walked mechanically, already tired out, though the sun had but just risen. Then, when she was about five miles out, going up a hill she heard the trot of hooves behind her; they fell into a walk, and looking over her shoulder, she saw a dogcart, drawn by a big rangy yellow horse, with an elderly woman sitting bolt upright holding the reins. She was wearing black and had a big straw hat. The yellow horse walked faster than Clementina, and as the dogcart overtook her the woman, sitting high up on the seat, asked: 'Going far, my dear?'

'Indeed I am,' replied Clementina.

'Care for a lift? I'm to Chesterfield.'

'Yes, please.'

The woman pulled her big horse to a halt and Clementina climbed up and sat down beside the woman, who introduced herself as Mrs Anson and told her that she was a widow and did a brisk trade as a pedlar of knives and scissors. She had boxes of them in the back of her cart – enough to last her until Easter when she would return to Sheffield to lay in a fresh supply. She drove from town to town, put her horse and cart in an inn-yard, and then went from house to house with her basket of cutlery. 'I go all over the Midlands – everywhere except Brummagem.'

Clementina in her turn told Mrs Anson about her own life, and in answer to questions let fall that her father had been transported for protecting the gypsies on his farm from arrest by excisemen. This was sufficient to win the confidence of Mrs Anson, who embarked on the following narrative.

'A rich gentleman called Charles Twiss started making knives and scissors in Birmingham. But they are trash – lose their edge. All Brummagem stuff is trash. You see, the steel isn't like Sheffield steel. That's the best in the world. While my man and I were peddling Sheffield knives in Birmingham there was no market for the stuff Mr Twiss turned out. So he sent a couple of fellows along to cudgel my husband and run us out of town. My man stood up for himself and fought back and stuck a knife in Mr Twiss's bully. But it went through his liver, and he died of it, and my man was hanged. So I daren't go into Birmingham now.'

They stopped for an hour by the road and shared a pork pie and drank a bottle of beer each. Mrs Anson paid. Clementina thanked her and was told: 'I like company, but I don't get much of it. You have paid me well for the food by sitting up here and listening to an old woman running on. As soon as I saw you I liked your face. I don't mind the Scotch, but I don't trust the Irish – all blarney.'

When they got to Chesterfield, Mrs Anson put her horse and cart in the yard of a small inn and before parting gave Clementina a glass of ale which she paid for. Clementina went on her way refreshed and recovered. It was only a little past midday, and she stopped short of Alfreton, where the woman at a farm said she could sleep in the hay barn if she did not light a fire.

In the morning she went to thank the woman, who gave her a glass of warm milk and, after looking at her, said: 'I wouldn't go through Derby. The miners are come in because they want more wages, and there has been talk of their smashing up the town hall. Goodness knows what may be going on today.'

Clementina asked how she could avoid Derby going south, and was told that she could take a side road just before Alfreton, which would take her to the river, and that there was a cattle drift on the other side which she could follow all the way to

Long Eaton. 'You'll meet a lot of miners. They are a rough lot, but they will not do a woman any harm unless they are drunk. Not like soldiers and sailors.'

Five miles led her to the river, which she crossed and came to the wide drift cut up into deep ruts by waggons that had straggled widely to avoid getting bogged. But there were wide verges of grass on either side. After walking five or six miles, she saw a flock of a hundred or more geese cropping the grass, and two girls sitting on the fallen trunk of a tree eating their midday meal.

'You have got a fine lot of geese,' said Clementina.

'They are in pretty good shape considering,' said one of the girls contentedly. 'We have driven them all the way from Kendal in Westmorland and are taking them to Nottingham,' said the other. 'We have only lost three. Two by foxes and one by a thief in a dogcart. He just picked up one of my geese, wrung its neck, and threw it in the back of his cart and drove off at a gallop. What could I do?'

Clementina sat down by them on a tree-trunk, opened her satchel and ate her hunk of bread and cheese. The girls gave her an apple and a drink of rather stale beer.

'How can a goose walk so far?' she asked. 'It must be a hundred and fifty miles.'

'Like this,' and the girl picked up a bird that was lying at her feet and showed Clementina that the webs of the feet were shod underneath with a layer of pitch. 'We spread the pitch on when it's soft, but not hot enough to burn the web, then plunge it into cold water. And we cut the quills of one wing so they can't fly away. I lead the flock and Susan hustles them along behind.'

Susan lifted the bird on to her lap and kissed its head. 'That gander's my favourite. He follows me around like a dog. I shall be sorry to let him go into a goose pie.'

'How many miles do you do a day?' asked Clementina.

'Four or five – sometimes six. Depends on the road. We've been four weeks on the road so far.'

'I have to do twenty-five or thirty, otherwise I would like nothing better than to have you as companions,' said Clementina laughing. 'And what will you do when you have sold your geese

121

in Nottingham?' The girls looked at each other and laughed.

'Susan thinks she'll stay in the South if she finds a sweetheart. I'll look for a waggoner who'll take me back North. I don't fancy marrying a coal-miner.'

That night Clementina got beyond Sandiacre. It had been a fine day, and once more she slept undisturbed by a river. When she woke and went down to it, she was surprised to see the backs of a row of men sitting on stools all along the bank, fishing. They must have come down the path close to which she was sleeping without disturbing her. She chose a place equidistant between two of them and splashed her face, filled her pot and greeted them with a 'Good morning.' Neither turned his head or spoke, but both went on stolidly staring at their floats in the stream. For all the interest they showed, she might have been a cow come down to drink.

That day, keeping to small roads, she passed by several miners and groups of idle men, but none molested her, or even spoke to her. But at last she got clear of that district, and stopped as it grew dark at a small inn at Codeby, where they gave her a good supper and a bed and breakfast for tenpence, and she washed her stockings and changed her linen.

Much refreshed she set off next day and, keeping to small roads, got beyond Fosse by the evening, where she slept out beside a mill-pond, with a big watermill at the far end. In the morning she had just made a little fire and was boiling her pot to make tea, when she saw a figure splashing in the pool and an old man, the miller, on the bank, shouting that there was a woman in the water, drowning.

Clementina ran at once to the edge of the mill-pond, wrenched off her boots, undid her skirt and waded in. The drowning figure was a girl. Clementina caught hold of her, first by an arm, then as the girl struggled and clutched at her, by the hair, and tried to pull her to the edge. Already she was out of her depth and went under. But she kept her mouth shut, and when she felt the gravelly bottom under her feet, jumped up, got her head out and snatched a big breath of air before she went under again. She rose once more, got another breath and went under again. She would have been lost then if Jasper had not plunged in and swum to her side. She felt him beside her, gripped his collar and got her head out. The dog turned round in the water and swam, pulling her ashore. Clementina still had hold of the girl's hair in her right hand, and holding Jasper's collar in her left, she began kicking; suddenly she was out of the deep water of the mill-race and lying exhausted in the shallow muddy water at the edge.

The old miller, who had done nothing but shout, then came round and helped her to her feet, and between them they dragged out the body of the unconscious girl. Clementina was soaking wet and very cold, her hair full of duckweed, her drawers and bodice covered in mud; but her first thoughts were for the girl. She told the miller to lift up her legs and she pressed hard on the girl's chest and forced open her mouth, trying to get as much of the pond water out of her as possible. Then she worked her arms up and down, pressing on her chest after the downward pull. Peter had explained that that was the way to get the half-drowned to breathe again. At last the girl, a draggled fair creature about seventeen, opened her eyes. Soon afterwards she was sick and, the miller and Clementina carried her into the mill-house and laid her before the fire.

A boy appeared, and the miller sent him off to the Hall to say that Miss Lucy, the daughter of the housekeeper, had nearly drowned herself, but was still alive. It was time for Clementina to look after herself – but all her clothes had been trodden into the mud or were soaked through. She collected her belongings and took them into the house, drank a swig of what whisky she had left, and then, since there was nothing else, wrapped herself in two corn sacks. She was making the girl on the floor comfortable, when she heard a pony cart drive up, and a minute later a well-dressed lady pushed open the door which she had tried to fasten, and exclaimed: 'Gracious me! Did you pull Lucy out of the mill-pond? I have come to thank you and to take you both back to the Hall with me where you can be properly looked after.'

'Thank you, madam. All my clothes are wet. I must make myself decent,' replied Clementina whose teeth were chattering.

'Don't stand shivering there. Wrap yourself up in this blanket, and I'll drive you back. We'll find you some clean clothes until yours are washed and dried.'

A few minutes later Clementina and the girl Lucy, both wrapped in blankets, were being driven up an avenue of lime trees to a neat country house of red brick with white windows. During the drive the lady introduced herself as Mrs Field and learned what she could not have helped noticing from her accent, that Clementina was Scottish. Also that she was called Mistress Lamond and on her way to see her husband, a sailor, at Portsmouth and that she was walking all the way. On arrival Lucy was received by her mother and packed off to bed, and Clementina shown into a bedroom where a maid was hastily lighting a coal fire.

'You rest in bed, my dear. And presently Alice here will bring you a hip-bath and towels and will help you to wash your hair. She always helps me. Get into bed now, and Alice will bring you a bowl of beef tea and a cup of chocolate and some breakfast. Have a good rest before you think about getting up. Alice, take Mistress Lamond's wet things down to the laundry and ask Mrs Ashby to wash them at once. But until they are ready, you must put on some dry things that Alice will bring you.'

Clementina, naked under her blanket, was in no state to refuse such kindness. When Mrs Field had left the room, she sat for a little while in front of the crackling fire with the blanket round her body and a shawl of Mrs Field's over her shoulders. She drank the bowl of beef tea and the cup of chocolate, and ate the plate of fried eggs and bacon that Alice brought her. Then she put on a clean nightgown and got into the bed that Alice had warmed with a warming-pan.

Alice came back, drew the curtains and said: 'I shall come back later in the morning, madam, and if you are not asleep, I shall put out your bath and first help you to wash and rinse your hair.' Then she tiptoed away. All this was so strange to Clementina that she felt that she had fallen into a dream world. But she could only accept gratefully what Mrs Field was giving her – and very soon she had fallen asleep in the warm bed. When she woke up it was to find that Alice had brought in a hip-bath and a big wash-basin and several brass cans of hot and cold water.

'Put on this dressing-gown, madam, and if you will sit at the table and bend over the basin, I will wash your hair.' Then Alice laughed and said: 'But before I wash it, I must comb out the tangles and pick out the duckweed. Excuse my saying so, but you look like a mermaid, ma'am.'

'Well, Alice, I am married to a sailor, so perhaps I am one. Not that I want to live in the sea.' And they both laughed together.

When the duckweed had been got rid of, Clementina was astonished to see that Alice was beating up the yolks of three eggs in a little basin. For a moment she recoiled from having egg-yolk poured on her hair, but then, saying to herself: 'In for a penny, in for a pound,' she bent over the big china wash-basin and Alice poured some of the beaten egg into her scalp and rubbed it in vigorously. This she rinsed out with warm water in a dirty brown stream, then emptied the basin into a slop-pail, spooned more egg-yolk into Clementina's scalp and repeated the process. After the third dressing had been washed away, Alice was satisfied. She gave Clementina's hair two more rinses, then dried it with a hot towel and wound another towel like a turban round her head. Then she pulled the hip-bath in front of the coal fire and filled it with hot water from a brass can.

'I have laid out your clothes on the bed, ma'am, and when you have had your bath and dressed, shall you please come down to Mrs Rose's room. Mrs Rose is the housekeeper, and is Lucy's mother. She wishes to thank you and hopes you will take luncheon with her.'

'Alice, you are a bonny lassie and I can never thank you and your mistress enough. Without her I think I should have perished of the cold.'

Alice left the room and Clementina for the first time in her life enjoyed the luxury of a hot bath in front of a blazing coal fire. The clothes laid out were plain and good, with two warm petticoats, black stockings and slippers and a black and white spotted dress. Her hair had never felt so soft and silky. She plaited it and wound the plait into a bun behind. Feeling very strange in these garments, so much newer and smarter than her old worn-out clothes, she went downstairs, noting the stair-carpet and the brass stair-rods, and the engravings on the walls.

At Clementina's appearance, Mrs Rose took her in her arms, kissed her, and burst into tears. Soon the whole story of the wicked Lucy was poured into her ears.

It was Mrs Field's nephew, Master Simon, who had turned the silly girl's head. He had come down in his new uniform for a week before joining his regiment; of course he had taken notice of Lucy, and she had let herself believe what she wanted to believe – that he would marry her later on ... the old, old story. Then when she found out that she had made a fool of herself, she went mad with grief and – one sin leading to another – had tried to drown herself in the mill-pond. Thanks to Clementina, Lucy had been saved from the crime of self-murder – perhaps now she would come to her senses. . . . There was a young man, the gamekeeper's son, who was ready to take her ... perhaps if recalled to her sense of duty in time, all might one day be forgiven.

This pathetic, but not unusual, story was related in all its details during luncheon, while Clementina and Mrs Rose demolished a steak and kidney and oyster pudding, with buttered turnips, drank several glasses of home-brewed ale, and finished with apple pie smothered in cream. And in the kitchen below Jasper was not forgotten.

An hour later Alice brought a message that Mrs Field would like to see Clementina in the drawing-room. More marvels to behold – but little time to take in more than the great carpet with its whorls of green and pink and chairs with backs of cross-stitch embroidery in wool and beads because Mrs Field had taken her by the hand and led her forward to introduce her to her mother, Mrs Cartwright, and to her husband, a red-cheeked gentleman with heavy black eyebrows, who stood cross-legged beside the mantelpiece. Clementina dropped a curtsey to each.

'Well, Mrs Lamond, you have saved us from a terrible tragedy, and it is not only Mrs Rose who is grateful and who admires your courage. . . . You come from Scotland, and you will find all the ladies of England are in love with your Scottish ballads that

Mr Scott has made them acquainted with. In Scotland you could make the story of poor Lucy and of Mistress Lamond into a touching ballad,' said Mr Field.

'Many of them are sad stories,' replied Clementina. She was wanting to say that if her clothes were dry, she would like to change into them and be on her way with no further delay. But for the moment there was no way of escaping Mr Field.

'I am sure you sing the old ballads, Mistress Lamond. We will not let you go until you have delighted us with a song in your native Doric.'

Clementina saw that the quickest way to escape from the drawing-room and to get on to the road was to comply with Mr Field's demands.

'Do you ken our poet Robbie Burns? I could sing you one of his songs.'

'Ah, the ploughman poet! No, I am not acquainted with his work.'

'He is a great poet, though much of his best verse is not fit for the polite society of ladies. This should be sung by a hand-some young man, as I ween your nephew Mr Simon must be.'

'Don't mention the scapegrace,' said Mrs Cartwright.

Clementina began :

> 'Green grow the rashes, O;
> Green grow the rashes, O;
> The sweetest hours that e'er I spend
> Are spent amang the lasses, O!
>
> 'There's nought but care on ev'ry han',
> In ev'ry hour that passes, O;
> What signifies the life o' man,
> An' 'twere na for the lasses, O.
>
> 'The war'ly race may riches chase,
> An' riches still may fly them, O;
> An' tho' at last they catch them fast,
> Their hearts can ne'er enjoy them, O.
>
> 'But gie me a canny hour at e'en,
> My arms about my dearie, O;

> An' war'ly cares, an' war'ly men
> May a' gae tapsalteerie, O!
>
> 'For you sae douse, ye sneer at this,
> Ye're nought but senseless asses, O:
> The wisest man the warl' saw
> He dearly lov'd the lasses, O.
>
> 'Auld Nature swears, the lovely dears
> Her noblest work she classes, O;
> Her prentice han' she tried on man,
> An' then she made the lasses, O.'

Mr Field was loud in his applause and Mrs Cartwright joined in with: 'The last verse makes us forgive the freedom of the others. But I am afraid your song was a plea for the forgiveness of my grandson.'

Clementina turned to Mrs Field and said: 'I can never thank you enough for your goodness. But I am anxious to be on the road, or I may not reach Portsmouth in time. So, if my own clothes are dry, I will thank you once more and be on my way.'

However, on Mr Field inquiring whether her way did not lie through Oxford, his wife explained that they were going to a wedding at Boar's Hill and could drive her as far as that next morning.

After an early supper with Mrs Rose, Clementina asked to see Lucy, but the girl had been given an opium pill and she was still asleep next morning when Clementina arose, after a night of luxury such as she had never before enjoyed, sleeping in a soft bed under an eiderdown quilt, and with a glowing coal fire in her bedroom.

CHAPTER EIGHT

FROM Boar's Hill she hurried along the road to Oxford, seeming more like a gentlewoman than a vagabond walking the roads; she had a satchel at her back, a stout stick in her hand and Jasper following at her heels.

Soon after she had left Oxford, it began to grow dark and rain fell. As she passed through a village, the shower increased to a sudden downpour, and she took shelter in the porch of the church. She had not been standing there long, watching the puddles forming in the road, when an old clergyman, wearing black breeches and gaiters, came out of the church door. He stopped and looked at her questioningly.

'I am sheltering until the worst is over, but perhaps....' said Clementina.

'Perhaps what?'

'Perhaps you can tell me whether I can find a lodging for the night in the village.'

'Are you a respectable woman? And what are you doing here?'

Clementina laughed. 'I have a certificate of my respectability, if you wish to see it. I am walking to Portsmouth to see my husband, a seaman in the navy.'

'Well, well, well ... I will look at your certificate ... and if you are indeed a respectable woman, I will ask my house-keeper what can be done for you.' The old gentleman's accent was so unlike anything that Clementina had met with, that she could scarcely take in his words. The violence of the rain had moderated, and she followed the cleric down the path and through a wicket gate to the rectory and then into his study, where a fire was burning in the grate, and an oil lamp illuminated the writing-table.

Clementina then opened her satchel and took the Reverend

Baird's certificate of her respectability out of her purse and handed it to her host, who read it carefully. Then he folded it up and handed it back. He was frowning and his eyes flashed as he said:

'But, my good woman, you are a Presbyterian. I cannot do anything for you. In fact I think it is a piece of gross impertinence for you, a Calvinist, to expect assistance when you do not belong to the Established Church.' With these words, the Canon showed Clementina to the door.

Rain had begun to fall again, and it was already dark. When the door had closed upon her, Clementina turned back and walked quietly round the rectory. Through a misty window she could see a woman washing dishes. Then, projecting into the garden, there was a glass conservatory. She tried the handle of the door; it was unlocked, and she and Jasper went in. It was pleasantly warm, and a faint light came from a coke stove. Clementina felt about, found a bundle of fruit netting which would serve her as a pillow, lay down and fell asleep.

She was woken by Jasper moving about, and seeing that it was almost dawn, she got up and made herself a cup of tea, boiling her little pot on the coke stove; and with it she ate a big slice of fruit cake that Mrs Rose had given her. Then, after inhaling the perfume of a pink carnation, she went out of the front gate of the rectory and set off along the road to Dorchester. There was a ground frost, the sun came up as red as a Dutch cheese, the puddles on the road were sheets of thin ice which crackled underfoot. Jasper startled a rabbit on the verge and caught it in the next field. He brought it to Clementina, who stowed it away under her cloak and hurried on.

As the sun rose and the shadows of frost under the trees disappeared, it grew warm, and almost for the first time on her walk Clementina was aware that it was springtime. She rolled up the rabbit in her cloak and strapped it to her satchel. Then she made rapid progress and felt gay and mischievous. She was delighted by the way in which she had got the better of the Canon by sleeping in his conservatory and being warmed by his coke fire.

Presently she overtook two small boys of about eight or nine years old dawdling along the road. She called out a good morning to them, and they looked at her and Jasper and, liking what they saw, ran up and began marching along one on each side of her.

'Where be you a going to, missus?'

'Portsmouth.'

'Why be you going there?'

'To enlist in the navy.'

'They don't take women, do they?'

'I shall cut off my hair and wear a man's clothes.'

'Coo!'

They looked up in her face in rapture to see if she was serious. Then they stopped for a moment to consult and then ran back to her again.

'Can we come with you, missus? They take boys like us, doesn't they?'

'Do you swear to keep my secret?'

'Yes, missus.' They nodded their heads and resumed their stations.

'You mustn't call me missus.'

'What um call you then, missus?'

'Captain Carey.'

'You won't be a Captain in the navy, will um you, missus?'

'Not for the first year anyway.'

'Why are you Captain, then?'

'I'm a Captain in the army, but I've deserted and am going to try the navy instead.'

'Coo!'

But in less than a mile Clementina's rate of walking proved too much for her young friends. She was going up a hill at a good four miles an hour and they protested.

'You go too fast, Captain.'

'Let's get a breather, Jim.'

'I'll look out for you on the quarterdeck, when I'm a lieutenant and you are midshipmen. But keep my secret or it will be the cat-o'-nine-tails,' Clementina called out, as she strode off, leaving the two boys seated on the turf at the side of the road.

She was in the mood for walking and pushed on fast, only

stopping for five minutes at a pot-house to drink a pint of mild ale and eat a thick sandwich containing rings of raw onion and a slice of cheddar cheese. She got into Reading before evening and walked straight through it, taking the Alton road out of the town.

She kept going, until seeing that the sun was casting long shadows, she shook off her resolution of going on and on. She must not exhaust herself and collapse before she reached her goal. Her road ran through an oak wood full of flowers, which in Scotland and the North grow on moorlands as well as woods. 'Windflowers', she called them. She climbed over the ditch into the wood, went through the trees, and came to a ride, where she turned off into an open glade under some big oaks. Half an hour later, when it was already owl-light, she had lit a fire and was cooking Jasper's morning rabbit, when there was the sound of breaking rotten branches and heavy footsteps, and a man carrying a gun came up. He seemed surprised to find only one person, and that a woman.

'Has your Joe just run off? I'll be taking him to lock-up. Douse that fire and be off, you damned tinker's whore. And I'll shoot that dog of yours.'

He spoke with a Scottish lowland accent in the tone of a man accustomed to being obeyed.

Clementina seized Jasper, and, jumping to her feet, held the big dog in her arms.

'Put that dog down, or you'll get shot yourself.'

'You would hang for that – so you can't scare me.'

The gamekeeper laughed.

'I've two spring guns set by the pheasant coops, and I'll tell the magistrates that you got yourself shot while trespassing.'

'Shoot awa', you damned ugly scoundrel.'

The man smiled and asked:

'How come a Scottish whoor should find her way this far south?'

'I'm a respectable woman, and I carry a certificate from our Minister. What's your name, you scoundrelly Scotsman? I trust I'm no kin to you.'

'MacArthur.'

'A bluidy Campbell.'

The gamekeeper laughed.

'But where are you from, missus, lighting a fire in a pheasant preserve and roasting a poached rabbit with a certificate of your respectability in your pocket? I never heard the like of it.'

'I'm walking to Portsmouth to meet my husband, who was wounded in the battle of Trafalgar.'

'You can put your tyke down. I will not shoot him tonight, though I will if I see him tomorrow. He looks like a gypsy's dog.'

'Well, good night to you, MacArthur Campbell. I'll be on the road by sun-up.'

The gamekeeper laughed and looked at Clementina with something like respect.

'What's your name, missus?'

'Mistress Peter Lamond. I was Carey and am half Lindsay by blood.'

'And you have the presumption to believe that you can out-face me and sleep the night with a poacher's dog in my pheasant covert? And to beat that, you tell me that you come from the most rascally stock in the whole of Scotland and that you look down on the great Duke and the sons of Diarmid?'

'Just so. I have that presumption, for it's the bare truth.'

'Well, since I have said that I'll not shoot your tyke, I'll keep my word, and since you are my countrywoman, I won't drag you out on to the highway by the hair of your head. But be careful you go out the way you came in. I have five man-traps set and the two spring guns.'

MacArthur turned his back and walked back to the ride.

In the morning Clementina made herself a pot of tea and ate a fried rasher of bacon and a slice of fried bread. The air was soft and the sun warm. When she had breakfasted, she led Jasper out of the wood for fear he should go after a pheasant or blunder into one of the man-traps, if there were any, which she doubted.

She walked at first through woods to Odiham, and then up and down over rolling farm lands to Alton. Before the little

street came to the broad market-place, she passed by a pork
butcher's where a boy was loading up the box at the back of
the butcher's pony cart. The boy turned back to the shop,
leaving the tailboard hanging down, and just as she turned into
the main street Jasper came frisking up with a small cut of
loin of pork in his mouth, and his eyes gleaming with the knowledge of a deed well done. Clementina took the small square of
meat out of his mouth quickly. It would make four pork chops.
She wiped off Jasper's saliva and hid the meat quickly under her
cloak. For a moment she considered taking it back to the pork
butcher's. It would mean paying for it, which she could ill
afford, and attracting attention to herself. The pork butcher
might not be content merely with restitution. He might demand
punishment. Calling Jasper to heel, she turned quickly out of
the main street down a lane parallel to the street from Odiham.
A moment after she and Jasper had gone up it, the butcher's
boy came running out to look for the woman with the dog,
whom he suspected of stealing the chops. But they had disappeared. By compounding the theft, Clementina knew that she
was as guilty as any gypsy woman, and she hurriedly skirted the
town, and as soon as she was outside it, took a by-road to
Selborne. Not until the road was clear did she examine her
prize. It was a lovely bit of meat cut from the narrow end of
the loin, and Jasper had left scarcely a toothmark.

Clementina wiped it with her handkerchief, stowed it away
in her satchel and patted Jasper's head. At that moment she was
a gypsy woman like Sarah, and not the respectable bearer of a
certificate. With a splendid supper assured, she only stopped
once to buy a penny loaf of bread and to drink a pint of ale.
Then, as dusk was falling, she got to the common just short of
Froxfield Green, chose a sheltered hollow where there were unlikely to be man-traps, built herself a fire and toasted the four
pork chops. They were the most delicious food she had enjoyed
since her supper with Mrs Rose, and Jasper was rewarded with
the bones and little bits of gristle. After the chops she ate a
piece of new bread and of cheese, made herself a cup of tea,
drained her last drop of whisky out of a little bottle, wrapped
herself in her cloak and went to sleep.

It was the last night before she would reach Portsmouth, and she knew that she badly needed soap and water, and to view herself in a looking-glass, if she were to look like the respectable wife of a seaman and not, as the gamekeeper MacArthur had called her, a 'tinker's whoor'. On Froxfield Green there were cottages ranged round the common green, and she went from one to another in search of a woman who would allow her to wash in a basin of hot water and to make herself respectable. She knocked first at one door and then at the next, but the woman who opened would only listen to a few words and then would slam the door in her face. If it were a man, the door would be slammed at once.

The last cottage stood back from the green in a garden full of daffodils and was made of weather-boarding. Clementina knocked, and the door was opened by a young girl, who Clementina guessed was a servant.

'I wonder if your mistress would allow me the use of a basin of hot water? I have my own soap,' said Clementina. The girl was astonished, and turned back to consult with her mistress, who then came to the door. She was the most beautiful young woman that Clementina had ever seen, very fair, with golden hair that streamed unconfined over her shoulders. She was wearing a white lace dress that hung loose about her and revealed her bosom, which was only partly concealed by blue ribbons. Clementina stared speechless, but the beauty burst into fits of laughter. Then, making an effort, she said: 'You must think me very rude to laugh.'

'I know I must look like a boggart for scaring corbies,' said Clementina.

'Please forgive my laughing. It was uncivil, but yours is an unusual request.'

'I have walked from Scotland, and I want to appear neat and respectable when I meet my husband in Portsmouth. He is a sailor and was wounded at Trafalgar.'

'Walked from Scotland!' exclaimed the lady. Then, turning to the servant girl: 'Nellie, put the largest kettle full of water on the fire.' Then to Clementina: 'Now come in and sit down and tell me all about it, while the kettle is boiling.'

Clementina sat down and told her story, which produced a great many exclamations of surprise and admiration and also laughter. And she was made to accept some delicious macaroons – the existence of which was previously unknown to her.

The maid came to say that the water was hot and that all was ready, and Clementina was shown into what was evidently a young gentleman's dressing room, for there were men's gloves and stocks and boot-trees with beautifully polished top-boots. And the lovely young woman came in and lent her a brush and comb and a packet of hairpins and insisted on her using a cake of soap that smelt of geraniums. Clementina took advantage of the abundant hot water to have a good wash, all over. When she rejoined her hostess there were loud cries of admiration, though as a matter of fact Clementina was a plain woman compared with the beauty beside her.

'I have put a ribbon in your bonnet. I hope you will admit that it is a great improvement,' said her new friend. Clementina knew little about bonnets, but she accepted the ribbon graciously. As she poured out her thanks, and as they bade farewell, she noticed that the beautiful young woman was not wearing a wedding ring.

Clementina walked fast down a narrow road between woods, and by the afternoon was in the outskirts of Portsmouth. Thereafter she kept a sharp eye on Jasper. She did not want him to repeat his exploit at Alton and bring her a piece of meat from a butcher's shop, which might involve her in trouble with the law. After she came to the dockyard and a view of the sea, she turned back to look for a lodging. There were many houses with the words, *Bed and Breakfast*, on a card in the window. She chose one with flowers in the front garden and where the doorstep had been recently holystoned.

A woman of sixty or so opened the door and stared at her.

'I am looking for a lodging and have come all the way from Scotland to see my husband who is serving in the navy.'

The blue ribbon in Clementina's hat seemed to produce a favourable impression.

'Are you married to him?'

Clementina showed her wedding ring.

'Your dog must stay outside the house. The room with breakfast is a shilling a night. For that you can have a fire in your room, all the hot water you need and can cook your supper in my kitchen. You pay in advance.'

Clementina looked at the room and accepted the offer. It was too late that night for her to try and signal the sloop *Weasel*, or to inquire after it. Already the streets were full of sailors staggering in one direction, while women pulled them in the other. Her landlady invited her to share a supper of boiled bacon with boiled cabbage and boiled potatoes with a slice of warmed-up spotted dog to follow. She slept well after her long journey.

Next morning she made two little flags of white calico fastened to sticks, and putting them under her arm walked down to the harbour. Then, standing on the end of the jetty, she began signalling, spelling out, as Robert had taught her, the letters for sloop *Weasel*. But she had not finished the name of the ship when a rough voice challenged her with the words:

'What tricks be you up to?'

Clementina turned and saw a sailor with a cutlass at his side and a pistol in a holster hanging from the right-hand side of his belt. She explained that she was trying to signal the sloop *Weasel* to say that she was waiting to meet her husband, Able Seaman Lamond, and she added that she had walked all the way from Scotland.

'Give me those flags of yours,' and taking hold of them he threw them into the harbour. 'Sloop *Weasel* is sailing tomorrow.'

'Then I must get word to my husband at once.'

'I'll speak to the signals officer and get word sent. Sloop *Weasel* – A.B. Lamond. A private message will be two shillings.'

It was an enormous price to pay – but what could she do? Clementina took out her purse and gave the man the money. She did not trust him, but it would not help to show anger, for she was in his power. She turned back thoughtfully along the jetty.

Liberty boats were coming in, disembarking sailors; the crew backing oars and the boat sheering away to make way for the next one in line. She seated herself on a bollard just to the seaward of the ladder up which the liberty-men sprang like monkeys, and as they streamed away to the town, scarcely one looked back along the jetty at her, not ten yards away. She was looking down, watching every boat, and it was a shock when she saw that she had not noticed a man with his arm in a sling. His big hat hid his face, but she knew that it was Peter. As his boat came under the ladder she walked to the top of it, looked down and at that moment Peter looked up.

For a moment he stopped, staring at her transfixed. The man behind spoke, asking him if he couldn't climb because he was one-handed, but, without replying, Peter sprang nimbly up the vertical ladder, and Clementina grasped his left hand as he mounted the last few steps. Then she put her arms round his neck and embraced him. Accidentally she pressed hard on his wounded arm and she saw him wince as she kissed him.

The sudden expression of pain, coming at that moment, remained forever in her memory. The reason was obvious and physical – she had pressed on the wound – and yet, and yet the look of pain, coming at that moment, symbolised their relationship: his youthful severity, her gay abandonment.

She told him hurriedly everything: all of which he might have guessed. He told her nothing of his life, of the battle of Trafalgar, of the wound he had got in trying to board *Redoutable*. They were hungry and went into a nearby eating-house. Then she begged him to come back to the room she had taken.

'I want you to make love to me.'

'I do not want to give you another child when I am not there to look after you.'

'Love means taking risks.'

'I take risks every day of my life. But there is no love in taking them – quite the contrary.'

'The risk of another child – why, a child is a joy! You can be as careless of that as you are of the risk when you board a French ship.'

Peter gave a short laugh. 'I am not careless of the risk then. I take every precaution. In spite of which I got a slash on my sword arm.'

Yet Clementina's words made him feel guilty. Perhaps he did

not love his wife as the marriage service enjoined? And so, when she urged him again, he took her hand and they climbed in single file up the narrow stairs to her bedroom.

It was so long since Clementina had been made love to, it was so long that she was clumsy and unaccommodating and then desperate to repair her failure. Peter had not been faithful. He had allowed himself to be seduced by a Spanish girl, who could not have been more than sixteen. She had looked at him with such melting black eyes and now – much against his will – she was uppermost in his thoughts as he embraced Clementina. Indeed if he had not visualised that exquisite naked young body, it is probable that he would not have achieved the complete act of love for which Clementina – his legal wife – with her short body hardened by toil and only half unclothed – was longing. And this was for him another reason for guilt. He had sinned and he sinned doubly by letting the memory of that sin invade what was sacred, that which he had vowed to give to Clementina alone. He was sunk in sin. He bore the curse of Cain. He had killed many men. But he would not again compound one sin by another, by refusing his duty to his wife.

With the thought of duty, he unfastened his money belt and shook out eight golden guineas.

'It is all I have been able to save out of my pay as I have some expenses on board.' And he gave his wife six of the coins. 'That will more than pay your passage by ship to Leith.'

There were plenty of vessels plying from Portsmouth to London, and from there she would have to take another vessel to Leith. It would save her a month walking on the roads. Clementina was reluctant to spend money in such a way, but Peter persuaded her, and she was longing to get back to Isabella and young Peter so she finally consented.

Then, when they had come down the rickety stairs and walked together to the harbour so that Peter should not miss the boat taking him back, they went into a miserable pot-house, where each of them drank a tankard of small beer and ate a bit of bread and cheese – why, then everything changed.

Peter looked at his wife and was overcome with admiration for a woman who had walked all of five hundred miles, only

139

to see him for one day – for *Weasel* sailed at dawn. He saw her again with the eyes of the boy holding the rejected shoes: the boy who had fallen in love with her because of her gaiety and courage, her honesty, her strength. He made up his mind that henceforward he would be worthy of this brave woman.

In the meantime there was business to be settled. If he should be promoted to Petty Officer, he would try and send her a little money every month. Clementina told him of his mother's letter and of her reply; and he shook his head sadly and said that Clementina had done right. And then he said that his father must be made to pay for little Peter's schooling when the time came.

Up till then she had not spoken of the incidents of her journey, but suddenly she told him of the worst moment: when the kindly shepherdess had galloped off with her satchel, with her purse and her papers, and of how she thought that she had lost everything, and had then found all her treasure left in the middle of the road.

'Another woman would have turned back then – but you went on, and your courage was rewarded,' said Peter.

'I never thought of turning back.'

And as she told her story, the thought of her courage – of when she had leapt into the mill-pond to save the silly girl from drowning, of how she had outfaced the gypsy with the cudgel and won a piece of money from him – and the Scottish keeper with his gun and talk of man-traps – these stories set him in a glow, and he leant over the table and took her by the hand and said that he was a lucky man to have such a wife. The war could not last forever, and then they would be happy together again. Young Peter was lucky to have such a mother – luckier than he had been – and he hoped little Isabella would grow up to be as courageous and honest a woman as her.

All this praise, so entirely unexpected, coming from Peter, usually so severe and silent, overwhelmed Clementina. She blushed scarlet, tears came into her eyes, and she lifted Peter's hand and kissed it passionately – something that she had never conceived herself doing.

At that moment the other sailors in the pot-house rose up in a body. The boat was coming in, and any seaman who kept the midshipman in charge waiting was likely to receive punishment.

'Drink up your mug of beer,' said Peter. They went out. It was high tide, and there were only four rungs of the ladder for Peter to scramble down. Then Clementina stood watching until the boat full of liberty-men was out of sight.

'Fancy Peter thinking like that about me,' she said to herself. She was still glowing with his praise as she went back to her lodging. His parting gift had been a white lanyard on which she could lead Jasper.

CHAPTER NINE

CLEMENTINA had never been out to sea in anything larger than an open boat, and then never for more than an hour or two. Thus there was excitement for her in going aboard a brig, leading Jasper on his lanyard, in walking the deck, and going down to the cabin below. And then after she had come on deck again, there was the marvel of seeing the Fleet, of passing almost under the gun-ports of *Mars*, *Royal Sovereign* and *Bellerophon* and seeing the crowd of frigates and sloops anchored at Spithead with pinnaces and Admirals' barges bustling along from one of the great first-raters to another. The sun shone directly ahead, the Isle of Wight, a soft green stretch of land, lay to the right and the choppy waves were crested with foam. More sail was put on the brig as she turned up Channel with a following wind that made her lurch and hesitate before sliding ahead over the waves.

There were two other women on board – the wife of a naval lieutenant with a nursemaid and a baby. Clementina had come on board first and as the lady, followed by a nursemaid carrying the baby, came on deck, she greeted her with a 'Good morning, ma'am,' only to be rewarded by a haughty stare and by the lady turning her back on her. Clementina was therefore not sympathetic when, after the brig had reached the open sea, the lady turned pale and tottered down the companion, and did not appear again until three days later when they reached Tilbury.

But by then Clementina was herself feeling unwell, though not from sea-sickness. Her head throbbed, she kept nodding off to sleep, and the noises of the ship seemed continuous and unnaturally loud. She made an effort, packed her little satchel, went down to the dock, leading Jasper lest he should run off, and was directed to a ship which was, luckily for her, sailing next morning for Leith. It was still being loaded, but she was allowed to go on board, found a cabin and lay down at once on a bunk. The rattle of the winch as the cargo of sacks of wheat was being lowered into the hold was full of evil, like fiendish laughter, followed by a chuckle.

A woman came into the cabin, looked at her and her dog and went away. Presently she came back. There was an interval and she heard the ropes straining and the ship was heeling over. It was morning and they were at sea. Her head was bursting and on fire; she could feel the leather pillow under her head scorching, but she could not move.

Then it seemed as though that keeper MacArthur were in the cabin with her. Clementina wondered how he came to be there. She dared not move. MacArthur had set a man-trap beside her bunk. It was painted bright yellow. Its pink eyes, like those of a ferret, watched her without winking; its steel teeth were of blued metal, and a long green tongue darted in between them. Clementina made a great effort to sit up in bed, and then to her horror she saw the yellow man-trap, like a huge scorpion, move and then scuttle to a new position against the cabin door.

She was on fire: a red-hot iron seared her forehead and entered her brain, which bubbled like boiling tar. She tried to lift her hand to her head, but she was too weak and fainted away in the flames. The coarse sailcloth sheet on which she lay was soaked in her sweat. She lay in torment.

When she became conscious she knew at once that she was no longer in the cabin, or on a ship in motion, and that she was not wearing her own clothes. She was naked except for a short smock of brown holland that scarcely came to her knee, and she was lying on a canvas hammock laced with whipcord to a wooden frame which hung a foot or two above the floor. Later on, when she was strong enough to raise herself up and look down on the floor, she was glad that her hammock had no contact with it, for it was filthy and covered in cockroaches. But it was a long time before she could move, and soon after her first awakening she fell back into an uneasy sleep.

When she woke up, she put her hand to her forehead and found that it was no longer smooth, but covered in little bumps. Then, making an effort, she turned her head and saw that her shoulder was covered with a rash of red pimples. So were her arms. But there were only one or two pimples on her breasts and the rest of her body. She knew then that she had smallpox and guessed that she had been taken from the ship to some old hulk used as a lazaret. In this she was right, and her guess was confirmed when an old woman came with a bucket and, looking at her exclaimed: 'Aye, the pocks are come out thick. You were never much of a beauty, but now your looks are gone for good, and no one will call you bonny again. But you are a lucky woman to be alive. You were nine-parts dead when they carried you in here, and I thought that you would be no trouble but just putting you in a coffin. But it seems I was wrong. Now whatever you do, don't start scratching.'

With the eruption, the height of Clementina's fever was gone, and she was aware of herself and the things about her. The lazaret, as she had guessed, was the empty hold of an old rotting hulk, lit by an open hatchway. Its filthy wooden walls were streaked with iridescent slime where big orange and spotted slugs had left their tracks. The place stank of human excrement. By good fortune there were no others with her in quarantine. Had there been an epidemic, her chances of recovery in such conditions would have been poor.

The desire to scratch was intense, and, to help resist it, she put her hands flat under her buttocks. She dozed off but woke up to find that she had been scratching her face in her sleep and that her nails were bloody. When the old woman brought her a bowl of thin porridge she asked for a strap, so that she could fasten her arms to her sides and would not start scratching again in her sleep.

Fever returned: she was again on fire and visions assailed her. She understood that she was in the power of the sea. The fiendish waves built up and up, gathering to enormous heights and then came rushing and rolling, and their crests flickered with white fire. She herself was struggling in white flame, her body thrown hither and thither. She was choking; then for a moment she was free, and again the monster was rushing upon her to play with her as a cat plays with a mouse. Her battered burning body cried for peace, for the relief of death.

The hours crawled by and became days and even weeks as Clementina lay, itching intolerably and finding her physical weakness hard to bear and hard to believe in. It needed every ounce of muscle and will-power to slide up the hammock, or to turn on her side, and she could not get back into bed after using the bucket, unless the old woman was there to give her a leg up and hold the hammock steady. Sometimes she gave way and scratched, usually only her arms or her scalp – but when she did so, the pustules or pocks became poisoned. Finally when they had all broken and healed, she began peeling. It was then that she was most infectious. And it was not until a week after peeling had stopped that an old apothecary, who was nominally in charge of the hulk, allowed her to wash and put on a new clean smock, before coming ashore. There she put on a set of new clothes, as her old ones had been burned and were in no fit state to save. The seamen on the brig and the old woman in the lazaret were honest, and there had been enough money left for the old hag to buy her a shift, a blouse, petticoat, stockings, skirt, shawl and boots, though the shawl and the boots were second-hand.

Clementina picked up her satchel, lifted it on to her shoulder and walked out into the street. For a moment she wondered if she had the strength to walk, for she could scarcely stand. She began unsteadily, keeping to the water's edge. She hoped to find a ferry that would take her across to Burntisland.

Suddenly there was a whine of recognition and a bounce that nearly knocked her off her feet and there was Jasper! Jasper, licking her hands, twisting his body against hers, leaping up to lick her face with an affection almost too violent. And if she was feeble and worn down by sickness, Jasper was the opposite. She had never seen him more handsome. His coat was washed and brushed, and he was wearing a new collar she had never seen before. After their first demonstration of mutual joy, she became aware that Jasper was not alone. A short, thick-set, dark gentleman in a blue tailcoat and wearing breeches buttoned down the side of his calves had come up and was surveying Jasper and her with astonishment. And Jasper was looking first at her and then at the short gentleman and wagging his tail vigorously by way of introduction.

'That dog seems to know you, my good woman,' said the gentleman, and then noticing the look of surprise which had greeted his form of address, he took off his low-crowned beaver hat, revealing a bald head.

'Indeed, sir, Jasper is my own dog,' replied Clementina.

'The servant of two masters, to use Goldoni's title. When did you last see him, madam?' asked the gentleman, for there was something in Clementina's air, in spite of her tattered shawl, that made him revise his opinion of her station in life.

'I came with him from London by boat six weeks ago, but was struck down with the smallpox and carried unconscious into the lazaret from which I have only this minute come out.'

'That fits the facts exactly. The dog must have been set ashore, and I have been caring for him for the last month.'

'And very well too. He looks the picture of health.'

The old gentleman bowed. 'It is more than I can say for his mistress. You look exhausted and distressed. You must excuse my saying so, but I am a medical man.'

'I have not got back quite my full strength. But I shall recover it by walking – the open air will do me good.'

The old gentleman looked surprised. 'Walking where?'

'To my home and children at East Haven, beyond Carnoustie.'

'All this needs discussion. If you come with me we will talk it over with my wife. But I am forgetting my manners. I am Doctor Galiani, an Italian professor of anatomy.'

'I am Mistress Clementina Lamond. I had been visiting my husband, who was wounded at Trafalgar, when I was taken ill.'

'After a bad attack of smallpox you need rest. You will strain your heart walking so far. You must take the coach.'

'I have to cut my coat according to my cloth,' said Clementina.

'Well, come, I must look into this. See, the dog is getting impatient.' For Clementina had stopped and stood silent.

Doctor Galiani looked at her with a most charming smile. 'Tell me, what is the trouble?'

'I cannot enter a decent house because of the condition I am in,' said Clementina angrily.

'What do you mean?'

146

'I mean that I am verminous. I am dropping with lice,' Clementina almost shouted at him.

'Anyone coming out of that hulk is bound to be. I often pick up a louse from my poorest patients. But I am a doctor, and I will get rid of them for you.' Then, as Clementina was silent, he said: 'I am not letting you go off with the dog like this. What will happen to him if you fall ill on the road?'

Clementina bowed her head and followed him.

Doctor Galiani's wife was a tiny, frivolous Scotswoman whom he had recently married. She was rather in awe of him: he was a foreigner and a distinguished man, older than herself. Leaving Clementina waiting, he went and had a word with his wife in an inner room. Presently Flora Galiani came out with a very flushed face and told Clementina to follow her to the wash-house. There she brought a bucket and a hip bath and gave Clementina a quart bottle of spirits of wine and a sponge and a big pot of sulphur ointment. She was to strip naked, throw her clothes into the bucket, soak her head in spirit and sponge herself all over with it. Then she was to rub herself and her hair with sulphur ointment and put on a clean nightgown, after which she was to go to bed.

These directions were given sharply in a voice that trembled with indignation and ended with the words:

'That is what Doctor Galiani has *ordered*, and I have to obey him.'

Clementina was so overcome with shame that she thanked her meekly. When she had finished, she called out and was led to a bedroom and put between clean sheets. The doctor had ordered that she was to stay there until she had completely recovered.

This was not the first time that Doctor Galiani had behaved in this way. He had once brought in a sick man he had found in the street. Flora had submitted with an ill grace, and had made him promise not to do such a thing again. Now he had broken his promise and brought a verminous woman into the house. And his excuse was that it was not he that had introduced her but the dog! And he had hinted that perhaps the woman would let them keep the dog which without a doubt belonged to her.

147

As soon as Clementina had got into bed she was brought a glass of hot rum and milk, and after that a bowl of vegetable soup and a glass of foaming egg-nog, which the doctor said was essential, and which he had beaten up from three egg-yolks with his own hands.

It was only a little past midday, but Clementina fell into the first deep and comfortable sleep she had enjoyed for six weeks.

Doctor Galiani was a man of great benevolence. But Flora thought that he ought not to pretend to act like the good Samaritan. He was, if anything, a Roman Catholic, though he never wanted to see a priest or spoke of confession. He had adopted the dog with an enthusiasm which his wife shared. But to find a lousy woman in the street claiming to be the dog's owner and to bring her back was too much!

Next day Clementina was allowed to get up, but she smelled unpleasantly of sulphur ointment for the whole of her visit. Perhaps it was in order to prove that she was not a vagrant that she spoke of her mother-in-law's brother who was a professor in Edinburgh and asked the Doctor if he knew him.

'No, I don't. But you must write him a note and borrow your coach fare,' he replied.

'I would rather die in a ditch than ask him for a groat,' exclaimed Clementina.

'That insufferable Scottish pride! You are worse than Spaniards! I shall have to go and see him myself!' The Doctor was really pleased to go, since the existence of the Professor would be a proof of Clementina's truthfulness, of which Flora had been doubtful.

That evening he unfolded a piece of paper and read aloud:

I, Clementina Carey, wife to Master Peter Lamond of East Haven, Panbride, at present serving in the Royal Navy, do hereby acknowledge the receipt of three pounds Scots which I promise to repay within one year of the present date together with interest of six shillings, being at the rate of ten per cent of the aforesaid sum.

May 3, 1806 Signed:

Doctor Galiani laid three sovereigns on the table.

'What a man! Shylock should have been a Lowland Scot and not a Venetian Jew!'

Clementina laughed and said: 'I would rather have it that way, than as a gift. But we are not all that bad. My father was generous to a fault, and he was only half Highland, and my mother was of the Lindsays: too generous to live on this earth.' Then she took the pen and signed her name.

Armed with the loan, Clementina reserved a seat on the coach from Edinburgh to Dundee and from Dundee on the one to Montrose as far as Muirdrum.

Then the Doctor's wife, who loved buying things, took her shopping, during which they came near a quarrel, for Clementina looked at every halfpenny. However, she was made to buy a pair of well-fitting boots, a skirt and a little bonnet which suited her well, as well as such luxuries, unknown in Panbride, as a cake of Naples soap and a bottle of Mitcham lavender water. She refused to buy a shawl: she had two of her own knitting at the shippon.

That evening Doctor Galiani listened to her heart and was satisfied that it was normal. Next day he took her to the coach, first making her accept an old Italian silk shawl. In return for all his goodness she could only offer him Jasper. He was delighted. 'The servant of two masters,' he repeated. Goldoni was his favourite playwright.

Then, as they were waiting for the coach, he brought out a brooch of pearls and garnets set in silver gilt and insisted on pinning her shawl with it.

Clementina refused outright to accept it, until he said, looking sadly at her: 'That shawl of yellow silk and that brooch belonged to my first wife, who died before I came to Scotland. I have never given them to Flora because it would remind me too much of the past if I saw her wearing them. So you will be doing me a kindness if you will accept them. Flora has asked for the brooch and doesn't seem to understand why I will not give it to her. If you will accept it the matter will be at an end.'

Clementina thanked him and kissed him farewell, before he handed her on to the coach.

Clementina's bonnet, her yellow silk shawl and jewelled brooch, made a far greater impression on all her old friends and acquaintances in East and West Haven, Carnoustie and Panbride, than the disfigurement of a face pitted by smallpox. Any woman may have smallpox, but few can hope for a silk shawl and jewels!

But it would be hard to say which was the more upsetting to her son Peter. He preferred men to women, men in rough clothes who liked him and let him alone, to women who were always telling him to mind this or that. Women pretended to love him – and then instead of laughing at him like men, they would catch hold of him and smack him and look at him with hard cold eyes. Women tyrannised, and the women in grand clothes were by far the worst: Mrs Henderland and his grandmamma the worst of all. Grand clothes were more alarming than the features of grown-ups. So for a moment he fled behind Elspeth at the sight of a grand lady who was, and wasn't, his mother. Then he recognised her voice and emerged shyly to be caught up and hugged and kissed. But he was glad to be put down. Isabella, on the other hand, was delighted to be handed over to her mother and was fascinated by the bonnet and the brooch and the rich smoothness of the shawl. But when the four of them had walked to the shippon together, Clementina unpinned her shawl and took off her bonnet as soon as she set foot inside, and while she put them away in safety, Elspeth lit the fire and dusted the table, and they began a conversation that lasted for many weeks.

Not everyone was as eager to hear every detail of her adventures as was Elspeth, but Clementina led a more social life for the first months after her return than she had ever done before. Her walk to Portsmouth – five hundred miles – and her success in seeing her husband, were for many the glory of the Havens, of Carnoustie and Panbride, and Clementina was a heroine. That she had seen Peter so briefly added to the romance, that she had suffered disfigurement as the result of her devotion, made her more admired. It gave an almost Christian religious flavour to what might have been carnal.

One immediate and fortunate result was a complete reconciliation with Old Lamond. He appeared on the morning after her return with a magnificent crab and an invitation to visit the bothy and tell him her story – and then with admirable self-control let little Peter hug the leg of his breeches and push his curly little head into his great-grandfather's crotch.

Clementina was not able to accept his full invitation, because of the children, but two days later, when there was a rough sea, she went round alone and told bits of her story. When he asked how she managed to come back on the coach, she explained that Doctor Galiani would not let her walk and had gone round and borrowed three pounds from Elizabeth's famous brother – and when she told him the terms of the loan, she thought that the old man would have a seizure of apoplexy. He laughed until he was black in the face and then he pulled himself together and swore at the meanness of mankind – that any human being should exact ten per cent from a sick woman for a loan of three pounds and that sick woman his own nephew's wife!

'The meanest men are the most successful – for the world will be inherited by mean ungenerous men, who will sacrifice not only all that is noble and open-handed (that was why I loved your father, Clemmie), not only everything that is noble, but even the barest decency, to gain a few groats!'

From then on he kept Clementina well supplied with fish, and crabs and lobsters, and salads from his garden, and she repaid him by popping in to the bothy when he was out in his boat, to shovel out part of the ashes that were mounting high on his hearth, to wash down the floors and impound dirty cloths and shirts and linen which later on she returned washed, folded and ironed.

One evening, before it was actually dark, for the days were getting near their longest, there was a tap at the door. Clementina had just put the children to bed and they were asleep. She went on tiptoe and opened the door. Donald Hossack, huge in his blue jersey and full blue breeches with white stockings gartered above the knee, and wearing slippers, was standing there, and there were men behind him.

'Excuse us, Clemmie, but I've brought the crew of *Patience*. Our wives have been telling us bits of stories – anyway Elspeth has been telling me, but if you are willing we would like to hear the tale out of your own mouth.'

'Come in, come in,' said Clementina and they trooped in, filling the tiny room. Huge Andy Gatt and Willie Windram sat on the floor.

'If you've got a mug or two and a jug of water, we've brought some whisky.'

'We want to hear about your walk to Portsmouth, but first we want to hear about Peter.'

'I brought them along, Clemmie, because I know you can't leave your bairns, just as Elspeth can't leave ours of a night. And it seems the only way for us to hear what we want to know.'

Clementina brought out four mugs and two glasses and a jug of water. Willie Windram poured the whisky.

At first Clementina was shy, but Willie goaded her with questions until her modesty gave way. First she told them about the lucky chance of meeting Peter: of how he was one of the crew of the *Victory* and had got a sword slash on his right arm while trying to board the *Redoutable* – but that he would say very little about the fighting. Then she told them, beginning to enjoy the telling, how she had pulled the girl Lucy out of the mill-race and come out shivering with cold and covered in mud, and had been made to sing Robbie Burns's song: 'Green grow the rashes, O' to the English gentlefolk.

'That was never Robbie Burns's song. My great-aunt used to sing it before Robbie was born,' said Andy Gatt unexpectedly.

'Aye – but Robbie added a verse or two about the lasses, O,' said Willie.

'Well, shut your mouth and let Clemmie go on,' said Donald. So she told them about the Scottish keeper, MacArthur, and how she had outfaced him and that he had gone away threatening her with his man-traps. But best of all they liked the story of the clergyman near Oxford who had turned her away into the rain because she was a Presbyterian, and how she had walked round the side of the rectory and spent the night snugly in his conservatory and cooked her breakfast on his coke stove.

They roared that she was a marvel, and encouraged by their laughter and with a second glass of whisky in her hand, she told them the story that Peter had liked the best: of how the mounted shepherdess had galloped off with her satchel and all her possessions – of how she had lain down under a stone wall and cried until it was too cold and wet to stay there longer and how when she pushed on she found her satchel a few hundred yards down the road, but at first it had scared her as she had mistaken it in the moonlight for a black dog. After they had asked a few more questions about Peter, they got up to go. If Willie had been alone, she would have given him a special twinkling look, but with the whole crew there could be no favourites. As they went out each of the men gave her a slap on the shoulder and as he wished her good night, Donald Hossack said that the war would soon be over and Peter back, and they moved off, taking care to leave not only the empty whisky bottle but another one three parts full, behind them.

Clementina soon recovered her health and even part of her looks. For her hair grew again, and the thin wisps were filled out with a thick growth. The colour came back into her pitted cheeks, and some of her gaiety came back with it.

But telling stories and sipping whisky would not fill the larder: she must earn her living.

One day Minister Baird told Clementina that he had something to say to her after the service. So she waited while the congregation dispersed and then followed him into the manse.

'Here in Carnoustie we are planning to start a school for the youngsters. It is too much to expect a small child to walk to Panbride and back and to do a day's work. It will be an infant school for the bairns between five and ten years old. I have talked it over with the Panbride folk, and Master Lamond told me what I should never have guessed, that you are advanced in the mathematics, that his son Robert had given you lessons, and that you had gone on with your studies after marriage. Master Lamond said that we could not find a better mistress for the school than you. So our School Council have agreed to offer you the job for one term on trial – which means from next Michaelmas to Christmas – for the sum of nine pounds a term. And your young Peter will not have to pay his twopence a week.'

Clementina accepted eagerly, though it would mean buying a pony and trap and driving over to Carnoustie every morning and back in the afternoon for five days a week – six if she took Sunday School.

She began at once to prepare herself for her new employment. Elspeth minded the children for a day, while she went into Dundee and bought herself a dress length of grey alpaca sprigged with white flowerets, a paisley shawl, flannel for winter petticoats and a pair of gloves. These purchases exhausted her savings, and the next big one had to be made on credit. Fortunately the Romanies trusted her, and it was from one of them, who had been acquainted with her father, that she bought her pony and a light trap. For the sooner the animal was used to her the better. He was an elegant little grey gelding with dappled hindquarters and a very long silvery tail – disadvantageous in one way, since every brook fisherman who saw it would come begging for a few hairs for trout casts.

During the day that summer she had to lay in all the usual stores, and five times as much hay and glean several sacks of oats, for the pony, whom she had called the Spreckled Laird, a name soon shortened to Spreck.

A week before the Michaelmas term started, Elspeth Hossack came to the shippon. She had something on her mind and at last she blurted out: 'You ought to know, Clemmie, that there are those who don't like you being made teacher. They are Carnoustie folk. They don't like your being friends with the gypsies and your speaking Roman. And they haven't scrupled to bring up your father being a convicted man, and that Mother Carey was a witch – and a famous one at that. They went to protest to Willie Baird, and he told them the points they raised made him think more highly of you. He said that you had freed yourself from your early associations, that you had taught yourself reading, writing and arithmetic, though taken from school so young, and that you had married Peter, who was the finest young man in Panbride and had proved yourself a devoted wife.

'Then last night Willie Windram had a fight and knocked out one of George Leman's front teeth, because George said that you had put a spell on Peter, and that it was witchcraft that made him marry you, a fisher-lassie older than himself, when he might have had an Edinburgh beauty with a fine dowry. And then he said that Peter had got himself pressed on purpose to get away from you. So you see you have enemies, and you must be prepared for a fight.'

'Willie is a good and loyal friend, but I doubt if he has made my task easier. If the Carnoustie folk are against me, I should do better to withdraw,' said Clementina.

'I just don't know what advice to give you. The mothers of young children are kittle cattle and could make your life a hell.'

'And I've just bought myself that pretty pony from Randal Boswell. Peter already loves him. I suppose I shall have to sell him and the trap back, as I promised to pay at Christmas. And then I've made myself a smart frock and three petticoats to bear the cold of the schoolhouse in December!' And Clementina burst out laughing.

Suddenly serious, she said: 'You are a dear friend to have come with the bad news, Elspeth. She who does not tell you and watches you blunder in ignorance – who makes a pretence of not wishing to hurt you, but in secret is enjoying your humiliation, because withholding the bad news feeds her sense of power – she makes herself an enemy who is unforgivable, for whom I would lie in wait for years longing to hurt her, as deeply as she has hurt my pride.'

'Who are you speaking of, Clemmie? Whoever did that to you?' asked Elspeth astonished.

'It was Agnes, that tall handsome Highland woman who would live a month or so with my father – then go off and come back again. She loved me but she loved power more. I myself meant nothing, really. She knew to the day when Mother Carey planned to hand me to the Devil and she never said one word. And I had trusted her and admired her. I was put on my guard by chance. And then I found that Agnes had known and hidden the truth. I never spoke to her again, for I saw that she was worthless. And I told my father, and he broke with her.'

'What happened to her then?'

'She had picked up with a sergeant some time before, and

followed his regiment out to the Peninsula, and I suppose she is living with him there now.'

Next morning Clementina had decided that it would be cowardly to withdraw and that with the backing of the Minister and School Council, she would be able to stand up against the hostility of the Carnoustie parents and probably win them over. But about the middle of the morning there was a knock at the door, and there was Mr Baird. After he had been invited in and taken a chair, he said: 'Mistress Lamond, I have come on the most disagreeable errand on which I have ever been sent, and one which is in my opinion shameful and disgraceful. But by a majority vote of one, the School Councillors have sent me to tell you that they do not now think that you are a suitable person to be the mistress of the new school. Not because of any fault in you, but because of the ignorance and prejudice that exists among some of my parishioners who are parents of the children. They have agreed to compensate you for dismissal with so little notice, and I therefore offer you the full wages for one term – namely nine pounds.'

Mr Baird took a purse out of his pocket and laid nine sovereigns on the table.

Clementina said nothing.

After waiting for her to speak, Mr Baird at last continued: 'It is disgraceful – but the fact is that seven of the families in Carnoustie have been persuaded, by interested parties, that your early association with the gypsies and the fact of your father's having been transported to Botany Bay, are reasons which make you unsuitable. Believe me, Mistress Lamond, I have done all that I could. I told them that your association with gypsies was in your childhood and that you now ...'

Clementina interrupted him.

'I think that my best and most loyal friends are gypsies; Romans as they call themselves. Pyramus Lee's daughter and her sweetheart came back at the risk of their lives after my father was taken, to offer me a safe home, and Pyramus and his wife are friends I would never repudiate. I owe more to them than to anyone in Carnoustie, West Haven or Panbride.'

Mr Baird was greatly shocked by her words.

'What you have just said would have made it hard, if not impossible, to argue against those opposed to your appointment.'

'Well, you can spare your breath on my behalf, Mr Baird. I have little doubt that it is to you that I owe the offer of compensation. But I would rather not be paid for work that I have not performed.'

The Minister was astonished by Clementina's refusal of compensation. He was also pleased – for though he would never have allowed her to guess it, four out of the nine pounds came out of his own pocket. He felt, however, that he must not agree to her refusal without giving her time to consider it.

'Mistress Lamond, your are a proud woman, and your pride is of the kind to sustain your high standards of conduct, and which I cannot therefore altogether condemn. But I ask you to think again.'

'My decision is final, sir.'

'I feel sure that you have been put to expense in preparing yourself for your new situation.'

'Yes. I have bought a pony and trap. But I can sell them. And the things I bought to make myself decent were needed.'

'Will you not allow me to offer you a small loan to tide you over?'

'Yes, Mr Baird, if you would lend me the sum of three pounds until such time as I am able to repay it. Peter is entitled to prize money, part of which will be paid to me.'

Mr Baird, who had picked up his sovereigns, put three of them down again, and departed, leaving a proud and angry woman in the shippon. She knew that she would have had Peter's approval of her refusal to accept compensation for having been treated unjustly.

As soon as Mr Baird had gone, she wrote:

Dear Sir,

I am fortunate to be able to return your loan of three pounds sooner than I expected. Please find three sovereigns enclosed with interest at ten per cent for six months, to wit three shillings. I shall be obliged by the receipt of an acknowledgement cancelling the debt.

Your obedient Servant,   Clementina Lamond

This she put into a little box with the coins, which she wrapped in white linen fastened with sealing wax and fishing line and confined it to the guard of the stage coach, who gave her a receipt for it.

Clementina's life returned to its ordinary course. But as the children grew bigger she became poorer and had to work harder. She did not at first send either of them to school, but taught them herself.

It is not easy for a single woman with two children, and one a baby, to support herself. But it is possible for a cottager who pays no rent to be almost self-sufficient and that seemed to Clementina what she must learn to be. The summer was the time to lay in stocks for the bleak and barren winter. She had a nanny goat called Kirstie who would have a kid in October, and so would be giving milk in the winter, but she must lay in hay and straw for bedding. She must build a stack of logs and peats for firing to last a year. Autumn, after the great storms which littered the beach with driftwood, was the time for that. Old Lamond had given her enough land for a potato patch and a kailyard: when the potatoes had been dug and were safe in a pie, she would sow the patch with turnips for spring greens. And Old Lamond gave her all the fish she wanted. So she split, salted and smoked haddock, cod and eel, and had them hanging like lines of dirty linen inside the chimney, where they would dry and harden.

She was given a cask and packed it with herring in brine. Sugar, loaves, flour, a big skin of lard and a hundredweight sack of oatmeal, she had to buy. Also oil for the lamps. The Minister, William Baird, gave her a big jar of honey, for he kept bees. She was working hard from early morning till dusk, with little Peter running beside her, thinking to help her in all her tasks. Isabella slept in her basket cradle, or woke up whimpering.

All these occupations kept Clementina happy, and on fine days Old Lamond could hear her singing and would come quietly up to his fence to listen and then walk back reflecting that it didn't take much to keep a female creature happy: just her young ones following her about. It was the same as a ewe with a lamb, a cow with a calf, a mare with a foal and a woman with a bairn. When they had little ones they could do without a mate – but a man was not a full man unless he had a woman – and it was high time he himself had one. Since the gypsies were gone, he had been too much alone. He needed the touch of a woman's body lying beside him. He was eighty-four.

But though women had not the freedom of men, he thought that their lives were happier. A man in Clementina's position would be eating his heart out, his ambitions thwarted, as he himself had done in the past years. For he had fought on the wrong side at Culloden – that which had been defeated – and as he would not play the part of a turncoat, he had been forced to keep hidden. The smuggling had been something – it was against the Hanover rats – but he ought to have been a soldier. But the days when the Scots and the Irish could fight for King Louis were long since past, and the Stuarts were finished.

When the herring were all gone, and the men were line fishing, Clementina would earn a few pence baiting the snoods with mussels. Donald Hossack gave her the big job of sewing a new suit of sails for *Patience*, and of patching the old sails where they were torn. And when she had put little Peter to bed, she would sit up knitting the long and thick fishermen's stockings for sale to single men or widowers, though the steadier fellows knitted their own stockings themselves.

By autumn the shippon was well-stocked for the winter: her children and she would not starve or lie shivering in the dark. And the sail-making and the knitting brought in a bit of money.

Winter evenings were also employed in teaching Peter his letters and to count on his fingers. By Christmas he could read his own name and words of one syllable. When he was four years old it would be time to teach him to write and then to add up and subtract figures. She read him bits out of the Bible, those she liked best herself, about Noah and Balaam's ass and Samson killing the Philistines with the jawbone of an ass, and about the men who lay on their faces to drink, and the more watchful ones who took up the water in their cupped hands. She taught Peter to pray for the safety of our sailors out at sea, for our soldiers on land, for the defeat and confusion of the

French and for the health of the Royal Family.

Three years passed by with no outstanding incident except that a fisherman on one of the smaller boats at West Haven was drowned after losing his balance and falling overboard wearing heavy sea-boots – and closer at hand, that Old Lamond got a tinker's wife to live with him for a month, after which he chased her out of the bothy, for her sluttish habits.

'Maybe I'll have a lassie or two on a summer's night in the hayfield. But it's only an old fool like me who would let one into the house, messing everything up and drinking the whisky. I could not find a spoon or a fork, or the salt-cellar, while that tinker's whoor was in my house.'

Even before she had been disfigured by the smallpox, the old man had never looked at Clementina with a lustful eye. This was not because of a taboo against incest, or because if she had allowed herself to be seduced it might have caused great unhappiness and broken up her marriage and caused a great scandal: such considerations did not weigh with the old reprobate. It was simply that he was perfectly content with their relationship and would not have had it different. Any attempt to change it would have been as hateful to him as it would have been to her.

The days lengthened and spring, more bitter than winter, came with its east winds and snowstorms. A hurricane lifted the thatch and Willie and Donald brought ladders next morning to patch it and fasten it down. Year succeeded year: there were too many grey hairs in her head for her to pluck them out one by one. And then one day the guard on the mail coach sent witless Simon with a letter from Peter franked from Plymouth.

It was the spring of 1812, and Napoleon was gathering his immense army to invade Russia.

H.M. Sloop of War *Dispatch*
Plymouth, Devon

My dearest Wife,
    I am happy to inform you that, thanks be to God, I enjoy reasonably good health and that I have been greatly honoured

by being promoted to warrant officer with the rank of Master and appointed Master of the Sloop of War *Dispatch*. She has been in several actions and my information is that we shall shortly be sent to American waters to protect our merchant vessels from attack by privateersmen. I pray constantly for you and my little ones and at long last I am able to send you some support. The other halves of the Bank of England notes enclosed will follow by the next post. My love to Peter, who must be a fine lad by now, and to little Isabella.

Your affectionate husband

Peter Lamond

Address any letter to Peter Lamond R.N.
Master of the Sloop of War *Dispatch*
Plymouth Dockyard, Devon.

Enclosed in the letter were the halves of two ten-pound notes cut so that only half of the serial number of each was included. Three days later the missing halves arrived. Clementina pinned them together.

The news of Peter's promotion had to be conveyed to his parents, and Master Lamond would be the best person to change the banknotes. So, after confiding the children to Elspeth, Clementina put on her alpaca dress and paid her first visit to the Lamond House in Panbride since she had taken Robert there on her pony just fourteen years earlier.

A little maid opened the door, and Clementina said that she had business with Master Lamond. Leaving her standing there, the child hurried away and after a long pause returned to ask her to step in. Clementina noticed to her surprise that the house no longer seemed grand. The carpet in the passage was worn out, the walls needed a new coat of whitewash, there was dust in the corners and dust on the frame of Robert Bruce and the spider.

And Master Lamond, who was waiting for her in his counting house, had gone to seed also; his always white face had acquired a blueish tinge, his eyes had sunk deep into his skull, the little fringe of hair at the back and sides of his head was so white and clipped so close that his baldness seemed complete, and the corner of his mouth twitched. But he was hospitable and greeted Clementina affectionately. She had been left waiting so long at the door because he was asleep, and the little maid was shy of waking him.

Clementina handed him Peter's letter, and after putting on his steel-rimmed spectacles, he read it over twice.

'Peter's promotion does not surprise me. It will bring great changes in your position and manner of life.' He took the two notes, went to a safe and counted out twenty golden sovereigns – more money than Clementina had ever seen before.

'It is a matter for pride for us all. But it will make big changes. I had been counting on Peter returning to skipper *Patience*, or at least to take over the management of the curing sheds. That he will never do now. After Bonaparte's final defeat, which cannot be long delayed, wider prospects will open for Peter. And you will take precedence of the ladies of East Haven.'

Here Master Lamond gave a little dry laugh, to show that the subject of precedence was humorous. Then he thanked Clementina warmly for coming to him at once, inquired after his grandchildren and without offering her any refreshment, saw her to the door. Elizabeth had not appeared.

It was not meanness, nor the fear of a scene with his wife, which was responsible for this neglect of hospitality. In an ordinary way he would have given her an oatcake and a cup of tea. But he was disturbed by the news. He had counted on Peter to succeed him after his discharge from the navy. Now he was faced by having to decide whether he should sell the business or continue carrying the burden. He no longer had the stamina of a young man, and he knew that he was failing in health. He sat thinking, or trying to think, for a long while, but he could not decide, and put off action from week to week until it was too late.

He did, however, go to the school in Panbride and call young Peter over to him. The lad was nine years old.

'How often does the sun go round the earth?' his grandfather asked him.

Peter looked at him doubtfully.

'I canna answer that question. But the earth goes round the sun once every year. Is that what you meant to ask?'

'Who was James VI's father?'

'Darnley. He was Mary Queen of Scots' second husband, a great-nephew of Henry VIII of England, which is why our King James became King of England.'

'Well, you know a thing or two. Here's a fourpenny bit for you.'

'Thank you, Grandpapa.'

Master Lamond drove down to East Haven two days later and surprised Clementina, who was digging potatoes, by telling her that he would pay all the expenses of sending young Peter to school in Edinburgh. He did not add that it was with the hope that the boy would eventually take over his ownership of the fishing boats and the curing sheds. That would mean carrying on himself for another ten years.

The change in her son's and in her daughter-in-law's social position was felt by no one so much as Elizabeth. She wondered if she should renew her attempt at reconciliation – though it would have to be on very different terms.

Silent now were the tongues of the ill-wishers who had made accusations of gypsy association, of a convicted father, and even of witchcraft, against Clementina, now that her husband was the Master of a sloop in the navy. The news made a greater difference to Clementina's manner of life even than the twenty pounds which had accompanied it.

For though only a warrant officer in rank and below any commissioned officer in the Admiralty lists, the Master comes after the Captain in the ship when she is afloat. He is next to the Captain in authority, for he is the most experienced seaman on whom the Captain relies. It is the Master who navigates her across the oceans and puts her into the chosen harbour. The Captain fights the ship, but it is the Master who lays her alongside the enemy when they board. It is he, not the Captain, who can mark her position at any time upon the chart. The importance of the Master in any ship of the Royal Navy was known to every man and boy in East and West Haven. All were impressed, but the crew of *Patience*, though they rejoiced, were not surprised. Indeed they wondered that the promotion had not come earlier.

Six months later Master Lamond died, having left his dispositions as regards the curing sheds and his fishing boats too late. Though he had also made no provision for continuing to pay his grandson's school fees, the governors of the school were prepared to keep the boy on until such time as his father was able to pay them. Peter, Master of the *Dispatch*, was not able to attend his father's funeral: the ship was in American waters pursuing American privateers. Yet Peter managed to write home twice.

In June 1815 came a letter from Edinburgh with news that was to bring a great change in Clementina's life.

His Majesty's Brig-Sloop *Cherokee*
Leith, 1st June 1815

My Dearest Wife,

Thanks to the interest of my former commander, Captain Galloway, and with the concurrence of Captain William Cobbe, who prefers an Englishman as Master, I have been appointed Master of H.M. Brig-Sloop *Cherokee*. She performs guard and defensive duties and is likely to be stationed for some time in the Firth of Forth. My duties as Master are not likely to be exacting in these circumstances, and I hope I shall be able to visit East Haven during the coming months. I went to see my son Peter at his school and there heard the sad news of my father's death. Young Peter is growing into a fine fellow and his greatest chum is a French boy and a Vicomte to boot!

My love to little Isabella, whose acquaintance I am eager to make. I don't rate Boney's chances very high, but all depends on the Duke of Wellington and the coming battle.

Your affectionate husband,

Peter Lamond, R.N.

I have written by this post a letter to my mother and am also going to see my father's solicitor in order to learn the details of my father's will.

Before Clementina had replied, or Peter had visited East

Haven, the news of the Battle of Waterloo reached Scotland, and it was still June when Peter wrote again.

H.M. Brig-Sloop *Cherokee*
Leith, 26th June 1815

My Dearest Wife,

As you will have heard, the war is over and with it I trust my active service in the Navy. I have already spoken to Captain Ramage of my wish to retire on half-pay, to which he has assented with the most noble sentiments of regret at my leaving the ship. I shall of course stay on until a qualified officer is appointed to *Cherokee* in my place.

I have already found an empty cottage for sale at Dysart. It has a paddock and large kailyard, so that you will not feel too cut off from your country pursuits. I wish you and the child to move there as soon as the legal formalities have been completed next week.

The best way to move our furniture and household belongings is by sea. Donald and my old crew should be able to move all our possessions at the shippon to Dysart in two journeys. If the weather continues fine and the sea moderate, I shall expect you not later than the 16th July. Go and see Donald and make the arrangements immediately.

Please give my compliments to my Grandfather, and I hope he keeps his health. Peter's French chum is already talking of returning to his native land after his father, the Duke, has been able to settle into his château, but in my opinion it will take some months before it is safe for him to return.

Give my love to little Isabella whom I am longing to hold in my arms.

Your affectionate husband,

Peter Lamond, R.N.

My reason for choosing Dysart as our residence is that it is within a short sailing distance of Edinburgh, where I hope to obtain employment and pursue my studies, and that life there will be within our means.

CHAPTER TEN

THE DAY fixed for the move was fine and clear with a good breeze. Donald and Willie ran *Patience* down the bank and set her afloat. There then began the carrying of all the household stuff from the shippon to the top of the shore: curtains, bedding, pots and pans, all were set down among the marram grass and sand. They were then carried down by Willie and stowed away in the stern and along the gunwales by Donald. When all was loaded, tarpaulins were spread to keep all dry. After that some of the pieces of furniture were tied down on top. Then Kirstie, the nanny goat, was put on board and tied firmly to a ring in the bottom of the boat so that she could not waltz around or jump overboard.

Isabella, carrying the tom-cat (another Thomas), took her place. Donald took his seat in the stern and the other four men ran *Patience* out and clambered aboard, just before the water reached the tops of their seaboots. A few strokes of the oars took her beyond the mouth of the channel. Then, as *Patience* rocked uneasily, the sails were hoisted. They drew at once and she forged ahead, the oars were shipped and the waves slapped against her side and the spray came in sudden gusts to sprinkle the faces and clothes of Clementina and Isabella, who went wild with delight.

The wind was east, and when *Patience* had made sufficient offing to clear Fife Ness, she was able to sail south with the wind on her quarter.

For a time *Patience* pitched, dived into the waves, rose splendidly, and sheets of spray swept over her, each greeted with shrieks and howls of excitement by Isabella. Presently Willie Windram brought out a basket, and the little girl and her mother were offered shrimps, lobster and chicken, with scones and slices of fruit cake to follow. There was general laughter when an extra-violent sheet of spray knocked the leg of chicken that Clementina was holding out of her grasp and sent it flying overboard. A dram of whisky for the men and a drink of buttermilk for mother and child ended the meal. Isabella, sated, lay down amidships on a roped bundle and soon was asleep. She was still asleep when they passed the Bell Rock and then turned, with a following wind, past the Isle of May into the Firth of Forth. First Anstruther and Pittenweem slid by close, then they headed across Largo Bay, and Dysart showed up. As Donald ran *Patience* alongside the jetty, Clementina saw a tall figure in naval officer's uniform standing upon it with a telescope under his arm. It was Peter, who had been watching for their arrival.

It was low tide, so as Andy tied up, Peter was standing up above them and looking down. He gave Donald a warm greeting, then words of thanks to each of the four men before he turned to Clementina, helped Isabella to climb the ladder and folded the shy girl in his arms. Then, in time, he put her down to give his wife his hand as she stepped off the vertical ladder on to the quay. He gave her a brief embrace and turned again to Isabella, holding her at arm's length to look at her, then laughing, patting her on the head, he gave himself to the business of where *Patience* should be unloaded and pointed out the little house which was now his home.

If he were shocked by his wife's pockmarked features, she was shocked by his lean face and the stern expression it assumed in repose. But he was full of affection as he led her from the harbour quay to a little house at the end of the street. It overlooked the sea, and she was delighted to find an orchard and garden behind it. Willie followed them, leading Kirstie. Then came Donald carrying a sack. With the willing hands of the five men, *Patience* was soon unloaded. But though Peter was gentle and quite obviously happy, there was behind all his words a tone of authority. The habit of command could be felt as he told Willie to set the chairs in the living-room and Andy Gatt to carry the pieces of the bedstead to an upstairs room and to put them together, before going back to fetch mattress and bedding. All the men were aware that a distinction in rank had come between them and the boy they had chosen, as equals, to be their skipper. But they did not resent it – indeed it confirmed them that they had chosen rightly all those years ago. For they were, all five, real men, valuing work well done above other things. They respected professional skill, and knew that a hierarchy of authority and subordination is necessary for its execution and the safety of all. Not one of them had been out of sight of land for more than a few hours, or in a sudden squall. They had only sailed in open boats in rough seas with three sails set at the most. But their young skipper could handle a full-rigged ship with upwards of twenty sails set and take her safely across the oceans to any port in the known world. And he had fought the French and the Spanish and, what was more than either, the Americans. The fact that these gifts had brought a distinction in rank was right, and their awareness of it made them respect themselves the more.

A second boatload, with Elspeth's brother in Willie's place in the crew, brought the rest of the furniture from the shippon. Before its arrival, however, Willie had driven over the pony and trap and was taken home on board *Patience*.

There were very busy days moving their few sticks of furniture from room to room. Then one day there was a surprise: a knock at the door and there was Duncan.

'We've brought a few bits more for you: and you may say there are honest people in the world. For they have been keeping things that came out of the croft, so that the bailiffs could not seize them, for all of thirteen years, and now they know you would be glad of them, they have sent you what hasn't got broken or worn out.'

And Duncan was followed by Donald and Willie carrying the Spanish tallboy that had been the one really good piece of furniture in the croft and had come from Lord Lovat's castle. Then came Andy Gatt with two of the ash chairs, and then Duncan and Willie and Donald, with the weight of the old dresser between them.

'So it was you who hid them: I always thought it was my Auntie who flew away with them.'

Duncan laughed: 'She might have done – though these bits are a bit heavy to carry on a broomstick. But we were beforehand with her. Everyone loved David: he had been openhanded and had helped all his neighbours, and when the time came

168

there were those who were ready to hide his things in their byres, when the bailiffs wanted to seize them. They made use of the farming tackle, which was all worn out seven years since. And what china and glass there was got smashed long ago. But when your grand Peter comes back in his uniform with his cocked hat, you can tell him you didn't come to him quite empty-handed. These are missing parts of your dowry which would have been a better one except for the damned excise men.'

The crew of *Patience* stayed, while Clementina scratched up a meal and sent Isabella round to buy a gallon of beer, as Peter's little keg was empty and he had not bothered to get it refilled.

'And did you arrange all this, Duncan?' asked Clementina.

'Well, Willie had the biggest hand in it – in getting the things stowed away safely in the first place – and then when he came here the other day and saw how bare your house was, I went round telling the kind folks who had hidden them that the time had come for their return.'

'And were they all that willing to part with them?'

'There was one old body who had fallen in love with the tallboy and had come to think it was her own. She asked a heap of questions : "Were the rooms in your house big enough? Would it look well? Would it not give your neighbours a wrong idea of you?" At last I said to her : "Mistress, if you have a mind to steal the tallboy, it's clear that Willie chose wrongly. But if you want to argue it out with Clementina Lamond, I'll take you down to Dysart and you can measure the rooms." That settled her.'

Peter was impressed when he returned, not so much by the pieces of furniture as by Duncan Hossack and his own crew's secrecy. 'They are close devils, those East Haven men : they never told me one word about it. I always thought it was your wicked Auntie who had given the things away to the women in her coven.'

Young Peter was brought over in the naval pinnace the following Sunday to see his new home. After that he became a weekly boarder at his school in Edinburgh, and Isabella went to the day school in Dysart. Accustomed to running about wild at East Haven, she was unhappy. She complained, and when reproved showed her feelings by scowls and poutings. One Saturday Peter was allowed to bring his friend the Vicomte de Serignac with him, and to the astonishment of his parents chattered away in French to his visitor. For the first weeks Clementina felt much as her daughter did, but she could not express her feelings by scowls. For years she had longed for her husband, but now that she was living with him they were seldom together. Peter was on duty for much of the time, and when *Cherokee* was at sea, he slept on board. She rarely knew when he was coming to Dysart. It was not his fault, for he did not know himself and could not communicate in advance of his coming. She often spent the evening hours with an old telescope scanning the Firth for the naval pinnace which might bring him.

And when he did come, he usually spoke little, except for peremptory commands or words of praise. And his praise often annoyed her more than a direct order.

'Does Peter think I'm wanting in the head? How else could anyone have done it?' she commented inwardly. The war had come between them, as often happens. He could not speak of the war which had changed him. He never spoke of it. And he expected obedience. But a disagreement arose on which Clementina would not give way.

It was a mild evening. Peter had come early, but would have to go back on board that night. The crew of the pinnace had been dismissed. Two were playing a round of golf in the evening light, four were playing bowls and the others were sitting with mugs of beer watching them. Isabella had run off to play on the beach with schoolfellows. Peter and Clementina were sitting on a bench on the orchard side of their cottage. Suddenly Peter leapt to his feet and dashed at Kirstie, who, innocent of ill-doing, was chewing his cocked hat.

As he dashed towards her, the nanny goat bounded away carrying the cocked hat in her narrow jaws. Peter pursued her for some little while without success. It was ridiculous to see the goat bounding forward every time that the man in his uniform had nearly reached her. At last she dropped the hat; Peter picked it up and came back and saw that Clementina was laughing at him. He was in a rage: she had never seen him so angry.

'Get rid of that goat before I come here again,' he snapped, looking at her with icy fury. The hat was beyond repair. Kirstie had bitten through and masticated one of the peaks. As his wife did not reply, Peter repeated the order: 'Do you hear? You are to get rid of that goat first thing tomorrow.'

'No, Peter. That I will not do. Kirstie gives milk for Isabella and my parritches. We cannot do without it.'

'I tell you that I will not have that beast around. You are to get rid of her, you understand.'

'No, Peter. Kirstie is in full milk and she stays.'

'Do you mind that a wife has to obey her husband?' said Peter angrily.

'Only in what is reasonable,' said Clementina. There was a silence. Then she added: 'I will put a chain on Kirstie and tether her when you are here. And give me the hat, I might....'

'No. It is destroyed. And how am I to go aboard *Cherokee* hatless? I cannot salute a superior, hatless.'

'If Lord Nelson had lost his hat, would he have minded it as much as the Master of the *Cherokee*? I remember your telling me about the Marquis of Granby whose hat blew off, and whose wig blew off, and he went on "bald-headed at the enemy".'

Peter flushed and was silent.

'Stay here an hour or two longer and go on board in the dark.' Clementina took her husband by the arm and drew him towards her. 'You looked so funny chasing Kirstie that I could not help laughing. I am so sorry.'

Suddenly Peter's whole expression changed.

'You were right to laugh at me. It is I who should be sorry, for I lost my temper. I am getting too much in the habit of it.' And he pulled his wife into their cottage. When Isabella came back half an hour later she found the doors bolted.

On 30 August 1815, a new Master was appointed to *Cherokee*, and Peter was able to go on half-pay – five shillings a day. He was accustomed to laying out the course of his ship in the log-book, and he had always had a gift for mathematical drawing and geometry. Thus he hoped to be able to double his income by getting in the naval architect's office. If he did the Lamond family could manage comfortably on fifteen pounds a month.

There was prize money due to him and part of the sale of his father's property should come to him.

With Peter on half-pay, everything was changed, and Clementina was a happy woman. The cocked hat and the swords and pistols were put into the loft where Kirstie and Isabella and young Peter could not get at them, and the blue tailcoat and the four pairs of white duck trousers cleaned and ironed and laid up with bunches of woodruff to make them smell sweet when next wanted.

One of Clementina's first thoughts on going to Dysart was that she would be able to see Doctor Galiani and his wife again, and thank them once more for having taken her in when she was ill and feeble and for having bestowed so many marks of affection upon her. She would like to have news of Jasper, and if she could visit Edinburgh for a day, she might see all three of them. Now that Peter had retired from the navy there was another reason. She felt sure that the Italian doctor would like Peter and he might help him and advise him in his studies.

She spoke to Peter, then wrote, but added a footnote to the letter he was to deliver on his next visit to Edinburgh: a footnote which she knew that Peter would not have approved. It ran: 'Please detain my husband for a little while in conversation. He is deeply interested in the mathematical and physical sciences and though I am partial, I believe he is worthy of your friendship.'

It scarcely needed such words for Dr Galiani to beg Peter to enter his study, for his curiosity about the man to see whom Clementina had walked five hundred miles was great and he wished to judge whether he were worthy of such devotion. Peter's visit had an even greater influence than Clementina had hoped. For the old Italian doctor invited Peter to be his guest at a meeting of the Edinburgh Philosophical Society the following week and introduced him among others to Rennie. On the advice of that great engineer Peter paid a two-week visit to Glasgow to see the steam packet then under construction there which was destined for passenger service on the Clyde.

Moreover, during his absence, the doctor and his wife invited Clementina and Isabella to pay them a two-days' visit, and this was joyfully accepted. Isabella had heard much about the dog

Jasper, to see whom was the chief pleasure that the little girl looked for in Edinburgh.

Clementina had scarcely had time to respond to Doctor Galiani's greeting and curtsey to his wife, when Isabella began clamouring to see the dog.

'He is not here now,' said the lady, and then as the child's lips puckered and tears were threatened, she was given a slice of the cake that they were to have at tea. It was a cake such as Isabella had never seen before. The body of it was yellow with egg, it was full of brilliant red cherries, some sliced in half, others just discernible through the crumb. Then there were green slivers of angelica and plenty of currants, the whole not dry and crumbling, but moist and sticky and as delicious to eat as it was beautiful to look at.

'I'll keep a piece for Jasper, when he comes home,' said Isabella bravely.

'It's a strange story about Jasper. I'll tell it you while we have our tea. We hated parting with him, but the dog chose to go, and my husband has no doubt he is well looked after.'

At last, when the tea had been made and was drawing in a silver teapot covered with a red flannel muff and Isabella was devouring a second slice of cake which the old Italian cut for her, and the two women had settled themselves comfortably with their skirts falling around them, curiosity was satisfied.

'It is but two weeks since. I heard Jasper whining and scratching at the street door to get out, then the voice of a street-seller outside in the road. He was calling out: "Brooms and brushes and mats made of rushes. Who'll buy? Who'll buy?" And then Jasper became like a mad thing. He rushed from the front door into this room and threw himself against the window as though he would have broken the glass, then back to the door, barking and whining and scratching. I went to the door and, as he was so desperate, I let him out.

'The street-seller had gone past our house, about two doors down the street. Well, Jasper flew at him, and, as the man turned, bounded up into his arms, licking his face, and the man gathered that big dog up in his arms as though he were a woman. I stood in the doorway astonished, watching, and heard the man say "Jasper! Jasper!" And then he spoke to the dog in words that I did not understand. I called my husband then from his study. The man saw us watching him and came up to us, taking his cap off, and Jasper was running from him to us and us to him. He asked us if we knew anything about his dog. So, although he looked a rough customer, my husband asked him to come in. He marched in at the front door and sat down where you are sitting now. I must say I was horrified, and if Emilio had not been there I should have locked the dog in and asked my neighbour to send for the police.

'He was as rough a man as you could find anywhere: a yellow spotted handkerchief round his throat, little gold rings in his ears and – you won't believe me – there were tears running down his face. He just sat there with the dog's head in his lap – and really I believe he was weeping with joy! It shows that people of that sort sometimes have, or can have, tender feelings that one only expects in persons of refinement.'

'What nonsense you talk, Flora! He was weeping because he loved his dog, and the dog loved him too. I was much moved by it,' said the Doctor.

'He was Joseph Hearn, and he is a bad lot – but Jasper loves him,' said Clementina.

Madame Galiani looked at her as much as to say: 'So you are so low class as to know a street-seller!' But the Doctor said: ' told him the whole story of how I had found Jasper in the stree and through the dog had found you. And the gypsy knew wh you were and was coming to Scotland to try and find you an the dog! He said that your father had befriended his people. S in spite of Flora I decided that Jasper, or Rolando, must go bac to his rightful owner. I say I decided, but it was the dog who di really. Well, there was a sequel: about four days later th gypsy came back with a shawl that he wanted to give my wif She refused to take it, because she thought that it must be stole property. But he swore that it had belonged to his grandmoth and that he would not lie to anyone who loved Jasper. So I too it. I did not want to hurt the man's feelings or show I distruste him.' Doctor Galiani went and fetched the shawl from his stud

'You can see that it is a very old one: a very beautiful yello and red silk – but it is darned in one corner. He said that it was Spanish.'

'He was telling the truth, I think, for I have been told that Joseph Hearn's grandmother was a famous Spanish dancer.'

The shawl was held out and then spread over the ottoman. As Clementina looked at it, she felt herself blushing. Since the small-pox she blushed unevenly. Her throat and ears coloured but there were patches in her cheeks that did not. She knew that she could not tell the whole story. But she blurted out: 'I've seen that shawl before. What a beauty it is!'

'Seen it before! So the man must have been lying, and it was stolen goods,' said Flora Galiani; she was pleased.

'Oh, no. It belonged to Joseph's mother, who was Spanish, or half Spanish. I have seen her dancing in it.'

At these words Flora looked incredulous. Then she saw that Clementina was speaking the truth and had sunk still lower in her eyes. It was one thing to be a simple but uncouth fisher-lassie, but quite another to dance with gypsies.

The sight of the shawl had taken Clementina to her earliest memories. For, when she was three or four, Joseph Hearn's mother had been her father's mistress and had lived longer than most of them at the croft. It was talk among the gypsies after-wards that Joseph Hearn was probably Clementina's half-brother. That part could never be told, neither to Doctor and Madame Galiani, nor to Peter. All that part of her life had been over for a long while, yet she gazed longingly at the shawl, which was a proof that she could touch, of her father, whom she had loved, and of the lovely young woman arching her body back in the dance and clicking her castanets furiously. She had always been kind, and Clementina had loved her.

Doctor Galiani saw the expression on Clementina's face.

'You must have it. Perhaps your little daughter Isabella will wear it one day. Flora never will. And you did more for Rolando than we did.'

Clementina refused at first, though she longed for it. Then, when Doctor Galiani pressed her, she accepted it, and said: 'You will be shocked. But I loved those gypsy people when I was a child and had no other playmates. They were kinder to me than the fisher-folk have ever been, with one exception.'

The Doctor smiled. Of course Clementina was thinking of her husband. He was wrong. Willie Windram was the exception.

Peter was soon successful in getting a job in the dockyard at Leith where a vessel had been ordered for the wine trade. The head of the firm was an Edinburgh man, and he placed the order for the ship at Leith docks and not on the Clyde. It was on the construction of this merchantman that Peter was employed. He had bought himself a sailing dinghy and sailed from Dysart to Leith in the mornings – in winter starting off long before first light. His duties in the drawing office and in supervision were not very exacting, and he made friends with the master ship-wright and became his pupil. Fortunately the older man was as willing to teach as Peter was eager to learn.

He went also to Edinburgh University to learn what he could of mechanics. There was at that time no faculty of engineering, but men in the Physics laboratory were studying the expansion of gases and the principles of the steam engine. Thanks to Dr Galiani's introduction, he was able to make a friend of Robert Stevenson, the engineer, and the architect Rennie. He was eager, in an engineering works, to be shown a lathe and to watch the processes of casting iron and of tempering steel. Rennie liked Peter's company and explained the principles underlying the use of the arch and of trusses in architecture. He lent him the few books which he thought were useful.

These studies filled all Peter's waking thoughts, and in the evenings he began teaching Clementina the principles of naval architecture, the elements of mechanics and the construction of the steam engine, just as a dozen years before he had taught her the principles of navigation and the elements of astronomy. Most wives would have been bored, annoyed, or too slow-witted to understand what their husbands were telling them. But Clementina was not only an intelligent pupil but eager to master each subject. Sometimes, drawing out a diagram of the parallelogram of the forces acting on a roof, they would find to their astonishment that it was near midnight, and they would go to their bedroom smiling happily at each other.

Clementina well understood Peter's desire to get a job in ship-building: if possible the construction of a steam vessel.

On his visit to Glasgow he had met Symington, the man who had built a steam vessel for Lord Dundas to replace horses towing the barges on the Forth–Clyde canal. He had come back both excited and depressed. It was clear that the steam engine would and could be used for propelling ships. But the problems were great. To navigate a paddlewheel steamer in a really rough sea would be hazardous. When she rolled one set of paddles would dig deep, labour and turn her head, while the other set would barely touch the water. In practice it might be necessary to shut off the engine and depend on sail. And a paddlewheel steamer with the engine cut off would be cumbersome to steer. But if one wheel could be slowed – or even reversed – and the other accelerated, she would be very much more manoeuvrable than any existing ship. You could spin her round like a top!

The problem of gears was occupying the minds of many. It was how to adapt the variable speeds of the cogwheels of a clock and to engage and disengage them while in motion. For until the engine, keeping a constant speed, could turn the paddles faster or slower, it seemed to Peter that the strain at starting would limit the top speed obtainable.

One day Peter came back with sad news: he had been to the Galianis' house to return a book which the Doctor had lent him and the door had been opened by Flora in widow's weeds. The Doctor had been recalled to Italy on a business matter and the ship he was on had been wrecked and he drowned. Flora had been more forthcoming than usual and had invited him in. He was afraid that she might be left in distressed circumstances. But much depended on property the Doctor might have in Italy.

Clementina wrote a note of condolence but received no reply.

A year or two after they had come to Dysart, Clementina inquired about her old friend Grace and learned that her husband, Jacob Criggie, who had made his wife turn Clementina away when she was at the start of her walk to Portsmouth, was dead. Now that Grace was a widow she thought she would like to go and see her.

Thus, when Peter visited Glasgow again for a week, she set off to pay Grace a visit at Burntisland. It amused her to appear smartly dressed, driving her own pony and trap, with Isabella in her best clothes beside her. Isabella held the pony, while Clementina knocked. Grace came to the door and stared for a full half-minute.

'Why, it's Clemmie,' she cried, rushed forward and then checked herself.

'Goodness, you are smart, Clemmie. But you've lost your beauty – so have we all. Can you ever forgive me for turning you away from my door?'

'It wasn't you, Grace. It was your good man. He thought he was doing right, and now I hear he is gone to where all our sins are forgiven.'

The two women embraced, and when the pony had been unharnessed and put into an outhouse, and 'the little lady' Isabella kissed and admired, they went in and were regaled with buttered bannocks and blackberry jam and cups of tea, and Grace was invited to visit Dysart. Soon Clementina asked about Grace's neighbour Mistress Reekie and her two great sons, Alastair and Angus, one in red and one in blue. Well, Mistress Reekie had died three years before and the greatest scandal that Burntisland had ever known had followed a year after.

'Alastair married a girl from Pittenweem – a real baggage of a fishwife. Within a month it was known that she was bedding with both of them. The Minister called to see her, and the girl did not deny the story: she just said she had married the wrong man. Alastair was not much good in bed, but Angus was fine. So the Minister preached a sermon against them, and they sold the cottage and packed up and the three of them sailed off bound for no one knows where. But they are thought to have gone north, perhaps to Orkney or one of the Islands.'

As Grace told this shocking story, her eyes sparkled with delight. 'Wasn't it terrible of her to say that Alastair was no good at it, but that Angus was fine?' And she burst out laughing.

'What does astonish me is that Alastair went with them,' said Clementina.

'You could not expect him to stay on alone with everyone repeating that story. Besides, they had always shared in everything and could not live without each other. They needed two men to sail their boat, and Rosie needed two men, even if one of them was "left-handed at it", as she said to me. I think it's all for the best.'

Now that she was a widow Grace was her old self again.

'If I were to live my life over again, I wouldn't have been so jealous about Alan, but should have let you and Elspeth each have your turn.'

Clementina hoped that when Grace paid her visit she would not scandalise Peter. By the time of the visit, Clementina knew that she was pregnant. She asked Grace if she would come over and stay when it was time for her to have the baby at the end of the year, and this was arranged. Grace had no children of her own and was free to come and go as she liked : her neighbours would look after her fowls and her cat.

When the time came, Peter, who had been employed in building the vessel for the wine trade, had been invited to sail in her on her maiden voyage. The ship had been completed and launched in the summer. Then she had been fitted out. After the sailing trials changes had had to be made in the rig, and then, though late in the year, Peter had been invited to go as temporary Master and Navigator to deliver her to the purchasers at Xerez. He would be paid handsomely, and he had a pride in the ship. For these reasons he accepted the invitation, although it meant leaving Clementina alone in the last months of her pregnancy. He would return through Spain and France overland and believed he would be in time to be with her when their child was born.

So Grace Criggie was invited to come earlier and stay longer until Clementina was quite recovered from having her baby. Grace was all the more pleased to come, as she had friends living in Dysart. Jacob Criggie's sister had married a grocer named Huntley, and though he was a man more interested in the flesh-pots of this world than in food for the spirit, he had remained a friend of his brother-in-law. Visiting Clementina would be all the more agreeable because she would be seeing the Huntleys.

Clementina had never felt better in her life. Christmas came, and there was still no sign of the return of Peter, and the women both hoped that the newly built vessel would escape the violent gales that had been raging for a month. On Christmas Day there was a big fall of snow, and Grace and Clementina took turns at shovelling a pathway to the road and another round the back of the house to the pony's stable.

They went together to chapel and nearly froze to the seats of the pew. Then on Boxing Day they were invited to a supper party at the Huntleys'. It was a large and noisy gathering, and when the meal was over, Clementina, who began to feel unwell, went alone into a little room used as a counting house behind the shop. In spite of the rowdy party with drunken voices bellowing bawdy songs, she was nearly asleep when old Mrs Huntley came in to say: 'I think Grace had better be taken home: she has come over queer.'

Clementina roused herself and found Grace with a pale face and her clothes in disorder, lying in the arms of a young fisherman from Pittenweem, whose girl, Susan Huntley, was shouting insults at them. Grace was hopelessly drunk.

'Andy and Bob Ritchie are still fairly sober; I'll get them to help with her to your place.'

So they went out into the snow just before midnight with the two men slipping and sliding, and pulling and pushing, and dragging Grace by the arms.

'Don't wake the child. You can leave Grace down here in the living-room,' said Clementina. The men dumped her on the settle by the fire, and Clementina pushed them out and shut the door quickly with no word of thanks, for it was perishingly cold with it open. Clementina covered Grace with a rug, put a bucket beside her and made up a big fire. Suddenly the pains came on. She thought for a moment of going out to get help. But there was no one at the Huntleys' in a condition to give help – and, except for them, all Dysart was asleep. Then if she slipped and fell in the snow she might never get up again.

She struggled up to her bedroom where there was a fire laid in the little grate and lit it. Luckily she had a large supply of candles. She lit several and lay down, delaying undressing until the room warmed up. There was a wave of pain. She stuffed a sheet into her mouth and bit it through. It was all she could do not to scream or groan. But at all costs she must not wake

Isabella. When the pain moderated, she crept downstairs, filled her largest kettle and hung it on a pothook over the fire. Grace had been sick and was snoring.

As Clementina went up the stairs the pains came back, and she clung for a long time to the rope which served as a banister. Then the waters broke. She got back into her bedroom, shut the door and took off her clothes, dried herself and lay down on the bed. The pains came back and went on in waves of agony, tearing her apart for hour after hour while the sweat poured out of her body. Suddenly – she had no idea of the time it had taken – she felt the child's head between her thighs. Then the baby slid out into the bottom of the bed. It was at that moment that she needed her greatest strength. She was half fainting, sinking back. But that would never do. She forced herself to roll towards the child and, still lying on her back, picked it up. Seeing that it was alive gave her a quite new courage and new strength. Then she saw that it was a boy. But the cord held him, and she bit it through, as she had no scissors. She would tie it in a moment. She picked up the bright pink creature, streaked with blood and creamy white stuff, wiped his nose several times and finally carried him down into the living-room. She was so weak that it seemed she was moving about in a dream. But there was no more sharp pain : only an ache like bad bruising. She put the baby on the table, fetched the washing tub from the scullery and mixed a bucketful of cold water with the boiling water in the kettle. Then she washed him carefully. He began to cry, mewing like a kitten. She got thread and tied the cord again, dried him and wrapped him in the plaid Old Lamond had given her after her marriage. The afterbirth came away when she was going to carry him up the stairs and she disposed of it at once, throwing it on the fire. That was a mistake. At last she was able to carry the baby up to her room, strip the bloody sheets off the bed and throw them in a corner, then get in among the blankets and put him to her breast. He began to suck and went on for some time after she had fallen asleep.

Grace Criggie woke up with a cracking headache, a foul taste in her mouth, things whirling in front of her eyes, only to disappear leaving black spots which sank slowly across the retinas and then jumped back to the place from which they started. She lay for a little gazing at the ceiling, but a disgusting smell penetrated, and she turned on her side and looked around. The curtains had not been drawn completely and the room was lit by a ray of sunlight. Beside the settle on which she lay uncomfortably, was a bucket standing in a patch of drying vomit. And beyond there were bright stains: yes, it was blood. There were bloodstains round the hearth: something bloody had been charred in the fire, and part of the smell was explained.

Suddenly Grace realised that while she had been lying unconscious a murder had been committed in that room. She herself was in danger! She sat up, found a shoe that had fallen off, and picking her way carefully reached the door. It was locked from the inside, with the key in the lock. She unlocked it, slipped outside with the key in her hand and had the courage to wait long enough to lock the door. She felt very clever: the murderer must be within. Then she fled down the pathway between the banks of shovelled snow. Three minutes later she was knocking on the Minister's door.

He came to the threshold in his stockinged feet, wiping away a bit of parritch that had stuck to his lips, and blinked at her.

'There's been a murder at Master Lamond's house. There is blood splashed all over the floor and on the hearthstones. Master Lamond is away, you know, and Mistress Lamond and I went to a bit of a sing-song at Master Huntley's. I slept downstairs so as not to wake the lassie. Someone must have followed us in and murdered Clemmie. It might be one of Old Mother Carey's women – to get the unborn bairn for their devilment....'

The Minister looked at her incredulously.

'Clementina might herself have murdered the child she was carrying. I never thought of that!' said Grace. 'At all costs she must prove herself innocent of being an accomplice.'

'Most likely to have been a miscarriage. But I must look into it anyway,' said the Reverend Brotherston. Grace seemed to him to have taken leave of her senses.

Half an hour later four of the biggest of the Dysart fishermen had collected outside the Lamond house. One carried a fowling-piece, two carried cudgels and the fourth a few yards of fish-netting and a rope.

The Minister unlocked the door and the five men crept into the living-room. There was certainly blood. And then a bucket.

'Don't let that woman run off,' said Mr Brotherston pointing to Grace. Then he motioned towards the stairs and he and two of his posse tiptoed up to the landing. At the bedroom door the Minister proclaimed: 'Resistance is useless. We are armed,' and flung it open. Clementina was lying propped up in the bed with Isabella beside her and the head of the baby partly hiding her breast.

She stared at the Reverend Brotherston in astonishment and Isabella piped up: 'The kings and the wise men of the East have come to worship the babe.'

Colin Maclennan looked over the Minister's shoulder and laughed.

'That young lassie is about right. She has more sense than the rest of us.'

'When Mrs Criggie woke up she saw some bloodstains and came running to me with a story that either you had been murdered, or had murdered the bairn you were carrying. She is no great friend of yours, I'm thinking.'

'We'll send some of the women to clean the place up for you,' said Colin.

An hour later a boat put off with Grace and her belongings bound for Burntisland.

Three of the Minister's posse were married men. Their wives scrubbed out the living-room and lit the fire, soaked the blood out of the sheets in cold water and later washed and ironed them. Then they put Clementina into clean ones and gave Isabella her breakfast.

'I've got here a bit late in the day,' said the midwife who lived in Linktown. But she washed Clementina, bandaged her and would not let her get out of bed for three days. Clementina let the midwife have her way, for she had never been more tired and was content to lie in clean sheets with David close at hand in the cradle. She had decided to have her youngest called after her father.

CHAPTER ELEVEN

WHEN Peter returned he was very angry: angry with himself for having left Clementina at such a time in such company and in such a place. During the voyage he had been offered a more permanent job in the Leith shipyard, in the drawing office, and he at once decided to take lodgings for his family in Edinburgh, where he could be close to his wife and not cut off in stormy weather, when she might be most in need of him.

So the house in Dysart was put up for sale. Kirstie and the pony were sold too, for there would be no paddock or stable in the great city, and no garden. Clementina had to adapt herself to a new life. She missed the country and her garden, and time hung heavy on her hands, even though she had the new baby and Isabella to look after and the cooking, shopping and housework to do. What was worse was that the happy evenings of study with Peter were over. He was no longer concerned with theory, but with practice. Clementina could master the principle of the pulley, or of cogwheels, but had no notion of the need to oil the tool of a lathe, or of casting iron in moulds, or tempering and hardening steel. Such things were for men only, and could be learnt only by trial and error. Peter would come home tired by his work. Sometimes he brought back an engineer, and then expected Clementina to provide a good supper, to be smartly dressed, and to keep out of the way and prevent the children from interrupting the men's talk.

One day after she had received his two guests with her sleeves rolled up, not at all embarrassed, he said to her, after their departure: 'I think you should consult Mistress Galiani about your clothes: there has to be a distinction between the wife of the skipper of a North Isle fishing vole and the wife of the Master of a man-o'-war.' He would have spoken of her accent and told her that many of her expressions would be unintelligible to

Englishmen and even to educated Scots. But his lips could not frame the words – which were in any case unnecessary as Clementina was aware of the fact and was doing her best to pick up an Edinbro' accent and a genteel vocabulary.

Instead of risking wounding his wife's pride, he began to talk about his own future. He had been told of plans for building a steam vessel on the Thames. The engines were already being designed and would be of eighty horse-power: the most powerful yet made. There would be an opportunity for him to get to work in building her and perhaps it might lead to a command afterwards. But he had decided first to return to the navy for a short period of service as Master, so that he could offer his services in London as an officer who had only just left the navy, a man with most recent experience and not a man who had not been to sea for several years.

Young Peter was leaving school, and was apprenticed to a wine-merchant.

Shortly before he expected to be ordered to his ship, Peter came back to their lodgings, which were down by Leith docks, to say that he had met Mistress Galiani by accident, and that she had asked if he knew of anyone who would take the basement of her house – she was compelled to take in lodgers. He had told her that he was going to sea again and leaving Clementina and the two younger children for a time in Edinburgh, and the result of their talk was that Mistress Galiani would be pleased to have them as lodgers. He had agreed on the rent.

'I don't know how Flora and I will get on. But it seems to be a settled thing,' said Clementina.

'It is all furnished, and so we shall not have to take our furniture out of store. I don't think you need see more of Flora than you want,' said Peter, who was proud of having found a better lodging in a more respectable street than that which they occupied. Secretly he thought that the company of Mistress Galiani could not fail to improve his wife's knowledge of the ways of the world.

Such matters were trifles at the back of his mind. He was at the turning point of his career. If he could get the job of building, or supervising the building, of a ship on the Thames, a steam vessel, he would be a valuable man in the new world of marine engineering. And armed with a letter from the head of the Leith shipyard, he stood a good chance of the employment he wanted. Although he did not mention the subject of dress again Clementina realised that he expected her to appear in London, when the time came, dressed suitably as the wife of a sea-captain.

Till she went to live in Edinburgh, Clementina had worn nothing to support her breasts. Now, under Flora Galiani's guidance, she bought stays of whalebone, which were laced up behind and hooked in front. These stays encased her from her hips to her nipples, and in front was a stomacher, a hard triangular shield designed to press her belly upwards into the cage of her ribs. It had a point which pressed into her thighs when she sat down. Stays were torture to a body which had grown up in freedom. The bones stuck into her and bruised her bosom, which lay almost entirely exposed, upon the ledge they formed.

At first Clementina wore them obediently, as instructed, but they became so hateful that when Flora went out for the day, or when she knew that she was occupied, Clementina would pull up her dress, unhook the stays and hide them until Flora came in. Then she would put them on hastily. Once, when she was caught in the act, she made the excuse that she was about to wash her hair and did not want her dress to get wet.

Next to the discomfort of the stays, Clementina suffered from the embarrassment of feeling that she was naked. From infancy she had worn thick knitted woollen vests up to her neck, a multitude of petticoats under her skirt, and then a thick spencer and big paisley or Shetland shawl; home-knitted stockings to above the knee, and hobnailed boots.

All such protections against the cold and preservers of female modesty were now forbidden. She was to wear a thin cotton shift, which left her arms, shoulders and bosom bare. Then the hated corset, with its stomacher constricting her stomach and coming down in a point almost to the crotch. Above that a cotton dress left her shoulders bare while exposing her bosom in a frilly bag, and then flowed down, ignoring her waist, to below her ankles. She tripped over it and tore it if she made an unguarded movement. Then white cotton stockings and absurd slippers with a single strap over the instep: slippers which would fill with water at the first deep puddle in the Edinburgh streets. Otherwise pattens were necessary.

And when she went out, beside the basket on her arm, Flora expected her to carry a ridiculous little umbrella. On cold days she might wear gloves to above the elbows, carry a muff and wear a pelisse and, on her head, an absurd bonnet, looking like a gentleman's gigantic beaver hat. If it had not been firmly fastened under her chin with broad silk ribbons, it would have blown away. Her underwear, her handkerchiefs, her stockings, all had to be genteel, since she was no longer allowed to wash them herself. Gone were the days at Dysart when she lighted the fire under the copper, pushed the clothes and dirty linen around with a copper stick, fished them out of the scalding water, got the last stains of dirt out with a soapy scrubbing-brush and rinsed them again and again in cold running water. At East Haven the clothes had been spread on bushes to dry, at Dysart there had been a clothes-line, clothes-pegs and a clothes-prop. But now all went to the laundry. A list had to be made out and checked when the clothes came back, for the laundresses were thieves. Then the bills were exorbitant, and Clementina would have changed Isabella's petticoats more often had she been allowed to wash them herself. But in Mistress Galiani's house there was no place to hang them out to dry.

All this irked her, and she felt no spark of gratitude, particularly as she perceived how much Flora enjoyed laying out more of Peter's money than he could afford. Then to her horror, Flora spoke of the fashions changing. It was rumoured that flounces were coming in. So the money had not been spent in setting her up with new clothes which would last until they were worn out – and that was likely to be all too soon – but she was expected to embark on the perpetual extravagance of spending money on garments that she did not like wearing, or being seen in.

When Flora Galiani had visitors she would invite Clementina to come up and meet them, and when she excused herself, would say: 'Then we'll descend on you in your kitchen.'

Flora's wish to show Clementina off to her friends led to their first and final quarrel.

Clementina had taken off her hated corset and was rolling out some oatcake, when she heard on the landing of the staircase the loud lowland accents of Mistress Strabolgi, wife of Strabolgi of that ilk, saying: 'Well, you may exhibit the heroine of the march to Portsmouth, but I misgive that she was given more than one lift by waggoners on the way.' Then Flora rejoined:

'I have had that suspicion myself. But Clemmie has such an estimable desire for self-improvement, that I feel it my duty to encourage it.'

'How did you come to have her as a lodger? For you seem to have taken her under your wing.'

'Have I never told you the story of how my dearest Emilio was out for a walk when the dog Rolando rushed up to a woman – this woman – who was wandering in the street and recognised her? He thought the dog belonged to her, though we found out later that she was looking after it for one of her gypsy friends who was in prison. So thinking the dog belonged to her, dear Emilio brought the woman home. Of course, we wanted to buy the dog,' Flora paused dramatically.

'She was – my dear – filthy and verminous – I have never seen one of my sex in such a condition. Well, you know that Emilio was a saint – a sort of St Francis – and he insisted on my looking after her. Then it turned out that she had a husband who was in the navy. He had fought and been wounded on Lord Nelson's flagship, the *Victory*, when the hero was killed. Afterwards promoted to be an officer! Yes, what I am telling you is true.

'This woman, Clementina, is years older, and she had caught him when he was only a boy. A tragic, mistaken marriage. And it is only to oblige her husband that I have let her the basement. He as good as asked me to try and make her more presentable. In appearance there is nothing to be done, but I hope to teach her to wear decent clothes – to look respectable and improve her manners.'

'Well, Flora, I never knew you were such a good Christian,' came Mrs Strabolgi's screeching voice.

'Well, it was for the poor young man's sake. Clementina was much beneath him. His father owned several boats. While as a girl she actually consorted with gypsies. Her father was a smuggler who escaped the gallows and was transported. But in spite of this she seems to be honest and is trying hard to become a suitable wife for her husband – quite a remarkable young man. My dear husband actually introduced him to the Philosophical Society. I shall do all I can to make Clemmie worthy of him.'

Clementina had been frozen by this speech. A need at all costs to escape came upon her. She flung a shawl round her shoulders, and ran out into the street by the basement door, furious with anger. She had secretly known that the woman she had trusted and to whom she had submitted, had never been her friend – and yet was ashamed of the fact having come into the open by eavesdropping. Shivering with cold and flaming with fury, she walked about the streets of Edinburgh. It was time to fetch the children from the little dame school and she must make them their supper and put them to bed. Then she would tell Flora that she would no longer stay as a lodger in her house. She must send a letter to Peter to tell him that she was following him to London, and that he must find lodgings for her and the children, and then without waiting for an answer, take ship with the children from Leith to Blackwall.

Nobody can say how Clementina would have behaved, or what excuses she might not have made for leaving Edinburgh, if she had been given time. But as she went back into her kitchen with the two children, Flora Galiani came tripping down the stairs, with the questions: 'Oh Clemmie, wherever have you been? Mistress Strabolgi was here and had heard so much of you. She was so disappointed not to see you.'

'I overheard every word that you were saying to her about me and Peter, and I ran out into the street so as not to meet her. I am not to be patronised and hear my father looked down on. The Careys and the Lindsays are as good stock as you and your Edinbro' Straboogies.'

'Are you crazy, my good woman?'

'I will not stay here for you to exhibit. When I am gone you

can buy yourself a monkey to amuse your friends. I am not to
be made a monkey of!'

'You do not show much gratitude!'

'Am I to be grateful because I lacked the coach fare to Portsmouth and that my word is suspect?'

'We took you in....'

'You lie there. It was your husband, and he was a saint, who
helped me and saved my life. And I love and honour him.'

'And you have the impudence to wear that brooch that you
filched from him!'

'You know well that he could not have borne to see it on your
bosom because it reminded him of the woman that he really
loved. That is why he gave it to me. Call a constable if you
doubt my right to it.'

At these words Flora turned scarlet with rage and exclaimed:
'It is an ill-bred bitch that bites the hand that fed it.'

Clementina pointed to the staircase, and, seeing the look on her
face, Flora Galiani fled up it to her own part of the house.
Then she locked the door on the landing above the basement
stairs and after that put the chain on the front door.

Next day, without being able to communicate with Peter,
Clementina took a passage for herself and the children from
Leith to Blackwall. She went without saying good-bye to Flora
Galiani but left an envelope enclosing a month's rent in lieu of
notice.

Once they were clear of the Bass Rock the fog cleared and the
sun shone, and Clementina felt joyously happy. She strode the
deck bare-headed, wrapped in her old Scottish fisherwoman's
cloak; the gunwale dipped, the sails were full and hard as boards,
the cordage creaked, she staggered up to the windward side and
held on to the standing rigging. The Captain on the quarter-deck
called down to her merrily: 'Come up here, madam. You'll keep
drier now we have got into the open sea.' And already spray had
stung her face and wet her hair.

She climbed up the ladder to the quarter-deck and soon was
telling the Captain that her husband was a Master in the Navy
and that she was taking her children to meet him in London

where he was working in the office of a marine architect building a steam vessel.

'Is his name Peter Lamond?' asked the Captain. He had met Peter often, but he was very doubtful about steam vessels. 'I fear he's wasting his time – though maybe he's well paid for it; but the gentlemen who are putting up the money for building any steam vessel are losing it. It stands to reason that, in a sea, paddle-wheels will be worse than useless – and then there's the perpetual danger of fire from the furnace and of the boiler bursting. I would not risk my life on board a steam-vessel for double the money I earn now.'

Clementina spoke of the steam packets plying on the Firth of Clyde. 'Aye, a steam packet may do well on a river, or a canal, or on sheltered water, though even then there's the terrible danger of fire. But they will crack up or founder in a seaway.'

His words made Clementina angry. Her Peter would not give up his time to a chimerical idea.

'I'll be glad to know what you think about steam boats in five years' time, Captain Alexander,' she said defiantly, and turned away.

It was night by the time the ship had been towed to her berth on the river, and the Captain told her to stay on board and give the children a good breakfast, before she left next morning. She walked the deck excitedly, looking at the countless lights winding up the river and listening to the quiet voices of the men stacking the windlass bars and coiling cable ends.

It had not been her first long sea voyage, but it was her first landfall, and much had happened since she had come to herself on the quarantine hulk at Leith.

Next morning, with David in her arms and Isabella trotting beside her, she set out to find Peter. The Captain had pointed out the shipyard where he was working, but before she reached it she felt panic. The streets were no dirtier than in Edinburgh, the rain that fell no colder. The poor wretches in the street were much the same, but it was a strange city, and the people spoke strangely. A sudden terror came that Peter might not be working there. He might have gone back to the navy and be sailing to the other end of the earth. What should she do if he were not there?

And, even if he was, how would he greet her unexpected arrival? Until then, she had been carried along by her resentment against the woman she had believed a friend, but who had insulted her. But Peter might judge her behaviour differently. It was in this mood that she came to the gateway and inquired of a workman for her husband. The man looked strangely at her and grinned, and at that a spark of her spirit returned and she told him: 'Run to Captain Lamond with that message and don't keep his wife and bairns waiting in the rain unless you want to lose your job.'

A few minutes later Peter came out, still in his shirt-sleeves. Seeing him, Clementina bowed her head and said:

'You must forgive my coming, Peter. I could not stay a moment longer in the house with that woman.... She told her friends that my father ought rightly to have been hanged and called me a bitch to my face.'

Peter did not take her in his arms, or greet the children, as he might have done. He listened carefully, and the frown on his forehead showed neither sympathy nor even annoyance. When he had taken in the facts and their implications, he led his wife and children out of the rain into his office, kissed the children and gave Isabella a piece of string to make cats' cradles and David a sheet of paper and a coloured chalk. Then he called in a young apprentice and told him to lead them to his lodgings. He would come to them just as soon as his work permitted.

As Clementina followed the boy through the wet streets she wondered what she would find. Peter had said nothing. In his lodgings there would be a landlady, perhaps with an eye for her handsome lodger and resentful of the arrival of an older woman with children, and ready to pick a quarrel and make her life difficult. Peter's coldness was perhaps because of her.

But to her surprise the rooms, on one floor of a new house, were almost empty. There was a room with a large table covered with engineering drawings and a chair, with a coal fire laid, but not lighted, in the grate; a bedroom with one bed, an empty room beyond with no curtains in the grimy windows, and a kitchen with only a kettle, teapot and a saucepan half full of cold porridge. It was clear that Peter was living by himself and doing his own housework.

Clementina had hardly had time to take this in and begin a list of the hundred necessities they would need, beginning with a bed for the children even after her trunks and furniture had been brought ashore from the *Tropic Lily*, when Peter arrived and, to her astonishment, flung his arms round her and kissed her eagerly. She saw then that to kiss his wife was something he would not do in front of others. He was happy to see her. He snatched up Isabella in an embrace, he threw young David up, swinging him almost to the ceiling. She had done right to come: he had been longing to have them with him, and had only been waiting for the *Lord Melville* to be fitted out and ready for service, to write and tell her to join him. He was to be the ship's Captain. He had already been to *Tropic Lily* and arranged with the supercargo for Clementina's trunk and the furniture to be brought round without delay, and for a hot meal to be brought in from a nearby eating-house, so that the exhausted children should not be dragged out again into the streets, or left alone.

There was much to do. The single bed had had to be moved into the empty room for Isabella; as soon as the furniture arrived, the cot for David made ready; then the double bed she had brought put together in the room where Peter and she would sleep. Before that was finished the cookshop man had arrived with roast pork and cabbage and turnips, with a bottle of French wine, and, when the children were put to bed, quilts had to be tacked up over the window since there were no curtain rods. She was tired and dishevelled and dirty when she and Peter came to bed. But the touch of his naked flesh set her weeping almost hysterically, and she clung to him with passion. The strain she had borne so long was over. She would play her part, but with Peter there she would be safe and happy.

Yet, in spite of all, Clementina found in the next few weeks that happiness eluded her. It was not so much London with its dirt and hardness and cruelty, but the Londoners themselves that she came to hate. It was their yellow faces, their rotten teeth and bad breath, and the almost incomprehensible jargon in which they talked, and the foxy looks on the faces of the stallkeepers, when she revealed her Scottish origin with her first words. But at least in Blackwall there were no fine ladies to sneer and patronise her.

Before she had got used to London, all was changed, for the life of a sailor's wife is unsettled. She had scarcely found a school where Isabella could spend a few hours every morning, when the *Lord Melville* had completed her trials and was fit for service.

London to Calais direct with passengers and carriages, the superb and commodious steam packet the LORD MELVILLE, *Peter Lamond, R.N., Commander, of 220 tons burthen and eighty horses power, will commence running from her berth off the Tower to Calais every Wednesday and Saturday morning at half-past six precisely, returning from Calais on Mondays and Thursdays. Tickets, etc., etc.*

Clementina read the notice that Peter handed her in the *Morning Chronicle* with excitement and pride. Peter had reserved a cabin for her and the children on the *Lord Melville*'s maiden voyage.

The risen sun shone full in their faces as she puffed down the river: the decks were crowded, for every ticket had been sold, and the directors of the General Steam Navigation Company were on board, with their ladies. Clementina found herself being introduced to all of them. Although the passage was smooth, not all of them assembled at the Captain's table for luncheon. Clementina sat on the right hand of Mr Joliffe, the chairman of the company, Mrs Joliffe beside Peter, and Clementina heard herself listening to Mr Joliffe's views on the French: 'You would expect them to be broken-spirited now they have been beat, but not a bit of it. They have a strangely good opinion of themselves, but are always polite and obliging.'

Directly luncheon was over she went on deck and stationed herself behind the paddle-wheel on the starboard side of the boat, from where she could look back at England. The broken water tumbled out like a mill-race, and a gull stayed just above the stern without moving its wings. Although a jib and mainsail were presently set, the *Lord Melville* was not sailing. A cloud of black smoke was blown to leeward from her funnel, and her progress was marked by noise and fuss quite unlike a sailing ship, where there is no sound but that of creaking cordage, the slapping of the waves and the whistling of the wind. With the motion of a large water-beetle, the *Lord Melville* splashed her way onwards, and by the late afternoon the French coast was standing out, brilliantly lit in the declining sun.

From the moment that Clementina stepped ashore next morning, everything she saw delighted her. There were the familiar fishermen's boats drawn up, the nets drying, and a little crowd around the fishwife selling the catch that had only just been brought in. Compared with London it was a paradise, and when Clementina, next day, pointed out that as Peter had to spend from Saturday to Monday at Calais, they surely should spend the day of rest together, Peter, seeing what was coming, agreed.

'You would like to make your home in Calais, my dear?' he asked – and it was difficult for her to repress her joy, and to listen to the arguments in favour of their doing so.

'Young Peter's employers want him to perfect his knowledge of French before he is out of his apprenticeship; he can live with us. A knowledge of French may also be valuable for David, who will pick it up quickly, and it can do Isabella no harm. You and I will both prefer Calais to Wapping, as we were happier at Dysart than in Edinburgh, and my duties will be less, while in port here, than at Tower Bridge, where *Melville* will be coaling and I shall be at the beck and call of the agent and the owners.'

After the next channel crossing, Clementina and the children were left at a French inn, and she went house-hunting. When Peter came over they found one that was to let, close to the Place d'Armes. It was easy for Peter to go to the harbour, and for Clementina to go to the beach with the children and at midday, with the sun behind her, point out the cliffs of Dover. Every morning young Peter would go to the office of his firm, who had a branch where English visitors could taste their wines and give orders which, if they were large, would be shipped from Bordeaux.

Isabella took music and singing lessons, David was dispatched to a dame's school. In no time at all he had picked up enough French to play marbles and bowl hoops with his schoolfellows.

In the old garden of his school amid cat messes under the shrubs, he fell hopelessly in love, though he could not put a name to the feelings that Madeleine's corkscrew black curls and flushed dimpled cheeks aroused in him. Actually she was all dimples: in her fat little knees and elbows, wrists and ankles, cheeks and chin. She called him an English booby to her schoolfellows, but secretly was flattered by his slavish adulation. Then it occurred to her that she might do a work acceptable to God by converting him to the true faith. When David realised what she wanted, he acquiesced happily, and snuggling up beside her, he repeated 'Hail Mary, full of grace, your womb was full of Jesus Christ,' after her and longed to wind his fingers among the black curls framing her dark red cheeks. After this initiation, he was taken to the church with a crowd of other children and patted on the head by a pale and ill-nourished young man in a black cassock. To win Madeleine's company, David was ready to tell the beads of a rosary and to say a dozen Hail Marys.

Clementina soon discovered what was happening, but she was only amused. It was as good a way to learn French as another. She herself did her best to get a smattering of the language. Young Peter and the friends he brought into their house were her tutors – and she talked often to the fishwives on the quay and in the market. She had tried to ask for a skate to be skinned, and as the old woman hesitated, Clementina took the knife out of her hand and skinned it herself. The old fishwife was amazed and became her special friend and, after that, would keep special delicacies for her such as a salmon grilse that had blundered into the seine nets: and she told her how to cook the cuttlefish and squids that in Scotland they would have thrown away.

Young Peter deplored this friendship and told his mother that she was acquiring a Norman peasant's accent. At this his mother turned on him and poured out a few sentences that might have been used by the fisher-lasses in Forfar, with words and inflexions that the boy had almost forgotten.

'That's the tongue you were born to, and if I can talk like that to an old French fishwife, I'll be doing fine.' And they laughed together.

Two years passed at Calais and Clementina was talking French, and young Peter had long since left to be an assistant buyer of claret at Bordeaux, when one morning Peter said: 'We shall soon be moving again. I've been given command of our new steam vessel *George IV*. I am to take her to Gib or Malaga this winter, and I have been promised later on to be the first to take a steam vessel into the Baltic, to Lübeck and St Petersburg. But we shall have to wait until the sea there is ice-free.'

'I'm not going,' exclaimed Isabella. She was twenty-two: a tall, dark, beautiful girl who, after several flirtations, had secretly engaged herself to an Irishman, a dozen years older than herself, who had served as an ensign in the Peninsular war and who had, according to her account, behaved with extraordinary bravery.

Isabella's parents did not question Phelim O'Hagan's courage, but they thought poorly of his prospects – he lived upon a miserly remittance and his winnings at cards, and Clementina had got tired of his stories and of refilling his glass when Isabella invited him to the midday meal. In the evenings he frequented the Casino and the tables of the wealthier English visitors.

'I'm not going,' repeated Isabella, and stared her father in the face. To her astonishment he did not flare up into a rage. 'You will have some time to think it over, my dear. And I can rely on you to listen to your mother, and to use what sense God may have given you. I would not force you, and you are of age. But give your actions thought and remember that I love you and shall give you shelter. But ...' Peter did not finish his sentence. He had been about to say that he forbade O'Hagan the door, but had checked himself, as he guessed that it would only harden Isabella's determination to throw in her lot with him.

Isabella rushed out of the house: an hour later she crept in and shut herself in her room. Next morning as Peter and his wife were making ready to go to the Presbyterian chapel – David had already scampered off to mass – the Irishman appeared. Clementina set off to chapel alone. Isabella was shut in her room and the two men had a short interview.

Five minutes later Mr O'Hagan left the house.

Captain Peter might have overtaken his wife or at most missed a few minutes of the service. However, he did not leave the house, fearing that O'Hagan might return and try and see Isabella. His fears were groundless, and when Clementina questioned him later, he only remarked: 'O'Hagan wished to know what fortune our daughter had, or what allowance I should make her after her marriage. When he told me that it was unreasonable for me to expect him to support her, I wished him good morning, and he took up his hat and left the house.'

Later that evening, when Isabella appeared, her father suggested that she might like to cross the channel with him and spend a day or two in London, and then accompany him on *George IV* to Lisbon, Cadiz, Gibraltar and Malaga. This offer she rather ungraciously accepted. But once at sea she became herself again, and for the first time since she was a small child felt warm love for the reserved father she had feared during her adolescence.

CHAPTER TWELVE

THREE months later Peter had bought a house at Travemünde close to Lübeck. Number 190, Travemünde was a tall house with a brick half-timbered front, but otherwise built of wood, with a steep slate roof. It was the largest house that Clementina was ever to live in, and she fell in love with it at once. Although numbered it was not in a street. It stood a little back from the road on the other side of which was the estuary of the Trave. Further up the river there were shoals, and the harbour at Lübeck would not take so large a vessel as the *George IV*, which was therefore moored immediately opposite the house and not a hundred yards from its front door.

The plan of the house was simple. On each side of the entrance hall was a large room: on the right the kitchen, with scullery and outhouses behind, on the left Peter's office. A fine birchwood staircase led to the dining-room, over the kitchen, with a lift to bring up the dishes, and a drawing, or reception room, over Peter's office. Above were bedrooms and then attics.

But it was the garden and orchard, well-kept and full of fruit trees, which delighted Clementina even more than the house. For Peter its greatest merit was that by looking out of his office window he could watch what was being done on board his ship. For him it was the front of the house, for her the back. When they arrived the last snowdrops were in flower and daffodil buds shooting up. Some of the raked seedbeds were already sown with all sorts of vegetables she could not guess at, for Hans the gardener, who had been the caretaker while the house stood empty, could not understand a word when she tried to question him.

Peter had brought out his family with all their possessions and furniture in the *George IV*, but there was not enough to fill the big rooms, and much would have to be bought later.

Isabella actually demanded a piano!

Clementina had scarcely time to decide how the house should be arranged when Peter was off again on a last cruise to Lisbon and Gibraltar, taking Isabella with him again.

The weeks which followed were difficult. She could not speak a word of German, and she had to buy many things for the house and engage a maid and direct her. She could only reach Lübeck on foot, and yet it was constantly necessary to go there.

In all these difficulties David became her standby and her interpreter: he had a natural gift for languages, and seeing the affinity of German and English for such simple things as milk and bread and sugar, tried experiments gaily when his mother was tongue-tied.

So the necessities were got, and simple living made possible. On larger matters – buying chairs for the drawing-room and a bed for David, who was sleeping in Isabella's and would have to sleep on the floor – Clementina thought she must wait for Peter. But when he arrived there was no time for anything. The ice was reported to have broken in the Gulf of Bothnia and directly the *George IV* had finished coaling, she and David went aboard to set off on the maiden trip of the steam vessel to St Petersburg.

The sea was calm, the sun shone, but a piercing north wind blew the smoke from the funnel back over the quarter-deck, and the only way to escape the smuts was to go forward. For until he had got clear of the islands, Captain Lamond kept the sails furled and avoided tacking. Only when there was a side or a following wind, did he make use of sail as well as steam.

'Sail is only an auxiliary, sir,' he replied to gentlemen who complained of steaming into the eye of the wind. 'We shall be using it when we get further north and turn into the Gulf of Finland. Meanwhile we must put up with the bad quality of the Brunsbüttel coal.'

In spite of the wind, the *George IV* made good progress. The cabin below was comfortable, but on the second night out from Riga Clementina was woken by a bump and by a sudden swerve with one paddle backing water. She jumped out of her bunk, put on Peter's overcoat, thrust her feet into slippers and ran on deck. The sun had not yet risen: the rigging and deck structures were covered in hoar frost; there was a low fog ahead. Looking over the side she could see ice – an ice floe broken up into many pieces and on the nearest lay the body of a man on his back with his arms spread out. A big black-backed gull was pecking at the corpse. Looking over the side, Clementina could see the empty sockets of the eyes, and that the lips and most of the face had been torn off. She shouted at the bird, which looked up at her, but did not fly away, even when she waved her arms at it.

'Peter,' she cried, clinging on to the taffrail because for a moment she thought she was going to faint, or to be sick with disgust. 'Peter, shoot that horrible bird!'

Peter had seen the bird tearing at the dead body and ran down to his cabin, but by the time he had fetched his gun from the rack and loaded it, the corpse and feasting bird had been left far behind, the table of ice toppling in the wake of the steamer.

The fog lifted, and she could see crowds of seagulls gathered round black objects on the broken ice-floe. When the *George IV* had nosed her way slowly near to them, Peter raised his gun and fired a shot, and the birds rose screaming from the frozen corpses – but leaving one of their number wounded, flapping an unbroken wing beside the almost fleshless head and neck of a cadaver. The birds had begun tearing at the clothing, but the high leather boots defeated them.

'What is this? Where are we?' she asked Peter.

'In the Gulf of Finland, coming into Reval. But we shall soon have to pull up and wait for the pilot,' he answered.

For twenty minutes, with the *George IV* moving at quarter-speed, they pushed their way through the broken ice scattered with frozen bodies, lying where they had been shot down while trying to escape from their pursuers over the frozen sea.

The cold was so bitter that Clementina soon went below, and when she had dressed herself in her warmest clothes, she heard the paddles go into reverse. The steamer stopped, and when she went on deck, the pilot had come aboard. Like most pilots all over the world, he could talk a little English – more than enough than just to give directions to the helmsman. Clementina went and stood beside him at the wheel and asked him about the dead bodies on the ice. He looked at her blankly, pretending not to understand, and she repeated: 'Why were there dead men on the ice?'

The pilot did not want to answer, but she looked at Peter, who repeated her question. The pilot shrugged his shoulders and said: 'His Imperial Highness, the Tsar, sent two regiments of grenadiers and they killed over five hundred. The bodies you saw were those of men who were caught on the shore and ran out over the ice to escape. If they had had skates they might have done so, but there was no time for that. The Russians pursued them in three sledges drawn by ponies and shot them. Better not to speak of it in Reval, for the Russian soldiers paid for it. Their sledges kept too close together and the ice broke close to the shore as they came back. The sea is deep there, and the Russians in their heavy boots and overcoats were drowned, and so were the horses. Their captain was drowned too. The beach was crowded with men and women from the town watching, but no one threw out a rope, or even held out an oar, to pull in any of the men drowning almost at their feet. There were many there who would have pushed back any man who got out of the water.'

He said no more. They were at the dock side. Cables were thrown. Two sentries took position by the companion ladder. They were men in thick high boots of felt, long brown overcoats and black astrakhan hats, carrying muskets with immensely long fixed bayonets with triangular blades. And, behind them, dock policemen were walking up and down in long black coats with big sabres hanging back to front from black leather swordbelts. And then customs officers. Peter was allowed ashore, as was the Mate, who superintended the loading of deck cargo. And then, unexpectedly, a whole platoon of soldiers with their officers in long grey overcoats with scarlet revers and polished black wrinkled high boots marched down and came aboard. Then the paddles started turning: the cables were thrown and caught and coiled, and Reval was left behind.

There were no more corpses, and *George IV* steamed steadily north with the crowd of soldiers on the foredeck singing and laughing and some of them even dancing to the sound of a balalaika. Watching them, Clementina's mood changed. The Russia they were going to could not only be a land of murdered men being torn to pieces by seafowl. That aspect would be best forgotten. Nevertheless the cadavers lying crumpled on the ice stayed in her mind, and as horrible was the thought of the horses and sleighs crashing through the ice close to the shore and the soldiers weighed down by their heavy boots and equipment drowning a few yards from land while a line of men and women stood watching, with no one holding out a helping hand, or throwing a rope to save the life of a fellow-creature.

That contravened the great rule of the sea. It was as abominable as the Cornish wreckers: typified by the villain who had cut off Sir Cloudesley Shovell's hand as he was clinging to a rock, in order to steal the old Admiral's diamond ring. She knew that during the heat of the battle of Trafalgar hundreds of British, French and Spanish seamen had been left to sink or swim, but that once the fight was won, every effort was made to save the drowning sailors, be they friend or foe.

So Clementina spoke politely to the Russian officers on the quarterdeck in her best French, and then went forward with two of them to watch the Russian soldiers, who jumped and squatted and spun in the air, as their companions sang such strange rousing melodies, and the two men strummed on the triangular balalaikas.

Meanwhile Isabella was gaily talking French, and one of the officers volunteered to teach her a Circassian dance, the *Lezghinka*. Two of his fellow-officers laughed at him and said that he did not know the steps, so a common soldier was called aft and asked to show them all how it was danced in the Caucasus. He was a serious little man who took the subject of the dance as important. First he showed them the steps taken by the man – three to the right, three to the left, strutting round his partner like a barndoor rooster; then the woman swaying and waving her handkerchief provocatively; the man stamping as she circled round him, drawing his dagger and at the end of the dance throwing it point first on to the deck, where it stuck quivering.

When he had shown them the dance, he made them do it together – but often stopping them with a sharp tap on the officer's sleeve and a hand held up to the two musicians. Isabella showed more aptitude than her partner and won applause.

It was ice-cold on deck, but the dance warmed her, and she was surprised when Clementina, with her head wrapped in a tartan shawl, stopped the dance and told her to go below or her nose might get frozen.

Exactly twenty-four hours after they left Reval, they came in sight of Kronstadt, the island fortress that guards the mouth of the River Neva and the approach to St Petersburg by sea. There was a magnificent harbour with a granite wall, a line of men-o'-war of all sizes anchored in it, and a granite fortress with batteries of bronze cannon behind.

The *George IV* anchored in Kronstadt harbour, since the sandbanks in the river bed were liable to shift during the spring floods, and she was of too deep a draught to navigate the shallows. The soldiers went ashore, but not before one or two of the officers had begged Isabella to allow them to entertain her in the capital.

Since the steamer was not due to sail back to Lübeck for a week, Peter took his wife and daughter to St Petersburg to see the sights. He had been given an introduction to a fellow-Scotsman, Mr Nicholls, who was the manager of the very successful and fashionable 'English Shop' much patronised by the aristocracy. The two men took to each other at once and soon became firm friends. Both were practical men who loved work and every detail of their work. Thus, though Nicholls was a respected member of the English colony and a friend of the Ambassador, he still served behind the counter in his shop and it did not occur to him that such 'eccentricity', as the Ambassador regarded it, was demeaning.

Clementina felt stunned by the size and the splendour of St Petersburg. She knew the capital cities of Edinburgh, London (east of St Paul's) and Copenhagen, but she had not imagined a city on such a vast scale, built to impress the eye, and not a warren of little streets. But she felt anxious about her daughter.

Isabella had put on her finest morning dress, and as she walked through the streets was trembling with excitement and drawing deep breaths like a high-mettled racehorse.

It was a relief to Clementina to find herself being greeted by Mrs Nicholls, a red-haired woman whose eyes grew moist with emotion when they spoke of Dundee and Montrose. Mr Nicholls had found them lodgings, though he warned that they must expect to be devoured by fleas and bugs anywhere in the city. Then, although it was business hours, he led them to their rooms, which seemed clean enough at first sight, and promised to take them to watch a military parade next day.

They spent a disturbed night, for fleas were active, and one or two fiery swellings on thumbs and toes showed that bedbugs had also been present.

Early next day Mr Nicholls appeared and drove them to a palace with windows overlooking the parade ground, where they were introduced to the British Ambassador and, by him, to a Russian lady, the niece of the owner. Peter had fortunately put on his dress uniform as Captain of the *George IV*. Clementina wore a flounced yellow silk dress, and Isabella a very smart walking-out dress of sprigged muslin, long gloves and a bonnet like a coal-scuttle thrust back on her head with an ostrich feather falling among her dark curls. She looked ravishing. The Ambassador was cordial and smiled graciously as Clementina and then Isabella dropped their curtseys, and then he found them a place by the window from which they could get a good view.

Below them in one corner of the immense square, a small group of horsemen trotted out.

'Do you see the Tsar? He is a head taller than any of the others,' explained Mr Nicholls.

A band struck up and then was silent as a wild charge of Georgian horsemen came thundering across the parade ground, appearing and disappearing at full gallop. They wore red tunics partly covered in chain mail, with steel caps, and were armed with spears. To Isabella, who had read the novels of Sir Walter Scott, they seemed like a reincarnation of the Crusaders. These savage warriors were followed by companies of the Household Cavalry, who trotted across to the sound of their trumpets and kettledrums. Such perfect alignment of rows of carefully matched horses made them seem like toys. Each company rode upon identically marked animals: bay for one squadron, grey for the next, then chestnut, and black for the last of all.

They were followed by hussars, and these by lancers and wild-looking Cossacks in astrakhan caps. Last came field artillery. Then there was an interval, and the Tsar could be seen riding up to an officer who sat rigid while abuse was showered upon him; but though the Emperor screamed in anger, the distance was too far for a sound to reach the listeners, who could, however, see the Tsar strike the man with his riding whip.

After an interval the horse artillery and their unfortunate captain were dismissed, and a brass band was heard approaching. The band was followed by the colonel of the regiment on a white horse, behind which came serried ranks of grey-coated infantry, each battalion headed by its mounted officers reining in their caracolling steeds. As each battalion passed the saluting point, an enormous shout was heard. Nicholls explained that the Tsar had called out: 'You have done well, my children,' and that the soldiers had shouted back: 'We will do better next time, Our Father!'

The review lasted for five hours, and Clementina began to long for a cup of tea. Even Isabella was sated by the spectacle of no less than ten thousand uniforms: for that was the number of the troops taking part. But at last the parade was over, and it was possible for the Scottish party to go back to the Nichollses' house and enjoy a home-made bannock.

Isabella was angry: she had been told that there would be a ball after the review and a young officer had begged her for a dance, taking for granted that her party was among those invited.

'Could we not have stayed, Mamma?' she complained.

Her words were overheard by her father, who said severely: 'We are greatly indebted to Mr Nicholls for obtaining permission from His Excellency to accompany him and watch the review. The invitation did not extend further and I am sure you would not wish to thrust yourself forward, my love.'

Isabella was not comforted when her mother remarked: 'I

have as little inclination to see great people as they have to notice me.'

Very different from the rich ladies of St Petersburg were those who excited Clementina's interest. At dinner she had heard Mr Nicholls say in deprecation of young Count Tchernavin (the officer who had tried to teach Isabella the Circassian *Lezghinka*) that since his return he had spent almost every evening either gambling or with the gypsies. Later, when Clementina was alone with Mrs Nicholls, she asked about them. All the good lady could say was that it was a recognised thing for rich young men to go and drink and watch the gypsy girls dancing. She knew where their village was, but she had never been there.

'I should like to visit it and will drive out there tomorrow.'

Mrs Nicholls thought it a most strange suggestion which might have unpleasant consequences.

'If I drive there in the middle of the day there can be no harm in it. I shall not ask Count Tchernavin to escort me.'

'Vassily, our footman, who is a strong fellow and knows a little English, must go as your bodyguard and interpreter, and you had better take a bag of kopecks, as they will certainly beg a great deal.'

Clementina did not reveal that if Russian gypsies spoke Romany an interpreter would not be required. She set off next morning and much to her surprise found that the gypsies actually did live in a village. There were a number of covered carts and one or two tents, but there were log cabins arranged on each side of a large pond with a swollen stream running through it. The sun was warm, but the ground still covered with hard-beaten snow. Telling Vassily not to accompany her, she walked across the snowfield to the nearest of the log cabins. The fur shuba and the fur hat she was wearing made her feel uncomfortably warm. The arrival of her sleigh had been noticed, and several of the doorways were filled with the heads of wondering spectators. There was a young woman with a sulky, indeed rather hostile, expression at the door of the nearest cabin.

'May I visit you? I come from Scotland,' Clementina asked

in Romany. The young woman stared in amazement.

'I have never been to that place. Which province is it in? How is it that you speak Roman?'

The accent was different, one or two words puzzled her, nevertheless they understood one another and soon got talking.

Clementina explained that she had come to Russia on a very big boat and would soon go back to Germany. The gypsy girl knew about Germany. Her uncle had been taken for a soldier and had been sent to Germany and to Paris.

'Come and see his wife. She can talk to you about Germany.'

Although Clementina did not want to be told about Germany, she followed the young woman round the house. And there, on the next doorstep, sat an enormous brown bear, holding a human baby in its arms.

Clementina gave a cry and was darting forward to snatch the child away, when the young woman took hold of her and held her back, laughing.

'Haven't you seen a bear holding a baby before?'

'No, I have never even seen a bear,' Clementina confessed.

She saw that the bear was chained to the doorpost. He was huge, and the baby was tiny, wrapped up in swaddling clothes, and the bear held it in his folded front legs at the ends of which were long, curved, black claws.

'Misha is a very good nursemaid; he would never hurt a child,' said the gypsy.

Clementina stared, and the bear, lifting his snout, stared back out of his little eyes.

'Not all our bears are to be trusted like Misha. Some years ago a child was hugged to death. I don't think the bear meant to hurt the boy, but they had to keep the children away from him after that. In the end he was killed as too much trouble. Here is my Auntie.'

A bent old woman came out, and her niece introduced Clementina.

'A lady has come from Scotland in Germany. She speaks Roman.'

'I don't mix with any of our people who live with the Russian Gorgios,' she said, scanning her with hostility.

Clementina began to explain that she was not a Roman, but had learned the language as a child. The old woman remained hostile.

'All the Romans in Scotland loved my father. Their king, Pyramus Lee, called him his brother.'

'There is too much of that sort of thing,' said the old hag and, turning her back, went into her cabin and shut the door.

'Come back to my house, and I will give you a glass of kvass.'

They walked back past the huge bear, which was gently rocking the baby.

'I suppose Misha is a she bear,' said Clementina.

'No, indeed! She bears may be dangerous nursemaids. They try to get the baby to drink their milk and a man who has been suckled by a bear is never to be trusted. Such men are always treacherous. And if it is a girl child, she grows into a clumsy and cruel woman. Contrariwise, if a woman suckles a bear cub, she can do anything with it when it has grown up.'

'Have you ever...?' Clementina began to ask.

'Good God, no! They have teeth that nip and they pull at you terribly, I'm told.'

Her new friend, who was called Euphemia, gave her a glass of kvass, and Clementina was just leaving when a man came up and accosted her.

'That footman tells me you come from England, Sister.'

'Yes I do.'

'I ask because I met a clown at Nijhni. He was Welsh and could talk a little Romany, and we made friends. I love him, so when you meet him, tell him that I often think about him and greet him from me. His name is Arthur Evans, and mine is Apollo Kantarovits.'

'I will surely. And I will tell my Roman friends in England about all of you in Russia.' They smiled and parted.

When she was being driven home, Clementina found that her pocket, hanging inside her placket-hole, was full of kopecks. Gypsy children had looked at and had followed her at a distance, but none had run up to beg. Yet the streets of St Petersburg were swarming with beggars. Clementina would have asked Vassily to say nothing about her visit, but reflected that it would be asking too much and that her wish to keep it secret would add interest.

When Clementina told Mrs Nicholls about the bear holding the baby, that good lady was horrified.

'What savages. That must be stopped. I will speak to our friend the Nachalnik and get the police to act. It is appalling to think of.'

'Please don't do anything. I was as horrified as you, when I first saw it. I would have snatched the baby away from the bear if Euphemia had not stopped me. Those gypsies know their bears.'

Clementina could not restrain her hostess, who rushed off at once to the police station. The young efficient Nachalnik promised immediate action. But next day it rained; the snow was melting fast, and it was impossible to reach the gypsy encampment, either by carriage or by sleigh. A week later, when the roads had dried, the subject was forgotten.

Clementina had learned her lesson, and when the British Ambassador's wife, giving her a peculiar look, asked about her visit to the gypsies, she had her answer ready.

'I believe in palmistry. I had my hand read by a gypsy in Scotland and most of what she said has come true. I heard that there was a woman here who could read one's hand and I wanted it done again.'

The Ambassador's wife looked relieved: a subject for scandal had been averted, and the Captain's wife would not bring discredit on the British community. Anyhow the ship was sailing very shortly.

On the voyage back to Lübeck, trying to be polite to Russian women who treated her as an inferior, and talking to them in her bad French, often no worse than theirs, Clementina made up her mind that she would not go on any of the subsequent voyages to St Petersburg and told Peter that in future she would live all the time at Travemünde. She added that she thought that it would be better if Isabella stayed with her. Russian officers in their uniforms had turned her head. If she had to marry a foreigner, it would be better to have a solid German merchant for a son-in-law.

Peter disagreed: 'Isabella is very useful to me, owing to her command of French. She is a valuable interpreter with the passengers on board, and her gaiety and sweetness keeps everyone happy.'

'I am afraid that she may get ideas above her station in life,' said Clementina.

'We can trust Isabella to conduct herself with propriety. Remember, my dear, that she is a woman of twenty-three years old. I think that she should accompany me if she so wishes.'

This conversation was a reversal of their usual attitudes. It was almost as though they had changed their natures, and success and authority had melted the austerity and reserve of Peter and had frozen the light-hearted adventurousness in Clementina.

Actually she guessed that though Peter was proud of her and loved her, he was not altogether sorry that his plain wife, her face pitted with smallpox, and her broad Scottish accent, should elect to stay in Travemünde and look after David while his gay and beautiful daughter sat opposite him at the captain's table, entertaining distinguished passengers in fluent French.

So it was settled, and for that summer Clementina led a happy and peaceful existence. Every morning she rose early, ate her breakfast with David – a breakfast of parritch, buttered kipper or haddock, oatcake and marmalade and cups of strong tea. Then, after David had gone off to school, she would wash the dishes, make the beds and go out into her garden to hoe between the rows, and gather whatever was in season: broad or runner beans, strawberries, raspberries, red and white currants for David's tea. On half-holidays she would go out with David in their row-boat, and while she sculled, he would fish with a long line trailing behind, trolling. Once to their astonishment he caught a big sturgeon, which took hours to play and get on shore, for it was like a log of wood in the water.

David's companionship in Travemünde had, from their first coming, led Clementina to indulge in make-believe games with her son's participation. They were a kind of day-dreaming, in which the two pretended that they were refugees hiding after being defeated in battle. Scott's novels were the basis of these games for David, but for his mother it was an indulgence of a life-long hankering after a gypsyish life.

Sometimes they would steal out along the banks of the Trave, having, in their game, to keep out of sight of their German neighbours who were the enemy. Sometimes David would be Bonny Prince Charlie and Clementina Flora MacDonald; sometimes the make-believe would be taken from *Rob Roy*. And when David grew too old for such pretences, Clementina would, in solitude, live in a dream world until she suddenly realised that she had not made the bannocks she had intended.

Then there were the dreams of the garden. Why should she not plant seakale and make an asparagus bed? They might need protection in very hard winters: but they liked salt and a load of seaweed spread upon either would do no harm. She would write to her son Peter, at Bordeaux, for that French lettuce that old Peter used to grow at the bothy which did not bolt in summer, and for those beans without strings, climbing haricots. And next time her Peter went to St Petersburg she would ask him to buy seed of those melons that everyone was eating in summer.

The steamer from Hull had been delayed, so the *George IV* had to wait, anchored in the Travemünde roads, for the passengers arriving by coach from Hamburg and booked on to St Petersburg. When she had finished coaling and the decks had been washed down and holystoned and all was in apple-pie order, Peter was free to spend his time with his family until the passengers arrived. The apples in the orchard were ripe, and he picked them, while Clementina stood below, steadying the ladder and taking a full basket from him and handing up an empty one.

Looking down into her joyful face, he smiled and said: 'You would like to turn me into a farmer instead of a sailor.'

Their eyes met and Clementina laughed but did not reply.

'You have never much liked the sea.'

'What reason have I had to like it?' she asked.

'Well, it has brought you here from East Haven and given you this house and orchard, instead of the shippon. But perhaps you wish you were back there?' he said, as he climbed down and they shifted the ladder to the other side of the tree.

'That is not fair, Peter. The pride I take in you is the next thing after my love for the children. And I have enough reason to be proud of you.'

'Thank you, my dear. All the same you would be as happy if the *George* were *Patience* and St Petersburg Arbroath. And you would rather young Peter and David did not follow the sea.' Peter climbed the ladder smiling to himself.

'Who can tell? I am happy the now. But here comes the postman with a letter.'

'That means the passengers will be here soon. For the mail comes on the boat from Hull.'

Letters from England were rare things, and the postman, getting no answer to his knock and seeing a basket full of apples, walked round into the orchard. Peter came down the ladder and drew out his sheath knife to cut under the seal. He started reading, turned very pale and fell back on to the ladder. Then sat down on the wheelbarrow and put his hand on his heart.

Clementina looked at him and felt afraid. She ran to the house and came back with a bottle of whisky and a tumbler. She poured out the spirit and held it to his lips.

Peter took a sip, then brushed it aside and said: 'Thank you. I am all right, but that letter has brought terrible news. At the end of the season, Mr Joliffe is selling my ship.'

'Selling her!' exclaimed Clementina.

'Yes, selling her and dismissing me. As you know, Mr Joliffe and his friend Mr Banks put in a tender for pulling down and rebuilding London Bridge. Now their tender has been accepted, and they will need every penny of capital they can raise. So they have sold their steamships to the government. This letter is telling me that at the end of the season – that is after two more trips to Russia – I am to deliver my ship to the purchaser and that I am dismissed from their service. In a month's time I shall be without a ship.'

Clementina embraced her husband, who took his hat and

went out for a walk. She finished the whisky he had brushed aside. She did not mind for herself being poor again; but it was a terrible thing for Peter. Anger rose in her, and when David came home from school, before his father had returned, she poured the news out indignantly. David ran out after his tea, and that evening they received an unexpected visit from the fathers of two of their son's schoolfellows. David ushered in Herr von Duhn and Herr Behnke and introduced them to his father. They were full of apologies, but they understood that he was sailing at dawn and they had important questions to ask. They were ill at ease. Then David explained that he had told his schoolfellow Wilhelm Behnke about the sale of *George IV*, and this visit was the result. Peter looked severely at his son when he confessed to this indiscreet gossiping. But Herr von Duhn interrupted to explain that they came on business. Was it true, he asked, that the *George IV* would no longer be sailing regularly from Lübeck? Peter told them that, indeed, it was the case.

The long and short of the matter was that they, and the Burgermeister and the chief banker, all felt that the discontinuance of the service would be a severe blow to the town. The town councillors had only recently agreed to spend the money necessary for dredging the harbour and building a dock alongside which a ship of *George IV*'s size and draught could berth. When it had been constructed, it would no longer be necessary to anchor off Travemünde and load and unload cargoes from and into lighters. This would be an economy and lower the price of imported goods, and the money saved would pay the interest on the cost of dredging and dock construction. But without a ship like the *George*, sailing regularly, the scheme might have to be abandoned: Lübeck would sink in importance, and Kiel and Neustadt get all the trade. And at this point they scowled at Peter as though he were responsible. Peter told them that he agreed with all that they had said, but the owners had decided to sell, and he was helpless in the matter.

They grunted sadly, and then Herr Behnke said that although it was such short notice, they had come to say that if Captain Lamond could buy another steam vessel to replace *George IV*, they would be glad to invest in her and become part owners.

Peter explained that there were no suitable steam vessels for sale and that to maintain the service it would mean building not one, but two ships. He would be delighted to be commissioned to construct them, but it would probably need more money than they were prepared to lay out. The Germans scratched their heads.

'Perhaps some of the Russians would contribute. The service is as important to St Petersburg as it is to Lübeck,' von Duhn pointed out. He thought that the Lübeck consortium could raise a third of the sum Peter had mentioned, if the Russians could provide the rest.

Peter said that he would do everything he could to raise money in St Petersburg and that he would design the two ships and supervise their building, on condition that he was paid an architect's fee and given a contract to be captain of the Baltic vessel. After he had shown the Germans to the door, he went into the kitchen and told Clementina. She saw that he was a changed man, and when he went on board at first light next morning he was more excited than she had seen him for many years. Isabella went with him. She had been invited to stay with the Nichollses. And it was on Nicholls that Peter most relied for introductions to Russian capitalists, who would put up the money. If they did not, it would mean leaving Travemünde.

Clementina waited most anxiously for his return, yet it did not prevent her from making jam and pickling mushrooms in German fashion. But she had little hopes of a quiet life of retirement.

The *George IV* reversed her paddles and an unseen seaman picked up the buoy. Then her anchor rattled down. The companion ladder was lowered, and the passengers descended into the sailing barge which would take them to Lübeck. Their luggage, enclosed in a rope net, swung to and fro from a derrick and was guided into the hold of the barge. A rope was thrown, the barge pushed off, and almost immediately the Captain's gig was lowered, and Peter came ashore. He sprang out as it touched land and walked rapidly up the path, meeting Clementina hurrying down, half-way. She had waited to wash the garden soil from her hands, to tidy her hair and to put on a bonnet. It was an iron discipline that she imposed on herself. One glance at Peter showed her that he was in good spirits – but also that he was looking thin and ill.

'All seems to be going well, my dear,' he said taking her in his arms. 'The Emperor was much annoyed at the sale of *George IV* and had spoken to our Ambassador, trying to prevent it. So when I put forward the project of building two vessels to replace her, it was very well received. The contract has not yet been signed, but is now being drawn up. I shall be commissioned to build two steamships for the service. I have promised to get them built by the opening of next season, which will not be easy. I shall command the one trading the Baltic. All that worries me is that both ships will sail under the Russian flag, and that I shall be an officer in the Russian merchant marine, such as it is. As the Russian merchants are putting up two-thirds of the cost, it is not unreasonable that the ships should sail under Russian colours, but it means I shall not be protected by British maritime law. We sail again immediately the passengers arrive, so I must see our friends here without delay.'

Clementina did not speak of her vanished dream of a peaceful life of retirement. A message was sent to ask that David should come home at once to serve as interpreter, and directly Peter had had a cup of tea and a buttered scone, they set off to Lübeck to meet the Burgermeister, the bank manager and the other merchants who were taking a share in the enterprise. Contracts had to be drawn up, oaths sworn, signatures witnessed. Peter sailed next morning. He felt that the fact that German merchants had invested a third of the capital was some protection against future arbitrary action in Russia. Moreover he was still a Master in the Royal Navy, though on half pay.

Meanwhile Clementina had to close up the house at Travemünde for the coming winter, put David in a new school in Lübeck where they took boarders and pack up all the household equipment she might need in England, including a fine collection of pots of jam, smoked hams and glasses of brawn and potted meat, dried sausage, apples and a little barrel of Swedish cranberries. Peter would be sure to say that she was taking too many provisions with them. All was ready to be taken on board for life in England. She hated the thought of the yellow Thames, the filthy little streets, the cockney features that would replace the placid German. She hated leaving her vegetable garden, even though it would soon be covered in snow, and not knowing whether she would be back in time, when spring came, to rake seed-beds and sow seeds. Old Hans would have to do what he could. The sow, the young porkers, the ducks, hens and geese would have to be sold. It was lucky that she had not bought a young Friesian cow after all.

Actually when the *George* returned from her last voyage to Russia, her Captain's mind was too much occupied to pay attention to household details. Everything was loaded on board as rapidly as possible, and they were away for England. Once they were clear of the islands Peter left navigation to the chief mate, and spent every spare moment either in the chart-room or, footrule in hand, measuring all the timbers of *George IV*.

He had already made several decisions: the two boats were not, as formerly, to be twin ships. The *Alexandra*, sailing from Hull, was to be of deeper draught and of greater capacity. She had not to fear the shoals of the Gulf of Bothnia. The *Nicolai* was to be of shallower draught, but to have greatly reinforced bows so as to be able to break through pack-ice if necessary.

On the second day out, the sea became rough, and Peter went on deck to take command. When he returned to the chart-room, he was surprised to see his wife looking over the plans of the *Nicolai*.

'Well, my dear, you see the ship shaping from my plans. They are not totally mysterious, are they?'

'No, Peter. But I have a suggestion to make'

Peter was surprised, but listened carefully.

'Your companionway – your staircase – is either not wide enough, or else it is too wide. It is not wide enough for a gentleman to descend gracefully with a lady on his arm when they are comfortably in port – but it is too wide in a seaway, like the present, when a passenger needs to grasp both rails of the banister firmly with each hand, so as to descend in safety.'

'You mean that I am cramping my passengers when they are in port and not giving sufficient protection when they are at sea.'

'Exactly.'

Peter looked at the plan silently.

'The companionway from the upper deck, and from the main deck below to the first class, must be wide enough for two people to pass each other comfortably,' she said. 'But wouldn't it be possible to put a rail in the centre dividing it into two? It might even be removable.'

Peter nodded his acceptance of her suggestion. He did not thank her, but after that he asked his wife's advice on all points which had to do with the comfort of the passengers, and the equipment and the planning of the galleys and state-rooms.

Then, before they landed in England, he said to her: 'My dear, I want you to be responsible for the entire interior decora-tion of the two boats I am building; for the purchase of every-thing needed for the bunks and cots, sheets, blankets, pillows, basins; also for the provisioning of the two ships. Otherwise I do not think that we shall have them ready in time for when the ice breaks up next spring. Of course, you can leave most of the outfitting to the chandlers. But it needs someone to keep an eye on them, or they will provide inferior stuff and over-charge.'

Clementina set to work immediately. 'The expense is bound to be very great and I trust it has been allowed for.'

'Time is more important than expense,' Peter repeated over and over again, when she questioned him. 'And the quality must be of the best. My Russian backers will expect that and not grudge a few thousand roubles.'

Though frugal, Clementina was thorough, and she was not above asking advice from all sources: the ship's cook, a stewardess and a London plumber. And then, of course, she asked, in Peter's name, for an estimate from two ships' chandlers.

The estimates sent in were by all standards very high, and though the prices for various items differed, the final amounts were the same within a few shillings. Clementina thought those for the ships' linen were far too high, and the samples of its quality second-rate and inferior to what she had bought for her house in Calais.

'I'm going to Leeds, or Manchester, to find what we need there, without employing these middlemen. And I'll go to Sheffield for the silver and cutlery.'

Then when Peter queried her wisdom, she replied: 'I shall save more than the coach fare, get better goods and immediate delivery.' Peter wrote her out a credit note on the Bank of England.

While his wife busied herself with lists of ship's equipment, Peter devoted himself to organisation. Even before the keel had been laid he had hired two joineries where the interior woodwork could be made, so that when the hull was complete decks could be laid, partitions put up, and bunks in the cabins put at once in place from timber already cut to size.

In the midst of all this Clementina received a letter which had been forwarded by the Minister in Panbride to Calais, and from Calais to Lübeck, and which had come originally from Australia. At first she thought that she should refuse it, as the charges were heavy; then she saw that it must concern her father and paid.

She opened the letter and read:

Dear Madam,
I have to inform you that your father David Carey is deceased. In his will, here enclosed, he left you the sum of twenty-five guineas which I remit in a draft on the Bank of Scotland. After liberation on parole, your father met with good fortune as a sheep farmer. He married a widow, Elizabeth Lyall, and was generally respected and I may add loved in our community. Like many men of equally noble connections he adapted himself rapidly to life out here.
Your humble and obliged servant
William McHenty

When Clementina took the letter to Peter, he read it and

burst out laughing at the reference to her father's noble connections.

'He was always great on being a gentleman. Do you remember that you had to buy him velvet breeches and a ruffled shirt and buckles to his shoes in order to go decently to the gallows? He only agreed to our marriage because my old rogue of a grandfather fought on the wrong side at Culloden.'

'I don't know why you say that, Peter. He fought for the rightful king.'

'Well, he fought on the losing side and had to keep hidden afterwards.'

'He was very good to me after you were pressed, and I loved him. He told me, I remember, that you were not good enough for me,' said Clementina.

'Well, he was right about that, at all events,' replied Peter, laughing.

CHAPTER THIRTEEN

PETER had chosen the Butterley Ironworks Company to design and manufacture the engines of the ships he was building, in preference to Boulton and Watt, whose order book was full. Then, after having contracted for timber and engaged shipwrights and a competent foreman, he went to visit the Butterley Company in Derbyshire. Clementina and he therefore took the coach together at crack of dawn to Derby, where they stayed the night at the York Inn. Next morning Peter went as far as Swanwick and Clementina went on alone to Sheffield. This was a great adventure for her. She was travelling the same road, though in the opposite direction, as that on which she had walked to Portsmouth. Thinking of that time so long ago, naturally brought to mind the woman who had given her a lift as far as Chesterfield, and who peddled scissors and cutlery which she bought in Sheffield. Her name, Clementina remembered, was Mrs Anson. She was only a few years older than she herself and might be alive, and her advice could be valuable. So, on the coach stopping to change horses at Chesterfield, she found her way quickly to the small inn where Mrs Anson had put up her pony and cart and went in to ask after her. Yes, said the landlord, he remembered her perfectly, but she had given up coming six or seven years ago. He had heard, however, that she was still in the cutlery trade, but in Sheffield.

Thus encouraged, Clementina went on again, and, after taking a room at an inn in Sheffield called the 'Rutland', she went out to look at the town, and to ask at every cutlery shop she came to for Mrs Anson. But it was late, the shops were closing and street lamps being lit. Next morning she went to a wholesale firm of cutlers and asked if they had ever had dealings with a Mrs Anson, and was she still alive? At the mention of the name, the manager came forward and said, indeed, yes, Mrs Anson had a little shop of her own and had gone in for silver as well as cutlery. Then, turning to a boy, he said: 'Johnny, take this lady to Mrs Anson's shop in Bridle Lane.'

The shop was small, hidden in a back street, and there was a strong steel grille in front of the window, behind which were some silver teapots and a case of spoons of good quality. Clementina gave the boy threepence and walked in. A young shopman greeted her, but she brushed past him to speak to an elderly woman.

'Mrs Anson, do you remember giving a lift as far as Chester-field to a young Scottish woman? It was the year of Trafalgar.'

'I cannot say that I do. That is a very long time ago.'

'You were selling scissors and knives, and you told me about your husband.'

Mrs Anson looked grim. 'But what can I do for you now, madam?'

'I was that Scottish fisher-girl walking to Portsmouth to meet her husband. He is now building two steam vessels for Russia.'

'We have both risen in the world, I see.'

'I have come to ask your advice about buying an entire set of silver for the Captain's table, and silver plate for the rest.' Together they went through the list of what would be needed which Clementina had made on the homeward voyage of the *George IV*.

'That is a very large order to give to a small dealer like me,' said Mrs Anson. 'I can tell you where to go.'

'No, you buy for me, and take a reasonable commission. I would rather deal with you, because I believe you are honest.'

'You will be putting a lot of money in my pocket.'

'One good turn deserves another,' replied Clementina.

Leaving Mrs Anson to execute the order, she took the after-noon coach to Leeds. There after taking a room at the inn, she went to the market. There were many booths selling linen and cotton goods. She was looking at some sheets when she noticed a gypsy woman, in a long brightly coloured dress, standing beside her, also looking at the goods on display. It was Sarah!

Clementina was astounded. While she herself had been dis-

figured by smallpox and had grown into an unattractive age-
ing woman, the companion of her childhood had matured into
a woman of exceptional beauty. Clementina looked at her for a
full minute in order to be certain that it was Sarah indeed.
The skin was deeply tanned, there were a few grey hairs among
the dark locks, her face was thinner, the cheekbones and jaws
prominent, her thin lips showed perfect white teeth.

'Sister, I am glad to find you,' said Clementina, speaking in
Romany. The woman whirled around, stared and gasped in
astonishment! 'Clemmie! I should not have known you but
for the voice.'

Her eyes sparkled, delighted and very much alive. She
hesitated for a moment, and Clementina stepped up to her and
putting her arms round her, gave Sarah a kiss and a hug. But
all the time she was marvelling at her friend. Her figure, in
spite of childbearing and hard work, was lithe and thin. When
Clementina released her, Sarah laughed and held out her hands:
the fingernails were broken, but there were two silver bracelets
on her wrist. They took each other by both hands. People were
beginning to stare at the two oddly assorted women.

'The stalls are closing. Come and talk in our covered cart.'
The gypsy encampment was close by, in a field not yet built
on. Ponies were grazing, children running about. A woman was
carrying two buckets of water. Sarah led the way to a handsome, beautifully decorated caravan. She put a kettle on a
smouldering fire, threw on some sticks and soon made a pot of
tea.

They sat then, Clementina telling her story – she had more
to tell: of how she had reached Portsmouth and seen Peter
and all that had happened since.

When it came to Sarah's turn, she said that Pyramus had
died three years before. She herself was a widow for the second
time, but she had a young Joe – and they were off next morning
to Birmingham to stock up with buttons and tinsel and tinware.
They had been buying a stock of linens with slight faults in
them and were going on to sell their purchases in Wales. They
would buy ponies there and take them to horse fairs.

'Like the one at Appleby?' asked Clementina.

'Yes. That was a good place. But I have never much liked to go there since Jonathan broke his neck.'

Then, before they parted, she capped Clementina's story about the bear nursemaids and the girls who were coarse and clumsy and ill-tempered because they had been suckled by a she-bear.

'There is an Indian woman, called Kardar, in Wombwell's circus. She is a snake charmer and on cold nights she always takes her python to bed with her, so that he should enjoy her warmth. Just think of that! She sleeps with that great snake on one side of her and her lover on the other.'

'He's a brave man. Don't they ever quarrel?'

'I expect he knows better than that. But if that woman strangled her lover in his sleep, she would have a good alibi, wouldn't she?'

'Do you ever want to strangle your lovers in bed, Sarah?' Clementina asked, feeling rather daring.

'Sometimes. Don't you?'

It was getting dark. Clementina had a feeling that there was a man outside, waiting until she should go away. She said good-bye, and Sarah held her by both hands. Then she found her way to the inn where she had booked her room.

She ate a pork pie and drank a glass of stout and then went to the bedroom. But instead of undressing, she threw herself down suddenly, more unhappy than she had felt for many years. She looked at her own life, and what she knew were wicked thoughts assailed her.

Then coloured lights like catherine wheels turned before her closed eyes, and figures like the points of the compass, but angled, interfered with her vision when she opened them. She took off her clothes and crept into bed, but instead of soothing sleep, her head was full of racing thoughts and visions from the past. She saw the tree, 'Carey's Castle', which Sarah and she had made their fortress. Then sweet water began running in her mouth, and she was only just in time to seize the chamber pot and be sick.

She felt better afterwards, and the catherine wheels disappeared. But her thoughts went on, uncontrolled.

When they were little girls, most people would have said

that she was prettier than Sarah. Now, even if she had not been marked by the smallpox, she was a plain woman growing old. And Sarah, who ought by all the rules to be a broken-down hag, was a woman whose beauty had grown with the years. If it had been Sarah who had been marked by the small-pox and not her, the gypsy would still be far the more beautiful. Clementina thought of this not with jealousy but with wonder. Suppose that when Sarah had risked prison, or transportation, or even hanging for herself and Jonathan, suppose that then she had accepted her offer, had climbed into the dogcart and had been driven off to the life of a nomad, what would she be like now? And perhaps Peter would have been happier with a girl who wanted to rise in the world and would have done him credit sitting at the Captain's table and entertaining the grand folks going to St Petersburg? But when her mind wandered to what kind of a man would have made her happy, if she had thrown in her lot with the Romans – then she pulled herself up short and tried to fill her mind with prayer. But prayer was no answer. It was wicked of her to have a longing for a free life with no duties. For it was men like Peter who were changing the world, who shrank from nothing – who worked to fulfil God's will and make a new world. By marrying Peter she was helping, as much as a woman could, to bring that world into being. Whereas Sarah was not even aware that the world was changing, and if she were asked, would only wish that there were fewer changes, and fewer police, and that wilder, more primitive times should return. Was it because Sarah had no duties that she was more beautiful? Exhausted with self-questioning, she prayed again, thanking God that she knew where her path lay and would do her duty in any station of life in which it pleased God to call her. Next morning the only noticeable result of the moral struggle was that, after eating a pair of kippers for breakfast, she refused a plate of scrambled eggs. She had made up her mind that although she could not hope for Sarah's lean beauty and lithe figure, it would be better if she ate less.

She went to Marshall's, the wholesale linen-weavers, directly afterwards and handed in her list of requirements.

'This is quite normal,' said the manager, and after she had chosen the qualities she wanted, he told Clementina that he would be able to give her an estimate in two hours' time. Clementina went back to the field where the gypsies had camped, but it was deserted; then to the market, where she bought a few things, and then back to Marshall's warehouse. The estimate was just over half what the ships' chandlers had quoted: the quality was far superior, and Clementina accepted it and after paying a deposit and arranging for the goods to be delivered in the spring, when the ships had been launched, took the coach back to Sheffield feeling more cheerful.

Mrs Anson had been busy in her absence. She had obtained a rough estimate for the plated goods and for the kitchen equipment. But what was exciting was that she had the promise of a magnificent set of silver – for the Captain's table – second-hand, but each piece was marked with a capital H. Would that matter? For the first moment Clementina thought that to have silver that was wrongly marked would be impossible, then she suddenly remembered that Peter had said that the ship was to be called the *Nicolai*, and that the letter H stood for N in the Russian alphabet. She did not explain this to Mrs Anson, but hummed and hawed, and after Mrs Anson had been round to the silversmith and had got the price reduced for a cash payment, she bought the entire service. But until the *Nicolai* was fitted out it would be safer with Mrs Anson who would come delivering it herself to London, together with all the silver plate that had been ordered. Half would be engraved with an H, the other with an A for the *Alexandra*.

When Clementina arrived in London the following day, after a night spent in great comfort at the 'George' in Grantham, she found all in confusion. Peter had come back the day before and had at once taken a house in Bruswick Square East, and all their belongings had been moved from their lodgings. And with Peter was an unknown young man from the Butterley Ironworks who would be living with them. He was to design, build and instal the engines for the two ships. Joe Hedley seemed so much too young to be entrusted with such work that Clementina at first thought there must be a mistake. She liked him at first sight: he was so gay and friendly, so helpful in all practical details, and so light-hearted, helping to carry the furniture from room to room as Clementina wished, and making the hanging of a mirror or the placing of the kitchen table a joint affair. He spoke with a Geordie accent, as he came from Newcastle-on-Tyne and was often as puzzling to the London kitchen maid as she was herself – and at such a moment he laughed with such charm and sweetness that everyone felt happy.

Peter had an office at the dockyard, but Joe said that it was not a good place for him to work, as men kept coming in and out to ask Peter questions, and that he must have a room in which he could work alone. He was given the back room of the new house, overlooking the garden, and a big table was put in on which he could make his drawings. He sat there silently working all the morning, making mathematical calculations and then standing up with his T-square, drawing diagrams for the bearings of the driving shaft, or of the attachment of a paddle-wheel. Then, when Peter returned from the dockyard, Joe would discuss the results of his morning's work and the modifications which he thought necessary in Peter's plans.

Having him in the house with her made Clementina feel that he was one of the family. In the middle of the morning she would go into his workroom carrying a cup of tea. Sometimes he would not look up from the notebook in which he was making calculations; at other times – when he was making a drawing for instance – he would smile and thank her so sweetly that she would go back to the kitchen feeling happy for the rest of the morning.

One day she said to Peter: 'Joe reminds me of your brother Robert.'

'He laughs much like him. I noticed that directly I met him, but Robby had not got such a head on his shoulders. Joe is the cleverest man I have ever met. Every day he is inventing something new. He is putting a steam pump into the *Nicolai*.'

To her surprise Clementina was happy in the little house in Brunswick Square East. There were two things which made her so: the work of having to fit out the ship and furnish it, and having Joe living with them. Her success in buying plate and linen led her to buy the least possible from the chandler who battened on the ignorance of seamen, and to make all the purchases of blankets and pillows, china and saucepans, chairs and tables, lamps and glasses herself. In the evening she would talk over what she had bought, and the prices she had paid, with Peter and Joe and feel proud of their approval, and then listen in her turn, with more understanding than most women, to their discussion of the progress of work on the two ships.

One day she remembered her unhappiness after meeting Sarah and how she had envied the gypsy woman's way of living. And now with Joe and Peter she was perfectly happy and felt it was a privilege to have a man like Joe, who was inventing new uses for the steam engine, living under the same roof. Yet Sarah's beauty and the image she called up of early morning, the dew on the grass, the smell of the wood-fire, the hobbled ponies, woodpigeons cooing and then clattering their wings as they flew out of the ashpoles in the copse: that was something which she longed to enjoy, a secret part of her that she could never share with anyone – least of all with either of the two men with whom she was living. Nor could she speak of it to her children. With her son Peter she was not sufficiently intimate, nor could he understand. And such a feeling was the last thing she would hint at to Isabella who needed all the moral influence that she could exert. And David was still a schoolboy.

Meanwhile the weeks went by in yellow, foggy, muddy London, and the hulls of the two ships rose slowly in the dry dock. It seemed impossible that the *Nicolai* should be ready to sail in time to arrive directly after the ice broke up. One day she ventured to ask Joe whether he thought that there were any likelihood of it. He was sitting at his table drawing, and she had just brought him a cup of tea. He looked up and laughed.

'You, if anybody, should know better than to doubt whether Peter can do what he has planned.'

'It is spring already: it seems impossible.'

'The boiler goes in tomorrow, the masts before the end of the week. Then the carpenters take over. All the planks for the decks are cut and numbered. Peter has worked out every detail. It is just a question of fitting the bits together like a puzzle.'

'So you really think it can be done?'

'Yes, if your furniture men are ready to lay the carpets and hang the curtains. You haven't forgotten tables and chairs as well as cots and hammocks?'

'Thank you for reminding me that we shall need them, I might have forgotten,' replied Clementina mischievously.

The *Nicolai* would be finished in time, but it was clear that the *Alexandra* would not.

Both ships were launched and towed down the river, and anchored off Tilbury. The new Captain of the *Alexandra* had not collected his full crew and there were details that he wanted altered. But passengers could reach Hamburg by other routes. The *Nicolai* was the more important. Peter and Joe took her out for her steam trials while men were still laying carpets in the lounge.

One afternoon there was a knock on the door in Brunswick Square East, and when Clementina opened it she saw a young man on the doorstep. He had golden hair brushed back and falling in ringlets behind his ears, and golden brown eyes. He looked at her for a moment before giving her a winning smile and saying: 'My dear, will you go and tell your mistress that her brother, from Australia, has come to see her? Try to break it gently to her, will you? I have come a long way to see her and don't want to be turned away from the door.'

The last words were a joke. It was inconceivable that a young man of his appearance and charm should be turned away from any door. But at the end of his speech something in Clementina's look pulled him up. He struck his forehead dramatically, and before she could speak, exclaimed: 'Oh, my sister, what a fool I am! Please, please, forgive me, if you can. May I embrace you as your brother George? I loved your father as though he were my own, and that surely is a bond?'

And then he took Clementina's hand and kissed it and then drew her to him and kissed her on the cheek. She had not said a word. She was stunned. To find such a charming, handsome young man, carelessly dressed in fashionable clothes, standing

229

on her doorstep and claiming her as his sister, left her speechless with astonishment.

'Are you Elizabeth Lyall's son? Oh, I am so glad that you have come,' she said at last and, taking him by the hand, drew him into the passage. A few minutes later he was sitting at a little table with a slice of fruit cake and a decanter of port in front of him. He refilled his glass again and again and was laughing at his own enthusiasm as he told her about kangaroos and wallabies, and the blackfellows who could throw a boomerang so that it would come back to the hand of the thrower if it missed the bird at which it was aimed. He would show her one that he had left at his inn and teach her how to throw it. And then he took out an old snuffbox in which there was a nugget of gold and some gold dust that he had washed out of an Australian river. By the time that Peter had come back to his supper Clementina was half in love with George.

With Peter he was deferential, without ceasing to be entertaining – and he actually made Peter laugh. He talked about David Carey with a mixture of respect and love and humour, describing the strength and grandeur of the old Scotsman, how he was fond of talking about the execution of his noble kinsman, Lord Lovat, and then how his bloodshot eye always lit up if a pretty girl came into the room, even in the last years, when he could only walk with the help of two sticks. Clementina listened breathless, and sometimes wiped away a tear from laughter and sometimes one from sentiment.

'Oh, you bring him back. I loved him, for he was a full man!'

To her surprise Peter nodded agreement. He spoke of his own grandfather and the bothy. The last thing he had heard of him was that he had been shooting his neighbour's hens when they came to scratch in his gardens: and he was a hundred years old! Then he summed it up with, 'There was a great air in many of those scoundrels. Wicked old men, no doubt, but such as one meets in the Testament.'

Joseph Hedley was away at Butterley and the three were alone. They ate the supper Clementina had provided; then she suggested a glass of whisky, and once again George Lyall drank up one glass after another. When bedtime came Clementina would not hear of George going back to his inn. He must stay the night. Joseph Hedley's bed was made up; it was no trouble. Peter added his own invitation, and George went rather unsteadily to his bedroom, Peter lighting his way with a candle.

Next morning George came down as fresh as a daisy and began singing as he washed in the scullery.

What shall we do with the drunken sailor?
What shall we do with the drunken sailor?
Stop his grog and make him sober. Stop his grog and make him sober.
Set him polishing up the brasswork. Set him polishing up the brasswork.
Aye, Aye, Up she rises! Aye, Aye, Up she rises!

At breakfast he said that he was taking the coach to Bristol to see some of his mother's family, who lived on the Welsh border. And then, just as Peter was leaving to go to the dockyard, he asked him: 'You couldn't help me to a ship, Peter, I suppose?'

'But you are not a sailor, are you? You don't want to serve before the mast, I take it.'

'I was a mate of a brig sailing to Van Diemen's Land.'

'I should never have guessed it. Well, I'll bear you in mind.' And Peter was gone.

That evening Clementina said: 'It would be a pleasure if George were one of the crew of *Nicolai*.'

'I don't know what sort of an officer he would make. He hasn't the cut of a seaman,' answered Peter.

However, ten days later, when the *Nicolai* was almost due to sail, George Lyall reappeared. He was very cheerful and had amusing stories to tell about the Welsh, but he did not refer to his own future, or ask Peter if he had found a ship for him.

He stayed to supper, drank three glasses of claret for every one of Peter's and of Joseph Hedley's so that Clementina opened another bottle. Then came a surprise announcement.

'The man I booked as Second Mate for the *Nicolai* has got the jaundice. When he recovers, his job will be waiting for him, because he and I have served together in the navy. But if you would like the post of Second Mate for a month, or perhaps two, I shall be pleased to have you.'

George Lyall accepted with delight. 'It will be wonderful to be serving with my sister on board ship.' He left early to put his kit together and buy oilskins and seaboots. They were sailing next day.

Joseph Hedley was present and made round eyes of surprise when Peter invited George to join the ship. Even in that moment of delight Clementina could see that, for some reason, Joseph had a low opinion of her brother. 'If I were twenty years younger I should think him jealous,' she said to herself with a chuckle.

Next day George came aboard all smiles.

'This is just wonderful, Peter,' he exclaimed, as they puffed down the estuary of the Thames.

'On board you call me sir, and I call you Mr Mate,' said Peter. But there was no unkindness in his voice.

That night Peter had taken the middle watch and, on leaving the quarterdeck, remarked: 'The sea and wind are rising. You will soon have to take sail off the ship, Mr Mate.' Then he went below, but because the weather looked dirty he only took off his oilskins and seaboots when he lay down. Clementina in the cabin was woken up by the rolling of the *Nicolai* and had to hold on to the edge of her bunk in order not to be rolled out. She climbed out and dressed herself with a vague presentiment that she might be needed. They were steaming north and the wind which had been south-east was veering to south-west. The engines were running at half speed.

The ship's motion increased, she was rolling and going further over each time a big wave hit her. Suddenly there was a crash, and Clementina lost her balance and was thrown across the cabin on to Peter's bunk.

He woke and instantly got hold of one boot and pulled it on while Clementina chased the other into a corner of the cabin. Directly Peter had got it on, he went quickly on deck, and it seemed then as though *Nicolai* were going over on to her beam ends.

The mate had left furling the sails late, and there were still four or five men aloft, clinging to the yards for dear life. But the foresail had jammed, and it was the wind acting on this sail which made the ship yaw this way and that and prevented the man at the wheel from keeping her on a steady course. The mate had disappeared and the only sailor on the quarter-deck was a young lad.

Peter gave the order: 'Cut that sail adrift,' and then looked at the white-faced boy beside him. At that moment Joe Hedley came on deck, closely followed by Clementina.

'You take charge, Joe,' shouted Peter. The young sailor had shifted his grip on the rail and was watching silently as the *Nicolai* rose and the seas poured off her main deck. In an instant Peter was down the ladder and running forward. He had got to the foot of the bowsprit when the bows were buried again, and the seas were sweeping the deck. Everything forward of the quarterdeck disappeared in a smother of foam. Clementina had made an instinctive move to follow him, but checked herself as she saw that she would be swept overboard before she could reach him.

Nicolai came up on to an even keel as the wave swept past, but for what seemed minutes to the watchers, hanging on to the rail of the quarterdeck, there was nothing visible but a white sea of foam. Then as the ship rolled, before plunging into the trough below, the seas poured off and Peter became visible, crouched and clinging like a cat. A moment later he moved, crawling along the bowsprit and had got perhaps half way, when the next great wave tumbled over the ship and everything disappeared. Again there was a very long wait, and then the ship seemed to roll the water off her back and Peter was crawling again and had reached the foot of the sail before the next wave came. Directly the ship lifted again there was a crack like the shot of a gun and the sail was flying loose like a flag.

Twice more Peter was buried as he crawled back. Then when he was more than half-way along the deck, he stumbled and fell. A little knot of sailors had appeared from nowhere and were watching. Three of them ran out with a line and caught Peter and the other men hauled them back like porpoises out of the seas roaring across the deck.

233

Then Peter was handed up the ladder on to the quarterdeck. He was limp and offered no resistance. Clementina ordered two of the men to carry him below. With the help of the steward, Clementina got him out of his jacket, and pulled off his boots and then his trousers. Then she ordered the cook, Sam Harrington, to bring some hot rum with sugar in it, while she cut off the singlet with her scissors. She lifted his head when the rum and molasses was brought and made him swallow some. The steward brought hot towels. Then Clementina spilled a bottle of embrocation over him and began rubbing and pummelling his naked body.

The steward, who like almost all the crew had never sailed with Peter before, gazed at his lean naked body and noted the white scars on his arms and a jagged white stripe on his ribs where the splinter from an American privateer's carronade had struck him.

'By all that's holy, the Captain's been a fighter,' he ventured, but Clementina did not look up or reply.

At last Peter opened his eyes. He was silent for a long time. Then he clearly recollected what had just happened, for he said: 'Aye, she's steering better now. It was that foresail made her yaw.' Then, looking at his wife and realising that he was lying naked under the blankets, he asked: 'How long have I been like this?'

'About two hours.'

Joseph Hedley came down soon afterwards. 'Where was Mr Mate?' asked Peter.

'He was being sick in the chart-room. He says he would never have taken a job on a steamship, if he had known how they steered.'

'He hasn't got his sea-legs, I suppose,' said Peter mildly.

'He didn't get here overland from Australia. He had time enough to get them on the voyage of three months,' snorted Joseph.

'How's she going now?' Peter asked soon afterwards.

'Riding the sea like a duck. Engines at half speed. Sea and wind moderating.'

Peter was on deck again less than two hours later to relieve

Jacobsen, the First Mate, on watch. All that he said to George was: 'Mr Mate, never leave the deck again while you are in command. I shall overlook it this once.' Then he asked for the men who had pulled him out to come aft. Three sailors, one an old man with a white beard under his chin, came on to the quarterdeck.

'How was it?' asked Peter.

One of the younger men pushed the old man forward, but he would not speak. Then the third man said: 'Well sir, we was watching you. We aloft holding on to the yard. And old Douglas here said: "Come on, mates, we'll get him," for you had let go your hold. So we dropped down after him and he got hold of you. Smithie and I held tight to Doug, and he held tight to you. Then we got you up on the quarterdeck, and Smithie and I carried you down. Old Doug was all in by then.'

'All right, the now?'

'Yes, sir. Master Hedley sent us down to the galley and Mr Harrington looked after us.'

Peter dismissed them. It would have seemed as out of place for him to thank them for saving his life as it would have to them to thank him for saving the ship. But Clementina would not speak to George Lyall, or look at him.

Nicolai I steamed slowly up the estuary of the Trave and picked up moorings just outside Number 190 Travemünde. In honour of their arrival the whole town of Lübeck and its suburb were bedecked with flags. There were massed decorations of flags and flowers at the Travemünde landing-stage. All the church bells were ringing, and that evening there was a grand display of fireworks, followed by a grand dinner party in the Rathaus. George Lyall was still feeling too ill to attend and did not even come ashore.

Before putting on her silk dress and the yellow Spanish shawl and brooch given her by Dr Galiani, Clementina only had time for a short look at her garden and a word to Hans about sowing peas and beans and planting out the seedlings that he had raised in boxes.

In the Rathaus there were speeches between each of the courses. First the one of welcome and triumph by the Burger-

235

meister which was followed by cabbage soup with shrimps. Then a speech by the editor of the *Gazette*, then boiled sausage with dumplings. Then a speech by the principal banker, which was of more importance, because it contained an estimate of future profits. Then roast sucking-pig stuffed with buckwheat; then a short speech on how much Lübeck and Europe owed to the Hanoverian succession, and then pancakes with cranberry sauce, after which Peter got up and spoke a few words in English, which were translated to the company by young David and which elicited tremendous applause.

The passengers from Hamburg had arrived that night and had gone on board during the speech-making. So there was no question of Clementina sleeping ashore and looking at her garden next morning, for they sailed at dawn.

There was no wind, the sea was smooth, but it was intensely cold, and Peter wondered whether the ice which was reported to have broken up, might not be freezing over again. George Lyall had recovered and Clementina forgave him. He would, she knew, never have succeeded in cutting the foresail adrift. He would merely have been swept overboard and drowned. Perhaps it was as well that he had been prostrated by sea-sickness, and if they were to live side by side upon the *Nicolai*, she could not refuse to speak to him.

He brought out a boomerang and threw it with great skill. It went spinning out over the sea, rose high unexpectedly, and then came spinning back. George did not attempt to catch it, but it fell on the quarterdeck and went sliding along until it came to rest in the scuppers. But on the third throw it hit the standing rigging ratlines and rebounded into the sea and was lost. George only laughed. He was himself again and as charming as ever. Clementina wondered whether Isabella might not fall in love with him when they met in St Petersburg.

The following night Peter took the first watch. It was bitterly cold and he would be glad when the four hours were over and he handed over to George at midnight.

The bells struck and soon afterwards the cook, Harrington, appeared, looked around anxiously, and then pulled George Lyall, thickly dressed in fur coat and fur hat with ear-flaps, after him on to the deck. Peter, who had been speaking to the helmsman, turned abruptly and watched George stagger unsteadily across the deck, reach the rail and cling to it.

The ship rocked gently to a small wave, George's legs slipped from under him and he slid gently down on to the deck. Peter watched until after a little while the prone bundle managed to reach the rail and struggle to its feet.

Peter walked to the companionway and called down: 'Help Mr Mate back to his cabin.'

'Harrington. Fine fellow Harrington. Finest seaman on the ship,' George mumbled. 'Only fair to let you know.'

Peter walked the quarterdeck alone. It was brilliant starlight and ice-cold. After about three hours the *Nicolai* ran into freezing fog hanging so low over the sea that the stars were sometimes visible above it. Peter reduced speed to dead slow, and gave orders for the foghorn to be sounded every five minutes. He thought it unlikely that there was any vessel in the neighbourhood – unless perhaps a fishing boat becalmed.

It was the foghorn that woke Clementina. She lit a candle. Peter was not in his bunk; then she saw that it had not been slept in. That frightened her. Then as she dressed slowly the ship lurched on a sudden turn, and the starboard paddle-wheel stopped for a moment. Clementina put on her thickest coat and fur gloves and went on deck. Peter was standing motionless. He was so exhausted after eight hours on watch that he could not keep moving. He was frozen, but alert, and had spotted an anchored fishing boat, with not a sign of life on board but mercifully with a lantern at its masthead, and had avoided running it down. The *Nicolai* was on her course again but at very reduced speed when Clementina came on deck.

'Why are you here? It is George's watch,' she said. Peter did not reply. Clementina slipped off her glove and touched his cheek. She peered at him closer and saw an icicle glisten on his eyebrow. He just stood like a post. Just then the bell sounded and Jacobsen, the First Mate, a Dane, came on deck.

'Steward only just told me that you were taking second mate's watch, or I would have come up before.'

Peter gazed at him stonily and said in a hoarse voice: 'There are fishing boats about. Keep her slow,' and then after a long pause before letting Clementina lead him below, he said: 'Take her into Reval. I shall put Mr Lyall ashore.'

Once in the cabin Clementina repeated the remedies she had employed before, giving him a tumbler of hot rum and sugar, wrapping him in hot towels and massaging him with an embrocation of camphor and mustard.

Before he went to sleep he said: 'Tell George to put his things together. I am putting him ashore at Reval.'

'Why Reval?'

'I am dismissing him and don't want him hanging around St Petersburg after we arrive.'

Peter was right. She saw that he could not keep George as an officer on the ship. And he was right not to take him to St Petersburg, where he would charm everyone, and Isabella was bound to fall in love with him if she set eyes on him.

What she had to do was unbearable. She sponged her face with cold water and went and knocked at George's cabin door. It was ajar: she pushed it open. George was awake. She gave Peter's message: that he was dimissed the ship and would be put ashore at Reval, the nearest port, in a few hours.

'Yes, Harrington told me.'

Then as he said nothing and simply stared at her, she felt suddenly enraged and said: 'You have put Peter's life in danger twice and put the ship in great hazard. You were forgiven once.... You are not to be trusted.'

George said in a desperate voice which she never forgot: 'I know. Don't say any more. I can't help it.' Then he put his head in his hands and burst into tears.

Clementina left the room and went back to where Peter was asleep. Then she wept herself.

When Peter woke she was still weeping. He put on his clothes and then patted her on the shoulder.

'We all drank whisky as though it were water, and it didn't....'

'I know ... I know.... I'm giving him his pay for the whole voyage.' Peter unlocked his safe and took out the money.

238

Then he took pen and paper and wrote:

To Those Whom It May Concern

Mr George Lyall was shipped in London on board S.S. *Nicolai I*, as Second Mate and was dismissed in Reval for dereliction of duty and drunkenness.

Peter Lamond, R.N.
Commander of the S.S. *Nicolai I*.

He put money and certificate in an envelope and sealed it. 'Steward, give this envelope to Mr Lyall.'

Neither Peter nor Clementina watched George go ashore, where he was immediately surrounded by dock police and customs officials.

CHAPTER FOURTEEN

IF the reception of the *Nicolai* had been enthusiastic at Lübeck, that at Kronstadt was infinitely grander. She was the first steamship to enter the port under the Russian flag, and she was a ship of the latest design with most powerful engines. All the ships in the harbour were fully dressed with flags. The Tsar attended in person and was immensely gratified to see his name in Slavonic script upon the bows of the steamer. A band of the Marines struck up the Russian national anthem as His Imperial Highness, attended by an Admiral of the Russian fleet and several naval officers and the British Ambassador, went on board, where he was respectfully greeted by Peter who had thoughtfully supplied himself with what he believed was the full-dress uniform of a Captain in the Russian merchant marine. It was a dark blue double-breasted tailcoat, with epaulettes, a white stand-up collar and white nankeen trousers.

The Tsar graciously acknowledged the existence of Clementina and Isabella, who with Mrs Nicholls had rushed on board as soon as the ship docked. She curtseyed and was chucked under the chin, and Joseph Hedley was presented.

When the grand proceedings of the day were over, Mrs Nicholls gave Peter a letter which had arrived during his absence. It was from the Minister at Panbride and announced the death of his grandfather, old Peter, at the age of one hundred and four.

He read it aloud to his family and then said: 'He was just twenty-one when he fought on the wrong side with a parcel of Highland caterans, at Culloden. He was not much more than a Highland cateran himself.'

At this Isabella flared up. 'He fought for Bonny Prince Charlie, his rightful King. I am proud of him.'

'Aren't you proud of your father who fought for King George

beside Nelson on the *Victory* at Trafalgar?' Joseph Hedley asked mischievously.

Isabella turned scarlet. 'My father and Admiral Nelson would have fought just the same had there been a Stuart on the throne.'

Peter looked at her. 'That is the truth. I fought because I was pressed and had to do my duty. A Stuart, or old mad King George, would have been all the same to me.'

'Lord Nelson wasn't,' said Clementina.

'We were not talking of great men,' said Peter severely.

'I am afraid, Isabella, that I agree with your father. It was the greatest blessing that Bonny Prince Charlie was defeated. If we had had a Stuart on the throne, England would have had a revolution like that of the French and probably at the same time,' said Joe.

'After your father was pressed, old Peter was the only friend I had among the Lamonds. I loved him and we should have starved without his crabs and lobsters and haddock,' said Clementina.

But her great-grandfather, and on which side he should have fought on Culloden Moor, were of less interest to Isabella than the Autocrat of all the Russias. She had been overcome at the sight of him, and he had chucked her under the chin and had said to Peter: 'Is that lovely girl your daughter?' An odd question, since she had been introduced as such. Isabella's emotion was not unnatural, for Nicholas was by far the most handsome monarch in Europe: six foot three inches in height with classic features, but with a rather small mouth and the most formidable eyes. He was dressed for the occasion in the uniform of an admiral, his chest covered with medals and decorations, a sword at his belt, and a cocked hat which he had been forced to remove when he stooped to enter the engine-room. To Isabella, and to most women, he appeared like a god standing high above ordinary men. She poured out her feelings and was indignant with her mother when she said that she would not trust a man with such cold eyes.

Before the *Nicolai* sailed again, the Emperor had sent for Peter and Joseph Hedley and had ordered Peter to draw out plans for two steamboats for the Russian navy and had signed an order for their engines to be designed by Joseph and built by the Butterley Company. Joe had the temerity to say that building a man-o'-war was very different from building a passenger steamer, and that it might take as long as two years. The Tsar nodded agreement, and said that he personally would approve the plans. The question of the cost of the two ships was left to his naval advisers and the Russian treasury, but he agreed that money would have to be advanced during their construction.

When they got back on board, Joe was as usual in very high spirits – in marked contrast to Peter, who foresaw endless difficulties with Russian admirals. However, he set to work at once and spent every leisure moment in discussions with Joe bending over the drawing-board in the chart-room.

Once back in Travemünde, Clementina's life resumed its happy routine. Isabella became once more the hostess on board her father's ship. The *Nicolai* was a 'happy ship', for Jacobsen was a first class seaman, and the crew had confidence in their officers and respected them. But when autumn came, and St Petersburg was about to become icebound, a difference arose between the Russians and the German merchants who owned a third of the *Nicolai*. When the Baltic was icebound, the owners of *George IV* had always sent her on profitable voyages to the Mediterranean. But the plans for the two warships presented in September had not been approved. In vain did first Mr Nicholls, and then the British Ambassador, tell Peter that the only way to get the plans passed was by bribing the Russian admiral, who demanded a large share of the cost of their construction. Peter was firm and set his face against what he thought was a dishonest and exorbitant demand.

As things were at a stalemate, the only way was for Peter to remain at Kronstadt and for Jacobsen to assume command and sail the *Nicolai* to southern waters, which were not ice-bound.

The Lamond family therefore spent the winter in Russia, and in the coldest and most depressing part of it. For Clementina it was another minor disaster. All her livestock except her cat had to be got rid of. But as the garden would be under snow for at least a part of the time, she resigned herself without complaint, only regretting the winter vegetables: leeks, celery, turnips, Jerusalem artichokes and salads protected from frost, which she could not take with her. Peter rented a new dacha – or summer villa – from a naval officer in Kronstadt; and owing to its recent construction there were few fleas and no bugs.

Soon after their arrival, Clementina and Isabella were invited by a Russian lady of high rank to visit her in order to be shown her collection of jewellery. After all the precious objects had been sufficiently admired the visitors were dismissed without being offered even a cup of tea or a biscuit. Clementina described the visit, which had a good deal surprised her, to Mrs Nicholls who laughed and said : 'I have got used to it. All the great ladies in St Petersburg society will invite *anyone* – and by that I mean even people without titles, like you and me – anyone *new*. For everyone they know has been shown their treasures a dozen times over. When I first came to St Petersburg I was invited again and again and again to see collections of jewellery belonging to ladies in the height of fashion. I was once asked to come to admire a pearl necklace that my husband had bought in Paris and which had been in the window of our shop for over a month.'

'Among the fisher-folk in Scotland showing off to a poor neighbour would be thought bad manners. Of course we haven't pearls and rubies – at the most a paisley shawl. All the same it would seem to us to show – well – a lack of delicacy,' said Clementina.

'Delicacy! Why, you have put your finger on it, my dear. The Russians have many good points, but delicacy is not one of them. And there are no ladies or gentlemen either. There is probably as much delicate feeling in our watchman, Gerasim, as in all the princes and counts and grand duchesses at court.'

'Gerasim? Is he the old man with tangled unwashed hair and a beard all over his face, who keeps one awake at night, beating a board?'

'Yes, that is the Russian custom – to frighten away thieves and not to catch them,' said Mrs Nicholls.

'Why doesn't he get his hair cut? Or his beard trimmed? One can only just see his eyes. It can't be to keep warm, for it was just as shaggy when I saw him in the summer,' said Clementina.

'I asked him once,' replied Mrs Nicholls. 'And what do you

think he said? "It is God makes our hair grow, madam. Besides, if I had my hair shaved I should look like a younger man, and the sergeant might take me to be a soldier!" '

Isabella spent most of her time staying with the Nicholls family in St Petersburg and flirting with Russian officers with whom she was extremely popular. This was a cause of anxiety to Clementina. But with only a few words of Russian and not very good French and even less knowledge of the world, what could she do? She left it to Mrs Nicholls, who was not altogether dis-interested, as Isabella was a great attraction for the English shop and brought a host of young men who came pretending to want to buy, and actually buying, in order to ask if she were there. Peter was unhappy, reserved and silent. Eventually he realised that the plans for the ships would never be accepted unless he resorted to bribery. But he put off the evil day when he must give way, and slowly the admiral let it be known that, for patriotic reasons, he would accept less. But Peter grew thinner, and illness made him less adaptable.

The only member of the family who was absolutely happy was David. He spent his time tobogganing on the ice-hill and skating, at which he became masterly. On one occasion he was invited by a party of naval officers and cadets to skate across the sea to Finland.

Finally, as the frost was beginning to break up, Mr Nicholls came to Kronstadt with the news that Admiral Saltykov had been 'carpeted' by the Emperor, and was now ready to accept a mere thirty thousand roubles for his emendations to the plan, and that work could be begun on the two ships directly the news could be got to Butterley and Joseph.

The ice had broken up, but the *Nicolai* was late in appearing. Finally she steamed in, ten days late. It had been a disastrous voyage, although she had come back loaded with a valuable cargo of wines, silks and luxury goods from France and Italy. But the engines had broken down soon after leaving Venice. Sabotage on the part of a Turkish agent was suspected and afterwards proved.

The war between Russia and Turkey of 1828–9 had still a few months to run before the Treaty of Adrianople was signed after

Russian victories. Great hostility from the defeated Turks was only to be expected. Thus for the rest of the voyage *Nicolai* had to depend upon her sails, and owing to her paddle-wheel boxes she was a slow and clumsy craft under canvas alone. There was no port in the Mediterranean where the engines could be repaired. She was also frequently delayed by bad weather. It was not until she had sailed up the Thames to the dock at Blackwall where she had been built, that the Butterley Company were able to supply a new engine. The passengers at Lübeck had been left waiting until the cargo had been unloaded. Then, in spite of Peter's protests, the Second Mate, who was in no way to blame, was sacked and a Russian mate appointed. Peter delayed sailing until he had asked the advice of the British Ambassador.

'I am sorry to say that I can't help you,' said that diplomat with a smile that showed he was a happy man. Then, rubbing his hands together, he explained: 'You chose to sail under the Russian flag, Captain Lamond. In my opinion it was rash of you. But I cannot interfere between the Russian Government and its servants.'

The *Nicolai* broke her record on the voyage to Lübeck. The young Russian mate knew some German, and before the *Nicolai* set off on the return journey, Herr von Duhn called upon Peter to tell him that Herr Yershov had been to see several of the shareholders to say that, in his opinion, Captain Lamond had endangered her because he wanted to make a quick passage. He himself had spent the whole voyage expecting the boilers to burst.

Peter took no action. He felt that he had been warned and that the young mate, Yershov, though a competent sailor, was most likely Saltykov's spy. His restraint, and the trouble which he took to teach the young Russian how to handle a steamboat, particularly in bad weather, won the mate's respect, and from that time he did not intrigue against Peter, and relations with the Russian merchants remained good.

Clementina enjoyed a full year at Travemünde. She was proud of David, who was growing up as handsome as she remembered Peter. He had curly black hair and very blue eyes, rather an aquiline nose. He was good at his lessons, and, after a number of fisticuff fights, had become popular among his schoolfellows. One or two of them he liked to bring home to high tea or a dinner to taste such strange foods as cockyleeky, a fowl stewed with beef and leeks and lots of prunes, or a real haggis with rowanberry jelly, all of his mother's making.

Clementina spoiled her son, for with him she was carried back into her girlhood. Living in their own big house with a rich garden and orchard, there was not the hardship of her early years. But her tastes were the same. One day a swarm of bees settled on the branch of a damson, and David at once was eager to take it. With his face protected by a veil of black muslin, he shook them into a wooden bucket which he turned over and rested one corner on a brick. Then Clementina and he drove into Lübeck and bought a straw hive. In the evening with Hans encouraging him from a distance, he threw the swarm on to a board in front of the skep and escaped with only one sting. For a week or two Clementina and he went to look at the bees every morning, and were proud and interested in them. In the evening Clementina would help David with his homework, remembering what she could of Euclid and the trigonometry that Peter had taught her all those years before.

On one of Peter's trips that summer there was an unexpected passenger among those arriving from Hamburg by coach. It was Joe. He explained that he had received a letter from Admiral Saltykov to say that the boats now finished building must be fired by wood, when coal was not available. This would involve a stokehold of very much larger capacity, or else much shorter range for the ship. So he had thought it best to visit the Russian admiralty, and possibly get a decision from the Emperor himself, before modifying the plans. There was only a half-hour in which Joseph could visit the Lamond house before he went on board and the *Nicolai* sailed. He greeted Clementina with his usual warmth and then turned to Isabella. Her mother was surprised to see her face come alight with pleasure as she greeted him. It was a genuine spontaneous emotion, very different from the self-conscious provocative glances which she gave to her Russian officers and admirers.

Joseph was back again on the return trip of the *Nicolai*: he had seen the Tsar, who had decided that the original plans should be adhered to, and had ordered that an immense coal bunker should be installed at Kronstadt, the coal being brought during the coming winter in trains of sledges from the Don.

All this was only of interest to Clementina, because it meant that as soon as Joseph was back in England the ships would set off and that Peter wanted to take his whole family to Kronstadt to be there when the vessels arrived. She was more interested in Isabella, who kept close to Joseph and went to wave good-bye when he took the coach to Hamburg. And suddenly it came bursting out.

'Papa said I had better tell you myself. Joseph spoke to him on the way back. It will have to be a long engagement.'

'I was afraid it would be a Russian count.'

'I would not marry a Russian for anything. They spend all their time and money gambling, or flirting and eating chocolates and caramels. Joseph is a real man. He is changing the world and making it richer. And he never stops working.'

Clementina took her daughter in her arms and kissed her, something she had not done for several years.

Later she said: 'I suppose some Russians must work.'

'Only the serfs and the workmen. But I could not marry one of them, Mamma. They beat their wives and I don't think Joseph will beat me, do you?'

'It might be a good thing if he did, you hussy,' said Clementina laughing.

Once more she had to pack up her belongings and leave her garden, and this time just as the first fruits were ready. The strawberries were in flower; the early peas and the beans would be wasted – old Hans would benefit.

CHAPTER FIFTEEN

It was a fine day, one of those in early June when the sun shines and the waves sparkle and Russians at Kronstadt can believe themselves as far from the Arctic Circle as – one cannot say Naples – the Isle of Wight would be a more truthful comparison.

The harbour, the fort, the docks and all the ships tied up in it were decorated with flags, which hung idly from their masts, for there was not a breath of wind.

A narrow wooden pavilion had been erected opposite a landing-stage on the dockside. A band of marines marched out and took up position to one side of it. Presently two steamers approached the dock entrance. The foremost slowed down and yielded precedence to the one behind, which entered the splendid harbour and executed a circle which would bring it to the landing-stage opposite the pavilion.

A crowd had gathered; prominent among it were Peter and his old enemy Admiral Saltykov. Behind stood Isabella in red silk and David in a uniform with brass buttons and Clementina with her hand on his shoulder. The ship – a frigate – drifted near. There was a sudden burst of activity from the paddle-wheel; a rope was thrown and caught and the cable attached to it drawn in and looped over a bollard. The band struck up the Russian national anthem, and the Emperor, in the full uniform of a Russian Admiral, strode out of the pavilion. At his heels came the naval officer in waiting; a lieutenant wearing white gloves, girt with a sword and for some reason carrying a large telescope under his arm. The Emperor looked around with a cold glance. Admiral Saltykov stepped forward, followed closely by Peter, and in that order they walked up the gangplank on board the vessel, followed at a short distance by the British Ambassador and naval officers. The Tsar stepped on deck and at once halted, leaving the line following him unable to get on board, while he chatted with the captain of the vessel. He took no notice of Joseph standing beside him. After two or three minutes, the Captain led the Tsar over the ship, and the privileged line on the gangway were able to get on board. They followed the Captain, who was exhibiting the armament: two bow-chasers and nine cannon on each side, four in front of the paddle-wheel and five behind it. Then the Tsar inspected the crew drawn up in two lines, all in smart uniforms with short blue jackets with red braid, plenty of brass buttons and flat caps with ribbons worn at a rakish angle on their heads. The Tsar turned once or twice to speak to Admiral Saltykov, but ignored Peter.

Before the Imperial party left the dockside and embarked for St Petersburg, the British Ambassador hurriedly invited Joseph Hedley and Peter, Isabella and Clementina, to a ball which he was giving the following night. With this early warning, Isabella, with the help of Mrs Nicholls, was provided with an exquisite dress of white satin with dark blue flounces and a dark blue ruched edging to her very décolleté corsage. Her dark hair was done in ringlets, and she wore a necklace of dark blue sapphires that shone almost as brightly as the dark blue eyes above the jewels. And on her finger was an engagement ring of dark sapphires and pearls that Joseph had bought that afternoon.

The Lamonds and Joe went to the Ambassador's ball with Mr and Mrs Nicholls. They were greeted on the staircase by the Ambassadress, who appeared most friendly to the Nicholls family. Then Clementina, with a sort of stolid acceptance of her surroundings, walked into the immense ballroom, brilliantly lighted with huge crystal chandeliers. The walls were covered with paintings of partially draped nymphs, shepherds and goddesses. When she had taken in the room, she turned her attention to the company, and the first person she saw was Mrs Field, the lady whose housekeeper's daughter she had rescued from trying to drown herself. She was indeed standing only a few yards away.

Clementina was talking quietly to Mrs Nicholls when the Ambassadress pounced on them and led her up to the lady saying: 'This is Mrs Field, who arrived with her husband a fortnight ago to see their nephew Simon, who is assistant to our military attaché. Mrs Nicholls is the wife of the best ambassador that Britain has ever sent abroad. He has started a shop which provides all the great ladies in Russia with every luxury that London and Paris can offer. And here is her compatriot, the wife of the Captain of the steamship *Nicolai*. He actually designed and built the ship himself and the Emperor is much interested.'

Even had her name been given, it is doubtful if Mrs Field would have recognised Clementina owing to the disfiguration of the smallpox and the long interval of years. At that moment Captain Simon Field came up, was introduced and immediately asked Isabella for a dance.

However, before the ball opened there was a sudden hush. The musicians stopped tuning their instruments, the company hurriedly divided into two lanes, leaving the centre of the ballroom empty. The Tsar entered wearing the full-dress uniform of Hetman of the Cossacks. He was the tallest man in the room and appeared the most handsome, as he strode forward to where the British Ambassador and his wife were waiting. The ball was opened with the Emperor dancing with the Ambassadress. When the dance was over he was observed to be whispering to her and was at once led up to where Isabella had just returned to her mother, after her dance with Captain Field.

'You waltz, Miss Lamond?' he said, and without waiting for an answer, placed his hand on her shoulder and, as the band struck up, they began dancing. In a moment the floor was crowded with couples.

'I am pleased with your father's work and with that of Mr Hedley,' said the Tsar.

'May I tell him so, as I am engaged to marry him?' said Isabella, plucking up her courage.

The Emperor looked at her with his cold eyes. It was on the point of his tongue to say: 'I should not have told you that I was pleased, unless I expected you to repeat it.' But he suddenly gave a smile which transformed the marble hardness of his face: 'Tell him that I congratulate him on his engagement to you, young lady.' And, as the music ended, he walked rapidly away from her. After one more waltz he left the ballroom.

Mrs Field, like all the rest of the company, had seen the Tsar dancing with Isabella and conceiving the idea that her pock-marked Scottish mother must be a person of importance at the Court, said to her: 'What a lovely girl; quite the belle of the ball. What is her name?'

'Isabella, she is my daughter. I think the dress flatters her,' said Clementina.

'I should like to throw myself on your mercy,' said Mrs Field. 'We know no one in St Petersburg, or in Russia, except for the Ambassador and his wife, and that only because my nephew is an attaché. We live in a very humble way in Oxfordshire where nothing ever happens from one year's end to another and I feel quite lost amid all this grandeur. I don't know who is who, and am so afraid of committing a breach of etiquette. If you, who must know Petersburg society so well, would just tell me....'

Clementina interrupted the lady with: 'I know less than you, Mrs Field. My husband's ship sails tomorrow, so I cannot be of any help. But I am sure your life in Oxfordshire is more full of drama than that of the grand princesses and baronesses of St Petersburg. They love showing people their jewellery, and I think you will soon get bored by looking at pearls the size of wren's eggs and wish you were back in the Midlands.' Then seeing the disappointed look on Mrs Field's face, she could not resist saying. 'I hope Mrs Rose is keeping well. Give her my best regards. Good-bye.'

And Clementina walked away to join Peter, leaving Mrs Field staring after her.

The morning after the ball the Nicholls family and their guests rose later than usual, nor did they hurry over breakfast. The events of the previous night had to be discussed over and over again. At that time of year it is difficult to be sure of the time in St Petersburg as the sun rises so early and sets so late. It is the season of the 'white nights' of which Dostoevsky was to write half a century later.

Nicholas I had sent word that he intended to visit Kronstadt and discuss some subject with Joseph and Peter, and that they should not leave before his visit. Peter assumed this to mean that the *Nicolai* would not sail to schedule and sent word to delay passengers for Lübeck until further notice. It was not until the late afternoon that the Lamond family returned to Kronstadt with Joseph.

Peter was astonished to see a group of Russian sailors, with a pile of sea-chests near them, grouped round the gangplank and Jacobsen holding a pistol at the other end of it. Yershov, the mate, was waiting for them as they stepped ashore. He was in tears, and though he saluted Peter and bowed to the ladies, he was gulping with emotion.

He blurted out then that Peter had been dismissed from his command, that he, Yershov, had been appointed Captain and than an all-Russian crew was to take the place of the present one of British, Shetland Islanders, Germans and Norwegians. Jacobsen had, however, not allowed either him or the Russian crew aboard, until Peter's return. It was, as Peter could see for himself, a plain mutiny. And then as he surveyed the scene silently Yershov babbled : 'I owe my training as a sailor to you. I am proud to have served under you. But I have to obey the Imperial commands. This is not my doing, nor is it Admiral Saltykov's. . . . I could have used force to take over the ship from the mutineers and I have been afraid that the Emperor might arrive before you and see that his orders have not been carried out.'

'Have you those orders in writing?' asked Peter. Then, as the mate did not reply, he said : 'The Captain of a ship chooses the crew, and I have a contract with the owners for several years to run. Tell those fellows to stand aside.'

Then he went on board with his family and Joseph, saying in passing : 'Well done, Jacobsen. Have the gangplank run ashore. And, if steam is up, we'll moor her to that buoy out there.' After these orders had been executed, he told the Bo'sun to muster the men aft and addressed them as follows :

'As you know, this ship sails under the Russian flag, and I am wearing the uniform of a captain in the Russian merchant marine. This means that we have to carry out orders given us by His Imperial Majesty Tsar Nicholas I. I have been informed that His Majesty intends to relieve me of my command and appoint a Russian captain and an all-Russian crew. If this should be true, and I have only the word of Mr Yershov for it, I shall do my best to obtain compensation for our dismissal and for your repatriation at the expense of the Russian Government. It is because I have been given no evidence of the truth of this story that I have brought the *Nicolai* out here so that she should not be boarded on the dockside by persons without legal authority. When that comes, if it does come, you will have to obey whatever orders the new Captain gives you and I rely on you, in that event, to make no trouble. But, until then, all shore leave is cancelled.'

The crew murmured. A young sailor said: 'Thanking you, sir.'

'I leave Mr Jacobsen in command while I am on shore awaiting His Majesty's commands.'

Peter was then rowed ashore. The weather had turned misty and cold and he was not wearing an overcoat. He walked up to where Yershov was waiting beside the landing-stage where the Imperial barge would pull in. He did not greet or speak to the younger man, who made a movement towards him opening the palms of his hands, but said nothing. Clementina stood by the rail looking at the two figures. She had become used to Peter's extreme thinness; but now she was appalled by it. His uniform, which had fitted him perfectly when he had taken command of the *Nicolai*, now hung loose upon him. He seemed to be as strong physically as ever, but he ate little, though at short intervals he would munch a piece of biscuit or crunch a small bit of sugar, several of which he carried surreptitiously in his pocket.

She could tell even at that distance what the expression on Peter's face would be: his small mouth tightly closed and lips compressed, and a curious blend of contemptuous respectfulness and of authority in his look. Certainly the soi-disant Captain, Chief Mate Yershov, was not to be envied.

They stood there side by side in silence for two hours and then Yershov broke silence with: 'His Imperial Majesty cannot be coming this evening. It is getting late.'

'Mr Yershov, you have shown me no authority for your act

of insubordination. I therefore dismiss you from the ship.'

Yershov gazed at Peter with horror. He could not believe that the plan had failed.

'But that is not possible,' he murmured.

'You have heard what I said. Take yourself off,' said Peter in very clear precise accents. Then he waved to the *Nicolai* and the ship's boat, which had been waiting, pushed off to meet him. But he stumbled as he stepped from the dock stair and would have fallen, if the sailor standing with a rope in his hand had not caught him. He made an effort in the boat to rise but he had to be supported by a sailor who put his arm round the captain's shoulder. Then, when they reached the *Nicolai*, half-a-dozen strong arms were needed to lift him up the ladder and carry him below to his cabin.

For a moment he raised himself on his bunk and said to Joseph standing beside him : 'I have dismissed Yershov. A double game. I saw that.' Then he fell back and a fit of convulsive shivering seized him. Clementina had called for hot towels, but when she tried to apply them, the shivering had ceased, and his body was cold as ice. Peter was dead.

Peter's funeral was impressive. The Emperor sent a wreath of arum lilies and was represented by the naval lieutenant who had accompanied him when he inspected the steam frigates. The British Ambassador sent a wreath. The Nicholls family attended. The British shop in the Nevsky Prospekt was closed that day. From the moment that Peter's death was known, all the ships, both Russian and foreign, including all the ships of the Russian navy then in port, flew their flags at half-mast. When Clementina came on deck and saw this, she broke down and wept. This universal token of respect was something that she never forgot and often spoke of in later years.

The coffin draped in the Union Jack with Peter's cocked hat on top was carried to the Protestant cemetery by six sailors, and, as Peter had requested in his will, the burial service was that of the Church of England. Clementina, heavily draped in black (provided by Mrs Nicholls), followed the coffin with Isabella and David beside her. She moved as in a trance and occasionally wondered whether the funeral was actually taking place, and how soon it would be over. Behind the three members of the family came Joseph Hedley and the Emperor's representative, then the Nicholls family and then Admiral Saltykov and a representative of the Russian Admiralty. David, who had sharp ears, heard the latter say to Admiral Saltykov as the mourners walked back from the cemetery: *'Eh bien, cet Ecossais vous a encore vaincu, mais cette fois par sa mort.'* Yershov did not attend.

The day after the funeral, Joseph Hedley was sent for to Tsarskoe Selo and the Emperor, giving him audience, expressed his sympathy and ordered him to prepare plans for the Imperial Steam Yacht *Iskia*, about which he had also wished to consult Peter. Then he added: 'The Russian officer who attempted to take command of the *Nicolai I*, believing that Captain Lamond would resign his command and remain here to build the *Iskia*, acted without authority, and has been sent to Siberia on a life sentence to work in the mines.'

Two days before the *Nicolai* sailed eight days late, Captain Nico Wilhelm Stahl, a friend and neighbour of the Lamonds at Travemünde, was appointed the new Captain. He spent the two days in making an inventory of all the ship's stores for which he signed when he took over. There was no question of a Russian crew, or mate.

The ship was crowded on the voyage to Lübeck, and there were many complaints of bad service. Harrington, the cook, and many of the crew, left the ship on her arrival and made their way to Hamburg where they could find new berths.

CHAPTER SIXTEEN

DURING Peter's lifetime Clementina had often thought how different her life would have been if she had never married him : if he had been drowned in that ship wrecked off Norway – or if, after they had married, he had been killed at Trafalgar. Sometimes she had hankered after the life from which he had lifted her. But now that he was dead, it seemed as though the life they had shared, had been the only possible one.

When she looked at Isabella and Joseph she saw what a wonderful life it had been. Joseph Hedley, she knew, would rise above them taking Isabella with him. Joseph would become famous. He was already, perhaps, on the point of fame – but for David she hoped for at least a taste of that wild life that she would have lived but for Peter.

Almost as soon as they reached Travemünde, Joseph went back to England. Clementina thought that he might have stayed for a few weeks, if only for Isabella's sake. Moreover Joseph was a man who would have helped her transact business and make the right decisions. One day she said as much to Isabella, who rounded on her mother.

'Because he is always gay and seems light-hearted, you don't guess what Joe has to carry on his shoulders. The Butterley Company has to provide all the ironwork for the new London Bridge. That is a vast undertaking, and Joseph has to design what is needed and see that the casting and forging is well done. Then he must design and plan the Tsar's steam yacht, and that is where he needed Papa's help and experience. Then there is his own work, which has been almost at a standstill because of these ships. . . .'

'Well, you have been telling me about his own work and it does seem a great deal for such a young man,' said Clementina.

'You don't understand, Mamma. His own work is something

quite different. The steam pumps he invented can be adapted and enlarged. He foresees their use not only in coal mines and on every ship in the world, but he also has plans for draining the Fens with steam-driven waterwheels, like mill-wheels in reverse. Dutch windmills are out of date – like sailing ships and for the same reason. Then he is interested in lighting cities with coal gas, but methods will have to be found for cleaning it.'

'I hope all this won't make him forget that he is engaged to marry you,' said Clementina when Isabella paused. The girl almost spat at her mother.

'One of the things we talked about most was what sort of house we shall want to live in, and where it should be. Joseph will have to work in London a great deal, but I would rather live in the country. I am sick of cities after St Petersburg. I want a peaceful setting and my own garden. Joseph says they are talking of building some villas north of Holland Park, right out of London, at a place called Westbourne and he thinks we might go there.'

Isabella was still angry with her mother but she allowed her to embrace her warmly, something which she had not done for a long time.

A week after they got back to Travemünde, young Peter arrived. Her son was almost a stranger to Clementina: she had seen him only twice since he had left Calais, once in London and once at Travemünde, which he visited for a few days soon after his father had bought the house. She still thought of him as 'young Peter', a boy, though he was now twenty-eight and a man of the world. The close and lasting friendship with the Vicomte de Serignac, formed when he had protected the French exiled boy at school, had introduced him into the society of French exiles who had come back after the restoration of the Bourbons. As a result of living in France this son of hers was a man with manners very different from those of his parents. Where his father was habitually stern and reserved and was often embarrassingly silent, the son was always affable and sensitive to the feelings of others. Where Captain Lamond would either issue an order, or visibly restrain himself from doing so, the son would make a suggestion, and his suggestions were adopted with pleasure and gratitude, and not automatically or sullenly obeyed.

He was not so tall or handsome as his father, or as his young brother promised to be. But there was a lack of egotism and a disinterestedness that endeared him at first sight. And, whereas both his parents spoke broad Scots, and even Joseph was liable to relapse into his native Geordie dialect of Newcastle when excited, young Peter Lamond spoke like a member of the educated upper class of Englishmen.

These differences might have come between mother and son, but for the tenderness and love with which he took her in his arms, the warmth with which he kissed her and then led her, with an arm about her shoulders, to the little sofa, where he sat beside her, holding both her hands in his. The years he had spent in the wine trade in France had served him well. Now that he had returned to England he had retired from that business and had bought himself a house, Number 62, Ship Street, in Brighton.

Brighthelmstone, to give it its original name, was a resort made fashionable, when Prince Regent, by George IV. Peter had been made French consul, agent for the Customs, and, owing to his father's influence, agent for the General Steamship Company, none of which occupations took up too much of his time. He was also at ease in the fashionable society of the town. When a member of the French nobility visited Brighton, he sought out 'ce charmant Monsieur Le Mont,' who talked French without an accent and was intimate with many persons of rank. His knowledge of wine was also a passport, and more than one lord asked his advice on vintages, before replenishing his cellar.

On his arrival at Travemünde he took charge of all the necessary business. Captain Peter's will was proved and execution granted. He had left all his property to his dearly beloved wife during her lifetime and, after her death, it was to be divided equally between his three children. There were reasonable precautions to secure it for them in the event of Clementina's remarrying. His chronometer and one of his sextants he left to his son David if he should follow the sea; his silver watch No. 2653

258

by C. Harris absolutely to his son David. But apart from these legacies, Captain Lamond had left little. His mother was still living, and he had not received any part of his inheritance from Panbride.

Clementina had looked forward to happy years of retirement at Travemünde, cultivating her garden, watching the trees she had planted come into fruit, keeping a cow perhaps, and making her own butter. When her son told her kindly that this would be impossible, she would not have enough money to live there, besides which there was David's future to be thought of – she would not like, in any case, to bring him up a German – her face set firmly and she said: 'Yes. I see now that it was impossible.' And then, breaking off their talk, she went out into the garden.

She did not return, and it was geting near the time for the evening meal, although at that time of year it was broad daylight. So Peter went to look for her. He had guessed that she might be picking raspberries, but she was not among the canes. Then he caught sight of her seated on a bench near the hive of bees. He did not call, but walked towards her. She was sobbing and wringing her hands. He should have gone up to her then and put his arm round her shoulders and kissed her. But he thought she would hate him to know of her moment of weakness, and he turned and tiptoed away.

What had broken down Clementina's self-control was the sight of a row of seedling leeks, a second sowing, just breaking through the soil, each seedling like a little green whip-handle with a tiny lash bending over to the tip. She had sown them herself before their departure: so much had happened since, while they had been germinating in the ground. And no use now.

Yes, it was obvious that Number 190 Travemünde would have to be sold, and it was hoped that it might fetch as much as the thousand pounds which Peter had paid for it. Meanwhile his estate amounted to thirteen hundred pounds, which if invested in safe securities might bring in fifty pounds a year for Clementina, David and Isabella to live on – a sum which might be doubled if the house at Travemünde sold well. She would have also her husband's naval pension.

It would not be true to say that young Peter invited his mother, sister and young brother to come and live with him in Brighton. He took it for granted that they would make his house their home. After a suitable period of mourning, Isabella would marry, but his mother would continue to manage his house for him, and his young brother would go to school for a year or two in Brighton.

Peter was a model son: he was always affectionate and kind to his mother, and in fact loved and admired her. Yet she was not at ease with him, partly because she was afraid of embarrassing him in the eyes of his fashionable acquaintance. It was not only that they belonged to different worlds: but they spoke different languages, and the respect and deference that he paid to her seemed false and unnatural.

Isabella's marriage took place almost a year after she and David and her mother had gone to live at 62 Ship Street. Clementina had decreed that it must be a very quiet affair, but her words went unheeded, or rather they were over-ruled by events; for the announcement of the wedding brought a visit from an enthusiastic Russian count, who had travelled several times on board the *Nicolai* and regarded himself as an old flame of the bride's and an intimate of the Lamond family. He was staying with a friend and his wife, both Russians, and his joy at discovering that he had friends, or at least acquaintances, in England was such that Isabella could do no less than invite all the Russians to the wedding. Peter had also invited an equally aristocratic French pair, the Vicomte de Daunés and his bride, who were in Brighton on their honeymoon. Joseph brought a party from Pentrich in Derbyshire: Mr Brittain of Butterley Hall, who had asked to be his Best Man, and Mr Brittain's young sister, who was at once invited to be a bridesmaid. There was also the General Manager of the Butterley Ironworks and his wife and daughter. But the real surprise was the Hedley family from Newcastle who had come by sea and arrived two days early. It consisted of his mother and her sister and the sister's husband and Joseph's brother, the famous 'Steelhead' Hedley — so named because of the hardness of his skull, for he was a professional prizefighter.

Peter realised in time that the wedding was going to be on a large scale, and hired rooms at the 'Old Ship'.

The actual wedding was restrained, though smart: Isabella wore the white satin dress she had worn at the ball in St Petersburg with the addition of a veil, held in place by a wreath, and Joseph wore a black tailcoat with an embroidered satin waistcoat and a stock up to his ears. Peter gave his sister away. The Best Man wore a lavender tailcoat with a primrose-coloured waiscoat and very tight smalls. Clementina wore a black satin voluminous dress, with a black bonnet, and the white and gold silk shawl that had belonged to Joseph Hearn's mother, the Spanish gypsy dancer. She had it carefully cleaned and mended in two places.

But though the wedding itself was conventional and correct, the reception became high-spirited and noisy. First the company had to view the wedding presents laid out on a table in a locked room. In the centre was the chief and extraordinary glory: the present from the Emperor of Russia, a crystal bowl beautifully cut. The Butterley Iron Company had sent an entire silver dinner service, Mr Joliffe a silver salver and Sir Edward Banks a silver coffee pot. Herr Behncke had sent an ivory clothes brush, Herr von Duhn two silver egg-cups, and Joseph's brother 'Steelhead' Hedley contributed a watercolour painting of Durham with the cathedral in the background, which the Vicomte de Daunés, who was a connoisseur, pronounced a Constable. It was actually the work of 'Steelhead' himself, but he thought it better not to enlighten the Frenchman.

The wedding cake was cut with Captain Peter's sword. Healths were drunk, speeches were made; but it was not until after the departure of the bridal pair for their honeymoon on the Rhine, that dancing began and the Newcastle Hedleys came to the front. Once his distinguished brother had left the scene, 'Steelhead' came out in his true colours. He was a man of immense vitality and charm, and entirely unaware that few in that assembly could understand one word in three of his flow of witty exhortations. He danced, he made others dance, and he sang. The Russian count was a little jealous as he danced with his friend's wife – his mistress – but he resolved to outdo 'Steelhead', and flung himself into strange postures and made sudden leaps. The Vicomte de Daunés and his bride realised that in Albion it was fun to behave like the natives, and danced and giggled.

Then 'Steelhead' caught sight of Clementina sitting quietly in a corner and seized her hand, and cried out: 'Hoo's this then? Thoo a Scots lass and not dancen? Aweay up, Hinny, and partner me in a reel. Gettaway, lass dinnet shak' thy heid. Get thysel' stood up and let's aweay! And kilt that long skort o' thine up or I'll be treaden on it.'

She let herself be dragged on to the dance floor, and soon found herself dancing the polka, and the Lancers, and then a reel, and afterwards the Highland fling, after which she drank a couple of glasses of champagne and subsided breathless on a sofa.

She glowed in every limb, and she struggled to get her breath, dances in the summer evening in the horse-field came back to her: how she had loved dancing, and then the time when she had refused to partner Sarah because she thought that Peter would not like it if he knew she had been dancing with the gypsies.

It was too late to resent what she had lost because of Peter. She must think of how much she had gained – not wealth certainly – but honour and consideration. The Emperor's crystal bowl locked up with the wedding presents in the next room was proof of that. Yet, if she were asked, she would say that no woman in her senses should marry a sailor. But, of course, Peter had not been a sailor when she married him, but a fisherman. He had been his own master who slept on shore for most nights of the year, and who hauled his boat high up on the beach when there was a storm. Still, she would not have chosen a fisherman, if she had known. But, of course, nothing would have kept Peter down. He was one of the men who were changing the world – indeed they had changed it already. But it was shocking to think of all the money young Peter and Joseph must be spending on this wedding. She would as soon have had the dance round a bonfire on the Devil's Dyke.

Looking about her she saw David, looking savage. And then she saw that he was looking at his brother Peter, who had his arm round that pretty young girl – Elizabeth Brittain.

Peter was David's age, and she was that girl's, when she was so desperately in love with him – something unusual, as young girls are usually attracted by older, more experienced men and it is older women who are tempted by the innocence of a boy.

The wedding party did not break up until the manager of the 'Ship' had put his head in and told Peter that it was time to close: the waiters could not stay up all night.

What Clementina had observed – that young Elizabeth Brittain was much attracted by her elder son – was true. Peter was invited to look over the Iron Works and to stay at Butterley Hall, and after his return a correspondence followed. Three months later he was engaged and, a year later, he married Elizabeth Brittain by special licence, as she was still under age.

Once more there was a wedding party, but the resources of Pentrich in Derbyshire were not equal to those of Brighton; there was no wedding present from the Tsar, and none of the European aristocracy attended, although the Duc de Serignac sent an edition of Buffon's *Birds* bound in green morocco. Clementina danced a reel with 'Steelhead', but more important to her than the festivities was that the marriage meant that she moved from Ship Street into a little street in the east end of Brighton where she would now live with David.

This was a relief: she would no longer have to plan dinners of four or five courses when Peter wished to entertain one of his French acquaintances and no longer have to sit at the foot of his table trying to make conversation. It meant that she could live frugally, dress as she pleased, and if she avoided the front, Ship Street, the Steyne and the Pavilion, she was unlikely to embarrass her daughter-in-law if she were taking the air with some of her smart friends.

When she was living with her son Peter, she liked to go early to the fishmarket to buy one day a fine crab or, on another, some mackerel to grill or smoke for supper. But now on Saturdays and holidays, David and she would go out early before anyone was about, wearing their oldest clothes, and spend the day fishing off Black Rock, usually bringing home a basket of fish. If it were a dead low tide, they would go past Hove towards Worthing, and then peg out a long line baited with mussels on droppers a yard apart along its length – just what she used to bait and sell when she was living alone at the shippon. When the tide came in, it brought the fish with it. Clementina and David would go for a picnic, sometimes beyond the Devil's Dyke, or even to Henfield, and when they got back and the tide was ebbing, there was the intense excitement of finding a hooked fish flapping in shallow water, or lying flat upon the sand. For the most part they caught flatfish, dabs and soles, sometimes a skate or a thornback ray, and rarely a conger eel in this way. If it were the latter, Clementina would knock him on the head and cut him in two, throwing away the tail, too full of needle-like bones to be any good except for soup.

David was far too old for the make-believe games which they had shared at Travemünde, but they enjoyed kite-flying together on the Downs. Often he got into fights at school and he would come home with a cut lip or a bruised eye. He did not do well at school, finding it hard to adapt himself to English teaching after German, and the headmaster said that he was a bad influence, constantly comparing England with Germany, to the disadvantage of his own country. Though he was not expelled, he was taken away early from school. Then what was he to do?

Joseph was appealed to, and for three months David went to the works at Butterley. As he was idle, useless and unhappy, he was soon returned to Brighton. 'Engineering is not my line,' was what the lad, who was not yet seventeen, declared with a certain grandeur.

Peter suggested the navy; he knew a Captain who would take him as his 'servant', as the young gentlemen learning to be midshipmen were called. But Clementina knew too much about the sufferings on board ship to condemn her ewe-lamb to such a fate.

David then agreed to study law and was articled to a Brighton attorney, Mr Freeman, on the payment of a premium of three hundred and thirty pounds, which Peter advanced; the sum to be repaid out of David's share of his inheritance after his mother's death. He spent the five years there as unpaid clerk, dependent upon his mother, doing little work and wheedling sixpences out of her. It was difficult to resist him, for he was growing up even handsomer than his father, with the same head of black curls and deep blue eyes, but with a gaiety that reminded Clementina of the drowned Robert. But unlike his father or his uncle, David was selfish and believed that his good looks entitled him to the best of whatever was going. He was also given to self-pity, and to the habit of self-condemnation which often follows it. Everything, he felt, had conspired against him. He was so much the youngest of the family – his brother was fourteen years his senior – that although his father had left the money to be divided in equal shares after his wife's death, it was in Peter's hands and all decisions about his mother's investments and her way of life were taken by Peter. He, David, was treated as a child and not consulted when decisions were made.

Girls often looked at him provocatively, but that was his due. He seldom had the few pence needed to buy one of them a piece of gingerbread, or a bag of sweets and almost never the shilling needed to take her to the circus. Nor, with an old pockmarked Scottish mother living on a pittance, would it have been conceivable for him to ask a girl of his own class to arrange a meeting between their parents, so that they could meet each other respectably. Thus it was with pretty servant-girls, who did not expect much consideration, that he consorted – always keeping an anxious eye open lest he should be seen by his smart sister-in-law, or one of her friends, in such low company.

Yet the five years when David was working as an unpaid clerk in Mr Freeman's office in Brighton, and living with her, were happy years for Clementina. She could not expect to share the life of an exceptionally handsome young man, who would spend half an hour tying and retying his neckcloth, or in brushing his top-hat. But she could wash his shirts and see that they were spotless, polish his Hessian boots, and knit and darn his socks. She could cook his meals, bake his bread and oatcake and brew enough beer to last for two or three months. She ate and drank little herself – chiefly porridge and oatcake and fish and, before bedtime, a nip of whisky.

She regretted the garden and orchard at Travemünde, and

wished that she could keep a goat. But the tiny plot of land behind her house was only big enough to take a washing-line and a clothes-prop and was over-run by sparrows, pigeons and cats, and she could grow nothing except pot-herbs and a few flowers.

With age, time appears to pass more rapidly. So it was with Clementina. The five years while David was articled to Mr Freeman seemed to pass so fast that she could barely remember the events in their right order.

It was easy to remember when Peter's children were born: for little Brittain Lamond was now in breeches: but which year was it that Isabella had come to stay with her brother at Ship Street, when she was still nursing little Emily?

At the end of the five years in Mr Freeman's office David went to London to work without salary in the office of Mr Freeman's London agents, Freeman and Stuart. Clementina allowed him seventy pounds a year, on which he found it difficult to manage. A year later he got taken on as a Chancery Clerk and his new employers soon began to pay him – at first eighty pounds a year and in the second year a hundred, and in the third a hundred and twenty. This was not much, but it was something. But he never wrote to his mother and only visited Brighton occasionally, when the Law Courts were closed. Once when she was counting on his coming, he went instead to visit old friends at Travemünde.

Her anxieties about David grew: she knew from what Peter said that he had fallen into bad habits. All she could do was to put by every penny. She went out almost daily to the Black Rock. When the wind blew, she could hardly make her way along the wet slippery surface. But it was worth the effort, for she usually came back with a fish. Once or twice she went to the fish market not to buy, but to sell. For what could she do with fourteen soles that she had found that morning when she went to take up the line she had pegged down at low tide the night before?

Thinking about David in London sometimes kept her awake at night, until, cursing herself, she drugged herself to sleep with whisky.

One day, although it was in the middle of the term, David

came down. He was ill, and Clementina had learned enough from the ways of sailors in port, to know what the trouble was. David was full of self-pity and of shame. But Clementina firmly sent him every day to the hospital and paid the fees of a surgeon who had won fame among the debauchees of the Regency. The nearest that she got to talking openly to her son was to say that he should give up London and the law and live in the open air. For a full man should live out of doors, and the gypsies she remembered had all been healthy.

Her words had more effect than she had intended, for a few days later he said that he was going out to Canada to get his health back. He had met an old school friend who had agreed to go with him.

'Then I shall never see you again, David,' she said putting her hand on her heart.

'Oh, yes you will,' he replied kissing her. 'I shall make a farm in the wilderness and build a log cabin and you will come out and tan the beaver skins and fish in the lake.'

While he made his preparations, she sewed him a hollow money-belt, and when he looked inside, he found ten five-pound notes in it. He was soon gone: later his friend wrote that they had had a very bad voyage which had lasted between seven and eight weeks and the little *Snow* on which they had embarked had been driven by storms into pack-ice near Newfoundland. This friend, Edmund Parsons, said that he was staying in Montreal, but that David was going into Upper Canada among the Iroquois. This letter was brought by the girl that Parsons had written to and was shown to Clementina. After that she read what she could find about the Red Indians, which was a change from the Bible. She had never much cared for chapel-going, but now read a page of her Bible every night, much preferring the Old Testament to the New. For some reason she did not like the miracles. Ecclesiastes and Genesis and Job she read again and again, and could have quoted large parts of them by heart.

In the morning she did not usually get up until sunrise. Then she would blow up the embers – she wished she could buy peat in Brighton, but burned big logs of wood in an open fire for she had learned to hate the smell of coal-smoke on board all her husband's ships. It was coal-smoke, she said, that gave them the consumption. She had never known a Romany spending his life out in the open, to have the consumption. Nor one of the fishermen of her youth, nor an old-time sailorman. But three stokers on the steamers had got it. One of them had died at sea, spitting blood. The other two men got too weak for their work and had to live on shore. But she had not heard whether they had died of it or not.

When she had blown up her fire and put some sticks to it, she warmed up the porridge made of pinhead oatmeal. She sprinkled it with salt and took half a spoonful, which she dipped in the cup of milk she held in her left hand.

Later she would fry herself a fish if she had it, or smoke it in a tin box with oak sawdust. The Finns and Norwegians did that, and she had learned the ways of cooking in all the places she had been in. There was a dish she had learned at Calais: dandelion. You could find a dandelion anywhere. She washed it, chopped up the leaves and flower buds, sprinkled them with vinegar, then fried a rasher or two of bacon until it was crisp and then poured it and the bacon fat over the salad.

She laughed when she remembered how her husband had wrinkled his nose when she had first set it before him.

'You'll be trying to make me eat frogs next.'

And she had replied that frogs and snails were too dear for the likes of them, and that they would have to live entirely on mussels, like everyone else in Calais.

By the time she had finished her bit of fish, or her salad and drunk a couple of glasses of the red Bordeaux wine that her son young Peter was always bringing her, she would find herself nodding, and in a minute would be asleep.

Her mornings, like the mornings of most of the aged, were clear and vigorous. She would wonder whether she would go that summer to stay with Isabella and the children in Derbyshire. Joseph of course had made himself famous: he had lit Aberdeen with coal gas, he was building a bridge somewhere and was busy with his plans for draining the Fens. And to think that his brother was a professional prizefighter! Elizabeth, Peter's wife from Butterley Hall, had let that out. What a mix-up it all was! And in spite of the new world with their steam engines and coal-mines and factories, the common people were hungrier than they had ever been in her lifetime. A lot of labourers were starving and the poor-houses were filled every winter with the men the rich turned off their land to be kept by the parish.

But when she woke up after her nap – sometimes it only lasted five minutes and sometimes an hour – when she woke up she was unsteady. At first she was groping for the vivid colourful dreams which had filled those minutes. Most were of a far off time: Sarah and she were in their tree, Carey's Castle, and then she was leading a boy by the hand and, with no word spoken between them, they would be going either to a bedroom, or to that secret place between the straw stacks where she had once found her father with a girl. But before they got there ... she was awake, and there was only a spark left alight in the fire.

She would lean forward and poke and blow up the ashes and get on her feet and totter about and out into the garden, to see if the clothes were dry enough to be worth bringing in, for rain was coming. Horatio would accompany her, his tail straight up in the air, running just in front of her feet, and then suddenly stopping as though his aim in life was to trip her up. But she was watching him. Later she would give him a second meal, after which he would leap on her lap and poke her under the chin with his blunt head, and it was no good thinking of knitting with him there.

Sometimes she would just sit looking into the fire until it was time to bring out her supper of oatcake and cured cheese, an apple and then a drop of whisky, and a page or two of the Bible before bed.

She slept badly: memories came in the watches of the night: Willie Windram, always with a gift of some little thing when she was so poor after Peter was pressed – then singing in Mrs Field's drawing-room – that was funny – then the dead bodies floating past on the ice. And then she would wonder if the fire would last till morning and if she had remembered to put Horatio out. She had to climb out of bed and grope about, strike a light for a candle and look at the fire and at the empty cat-basket and return to bed, to think about canoes made of birch-bark, of beaver skins and of the Five Nations of the Iroquois.

There were good days when she would go to Black Rock and fish, and know in her bones that she was as strong as ever. She knew that death was coming: it could not be far off, but she was never for a moment afraid of it.

Then one day, a neighbour went round on a Sunday to catch Peter at luncheon, after church. She said that on Saturday Mrs Lamond had whitened her doorstep as she did every Saturday, but she had not come to Chapel – nothing unusual lately – but that her cat had been mewing at breakfast-time outside the door, and was still there now and had not been let in.

Peter hurried round; he had a spare key for an emergency and let himself in. His mother was still in bed, and he sent the neighbour for the doctor. But Clementina just asked him the time and only said that she must have overslept.

Then, while he sat by the bed she said:

'All my Roman has come back to me. I thought that the German had driven it out of my head. You know there are a lot of little rhymes and proverbs and snatches of song – lullabies to make the children fall asleep and charms and jokes about how to steal the farmer's pig. Just listen to this:

'Coin si deya, coin se dado?
Pukker mande drey Romanes,
Ta mande pukkeravava tute.

'Rossar-mescri minri deya!
Vardo-mescri minro dado!
Coin se dado, coin si deya?
Mande's pukker'd tute drey Romanes;
Knar pukker tute mande.

'Petulengo minro dado,
Purana minri deya!
Tatchey Romany si men—
Mande pukker'd tute drey Romanes,
Ta tute's pukker'd mande.'

While she was speaking the doctor came in, rubbing his hands, but Clementina went on with the Romany verses she had remembered.

'Delirium, gibberish – a very bad symptom,' said the doctor.

'Not gibberish but Roman,' said Clementina with a laugh.

'Not the Latin I learned at school,' said the doctor, intent on humouring her. 'Now let me hold your wrist ... pulse steady. Put out your tongue ... I'll leave some pills for the heart and I'll look in tomorrow. No immediate danger.'

'Ought she to go into the hospital?' asked Peter.

'She would be better there. I'll see if there is a bed free in the infirmary.'

Next morning Clementina woke early and full of energy. Put her in the infirmary, indeed! She took a piece of cheese and half the head of a cottage loaf in her basket with the lines and bait and set off to go fishing at Black Rock. She had not felt well enough to do that for some weeks. It was a rough day with a west wind that hurried her along. It might be too rough for fishing, but she knew an eddy where the fish sheltered.

But when she got to Black Rock she saw it was far too rough. She found a nook where she had a support for her back. Then the old woman sat down to watch the grey-blue waves explode in white towers of spray over the belt of rocks that held them back on that part of the coast. Often, after the roller broke, the wind swept the spray in, and the watcher's face was stung hurtfully and her clothes drenched. She would watch a leaden bar in the sea define itself into a wave, then grow to being a breaker that burst in towers of spray upon the rocks and rushed between them down any little channel, a pathway of boiling milk. Then, as the sea withdrew, the channel was left a dull blue, with a network of white bands of foam, like the brindled skin of a sea-serpent, all to be obliterated a moment later by another roller exploding on the rocks and come roaring down. And so without end. Men could build a steam yacht for the Tsar of Russia instead of a North Island vole, but they could not change the sea. Yes, all her life she had known that the sea was the eternal enemy.

The spray came in great dollops blown by the wind and struck hard against her cheek, but she could no longer feel it. Sea water had soaked through her dress to the skin, but she could no longer feel the cold after she had fallen back against the rock behind her.

THE END